Kiss the Bride

Kiss the Bride

DEIRDRE
MARTIN

CHRISTIE
RIDGWAY

LAURA
FLORAND

BRAVA

KENSINGTON PUBLISHING CORP.
www.kensingtonbooks.com

BRAVA BOOKS are published by

Kensington Publishing Corp.
119 West 40th Street
New York, NY 10018

All Kensington titles, imprints, and distributed lines are available at special quantity discounts for bulk purchases for sales promotions, premiums, fund-raising, educational or institutional use.

Special book excerpts or customized printings can also be created to fit specific needs. For details, write or phone the office of the Kensington special sales manager: Kensington Publishing Corp., 119 West 40th Street, New York, NY 10018, attn: Special Sales Department; phone 1-800-221-2647.

ISBN-13: 978-0-7582-7288-1
ISBN-10: 0-7582-7288-X

First Kensington Trade Paperback Printing: May 2012

10 9 8 7 6 5 4 3 2 1

Printed in the United States of America

Contents

Early Bird Special

DEIRDRE MARTIN

CHAPTER ONE

"How was your flight, hon?"

"Fine." Dana Fine squeezed her grandmother's tiny hand. They were in West Palm Beach Airport, waiting patiently for Dana's bags.

Dana had suggested her grandmother sit down while Dana waited by the luggage carousel, but Grandma Fine was having none of it. "I'm not an invalid, you know." Dana knew better than to push. If her eighty-year-old grandmother wanted to stand next to her while the carousel mindlessly looped 'round and 'round, Dana wasn't about to stop her.

Her grandmother was small but sturdy, her silver bob gleaming beneath the airport's fluorescent lights. Impatient, she pulled her glasses down to the end of her nose, squinting at her watch. "Your grandfather must be having a conniption, having to circle with the car."

"I told you, it would have been easier if I just took a cab to your place," Dana reminded her gently.

"Waste of time and money," her grandmother declared, patting her head to make sure every hair was in place. "Besides, this gives me a little more time with you."

Dana was immediately swamped in guilt. She hadn't been to Boca Raton to see her grandparents in two years, because she was always traveling. As the director of retail expansion for La Belle Femme, an upscale chain of boutiques for women, her job took her all over the world. This year alone, she'd been to London, Rome, and Geneva. She spent more time away than at home. She used to deny this, until she was at a barbecue at her friend Suzanne's house, and Suzanne's four-year-old daughter innocently asked, "Do you live on a plane?"

The question forced her to make a lifestyle evaluation, something she'd been avoiding. She wasn't going to lie: she had a great salary, a great wardrobe, and a great, some might even say "exotic," job. Unfortunately, she also had no husband and no children. She told herself she was okay with that, until she found herself starting to get teary holding her friends' babies. That's when she was forced to admit she wanted a family sooner rather than later. There was just one problem, and it was one she knew lots of women would kill to have: La Belle Femme was planning to open a store in Paris. If they did, it would be Dana's to run.

Dana felt a nudge in her ribs. "That one's gotta be yours." While she'd been daydreaming, everyone else who'd been on the flight had collected their luggage. There was just one large, lonely Coach suitcase riding the carousel.

"All right," she said to her grandmother, grabbing the bag the next time it came 'round. "Let's go find Grandpa."

"Probably having a conniption," her grandmother repeated.

Slowing her pace, Dana accompanied her grandmother outside. There, idling in front of the steel and glass airport, was her grandfather's taupe Lexus, the trunk already popped. Dana threw her bag in the trunk and climbed into the back-seat.

"What the hell took you so long?"

Dana's mood deflated, not because of her grandfather's gruffness, but because of the heat. She'd hoped he'd be blasting the air-conditioning, since walking out of the airport was like entering a blindingly bright, palm tree–lined sauna. Instead, the temperature in the car seemed warmer than the air outside.

"It didn't take us long at all," her grandmother countered, settling beside him in the front seat. "If you'd just found a parking space and waited with me like I told you, you wouldn't have had to circle."

Dana's grandfather muttered something unintelligible under his breath before smiling at Dana in the rearview mirror. "How's my girl?"

"Good, Grandpa."

"Good."

Looking at her grandparents, Dana noticed the differences two years had made: her grandfather, once a big, silver-haired bear of a man, looked a little more stooped than last time. Both of their spines were a little more crooked, and their age spots were bigger. The veins showing through tan hands were more ropey and prominent. The wrinkles on their faces etched deeper. But none of that mattered. They were who they'd always been: Grandma and Grandpa.

"How long have we got you for?" her grandfather asked, driving slowly down Jog Road, the ruler-straight avenue that would take them to Huerto de Naranja, the gated retirement community in Boca Raton where her grandparents lived. Cars driven by young, rich professionals flew by theirs, the drivers flipping her grandfather off. "Yeah, you go fuck yourselves, too!" her grandfather yelled.

"Idiots," her grandmother said. "Better safe than sorry, I always say."

"You're goddamn right." Her grandfather glanced at Dana again in the mirror. "We were saying—?"

"I'm not here long," said Dana, rummaging through her shoulder bag for some water. She chugged it down like a woman who'd been staggering through the desert for days. Thirst quenched, she sat back with a satisfied sigh. "Actually, I'm not completely sure. Three weeks, tops."

Her grandfather shook his head, prompting Dana's guilt to return. "Is it worth it? All this hopping around you do for your job? You look tired."

"Leave her alone, Sam," her grandmother said sharply.

"Who's bothering her?"

"C'mon, you guys." Dana leaned forward between the front seats, squeezing both of their shoulders. "No time for bickering. I'm just glad I'm here."

Her grandmother grinned. "So are we, doll." She turned to her husband. "Staying with us rather than at the Four Seasons in Palm Beach," she marveled. "Can you beat that?"

Her grandfather smiled happily. "Of course she is."

Dana leaned back again, feeling mildly groggy. She decided to be grateful for the small things: her grandfather would never acknowledge a request to turn up the AC, but at least he wasn't a horrible driver.

She closed her eyes, since there was really nothing to see apart from identical shopping centers, most of them boasting the same set of stores: a Publix supermarket, a Subway, a Rite Aid, and a bank. Sometimes you'd spot the occasional deli. That was it.

She was surprised by how short the ride was. No sooner was she on the cusp of sleep than they were driving through the condo community's gates and parking the car in its reserved spot.

Dana stepped out of the car, thankful she was wearing her sunglasses as the bright sun beat down. *Good old Huerto de Naranja,* she thought, where every condo unit and semi-detached house looked exactly the same. Same stucco walls, same adobe-tiled roof, same immaculately manicured flowers and plants lining the front walk. Nothing had changed since the last time she was here. But somehow, there was comfort in that.

Chapter Two

The next morning, Dana awakened at the crack of dawn to go running. She used the term "awakened" loosely; to be honest, she hadn't slept much. Her grandparents kept their condo warm enough to hatch chicks. Somewhere around three A.M., Dana had crept out of her bedroom and turned the thermostat down just a tiny bit. But an hour later, her room began sweltering again, and she knew one of them had inched it back up. It would be an unspoken battle for the length of her stay.

Once again, Florida's summer humidity smacked her in the face as she set off, making a point of remembering both her grandparents' address and the color of the car next to theirs. That way, she'd be able to find her way back if she got lost among the identical buildings on the identical streets. "I don't know why they chose to live there," Dana's mother had sniffed disdainfully when her parents left Manhattan for Boca. "It's like being dead when you're still alive."

Jogging down the silent streets, Dana wasn't so sure she agreed. What was wrong with wanting to be somewhere safe where there was beautiful weather all year-round? Or living within walking distance of your friends, whom you could hang out with all day long? Her grandparents seemed happy. Who was her mother to judge?

At any rate, Dana was glad to have a few days to herself before she had to start interviewing for the Palm Beach store.

She remembered when she used to find her job interesting. Now she found it tedious, except when she thought about Paris.

After an hour of doing laps, dawn had become more insistent, and Dana, coated in a thick sheen of sweat, started back to the condo. She was the only person out except for some tan, well-built guy in a muscle shirt, work boots, and battered blue jeans, staring intently at a line of azalea bushes as if they were a work of art. Dana made a U-turn the minute she saw him. She had no ID on her, no cell, no rape whistle. He was probably one of the maintenance crew, but still, she felt safer steering clear of him. You never knew.

By four that afternoon, Dana was no longer certain that choosing to spend the entire day with her grandmother had been such a good idea. So far, they'd spent the morning hours sitting by the clubhouse pool, where she'd been the only one who actually swam. They'd shopped at the mall, where her grandmother urged her to buy anything she wanted. But every time Dana picked something out, her grandma would give her a look that could wither a fresh flower. Finally, in capitulation, Dana let her grandmother buy her a shirt. On first glance, it wasn't that bad: a plain, beige women's button-down blouse. The problem was the epaulets. The blouse had gold epaulets. Dana had never worn anything with epaulets in her life, and she never would. The minute she got home, she was giving it to charity.

Luckily, the trials of the morning vanished when her grandmother took her over to her best friend Molly's for lunch late in the day. Dana had known Molly her whole life, and had always adored her. She was blunt and funny, and she had always treated Dana like she was in on a big secret. Molly made her feel special.

"Look at you!" Molly exclaimed as Dana and her grandmother came through her front door. "I can't believe it's been two years!"

"Neither can I," Dana's grandmother commented under her breath.

Molly, too, had aged since the last time Dana had seen her, but there was something timeless about her. Perhaps it was the mischievous glint in her eye, or the edgy pixie cut she'd always sported. Whatever it was, Dana had always found her inspiring. "I made your favorite," said Molly, cupping Dana's cheek the same way she had when she was small. "Tuna on rye bread, with chocolate milk."

"Oh, Molly." Dana hugged her. It meant so much to her that Molly remembered. Dana had stopped eating that meal years ago, but it didn't matter: Molly made it with love, and every time Molly made it for her, Dana ate it.

Molly motioned Dana and her grandmother into her small, white kitchen. Her condo wasn't broiling like her grand-parents', but it was a close second.

"Sit, sit," Molly urged as she regarded Dana's grandmother with a frown. "I swear to Christ, Adele, I'd sit in the Florida room, but it's too hot."

"Turn up the AC," Dana suggested.

"It's got nothing to do with the AC," said Molly. "It's that the room is all glass. The sun beats down, you fry. End of story." She looked at Dana hopefully. "How long are you here for?"

"Three weeks, tops. Why?"

Molly threw Dana's grandmother a significant look. It took Dana only a split second to figure out what was up. "*No*. No, no, no, no."

"Hear me out," said Molly.

Dana made a face as she poured out some chocolate milk for herself.

"It's my nephew, Josh."

"You never told me you had a nephew named Josh. I certainly never met a nephew of yours named Josh."

"He's my brother Greg's son. He grew up in Chicago. That's why you never met him: that branch of the family rarely came to New York."

Dana's grandmother shook her head, looking mystified. "I'll never understand that."

"Anyway," Molly continued, "Josh lives down here now. He's a big-time landscape architect, with a degree from Cornell."

Dana was unmoved. "So?"

"Why don't you meet him for a drink?" her grandmother suggested.

"What is the point of us meeting for a drink when I'm leaving in under a month?" Dana asked, cutting her sandwich in half.

Molly looked at Dana's grandmother with incredulity. "Would you listen to this one?"

"It's a *drink,* Dana, not picking out a china pattern," said her grandmother.

"Ouch."

"What's the harm?" her grandmother continued good-naturedly. "What, you want to spend every night with me and your grandfather, when you could be out exploring the nightlife, meeting people your own age?"

"Josh is nice," Molly continued. "He's good-looking, easygoing . . ."

"Then why is he single?"

"Why are you single?" her grandmother retorted.

"Adele!" Molly looked horrified. "That's not fair." She smiled at Dana, though her disappointment was obvious. "Look, it's no big deal. We just thought: two workaholics, it might be nice if, while you're here, you relaxed a little. God knows Josh could use some relaxation, too. He drives himself into the ground."

Dana considered the proposition before her. What was one drink? If they had nothing to say to each other, or if it was a case of loathing on first sight, the whole thing could be over and done with in half an hour. She hated to admit it, but her grandmother was right: it might be nice to have a drink with someone her own age. She had a few business connections in Palm Beach, but the thing about going for cocktails with business acquaintances was that you inevitably talked business. Hmm. One drink with a landscape architect with a degree from Cornell versus watching *American Pickers* with her grandparents. She supposed she could make the sacrifice.

"I'll do it," she said, "on one condition."

Molly's and her grandma's eyes lit up simultaneously. It was disconcerting. "What's that?" her grandmother asked.

"I want to see him first."

"Fair enough," said Molly, who had just chugged down her chocolate milk like it was bourbon. "Here's what we'll do. Adele, you call Josh."

Dana turned to her grandmother. "You know him?"

"Of course I know him. Everyone around here knows him. Like Molly said, he's a big-shot architect. I've met him many times."

Molly continued issuing instructions to Dana's grandmother. "Ask him if he can swing by your place tomorrow after work. Tell him that the white frangipani you have in the clay pot in the kitchen is wilting for no good reason, and you want him to take a look at it. Pluck a few blossoms, crumple them, and throw them to the ground. Make it look real."

Dana's grandmother stared at her. "I'm not an idiot, you know."

"When he comes by, introduce him to Dana," Molly continued. "A few days later, I'll see him and say something like, 'Oh, Adele told me you stopped by to look at her frangipani. Blah, blah, blah, blah, did you meet her niece, blah, blah, blah, she's new in town, it might be nice to go for drinks, blah, done.'"

"Wow," Dana deadpanned. "That summation is really encouraging."

Molly frowned. "You know what I mean."

"And what if he says, 'Not interested'?" Dana asked. The

thought rankled. And she hadn't even met the guy yet. For all she knew, he could be the world's biggest jackass. Yet here she was, already imagining herself being rejected.

"Doubtful," said Molly. "He's many things, but stupid isn't one of them." She glanced around the table. "Are we agreed on this? Josh stopping by?"

"You mean tricking Josh into stopping by," Dana pointed out.

"Who cares how we get him there?" her grandmother countered. "As long as he comes over."

"He will," said Molly.

Dana's grandmother touched her wrist. "Wear your new shirt."

Dana gave her a dirty look. "This is just introducing us to see if we want to meet for drinks at some point, right? It's not a setup for a date."

"You still want to look nice," said her grandmother. "That shirt is nice."

Dana thought fast; she'd rather meet this guy in her hole-filled sweats than wear the shirt. "I'd like to save the shirt for a real date, if that happens," she said, putting just the right amount of pathos in her voice.

Her grandmother looked thrilled by her use of the word *date.* "Completely understandable."

"So we're a go," Molly said triumphantly. "That wasn't too hard, was it?"

CHAPTER THREE

Does tying your own grandmother to a chair qualify as elder abuse? *Maybe not, if it's for her own good,* Dana thought, watching her grandmother anxiously pace the living room. As planned, a phone call had been placed to Josh Green, and he was stopping by her grandparents' condo around six. That in itself was not unnerving; it was the way her grandmother sounded talking to him on the phone, all helpless and coquette-ish on a level that would make Scarlett O'Hara proud. *Oh, Rhett. Rhett, please. Why, this white frangipani in my kitchen—I do believe it's dyin' a most piteous death, Rhett. Oh, please, do come.*

And now here she was, wearing a groove in the carpet as if awaiting royalty. "Where is he? It's six."

" 'Around six' means anywhere from quarter to six till quarter after six," said Dana's grandfather, eyeing his wife warily from the couch, where he sat thumbing through *The Palm Beach Post.*

"No, it means six," her grandmother insisted.

"If he'd meant six on the dot, that's what he'd have said."

Her grandmother looked exasperated. "Sam? Go over to your friend, Ernie's, please, and leave me in peace. You're frazzling my nerves."

Dana's potbellied grandfather hoisted himself off the low-slung couch and, forcing her grandmother to stop in her tracks, kissed her on the cheek. "Anything you wish, my moon and stars." He winked at Dana before beating a hasty retreat, at least as hasty as an eighty-year-old man could retreat.

Dana smiled to herself from where she sat on the couch with her feet tucked up beneath her, book in hand. She loved the way her grandfather still teased her grandmother. Her grandmother often seemed exasperated with him, but Dana and everyone else knew she truly wasn't. It was simply convenient shorthand between them that had been perfected over decades of being together. You be the know-it-all, I'll be the long-suffering one, and occasionally we'll trade places. Despite their seemingly adversarial stance, Dana had never once heard them raise their voices at one other.

The doorbell rang, and Dana's grandmother's halted mid-pace, raising an eyebrow. "Aren't you getting up?"

"He's here to look at *your* plant, correct?"

"And for you to get a look at him."

"I can get a look from here."

"So help me God, you make your mother look like she was an easy child." Her grandmother glanced at the front door in desperation. "Will you at least come over and introduce yourself?"

"Calm down, Gran. Of course I will. Now go answer the door before you have a stroke."

As her grandmother hustled to open the door, Dana chided herself for being nervous. So he was a big-time architect with a degree from Cornell. So what? She could picture his office: glass, minimalist, right on the water. Framed blue prints on the wall of some of his most successful architectural designs. A softly lit cabinet of trophies. A bonsai tree or two.

A deep, rich voice sounded in the hall. "Sorry I'm late, Mrs. Fine. That row of painting line hibiscus along the back of Building Five is dying, and I can't figure out why. Anyway, I had to replace them. Let's see what's up with your frangipani."

One point for Josh Green: he had a nice voice. Dana slowly uncurled herself from the couch, heading for the kitchen. She was almost there when she found herself enveloped by an unpleasantly earthy smell. A crew of maintenance workers was probably planting some flowers; Josh Green's opening the door had let the aroma slip inside for a moment.

She expected to walk in the kitchen and see a handsome man her age in chinos and a tennis shirt. Instead, much to her chagrin, it turned out that Josh Green was the early morning landscaper she'd seen staring at bushes the day before. Of course, that early in the day, he probably didn't stink of sweat the way he did now, and she was fairly sure his arms and legs hadn't been streaked with dried dirt and plant material.

He was crouched on the white tile floor, carefully examining the frangipani petals her grandmother had plucked, crumpled, and scattered as part of her and Molly's master plan.

"Hmmm." Josh picked up one of the plucked flowers, turning it over in his hand.

"You sure you don't have a cat or something that might have ripped them off?"

"No pets allowed, remember?"

"Right."

"I'm not worried about a few flowers wilting. The whole plant looks like it's wilting." Discretion not being her strong suit, Dana's grandmother didn't wait for him to respond before launching into, "Have you met my granddaughter, Josh? Her name is Dana."

Josh rose, and went to the sink to wash his hands. Drying them, he held out a hand to Dana. "Josh Green."

Dana hesitated before taking his hand. "Dana."

"Nice to meet you." He looked at his hands, checking them over thoroughly. "I can go wash them again with bacterial soap if you want."

Dana swallowed, embarrassed. "No, no, I didn't mean—"

"Dana's the director of retail expansion for the La Belle Femme chain of boutiques," her grandmother cut in. "She's overseeing the one that's opening in Palm Beach over Labor Day weekend."

"I think my boys are doing the landscaping there."

Dirt, sweat, and body odor—they were making it hard for Dana to focus on the light green eyes and brown curly hair she knew were there. She tried to picture him all cleaned up, but things kept jumping out at her: a gash on his forearm in need of a Band-Aid, a small swath of dried dirt on his cheek. It didn't work.

Dana's grandmother's eyes lit up. "Did you hear that, Dana? Josh's crew might be doing some landscaping by the store. That's exciting."

Josh caught Dana staring at a thick, dried patch of mud on his shoulder. "I'm betting you don't have a garden."

"I'm barely home," Dana murmured, mortified by her blatant scrutiny of him. As far as she knew, she'd never been so indiscreet checking a guy out in her life.

"That's too bad. Digging your hands down deep in the earth, creating something—it can be very gratifying."

"If that's what you like," Dana replied politely.

Her grandmother was beginning to look panicked. "Josh, did I tell you Dana was single?"

Dana's embarrassment skyrocketed. "Grandma."

Josh directed his attention toward Dana's grandmother. "Don't worry about the frangipani. Give it a little less water, okay?"

Her grandmother nodded as if God himself had spoken. "Okay, Josh."

"Good luck with the store opening," he said to Dana, looking and sounding sincere.

"Thank you."

"If you need anything else done, just call me, Mrs. Fine."

"Of course, Josh."

With that he smiled again, and left.

★ ★ ★

"So?" Dana's grandmother had her hands clasped together hopefully as they returned to the living room couch. "What did you think of him?"

"He's a glorified gardener."

Her grandmother blanched. "What? He's got a degree from Cornell."

"Then what's he doing out there digging in the hot sun? He's a gardener, Gran. You only know him because he's part of the maintenance crew here."

"That crew works for him, Dana. Plus, Molly already told you: he's an architect. A landscape architect."

Dana was silent.

"Fine, don't say anything. The important thing is, would you go for a drink with him if he asked?"

"Grandma, he looked like he came out of the swamp!"

"The man spends most of his time working outside for a living," her grandmother snapped. "You can tell how handsome he is beneath the dried mud."

"No, you can't!"

"Let me tell you something." Her grandmother did what was known in the family as "the point," crooking a bony index finger extremely close to her granddaughter's face. "I've talked to him, Dana. Many, many times. He's nice. He's smart. He works hard. And if you're seriously thinking about getting married and starting a family soon, Josh Green is the kind of man you want."

Chapter Four

"Goddamn it, man. It's so hot, it's a miracle I'm not tripping over my own balls."

Josh slowly nodded in agreement with Eduardo, the tall, wiry foreman of his top landscaping crew. "Hot" didn't even begin to cover it. Mopping his face with a bandanna that had been soaked in cold water, Josh hoped for some temporary relief. The problem was that with heat like this, the bandanna would be dry within minutes. "What happened yesterday with Mrs. Fine wanting to see you?" Eduardo wanted to know, looking irritated. "Another stupid complaint about her hibiscus plants not being uniformly red?"

"That's Mrs. Arbisser in Building Seven."

"Ah, you're right. I'm thinking of Cotton Candy Head."

"Right."

Josh shook his head good-naturedly. Eduardo was a damn good foreman, but sometimes, working at the gated retirement communities that were their bread and butter got to him. He resented that to the residents, he and Josh were just faceless gardeners who maintained their lawns and shrubberies. Josh could care less about what the retirees thought: he was making more money than he ever could have dreamed, and was designing enough landscapes on his own for private home owners that he was earning a reputation.

"So. Mrs. Fine—?" Eduardo pressed.

"She wanted me to take a look at the frangipani plant she has in her kitchen."

"And—?"

"Same old, same old." Josh grabbed an ice cube out of one of the coolers and began running it over his dirt-flecked face. "What she really wanted was for me to check out her granddaughter."

Eduardo nudged Del, the other guy on the crew, in the ribs. Del didn't talk much, but Josh didn't care about that, either. As long as the guy worked hard and had no criminal record, he was free to speak two words a day or two thousand.

"Are you listening to this?" Eduardo cracked. "She wanted him to check out her granddaughter."

"It happens all the time."

"Get the fuck out of here, *mijo,* you got it wrong. They want the girls to check *you* out. And take it from me: you don't have a chance in hell. If I were a woman, the last man I'd go out with is someone who looks like he's been rolling in a ditch all day. None of them would even walk down the street with you."

Josh shrugged. "I don't care. I don't need anyone's help when it comes to women."

"This kind of stuff never happens to me," Del muttered.

Josh and Eduardo stared at him in shock. This was the first piece of personal information he'd ever offered.

"It doesn't," Del repeated.

"Maybe if you talked more," Josh suggested.

"Yeah, and got two front teeth or something," Eduardo added helpfully.

Del still looked gloomy. "Maybe."

Josh waited to see if Del had anything else to add, but he didn't. "Like I said," he continued, picking up the thread of his conversation with Eduardo, "I don't need these introductions, but obviously, these women do. Which makes me wonder: what's wrong with them?"

"Maybe nothing is wrong with them," Eduardo retorted. "Maybe they're tired of meeting jerks."

"How do they know I'm not a jerk?"

"Because you've been vetted by Granny."

Josh rubbed the ice cube across the back of his neck. "The one I met yesterday was cute: petite, with big brown eyes and long blond hair. I might have gone out with her if the circumstances were different."

"Different how?"

"If she looked at me with the respect you should show anyone you were meeting for the first time."

"What, you expected her to be excited by a guy who shows up looking like a grave digger? You expect too much, my friend."

"Hey, it's not my fault. It's not like I ever know when one of these old women is going to ambush me."

Eduardo plucked on his lower lip. "True. Now I'm back on your side. Screw anyone who shows no respect for a hardworking man." He took his water bottle and squeezed some water over his head, his expression momentarily blissful as it trickled down his face and neck. "Do you know what she does?"

"She's retail director for some expensive chain of boutiques. She's down here because the newest one is opening in Palm Beach on Labor Day weekend."

"I hope she has some Valium and thousand dollar bills to make change with."

"Amen to that."

CHAPTER FIVE

Since the dawn of time, people have made sacrifices for those they love, Dana told herself. Today, hers was wearing the hideous beige shirt with gold epaulets in order to make her grandmother happy.

"We're gonna be late," her grandmother called out from the living room. She'd been ready to go to her friend's wedding for an hour already. Now she was driving Dana and her grandfather crazy.

"Calm down." Dana's grandfather's voice was gruff but affectionate as he called back to her from behind the closed door of the master bathroom. "We've got more than enough time."

Dana knew her grandmother: inside, she was cursing her grandfather up and down, mainly because she knew he was right.

Dana forced herself to again look in the mirror in her bedroom. Nice pants, nice heels, nice nails, nice hair, nice face, and then . . . the shirt. God, what was that show her mother used to watch? *The Love Boat*? Dana looked like she could be the first mate on *The Love Boat*.

She tried to put it in perspective. It was only a few hours of her life, and it was worth it to please her grandmother. Her grandmother's friend, Lois, was getting married to her "longtime" boyfriend, John. According to Dana's grandmother, it had been "love at first sight" about three months after John's wife died. Dana found the timeline shocking, until her grandmother explained something to her: what younger people might consider "hasty" nuptials didn't hold here. Here, everyone knew that they didn't have all the time in the world, and when a chance for happiness came along, you had to snatch it up as fast as you could.

"Grandma," Dana called out. "I still don't understand why I was invited to Lois's wedding."

"I told you," her grandmother called back. "Lois wants to meet you."

"What a bunch of crap," Dana's grandfather hollered. He'd joined her grandmother in the living room. "Lois has a grandson who's king of some computer company. She wants you two to meet."

Dana entered the living room just in time to see her grandmother pinching the ridge of her nose dramatically. "Shut up for once in your life, Sam? Please?"

He turned his palms up plaintively. "See how she treats me?" he asked Dana. "All I do is give her love, and what do I get in return? A kick in the ass."

"That's why our marriage has been such a success," her grandmother deadpanned. "Both the wedding and the reception are being held at the clubhouse," she told Dana. "It'll be nice."

Dana nodded, dutifully followed her grandparents to the door.

"Unless Ben Barry is there," said her grandfather, making a face. "Total moron. Trying to tell me the origins of World War Two."

Her grandmother sighed.

"I was a goddamn history professor for fifty years and he's telling me?"

"Ignore him," Dana's grandmother said.

Dana's grandfather fiddled in his jacket pocket for the house keys. "Oh, I'll ignore him, all right."

Dana looked down at her feet so her grandparents wouldn't

catch her enjoying their craziness. She was actually on the verge of a small giggle when she noticed the epaulets on her blouse were casting shadows on the sidewalk that made her look like a linebacker. It was going to be a long night.

Lois and Johnny stood beneath the wedding *chuppah* in the clubhouse's "reception" room, reciting their vows in quiet, almost shaky voices. Dana's grandmother had wanted to sit in the front row, but her grandfather insisted on sitting on the aisle seat somewhere in the middle in case he needed to "escape." Johnny, bald as an infant and sporting glasses the size of dessert plates, looked charming in a baggy suit that he'd obviously filled out in his younger days. Lois was attired in a modest, ankle-length, ice-blue dress with long sleeves of scalloped lace. Her dowager's hump wasn't as bad as Dana's grandmother claimed. There had been no walking the bride up the aisle, no relatives holding up the *chuppah* poles. The only family on hand was Lois's grandson. But the lack of relatives in no way detracted from the overwhelming sense of joy filling the room.

Watching the elderly couple recite their vows, Dana's chest constricted. She was moved by what an act of hope it was to join your life to someone else's at such a late stage of the game. But she was also sad, recalling every wedding she'd ever attended, every bridesmaid dress she'd ever been fitted for, every baby shower she'd ever helped plan. When would finding the right man happen for her? And what if it never did? Molly had never married and had been perfectly happy with her life. But she wasn't Molly.

CHAPTER SIX

"Gimme a break, Aunt Molly. I'm not an idiot."

Josh stole an affectionate glance at his aunt as the entrance gate at Huerto de Naranja lifted and he drove inside. When his phone had rung early this morning, he'd known immediately who it was. His aunt always called him early on Sunday morning, even though he had repeatedly asked her not to, because Saturday night was his one night "out on the town" and he usually got in late.

Last night, he'd met up with Eduardo at some new salsa club that his friend had been raving about. Josh was well aware he couldn't dance worth a damn, but some of the women there didn't seem to care. Seeing an attractive man, they were more than willing to try to teach him.

Josh was fascinated watching all those gorgeous, curvy women, so secure in their bodies and the power they exerted over men. He could have had his pick of any of them. He usually did. But for some reason, the uptight germ-o-phobe Dana Fine kept creeping into his head, a much-unwanted nuisance. He'd spent the last half hour of the night watching these women strut their stuff, betting there was no way Dana Fine could move like that.

Occasionally his mind would veer over to the image of her shaking her hips, but he was able to put it aright by thinking about her face, and the intelligence he'd seen there. She held a powerful position at work. Josh knew she couldn't have gotten where she was without busting her ass, the same way he did. She had to be smart and ambitious—two traits often used to describe him. Interesting.

The story his aunt had given him about why she needed him to accompany her to the wedding was so transparent, Josh couldn't resist teasing her. "You really expected me to believe you wanted me to come with you because Mr. Owalu from your reading group has the flu?"

"I don't know what you're talking about," Aunt Molly insisted as Josh opened the car door for her. She was always late, which meant they'd missed the ceremony. Josh was glad: he was tired, and the last thing he wanted was to sit through a wedding ceremony at a retirement complex.

"Don't bullshit a bullshitter," Josh continued, as his aunt gripped his forearm to pull herself up out of the car. "Knowing you, there's no book group, and there's no Mr. Owalu, either. The only reason I'm here is because Dana Fine is here with her grandparents."

His aunt peered off into the sunset. "I have no idea if she's here."

"Don't insult my intelligence, Aunt Molly. C'mon."

His aunt's shoulders sank. "All right, she's here. Adele told me things didn't go very well between you two."

"Dana doesn't seem to like dirt."

"That's why Adele and I thought it was important she see you all cleaned up."

Josh laughed. "Because God knows that's something I would never think of myself."

His aunt stared at him down the length of her beaky nose. "We don't have to stay long."

"Just long enough for Dana to check behind my ears for mold?" Aunt Molly gave him a dirty look as they began their slow march toward the clubhouse. "You owe me for this."

"If you like her, *you're* going to owe *me*," his aunt pointed out. "So there."

Josh looked out at the sun, a bright orange fireball in the

sky that was slowly setting. He felt lucky being able to wit-
ness something so beautiful every night. His aunt was right,
of course: if Dana Fine liked him, he'd be the one doing the
owing. But he doubted it would matter.

CHAPTER SEVEN

Dana really didn't like being rude to other people, but if Lois's grandson, Jay, didn't stop talking at her about how he'd built his company up with his own two hands, and how incredible his new luxury apartment on Williams Island was, she might be forced to abruptly say "Excuse me" and flee to the ladies' room. Dana might have given him more of a chance if he'd asked a single question about her, but he hadn't. *Maybe it's a sign,* Dana thought. *The universe is trying to tell me to forget all this old-fashioned love and marriage stuff and just go to Paris.*

Jay had started droning about the yacht he was thinking of buying when her aunt Molly entered the room on the arm of Josh Green. So that's why she'd been invited to the wedding. She sighed heavily with resignation.

"I'm sorry," Jay said, looking offended. "Am I boring you?"

Dana blinked. "What—no. Why would you say that?"

"Your sigh?"

"I'm worried," Dana lied. "My aunt just walked in and she doesn't look well. I really need to see what's going on. Excuse me."

Crossing the room, Dana wondered if her decision to use Molly as an excuse for flight was a wise one. Josh might think she was making a beeline for him. Now that he wasn't encrusted in dried mud, there was no mistaking how handsome he was. Classic features, as her mother would say. Hot, Aunt Molly would say. The deep tan didn't hurt; it made his green eyes really stand out.

Molly broke into a big smile at Dana's approach. "Dana! What are you doing here?"

Josh and Dana looked at each other with amused disbelief. "I'm here for the same reason Josh is," Dana said good-naturedly. "I was duped."

Josh pointed out the table where Dana's grandparents sat to his aunt. "Why don't you go sit with Mr. and Mrs. Fine and I'll bring you something to drink?"

"Don't spend the money. Water is fine."

She winked at Dana and began moving slowly toward the table, where Dana's grandfather was snapping at the pruny face of another man, who was snapping back. The dreaded Ben Barry. Little did the poor man know that if he kept challenging her grandfather on facts about World War II, he was going to find himself flattened like a tank.

Dana looked at Josh. "I just want you to know I had nothing to do with this."

"Well, I did."

Dana was caught off guard.

"I figured that if you got a good look at me when I wasn't caked in dirt, maybe a quick drink would be possible," he said dryly. He loosened his tie so she could see his neck. "See? No dirt."

"Josh." Dana was mortified. "I'm so sorry about that. But you didn't help things when you offered to wash your hands a second time."

"Did that rankle you? Good. It should have after you recoiled from me."

"I didn't recoil from you! I hesitated." Admitting it made her feel ashamed.

"Well, as you can see, I clean up real good. So, would you care to join me for a drink?"

"Sure." Dana knew she sounded smooth and confident,

but that wasn't how she felt. Thankfully, she was used to faking it with clients.

"Great." Josh looked pleased. "I vote we sit at the bar."

"I don't know. If we do that, a lot of casually walking by is going to happen."

Josh rolled his eyes. "True. I guess we'd better sit at the table." He frowned. "Too bad we can't just leave and go for a drink somewhere else, you know? It would save us having to choke down the rubber chicken."

Dana laughed. "I know. But that would be bad manners."

"Well, I'm just one step away from a grave digger, so I know all about bad manners." Dana stared at him frostily, and Josh backed off. "All right, I'll stop goofing on you. We're here. I guess we might as well try to enjoy it. I just ask one thing."

"What's that?"

"If my aunt calls me 'Joshie,' tell her you'll never speak with her again."

Dana extended her hand for a shake. "Deal."

"Good. Let's go."

Chapter Eight

"They think we're eloping."

Dana nodded avidly. "Oh, no bets, it's a given."

Her smile matched Josh's as they drove toward Delray Beach. They'd been eager to escape the reception, not just because the food was god-awful as predicted, but because it was hard to carry on a conversation when two old women were straining to listen to every word they exchanged, hope flashing in their eyes like blinding beacons.

She and Josh had laughed the moment they sat down at the table. Somehow, they'd been seated right next to each other. Go figure. When Molly and her grandmother weren't watching them with eagle eyes, they were lobbing what they believed to be vital information across the table at Dana and Josh like hand grenades.

"Dana, Josh designed the landscaping for the Fortnum Estate in Palm Beach," Molly boasted. "But he's not just an architect. He runs his own landscape contracting business too, called Green Thumb. Because his last name is Green."

"Josh, did you know Dana invented the corporate ladder for women at La Belle Femme?"

Other gems included: "Josh might get his pilot's license," "Dana wants a family one day," and "The *Palm Beach Post* called Josh the hottest landscape architect in town."

As dinner wore on, Dana was surprised to find her frustration growing. She didn't want random facts about Josh thrown at her by Molly: she wanted to hear about Josh from Josh. Josh appeared to share the same frustration: a few times over the course of the meal, Dana caught the glint of annoyance in his eyes when her grandmother started in on another spiel about Dana's stellar qualities. Josh must have wanted to know about her, too.

It was as if they'd made some unspoken agreement. As soon as dessert was over, Josh politely rose from the table, pulling Dana's chair out for her.

"Aunt Molly, do you think you can catch a ride home with the Westons? I thought it might be nice to show Dana around Delray."

Molly and Dana's grandmother shared a not-so-secret smile. "Of course I can get a ride from someone else," she assured him breezily. "It's silly for you two to be stuck in a room full of old people when you could be out on the town." She shooed them away. "Go, go. Have fun."

Dana kissed her grandparents, telling them she wouldn't be late. That was when her grandmother grabbed her hand and stage-whispered, "I'll be praying."

"You do that, Grandma," Dana whispered back. Amusement had replaced mortification. Maybe that was a good sign.

Their relief as they drove past Huerto de Naranja's gates was tangible. Brutally hot as the Florida days could be, tonight was one of those evenings when the humidity wasn't too awful, and there was even a whisper of a breeze. Dana stuck her hand out the passenger side window, relishing the feel of the warm wind racing through her fingertips.

"We survived intact," she said to Josh, turning to look at him. The sun-streaked, brown, curly hair, the deeply tanned skin . . . Dana could tell he was the type who thrived in the heat, who loved the feel of the sun beating down upon him. She wished she could say the same for herself.

"You okay with the temperature?" Josh asked as if reading her mind. "I could turn on the AC."

"I'm fine," Dana assured him, though she did feel what she hoped was a last, faint trickle of sweat rolling down between her shoulder blades. Then she remembered.

"Josh? I want you to know something."

Josh picked up speed. "This doesn't involve you telling me we're being tailed by your psycho ex-boyfriend, does it?"

"No. It's this hideous shirt I'm wearing. I didn't pick it out. My grandmother did. I wore it tonight just to please her."

Josh gave her a quick glance. "I hadn't noticed it."

Dana felt surprisingly insulted. "Really."

Josh looked her up and down. "However, I'm noticing it now. Nice epaulets, Dana."

Dana covered her face with her hands, steeling herself. "Go on. Let me have it. I deserve it after assuming you spend your life covered in muck."

"I do spend my life covered in muck, at least part of it. You thought having a drink with a guy like that was beneath you. But as you can see, I do have an intimate relationship with soap."

Dana uncovered her face to find Josh smiling at her playfully. He was enjoying teasing her, and she was enjoying being teased. Dana realized it had been ages since she'd felt so comfortable with a man. She worked all over the world, meeting all sorts of people. She was an expert at reading them. Josh Green was a terrific mix of confidence, intelligence, and humor. He was down-to-earth and worked as hard as she did. She flashed back on the image of her grandmother pointing a gnarly index finger in her face, upbraiding her about not giving him a chance.

"What was that Molly was saying about you getting your pilot's license?"

"I mentioned it to her once, six months ago," Josh said, undoing his tie and tossing it into the backseat. "She thinks it's one of my selling points."

"Does she try to sell you a lot?"

Josh glanced at her flirtatiously. "Why do you want to know?"

"Curiosity. Plain and simple."

"No, she doesn't try to sell me a lot. And even if she did, it would be a waste of time. I don't need to be sold. I think the women I date are more than capable of making a decision about me without my aunt having to list my 'selling points.' "

"I feel the same way." Dana rolled up the window a bit so her hair wasn't whipping around her face. "I don't need my grandmother trying to convince some guy that I'm worth spending time with."

"That's true."

Dana blushed. It had been a long time since a man had flirted with her outright, and she'd almost forgotten how good it made her feel. She felt happy, which was nuts. She hadn't even known Josh for twenty-four hours. And yet . . . She took hold of her runaway thoughts, forcing herself to remember who she was and why she was in Florida. One drink. That was all. She couldn't afford to let her long romantic exile go to her head.

Dana had been looking at and listening to Josh so intently that it came as a surprise to her when the car stopped moving as Josh pulled into a parking spot at the beach.

"This okay?"

For the first time since they'd met, Josh looked tentative. "I just assumed you'd want to take a walk along the beach. But if you'd prefer, we can skip it and go to downtown Delray first to get that drink. There's a lot going on."

"No, this is great," Dana assured him, because it was. She had promised herself that while in Florida, she would carve out some time to go to the beach. Her grandparents never went, preferring the swimming pool at Huerto de Naranja. "With a pool, you don't have to worry about sand creeping into every nook and cranny of your house, not to mention every nook and cranny of your body," her grandmother had opined. Dana didn't agree.

"I like coming here at night. It's really relaxing."

"I can imagine." Dana looked up at the sky. "It's a beautiful moon."

"It's a beautiful moon every night in Florida."

Dana regarded him with suspicion. "Are you sure you don't work for the tourist board?"

Josh laughed, bending to untie his shoes.

Dana followed, momentarily fretting over when her last pedicure had been. But her feet looked fine, her skin smooth, her toenails buffed and painted. Her vanity remained intact.

Meanwhile, Josh carelessly threw his shoes and socks in the back of the car.

He's rough on his clothing, Dana thought. First he'd tossed his tie over his shoulder, and now he was chucking what looked like an expensive pair of shoes into the back. She wondered if it came from years of throwing landscaping tools in the back of his truck. Casually tossing clothing didn't seem in character with being an architect. Weren't they known for being meticulous? Once again she was forced to remind herself that she really didn't know Josh at all.

Stepping gingerly onto the sand, Dana had assumed it would be cool now that the sun had gone down, but it still held the heat of the day. She and Josh weren't the only ones on the beach: it was by no means packed, but there were a lot of other couples out strolling. Not that they were a couple.

Dana reveled in the caress of the wind on her face, swearing she could taste the salt of the sea on her tongue. Though walking, she felt as though she were being gently rocked. For the first time in a long time, she felt completely relaxed.

Josh was eying her with interest. "You look hypnotized."

"I feel hypnotized."

"When's the last time you walked along the ocean, Miss

Dana Fine?" There was the mildest hint of scolding in his voice.

Dana smiled sadly. "It's been years."

"I'd lose it if I didn't live here."

"Why's that?"

"I love being outside as much as I can. I love the water. One of the great things about Florida is that it's warm all the time. So not only do I have the beach at my disposal all year-round, I can also work all year-round at something I love. I feel pretty lucky."

He pointed to a bank of lights far ahead. "I live in one of the buildings up there."

"On the beach?"

Josh nodded.

"I don't want to hear any more," Dana informed him. "You're making me envious."

"It's pretty sweet. But I busted my ass for it."

"I understand ass-busting all too well," Dana murmured, now thinking about his ass, and how it was probably anything but busted.

Silent, without a hint of awkwardness, Josh took her hand, prompting a small, sweet tingle of happiness inside her. She knew she should be leading with her head, not her heart, but she didn't want to.

"Tell me about your job," Josh said. "Every time I tried to ask you about it at the wedding, your grandmother would interrupt us."

Dana kicked up a small spray of sand. "It's not very exciting." She recited the facts.

"Sounds like a lot of travel."

"It is." She looked at the ocean. The steady, unvarying lapping of the waves was reassuring. "At first, I thought it was glamorous. Now it's just draining."

"But you had to know what you were getting into."

Dana smiled ruefully. "Actually, I had no idea at all." A piece of the tranquility she'd been feeling slipped away. "I needed a job when I graduated from college. Any job. As it happened, my uncle was working as an accountant for La Belle Femme, except the company wasn't called that when he started there. It was a small, family-owned clothing store called Hewitt's on Long Island. I don't know how, but he somehow managed to finagle a job for me as an entry-level buyer.

"When the owner's son took over five years ago, he decided he wanted to go after a very exclusive, upscale, female clientele. That's when the company was rechristened La Belle Femme and started to expand. He knew I worked hard and I had good people skills. Plus, I knew the ropes, so he made me director of retail expansion."

"Sounds exhausting," said Josh, grasping her hand just a tiny bit tighter, perhaps in reassurance. "But I've found exhausting is okay if you love what you do."

Dana hesitated. "That's the problem. I don't love it. I don't hate it, but I don't love it."

"If you could do whatever you wanted right now, what would it be?"

I'd get married and have a family, Dana thought without hesitation. But there was no way she was going to tell that to a man she'd just met, unless she was a woman who got her kicks watching men sprint away from her.

"I'd have to think about that," Dana answered in reply to his question.

A slightly more forceful wind swept in off the ocean, giving Dana a chill. Without even asking if she needed it, Josh removed his sports jacket, draping it over her shoulders. It was such a simple, thoughtful gesture, and it somehow made the world around her come into sharper focus: the moon seemed brighter, the sand beneath her feet more grittily delicious. When she broke out into a wide grin, Josh was right there smiling back at her, but his expression was also questioning.

"What's the big smile about?"

Dana blushed deeply, glad that he probably couldn't see that in the dark. "It's nothing."

"Right."

"You'll laugh at me if I tell you."

"Try me."

Dana stopped, drawing his jacket closer around her shoulders as if it could protect her from the vulnerability she was about to reveal.

"I was smiling because I'm glad you came to the wedding with Molly. I've really been enjoying the past couple of hours."

"Me, too." Josh looked around appreciatively. "I feel like we're in a movie. The setting is just so amazing."

"I know."

He turned so he faced her. "If this were a movie, this would be the part where I kiss you."

"And this would be the part where I let you."

Josh flashed a slow, seductive smile as he took her in his arms. Dana closed her eyes, waiting for their lips to make contact. The wait seemed to go on forever, even though it couldn't have been more than a few seconds before his lips brushed against hers. But she screwed it up: she was so happy, her mouth broke into a wide grin beneath his, effectively ending the kiss.

Josh drew back, regarding her with amusement. "What're you grinning about this time?"

"I just feel really happy. Goofy, almost."

Josh nodded thoughtfully. "I like that. Goofy is good."

Dana wrinkled her nose. "Really?"

"Yeah. I don't think I've ever had a woman tell me she felt goofy before. Giddy, yes. Intoxicated by my presence, hell yes. But goofy? No." Josh studied her face with concern. "You are, aren't you?"

"What?"

"Intoxicated by my presence."

Dana responded with another bright grin.

"That's it," said Josh, pulling her back into his arms. "No more smiling. It's getting in the way of my kissing you."

Dana laughed softly as Josh started out lightly kissing her mouth before moving on to butterfly kisses up and down her neck. But sweetness soon gave way to seductiveness as Josh's embrace grew tighter and his mouth more demanding. Maybe she was crazy, but Dana couldn't shake the feeling that he was holding on to her so tightly because he didn't want her to slip away. *I'm not going anywhere,* she longed to tell him. Dana was by no means an impulsive person. But something about tonight—the wedding, the moonlight, the steady whisper of the tide, maybe even the heat—had gotten to her. So when Josh gently bit down on her earlobe and asked if she wanted to go back to his place, there was no question in her mind what her answer would be.

CHAPTER NINE

I've never done anything like this before. The sentence was an endless loop in Dana's head as she and Josh drove the short distance to his apartment. Dana decided she would say it when their lovemaking began in earnest. Then she changed her mind: she'd say it before their first kiss at his place.

Driving the road along the beach, Josh had his hand on her knee, his fingers tightly twined through hers. Yes, it was like they were in a movie, the moonlight hitting the car so perfectly it gave it a magical glow. Josh glanced at her with the faintest hint of a smile.

"What?" Dana asked.

"Nothing."

"There must be something," she persisted.

"Your hand is so tense. Relax. In the movies, the woman's hand is never tense. Unless it's with anticipation."

"How do you know it's not anticipation?" Dana answered with uncharacteristic boldness.

"Actually, I don't." He untangled their fingers, his free hand now languidly sliding up and down her thigh.

"Am I allowed to do this?" he asked.

"Do they do it in the movies?" Dana replied, surprised to hear herself flirting. Josh made it easy.

"I think it depends on what the movie is rated."

"In that case, I vote we keep it PG for now so you don't crash your car."

Josh laughed.

Dana looked out the window. Maybe she wouldn't say, "I've never done anything like this before." Maybe she'd keep that tidbit her delicious secret. He probably knew it anyway: any woman who would accommodate her grandmother by wearing an epaulet-trimmed blouse was not the type to hook up with someone she'd just met.

Still, he hadn't seemed surprised when she'd accepted his offer to go back to his place. Dana had always been skeptical about the notion of fate. But for some reason, her path had crossed Josh Green's, and they were both smart enough to know that the ease and mutual attraction they felt wasn't something that happened every day. It would be foolish not to act on it.

"This is breathtaking."

Dana gazed at the ocean from Josh's tenth-floor terrace. To get to the beach from his building, all you needed to do was walk down a discreet path cut through tall beach grass. Between the whisper of a breeze and the moon showing off, glistening like ice across the top of the ocean, Dana couldn't remember the last time she'd felt so overwhelmed by the world's simple beauty. Her job rarely allowed her to slow down and take sights like this in.

Josh joined her at the railing, putting his arm around her as if it were the most natural thing in the world. *So handsome,* Dana thought. *The perfect leading man.*

"You like it?"

"What's not to like?" Dana felt embarrassed. "That sounds exactly like something my grandmother would say."

"Or my aunt."

"Must be in the drinking water."

"Speaking of which, can I get you anything to drink?"

Dana smiled contentedly. "No, I'm fine, thank you."

"Me, too."

Dana rested her head on his shoulder. She liked this movie. A lot.

"You smell great," Josh murmured, nuzzling his nose in her hair.

"Thank you." Dana looked up at him, smiling shyly. "If this were a movie," she said quietly, "what would happen next?"

"What's the movie rated now?"

Dana suddenly felt shy. "You decide."

"NC-17?"

Josh held out his hand to her, leading her back inside. Comfortable as she felt, Dana did begin to feel a flutter of nerves ripple through her body. *I've never done anything like this before.*

The wall of his bedroom that faced the sea was made entirely of glass, allowing the sunlight to pour in during the day and the moonlight at night.

"I have to admit something," Josh whispered as he took her into his arms.

"What's that?"

"I've been fantasizing about you ever since I walked into your grandmother's kitchen."

The tiny hairs on the back of Dana's neck stood up. It was thrilling, the idea that he'd already pictured making love to her. Dana, rarely the aggressive one, put her hand on the back of his neck and hungrily pulled his mouth down to hers. It was her way of telling him that his fantasy was about to come true. She could feel the atmosphere in the room charge, its sleek quietness turning into something more kinetic.

Josh tore his mouth from hers. The look in his eyes . . . Dana could see it wasn't just her lips he wanted to kiss. He wanted it all and he took it: Her cheeks. Her forehead. And her neck, where he treated her to seductive nips and bites. Teasing, but with a small sting of pain that aroused.

Dana's heartbeat was beginning to quicken when Josh

lifted his head to again gaze at her, his smile unmistakably mischievous.

"Much as I love your epaulets," he murmured as he slowly began unbuttoning her blouse, "I'm afraid they're going to have to go."

Josh's gaze was arresting as he slid the blouse off her shoulders, running his fingers up and down her bare arms, giving her goose bumps, but not the kind that you want to go away. Dana closed her eyes, smiling with sweet pleasure.

"Someone likes that," Josh murmured seductively as his hands moved to the back of her bra. "Maybe we should get rid of this, too."

His look became demanding as he unfastened her bra in one swift move and tossed it to the floor. Dana inhaled sharply, watching as he took her breasts in his hands, caressing them, before his index finger and thumb began gently squeezing her nipples.

Dana's eyes fluttered closed again. Her head dropped back as she reveled in the sensation of his hands on her, feeling her. Excitement surged through her when Josh knelt in front of her and began to taste her: a soft flick of his tongue against her nipple, a hard suckle, and all the while, those large, rough hands fondling her.

So good . . . Whimpers and moans escaped Dana's throat. She'd crossed over the line to lust. "You're driving me crazy," Dana whispered, unashamed of the urgency in her voice.

"That's the general idea."

Josh rose, his expression as greedy as she was feeling inside as he pushed her back on the bed. Dana found she couldn't escape the wicked thrumming between her legs that was making itself more and more insistent as she watched Josh unzip her pants and pull them down in one swift motion.

Josh groaned as he crawled back up her body to once again nip her neck and suckle her breast. His mouth was more demanding this time, more urgent. Dana's whole body was now pulsing with so much excitement she could barely contain it. Unable to stop herself, she began rubbing herself against him, gasping when she felt his cock straining through his pants.

"Josh . . ."

Words flew away as Josh reached down and slowly, with great deliberateness, began brushing his fingers across the wet fabric of her panties.

"I want you," Dana whispered fiercely.

"Patience," Josh whispered. "You need to learn patience."

Dana took a deep breath, but it was no good: Josh tortured her with a few more caresses before abruptly yanking her panties down. He lay beside her as his hand returned to its place between her legs, exploring her wetness. More and more, Dana was beginning to feel herself crack into pieces as her bucking hips met every thrust of his fingers.

Josh nipped her earlobe. "Do you have any idea how hard I'm gonna make you come?"

Dana wondered if he knew how close she was right now, how she thought she'd split out of her own skin when his fingers found her clit and began rubbing it slowly. She pushed against his hand, desperation racing through her. Josh quickened the dance of his fingers. She wasn't sure how much more she could take.

"Josh, please."

It was growing unbearable, the need of her body to release its passion. And Josh seemed to know it as he slipped two thick fingers inside her, moving them in and out while the pad of his thumb still teased her. Dana suddenly felt the heat of her body punch through her senses, erasing who and where she was. When she returned to herself, the breath-taking sight of Josh smiling beside her greeted her.

"Was that okay?" he asked, kissing her shoulder.

"Yes," Dana managed in a voice barely above a whisper. There were still aftershocks rippling through her body, and her own heartbeat was still swooshing loudly in her ears. Dana couldn't stop staring at her lover. She could see how happy he was to have pleased her, but behind his look of satisfaction, there was primitive desire in his eyes.

Dana reached down, pressing the palm of her hand against the bulge in Josh's trousers. She could see him fighting with himself as she began moving her hand up and down. "Do it," she whispered.

Josh reared up and rolled her onto her back while he hastily stripped off his pants, pausing only to reach into his night table drawer for protection. All the while, his eyes were devouring her body.

"You are so goddamn beautiful."

Dana moaned as Josh slid on top of her, pushing her legs farther apart with his knee until finally, Dana felt his cock inside her. He held still.

"Jesus, stop torturing me," Dana begged. "Please."

Laughing wickedly, Josh pulled back, thrusting back inside her slowly. Dana wrapped her legs around his waist, trying to savor the deliberateness with which he was moving, but she was finding it difficult.

"Faster," she pleaded. "Please."

"I want this to last," Josh replied hoarsely, his face buried in her neck as he began moving his hips against hers. "Fuck . . ."

Dana dug her nails deep into his back, their moans and groans the only sounds she needed to hear. The heat inside her was beginning to spike again as Josh pumped in and out of her. He lowered his head to suckle again, and that's when she exploded, strong and sweet. The sound of her coming incited Josh: he began pounding into her with all his strength, harder and faster than she thought a man ever could, until he cried out her name, his orgasm overtaking him in a series of violent shudders that Dana wished could go on forever.

CHAPTER TEN

Dana inhaled slowly, trying to regain her breath. She had hoped their lovemaking would be good; little did she know how great it would be.

Josh rolled off her with a smile, scrambling to pull back the bedcovers so he and Dana could sleep beneath the sheets. Dana thought he looked adorable, his tousled curls a mess. She wouldn't tell him that, though. You didn't tell men they were adorable, especially not right after you'd slept with them.

The ice-cold sheets momentarily shocked Dana's naked skin, but then Josh pulled her against him and warmth returned, the best kind there was.

"Thank you," Josh said, propping himself up on an elbow to look at her. Dana hadn't noticed it before, but his nakedness revealed just how darkly tanned his skin really was, those parts of his body kept from sunlight pale in comparison to the deep cocoa brown of his skin. Dana, not really having had a chance to appreciate his chest, ran her fingers over it now, pushing her palms against the solid wall of skin. She could feel his heart beating beneath her spread fingers. It was still a little fast.

Dana grinned at him, her goofy feeling beginning to return. "What are you thanking me for?"

"Letting me make love to you."

Dana was touched. "Don't be silly."

"I'm not being silly." Josh's tone, though casual, was heart-felt. "I don't do this kind of thing all the time."

Dana narrowed her eyes, unable to hold back her skepti-cism. "Yeah, right. A good-looking guy like you doesn't just snap his fingers whenever he's in the mood."

"My finger-snapping days are long over," Josh replied matter-of-factly.

"And why's that?"

"It gets kind of boring sleeping with women just for the sake of sleeping with them. And at the end of the day, I'm usually too tired to snap my fingers, never mind performing in the sack."

"I must be pretty special, then," Dana joked.

Josh reached out to caress her cheek. "I think so."

Dana tensed slightly, beginning to feel a little overwhelmed. "I don't do this all the time, either."

"I didn't think so."

"What does that mean?" Dana wasn't sure if it was a com-pliment or an insult.

Josh looked perplexed. "You look upset."

"Because I don't know how you mean it."

"How do you think I meant it? You've got to learn to re-lax, Miss Fine."

"I'm relaxed right now."

"Then get more relaxed."

Dana clamped her eyes shut. "Okay, I'm more relaxed. Now tell me what you meant."

"I don't think people who are looking to settle down go around having random sex."

"Who says I want to settle down?"

Josh looked amused. "Your grandmother was practically screaming it at me across the table, remember?"

Dana groaned. "I'd blocked that out. Sorry about that."

"Don't apologize," said Josh, sweeping her hair back from her shoulder.

"I guess you're right: there's no need to," Dana agreed.

EARLY BIRD SPECIAL 47

"It's not like this is a relationship or anything, and she's trying to pressure you."

"Right."

They both fell quiet.

Dana could tell he wanted to say something to her, but was mulling it over. Finally he asked, "How long are you here for?"

"Three weeks."

Josh looked disappointed as he brushed his lips against hers. "I like you, Dana. I don't want this to be a one night stand."

"Neither do I."

"How do you feel about spending more time together until you have to leave?"

"I'd like that," Dana replied, but she couldn't hide her uncertainty. "But I've never been involved with someone when I knew the clock was ticking."

"Neither have I." Josh sighed deeply. "But we've got three whole weeks. Why not enjoy it?"

And what if I enjoy it too much? Dana thought to herself. "You're right."

"There's just one hard and fast rule."

"What?" Dana knew there had to be a catch.

"You promise you'll never wear that blouse when we're out together. If you want to wear it around your grandparents' condo, fine. But if we're out somewhere and I see you in that blouse, the deal's off."

"I'll be breaking my grandmother's heart."

"Doubtful."

"No, it's true."

Josh kissed the hollow of her collarbone. "Then you'll have to break it, because that's my only rule—that, and we have a good time together."

"I think I can manage that." Dana snuggled up to him. "As long as you let me check your nails for dirt at the end of the day."

★ ★ ★

Dana had no idea how long they spent dozing on and off. But when Josh asked her what time she wanted him to set the alarm for, she suddenly found herself wide awake.

She sat up, looking at him. "I can't stay the whole night! What about my grandparents?"

Josh knitted his brow in confusion. "What about them?"

"What will they think?"

"That you're a grown woman?" Josh tried.

"I know, I know, it's silly." Dana felt foolish as heat crept to her cheeks. "I just think they'll be disappointed in me."

Josh sat up. "For having sex?"

Dana cringed. "Yeah. Yes. If I get home before they wake up, they won't think we fooled around as much as we did."

Josh's expression remained uncomprehending. "How old are you again?"

"Josh, it's irrelevant," Dana replied, getting flustered. "These are my grandparents we're talking about. My grand-parents. I don't think I could look my grandfather in the eye if he knew I stayed here all night."

"Okay, okay, relax. We'll throw our clothes on and I'll drive you home."

"Thank you."

He pulled her back down and rolled back on top of her, supporting his weight on his elbows. "When can I see you again?"

"Tomorrow night?"

Josh grimaced. "I've got a meeting with some clients to go over the blueprints for their garden. They want a waterfall. It's already been a pain in the ass trying to figure out where to put it without wrecking the landscaping that was done when they moved in. Day after tomorrow?"

"That would be nice." Dana's eyes lit up. "Let's go danc-ing!"

"Uh, no. I can't dance at all."

"You danced well before," Dana purred.

"Horizontal dancing is different. The minute you see me on the dance floor with Latino guys, you'll never want to see me again."

"Please? Just for a little while? I haven't been dancing in ages and I love it."

"We'll see," Josh mollified. "For now, I'd better get you home before your grandparents find out what a bad girl you really are."

CHAPTER ELEVEN

"Dana?"

Dana gasped, her hand shooting out to grab the shower railing so she didn't lose her balance and fall. It was 4 A.M. Her grandparents had been fast asleep when she got home from Josh's. Or so she'd thought, until her grandmother's voice unexpectedly cut through the patter of the shower.

Dana poked her head out from behind the shower curtain to find her grandmother standing in the doorway. "Grandma! I could have slipped and broken my neck! What are you doing up at this hour? Is everything okay?"

"Everything's fine," her grandmother replied, tightening the sash of her thick terry-cloth robe. "I just wanted to know why you didn't spend the night with Josh."

"Excuse me, what?" Dana was sure she'd gotten water in her ears.

"Finish your shower. We'll talk."

Her grandmother left, closing the door.

Stunned, Dana finished her shower, trying not to think of the conversation awaiting her when she was done.

She found her grandmother at the small kitchen table, doing the crossword puzzle from the previous day's *Palm Beach Post*.

Her grandmother glanced up. "Are you hungry? Can I make you something?"

"I'm fine."

"Tea?"

"I'm fine, Grandma, thanks." Dana slid into the seat opposite her. "Well?"

"Well what? What are you doing back here at 4 A.M., sneaking in like some kind of teenager?" Her grandmother's eyes went dark. "Unless Josh wasn't gentleman enough to want you to stay."

"Grandma." Dana cradled her head in her hands. "Why do you assume Josh and I—"

"Four A.M. shower?"

Dana's shoulders slumped. "Right."

"It's crazy that you didn't stay," said her grandmother, folding up the paper.

"I didn't want to scare you and Grandpa by being out all night!" Dana explained. "Plus, I was worried you'd think I was a slut. Or something."

"Oh, please," her grandmother said with a dismissive snort. "Like I didn't *schtup* your grandfather before we were married."

"I'm not marrying Josh."

Her grandmother ignored her.

"I repeat: I'm not marrying Josh Green. Don't pretend you didn't hear me, because I know you did. And while we're at it, I didn't need to know you slept with Grandpa before you were married."

"We did it like rabbits."

Dana's hands flew over her ears. "Oh my *God*! Please stop! You're traumatizing me!"

"What, you don't think we were young once?" her grandmother said indignantly.

"I never said that!"

Her grandmother gestured for her to uncover her ears.

"We better keep it down. You know what a crab's ass your grandfather can be if he doesn't get enough sleep." She folded her hands primly on the table. "Now. Josh."

"Oh, God," Dana groaned.

"We've established you've slept with him. Which means you like him. A lot. Maybe more than a lot, eh?"

Dana was determined to reveal nothing. "I haven't known him long enough for it to be 'more than a lot.' "

"Your grandfather and I fell in love at first sight."

Dana had never heard this before. "Really?"

"Yes," her grandmother said dreamily. "He was wearing a hat."

"You fell in love with him because he was wearing a hat?"

"Well, that and other things. My point is this, things can happen."

"I know." Her grandmother was so well meaning that Dana couldn't stay annoyed with her. "But it's not going to happen here."

"How do you know?" her grandmother pressed, looking mildly desperate. Dana changed her mind; maybe she could stay annoyed with her.

"Because I know. I'm only going to be here for three weeks. It doesn't make much sense to get seriously involved with someone when you have to leave in three weeks, does it?"

"Oh, please," her grandmother repeated, as if this were a minor thing. "What do you think long-distance relationships are all about?"

"Long-distance relationships work for couples who have been together for a long time, and then they have to be geographically separated for some reason. You don't meet someone, live apart right off the bat, and then try to build a relationship. It doesn't work that way."

"You're being obstinate."

"Grandma, please." Dana pressed her fingers to her temples. "I know you want to see me settle down. And that will happen one day. But not with Josh Green. We've agreed we enjoy each other's company, and that's it. When it's time for me to leave, I'm leaving."

"So, what you're telling me is, if Josh called you tomorrow and told you he'd suddenly fallen head over heels with another woman, you wouldn't care."

"No," Dana lied. "I wouldn't."

"I don't believe you."

"You can believe what you want. I'm telling the truth."

Her grandmother erased one of her crossword puzzle answers. "I told Molly you'd be stubborn about this."

"You were right, then. Stubborn and sane." Dana got up, stifling a yawn. "I have to get up in a few hours to check out the boutique space and start interviewing people, so I'm going to try to get some sleep." She kissed her grandmother on the top of the head. "Good night, Grandma. I love you."

"I love you, too, doll. Next time stay the whole night with him," she called after Dana as she headed back to her room. "Just pack an overnight bag and keep it in the car."

"I'll keep that in mind."

CHAPTER TWELVE

"Can I get you anything else, miss?"

Dana looked up at her waitress with a polite smile. She was sitting on the terrace of the Four Seasons Palm Beach, staring at an ocean that was almost too blue to believe. She'd just completed the first round of interviews for La Belle Femme. All the women she'd spoken with had impressive backgrounds in retail. She'd be interviewing more over the next couple of days, but if this first day was any indication, it wasn't going to be difficult finding staff for the new store.

"Just the check, please."

The waitress disappeared with a pleasant smile and Dana turned back to the ocean. She'd never interviewed potential employees *al fresco* before. She always did her best to put candidates at ease, and found sitting outside in the balmy breeze helped.

After leaving the café, she planned to check out the boutique renovation. The fixtures and furnishings were due in two days, the incidentals and initial stock next week. Dana would talk to the buyer about the inventory in a couple of days. Personally, Dana didn't relish having to cope with the crowds that she knew would be packing Palm Beach on Labor Day weekend. But an auspicious opening would cement her future in Paris depending on what the company chose to do.

She was dying to go to the beach. *Maybe tonight,* she thought, since Josh was going to be with a client. The thought caught her by surprise; they'd slept together once, they were keeping it casual, yet here she was, sounding like his girl-friend, working things she wanted to do around his schedule.

Dana paid her bill and began strolling down Worth Avenue, known as the Rodeo Drive of Florida. The heat was staggering, so she moved slowly. Armani. Hermes. Gucci. Cartier. Tiffany. Every parking space held a Rolls Royce, a Mercedes, a BMW, or a Lexus. Many of the people strolling by had little toy dogs. One older woman was pushing a bi-chon frise in a stroller. There were doggie drinking fountains on every corner. It seemed almost decadent.

At last she came to the future La Belle Femme. The windows were covered with mural sized reproductions of works by Aubrey Beardsley and Jules Cheret. The signs were up, using script that could have come from a Toulouse-Lautrec poster. In fact, the front door was covered by a Toulouse-Lautrec reproduction with the caption "Coming Labor Day Weekend."

Dana let herself in and quickly locked the door behind her. She pictured what the space would look like when it was done, the carefully placed Oriental rugs and velvet divans. Beautiful opulence straight out of Maxim's of the 1890's.

Satisfied all was on schedule, she decided to take a drive around Palm Beach. Staying with her grandparents, all she saw were the interiors of restaurants and stores. When she was small, Dana's mother always took her to the beach on their Florida visits. But Dana still had no sense of the area beyond the gated communities lining the ruler-straight roads where her grandparents lived. Her rental car had a GPS, so if she somehow managed to find herself hopelessly lost, she'd be able to find her way back.

A drive in the sunshine was exactly what she needed, especially since she'd be inside doing paperwork the rest of the afternoon. Maybe she'd see Josh and his crew at work when she returned to her grandparents'. *How pathetic.* First of all, Josh and his crew were responsible for the maintenance of multiple homes and communities. Secondly, even if she did see him, what was she going to do? Wave and call "Yoo hoo!" to him while he weed-whacked in the blistering sun?

Thoughts of Josh led to thoughts about her grandmother and how she'd ambushed Dana in the bathroom the night before. Dana laughed out loud. It was so typical of her grandmother, just barging in like that. She couldn't believe some of the things that came out of her grandmother's mouth, especially the sex stuff. But that was one of the things that made her lovable: her bluntness, and, every once in a while, her inappropriateness. No one could ever accuse her grandmother of being boring, that was for sure.

CHAPTER THIRTEEN

"So, you got laid this weekend."

Eduardo's leer as he hopped into the cab of Josh's truck made Josh laugh.

"Why do you say that?"

"There's no other reason to be smiling in heat like this, unless you've turned stupid over the weekend."

"I think I might've. Just a little."

Eduardo's eyes lit up as he rubbed his hands together in anticipation. "Tell me. This should be good."

Josh told Eduardo about his and Dana's adventure. The longer the story went on, the more unbelievable it seemed. Things like this didn't happen to him.

Eduardo lit a cigarette, looking thoughtful. "You've fallen in love," he declared.

Josh glanced at him out of the corner of his eye like he was crazy. "Whoa. No one said anything about love."

"Then where does the stupid part come in?"

"The stupid part is that I really like her."

Eduardo blew a stream of smoke out of the corner of his mouth. "You really like her. So?"

Josh frowned. "She's only here for three weeks."

Eduardo looked unfazed. "Big deal. You have *un idilio de verano* and then she leaves. No *morir de pena*, just good memories. What's the big deal?"

"Summer romances aren't for me. You know that. I'm an

architect, Ed. I like to plan things down to the letter. Even if we keep it casual to ensure there won't be any broken hearts, it freaks me out to be flying without a plan."

"But you do have a plan! The plan is to have a good time for three weeks."

"Still too many variables."

Eduardo shrugged. "Don't see her, then."

Josh was silent.

Eduardo looked alarmed. "I told you, man. It's *amor*. Am I right?"

"Maybe. I don't know." Josh hated being this imprecise.

"Let me tell you something." Eduardo took a deep puff of his cigarette and tossed it out the window, his expression deadly serious. "It's impossible to get to know someone in three weeks. *Fue amor a primera vista fue un flechazo,* what you call 'love at first sight,' it's bullshit. Doesn't exist. Lust, *lujuria,* at first sight, yes. But love? No."

"I didn't say it was love at first sight."

"You didn't have to." He tapped the side of his head. "I know what goes on inside a man's mind. Trust me. This girl has rattled your cage. It's not good."

Josh didn't argue. It was true. Dana was all he could think about. For the first time ever, he knew he was going to have to focus extra hard tonight when he went over plans with his client.

"Okay, I'm rattled," Josh reluctantly admitted.

"Very dangerous," Eduardo noted. "You can't keep it simple when you're all rattle, rattle, rattle."

"She won't know that."

Eduardo laughed loudly. "Women know everything! I couldn't even take a piss without my first wife knowing!"

"What the hell am I supposed to do, then?" Josh couldn't believe he was having this discussion. He'd never needed this kind of advice before.

"Three choices," Eduardo declared. "One: you stop it now. Two: you toughen up. Think with your dick, not your heart. Fun and sex. Keep telling yourself that. It's just fun and sex." Eduardo lit another cigarette. "Three: fall to your knees and propose. But allow me to remind you, *mijo,* you both agreed to casual. So get off Fantasy Island before things get complicated and her granny attacks you with pruning scissors. A handsome face like yours? She could do some real damage."

"Fuck you, Eduardo."

"It could happen." Eduardo lit another cigarette. "When are you seeing her again?"

"Tomorrow night. She wants to go dancing."

"Did you tell her you can't dance worth a goddamn?"

"Yup."

"I suppose she wants to go to a salsa club."

"Yeah."

"Okay. I can show you a few steps beforehand."

"Can't you and Marissa come, too?"

Eduardo's expression darkened. "Don't mention her. We broke up."

"Again? What, are you going for the world record?"

"I'll bring my cousin, Donna, instead."

"Great. Look, I don't need you showing me steps beforehand. I can figure it out."

Eduardo looked highly amused. "You've never been able to before."

"It's never bothered the women at the club before," Josh pointed out.

"You weren't dating any of those women."

"True."

"Look, if you can't perform, there will be more than enough men there who will be able to."

Josh looked at him stonily. "Is that supposed to be funny?"

"It is funny. Just leave everything to me. Eduardo knows how to party. A good time will be had by all."

Chapter Fourteen

It had always been the flirtatious energy flowing back and forth between dancing couples that struck Josh first whenever he went clubbing with Eduardo. The women in their high heels and sexy dresses out on the wooden dance floor, suggestive and confident; the men in their tight black pants and fitted shirts, reveling in their own *machismo,* because that was what the ladies wanted. And of course, the sensuality of the music.

The music was loud. It always was. And the club always smelled tantalizing, what with the mixing of God only knew how many perfumes and colognes. Josh kicked himself for not splashing some on before he left the house. He also realized he should have swallowed his pride and let Eduardo show him some basic salsa moves.

He was sitting with Dana at one of the small tables on the romantically lit balcony overlooking the dance floor. Dana was entranced by the dancing couples below. Josh realized that under the romantic, changing lights, she'd be amazed he was even able to master walking. The guys on the dance floor were moving their hips as suggestively as the women, yet there was no doubt who was in control. What had he been thinking? They should've gone dancing at some generic club. His dancing wouldn't be much better there, but at least he could count on one or two other guys to be as incompetent as he was. It wouldn't be as humiliating as what was about to come.

"This is the best mojito I've ever had," Dana said, sipping her drink happily. She looked so relaxed that for a moment, Josh's apprehension fled and the only thing left was appreciation for the smart, beautiful woman beside him. She was a knockout in a red halter dress and killer heels, her hair pinned up. He'd never been out with a woman this gorgeous in his life.

"Cuban rum," Josh explained. "The best. Drink it slow— they make 'em pretty potent down here, and if you're not used to it, you'll find yourself seeing three of everything pretty fast."

Dana laughed appreciatively. "I'll keep that in mind."

Her attention returned to the dance floor—specifically to Eduardo and his cousin, Donna. Josh watched enviously as the two of them twirled effortlessly. Dana was wide-eyed as she turned back to Josh. "They're amazing."

"In case you haven't noticed, everyone in here is amazing."

Dana looked worried. "I know."

"You sure you don't want to get out of here, find some place we can waltz?"

Dana smiled weakly. "I think once we get the swing of things . . . ."

"Your call."

Dana looked mildly deflated. *The woman wants to dance, you ass. She wants a taste of local flavor.*

Josh drained what was left of his mojito and stood, extending his hand to her. "Okay. Let's go for it."

Dana hesitated a moment, then rose. "Okay."

Josh could feel Dana's trepidation as they slowly walked down the balcony steps and he led her out onto the dance floor, picking a spot along the perimeter where he hoped their ineptitude wouldn't draw too much attention. His eyes scoured the room. Bodies in motion, perfect moves. *You can do this. You've been to places like this many times, you know how it goes . . . theoretically.*

Josh took Dana's hand. Trying to look confident, he

moved in imitation of some of the men on the floor, putting his left foot forward. Dana moved her right foot forward, crushing his toes with the spike of her heel.

"Oh my God! I'm so sorry."

"It's okay," Josh assured her, biting back a grimace of pain. He directed her attention back to the dance floor. "I think when I step forward with my left, you step back with your right."

"Then we both come back to center," Dana continued, studying the dance floor, "and then do the opposite . . . I think."

"Yeah."

They joined together again, managing the first steps correctly: Josh forward, Dana back. But when it came to doing the same move on the opposite foot, Dana, clearly overwhelmed by the expertise all around her, made the same mistake and spiked him.

Dana looked mortified. "I'm such an idiot!"

"It's okay, it's okay, it's okay." Josh looked at the sexy high heels that were making pulp of his toes. "You wear those at work? Aren't they a bit high?"

Dana looked sheepish. "I don't wear them at work. When we decided we were definitely going salsa dancing, I looked online to see what to wear, and the website said sexy high heels."

Josh leaned in and kissed her neck. "They are sexy. The dress, too. Especially the dress."

"I'm glad you like it," Dana purred.

Josh hated to admit defeat, and so soon, too. But if their attempts at salsa so far were a harbinger of the rest of the evening, he'd be in the emergency room by midnight with mangled feet.

Josh put his arm around her shoulder. "Look, I hate to say this, but I think we're in way over our heads here."

"I know." Dana looked guilty. "I shouldn't have pushed you to take me dancing."

"You didn't push me to do anything. I'm a big boy. If I really didn't want to be here, we wouldn't be here. I wanted to make you happy."

Dana kissed his shoulder lightly. "You did."

"Hey, hey! What's going on here? Where are the sexy moves, Green?"

Josh flashed his smirking friend a dirty look.

"We're hopeless," Dana told Eduardo before Josh had a chance to, "hopeless" not being the word he would have picked. She winced. "I keep stepping on Josh's toes."

"It's not just you," Josh admitted. "I'm not exactly Marc Anthony myself."

"C'mon, I'll show you some steps," Eduardo encouraged Dana. He looked at Josh to see if it was okay.

"Go for it." Smug as Eduardo was, Josh thanked God he was there to save the day. Even if he was showing Dana just a few basic steps, at least she'd be dancing a little.

Eduardo smiled at Dana. "It's all a matter of feeling the rhythm in your body."

Dana looked mildly embarrassed. "Okay."

Before Josh got a chance to be a gentleman and offer Eduardo's cousin a drink, she looked up at him apologetically and said, "I'd keep you company, but I promised someone else a dance."

"No problem. I'll go order myself another mojito and see how the dance master here"—he tilted his head in Eduardo's direction—"does."

Eduardo extended his arm for Dana to take. "Watch and learn, my friend."

Josh didn't watch and learn. He watched and grew pissed. Dana's lesson started off okay: she seemed uneasy at first, but Eduardo was a patient, easygoing guy. As she grew in confidence, she began to lighten up and smile.

The problem started when Eduardo came to the "feeling the rhythm" portion of the lesson. Like every guy in the place, his hips swiveled easily as well as sensually—no problem there, except Josh didn't like the way Eduardo was looking at Dana while he demonstrated. Dana copied him, but her movements came nowhere near Eduardo's in terms of smoothness, at least not at first. But the longer Eduardo tutored, the more she loosened up.

Eduardo was standing behind Dana, and with his hands placed squarely on her hips, the two of them moved in rhythm. It was at that point Josh decided he'd punch Eduardo's fucking face in. Striding out onto the dance floor, he shoved his friend's shoulder. "What the hell do you think you're doing?"

Eduardo blinked. "What does it look like I'm doing? I'm teaching your—friend—how to dance."

Dana looked appalled. "Josh, what's going on?"

Eduardo held his hands up in a gesture of surrender. "I was just showing her how to dance."

Josh was in his face. "Really? You sure looked like you were enjoying yourself."

Eduardo looked at him like he was an idiot. "Of course I was enjoying myself, you moron! I love to dance, and it's fun teaching someone else. Chill out, man."

"No, he's going to do more than chill out." Dana was furious. "He's going to get out of here and leave me alone."

Josh was astonished. "What?"

"How dare you come over here acting like you own me?" Dana fumed. She turned to Eduardo. "Can you give me a lift home when you're done for the evening? I don't mind waiting. I can catch up on some e-mail on my phone."

Eduardo squirmed. "Dana, you're putting me in a very uncomfortable position here."

"I'm sorry. I didn't think of that." She gave Eduardo a chaste kiss on the cheek. "Thank you for my short but fun lesson. You're everything a teacher should be: patient and kind. Very patient."

Eduardo smiled appreciatively. "You're welcome." As Dana walked away, Eduardo looked at Josh in disbelief. "Smooth."

"We'll talk about this at work," Josh replied, in no mood to hear it.

He followed Dana back to their table, putting his hand on her shoulder. "Can I talk to you a minute?"

Dana pulled her shoulder away. "No. There's nothing to say."

She picked up her purse to leave, but Josh blocked her. "Don't you think you're overreacting a little?"

"I guess that depends."

"On what?"

Dana's expression was arctic as she moved to sidestep him. "On whether or not you once dated a possessive macho ass-hole who was so insecure, he threatened every man who came within five feet of you. At least, that's how it started out. It ended with me being the one who was threatened. Apparently, I was a cocktease."

Josh didn't know what to say.

"Maybe now you'll understand why I have no use for macho bullshit. Excuse me, I have to call a cab."

"Saturday night at this time of night? You'll be waiting for hours. Let me drive you home."

Josh held his breath, waiting for the verdict. He hoped she said yes, since he still had things he wanted to say, though she'd no doubt find them pathetic now.

"Fine," Dana capitulated after what felt like an endless pause. "Drive me home."

CHAPTER FIFTEEN

Not the way I imagined the evening would end, Dana thought to herself wryly as she slid into the passenger seat of Josh's car. Her assumption had been that she and Josh would drink mojitos, get a little buzzed, dance, then end the evening by tearing each other's clothes off. Instead, she was being driven back to her grandparents' by a swaggering, macho jerk who brought back terrible memories.

Dana leaned forward, turning up the AC so high her earrings were gently swinging. She glanced at Josh out of the corner of her eye. His expression was determined, and it had nothing to do with driving. "You still want to talk about this, don't you?" she asked warily.

"Yeah, I do."

Dana thought she'd made it obvious why their evening had ended so abruptly, but then she realized the info might sink in better if she broke it down into bite-sized pieces for him.

"Then let's start by talking about Eduardo. You had no right to give him a hard time. He's your friend, and he was doing me a favor. Who the hell do you think you are, acting so possessive? You're not my boyfriend. And even if you were, you still wouldn't have the right to swagger out onto the dance floor and act like some macho jerk. We're not a *couple,* Josh."

Josh's eyes were glued to the road. "Yeah, I know that."

"Do you?"

"Yeah." Josh dialed the AC down a notch, turning slowly to look at her. "But I couldn't help it. It was driving me crazy, the way you were laughing and moving with Eduardo."

"Too bad. Do I really strike you as the type of woman who would go on a date with you, then turn around and flirt with your friend right in front of you?"

"It has nothing to do with you."

Dana laughed harshly. "I've heard that line before. Trust me."

"It's not a line, Dana. I felt totally emasculated—not to mention jealous as hell."

"Then you have a problem."

Josh looked frustrated as he jerked the knob for the AC even lower. "I realize I had no right to feel or act possessive. But I did, okay? And I can't take it back."

"You embarrassed me. You embarrassed your friend. Worst of all, you embarrassed yourself."

"Don't hold back on how you feel or anything, Dana."

Dana's temper flared. "Don't try to turn the tables and make me feel like I'm attacking you! Especially after I shared that charming little gem from my past with you!"

"You're right, you're right," Josh muttered.

Dana took the AC up a notch. "You're not my boyfriend Josh, you're my . . ."

". . . fuck buddy," Josh supplied dryly.

"If that's the way you think of it, fine."

Dana despised that expression. It made what they were doing sound so cheap. But that's what they were, right? Fuck buddies? She preferred the less graphic phrase, "Friend with benefits."

She looked out the car window, more worked up than she'd been in a long time. After their first night together, she'd thought they were both crystal-clear about their arrangement. Now Josh had muddied things.

"So, what do we do about this?"

Dana turned to look at him. His question was simple and direct—just the way she imagined an architect might respond. It wasn't plaintive, or angry. Just a simple, "We have a problem, now let's solve it" tone.

"I don't know."

Josh looked irritated. "Can you at least try to come up with a suggestion?" He waited. "Maybe elaborate on why you don't 'know'?"

"I don't know," Dana repeated stubbornly.

Josh revved the engine as they sat at a red light. "I need more than that."

Dana struggled to collect her thoughts. "I like you," she said as the light turned green and Josh peeled out. "But that macho thing tonight really put me off."

"I already explained it to you. You're a beautiful woman, Dana. Any guy who didn't feel jealous of Eduardo belongs on a slab in the morgue."

Dana considered this, trying to sort out how his oblique admission that he had feelings for her was really making *her* feel, beyond flattered. "I don't know about that. But in any case, it would be nice if you apologized."

"I'm not apologizing, because I'm not sorry." His expression carried not the slightest hint of guilt. "I'm embarrassed. I feel like a prize asshole. But sorry? No."

Dana peered at him with distaste. "You're one of those jerks who can never say 'I'm sorry,' aren't you?"

"I have no problem saying 'I'm sorry' when I am sorry. But I'm not."

"I see." Dana felt trapped. "You tell me you're not sorry, and then you have the nerve to ask me what we're going to do about this? It's not obvious to you?"

"I'm not that guy from way back who hassled you, Dana. Somewhere deep down you know that, whether you'll admit it to yourself or not."

Dana felt as if someone had just shoved a handheld mirror in front of her face, and she turned to look out the passenger window. "That irrelevant, Josh. I'm flattered you find me attractive, but I'm only here for two more weeks. I don't have time to deal with your emotional issues. We promised to keep things simple, and now they're getting complicated. We should end this now."

Josh considered this a moment. "You're right. It's the smart thing to do."

Unjustified annoyance bored through Dana. He was supposed to protest her wanting to end things, or at least put up some minimal resistance to her suggestion. After all, he claimed to really like her.

"I'm glad you agree," she told him coolly.

"I'm a reasonable person."

No disputing that. But Dana felt he was bullshitting her. Maybe she just hoped that. Either way, the speed with which he'd agreed with her bugged the hell out of her.

Josh pulled up in front of her grandparents' darkened condo. Now she had to come up with an excuse for why she was home so early. After all, she had a grandmother who had no compunction about barging in on her in the shower. For all Dana knew, her grandmother was already lying in wait, ready to strike.

Josh came around and opened the car door, ever the gentleman. Dana hated how uncomfortable she felt standing there.

She cleared her throat. "Thank you for . . ."

". . . a great mojito," Josh said with a grim smile. "I'm sad that we're not going to be spending time together the next couple of weeks, Dana. But I guess I understand where you're coming from. Good luck with the launch of the store. I'm sure it'll be a success." He walked her to the front door, kissed her cheek, and drove off.

I usually don't do this type of thing. Now she knew why.

Chapter Sixteen

Dana was relieved to find her grandmother wasn't lying in wait to ambush her. The last thing she wanted to do was recount the events of her evening. She crept into bed, trying to escape into sleep.

The following morning, Dana left early to get to Palm Beach for the next round of interviews, successfully avoiding her grandmother again. She deliberately got home that evening when she knew her grandparents would be out to dinner. She left them a note on the kitchen table, telling them she had a splitting headache and she'd see them in the morning. Then she went into her bedroom, locked the door, and got down to work on her laptop.

Dana was going over inventory projections when she heard a rustling. She looked at the door: a slip of paper had been pushed beneath it. Dana stared at it a moment, then got up from the bed and retrieved it. It said:

> *I know you don't have a headache. You can't hide forever. Sooner or later you're going to have to come out to pee or eat. I'll be waiting.*

Dana put her ear to the door. She thought she could hear her grandmother breathing on the other side. Dana's mother had always complained that Grandma was never happy until she'd squeezed every last detail of her personal life out of her. Dana had always been skeptical, thinking it was just her mother picking on Grandma. Now she realized she owed her mother an apology.

Dana's feet were silent on the silver shag rug as she tiptoed to the desk. Picking up a pen, she wrote back:

I don't want to talk about it now.

She pushed the note under the door, knowing what was going to happen next. The note re-appeared. It said:

Ha! I knew you didn't have a headache.

"Jesus Christ," Dana snapped, unlocking the door. She flung it open so violently it hit the wall. "You're right, I don't have a headache. But you're giving me one."

Her grandmother gave her a look of warning. "You shouldn't talk to me that way, Dana."

"And you shouldn't keep poking your nose in my business! I love how you assume it's about Josh. How do you know I wasn't fired from my job earlier today?"

Her grandmother looked sheepish for just a second. "You're right."

"What did you just say?" Her grandmother's honesty caught Dana totally off guard.

"You're right. I don't know if you were fired from your job. But if that were the case, you wouldn't be avoiding us. So tell me what happened with Josh."

Dana covered her face with her hands. "Oh my God." She looked back at her grandmother with pleading eyes. "You need to back off a little, Gran."

Her grandmother looked highly insulted. "I have wisdom, you know. Useful wisdom that might give you some insights—"

"Sometimes I wish I'd stayed at the hotel!"

Her grandmother's jaw set in a hard line. "Well, no one is stopping you."

Dana groaned. "Grandma, I didn't mean it."

Her grandmother didn't respond as she walked away to her own bedroom, silently closing the door behind her.

Good one, Dana thought. *Hurting your grandmother.* Wasn't this supposed to be a simple business trip? What an idiot she was; where did she get off thinking anything in the world was simple? She was thirty-two, for God's sake. She should know better by now. She sat back down on the bed and tried to resume working, but it was useless: her concentration was completely shot. She decided to watch some TV to help her wind down, and then attempt sleep. Tomorrow she'd apologize.

The next morning, Dana woke up extra early to go running. Her plan was to get back with enough time to shower and prepare breakfast for her grandmother as an act of contrition. It would go one of two ways: either her grandmother would wave the food away, and in a weak voice say, "I've lost my appetite," or else she'd cry and smother Dana in kisses. Either way, Dana was going to complete the *mea culpa* by telling her what had happened, as well as taking her out to lunch and showing her how the boutique was coming along.

She was just beginning to chop peppers for the omelet she was preparing when she heard her grandparents' bedroom door open and close. Dana was actually longing for her grandmother to appear; upsetting her had been weighing heavily on her mind.

"How's my girl?"

It was her grandfather.

"Let me guess," Dana said dryly. "She sent you out here as her emissary."

Her grandfather laughed as he carefully lowered himself into a kitchen chair. "She thinks I'm in the bathroom. But since she's busy Googling, 'What to do when your grand-child hates you,' I thought it might be good if I talked to you."

Dana hung her head for a moment before gesturing at the chopped veggies on the cutting board. "I'm making her fa-vorite omelet. The coffee is percolating away." She looked at her grandfather plaintively. "What else should I be doing, Grandpa?"

"Let me tell you something about your grandmother: she might come off as having balls of steel, but inside, she's a very sensitive person."

"I know that," Dana said softly.

"She loves you to death. I can't tell you how thrilled she is that you're staying with us." He pointed to a box of choco-lates on the counter. "Can you get me one, please? I'm already sitting."

"It's 6 A.M.!"

"Dana? Get me the chocolate. I worked hard all my god-damn life and now, if I want chocolate at 6 A.M., I'm hav-ing it."

"Fine," said Dana, doing her best to cover her amusement as she plucked a chocolate from the box and handed it to her grandfather.

"Mmmm, chocolate-covered cherry," he mumbled, chew-ing. "Back to your grandmother. She knows she's a nag. She knows she's critical. But she can't help herself."

"It's more than just being a nag," Dana lamented. "She's pushy. And nosy. And she's always got an opinion."

Her grandfather sighed. "I know. But don't you see? Giv-ing you advice makes her feel useful."

Dana paused. "I never thought of that."

"Of course you didn't. That's why I'm sitting in this *schmatte* robe talking to you. She needs to be needed, Dana."

Dana put down the chopping knife. "I feel awful."

"Look, I would have lost my temper, too," her grandfather admitted, glancing nervously at the kitchen doorway. "You've got all sorts of pressure what with opening the store, dating the weed-whacker—"

"I'm not dating the weed-whacker."

"Hooking up, casual sex, whatever it is you kids do. My point is, she just wants to take care of you. She just wants to see you happy. So if she went a bit overboard after you avoided her all day"—Dana looked down guiltily—"cut her some slack."

Dana found herself getting choked up. "I will. I promise."

"And PS, we never had this conversation. She'd cut my *pisher* off if she knew I was telling you what a softie she is." He waggled a hand in the direction of the chocolate box. Dana fetched him another candy, knowing she'd catch hell if her grandmother ever found out.

"My suggestion is this: apologize profusely, tell her you're glad you're staying here. Ask her to help you solve some problems, even if they're completely bogus. Everything will be fine."

"Thank you, Grandpa."

"I'll tell her I heard you stirring in the kitchen." He fumbled in his bathrobe pocket and pulled out a walkie-talkie. "Adele?"

There was a crackling noise before her grandmother's voice sounded. "Is that you, Sam?"

"Who the hell else would it be? I think Dana's up. Maybe it would be nice if we all had breakfast together."

"All right, I'm coming. Don't forget to wash your hands."

Dana held her tongue as her grandfather pocketed the walkie-talkie.

"You're a good girl, Dana. Now, hurry up and slip me one more piece of chocolate before she gets here."

Chapter Seventeen

"You tired? You want to sit?"

Strolling slowly up and down the consumer's paradise that was Worth Avenue, Dana was reminded that her grandmother was a champion shopper. After a nice lunch on the terrace at the Palm Beach Hotel (the staff now recognized her, which was scary), her grandmother insisted they go for a little walk. That was fine with Dana. But she didn't realize her grandmother was trying to achieve the world record for "Most Exclusive Stores Visited in One Day."

Her grandmother checked her watch, assessing her surroundings. "There's still a lot here I need to check out, Dana."

"Grandma, we don't have to do it all in one day. Besides, you live in Boca. You could come anytime."

"True. But I'm here now with my beautiful granddaughter, so why not take advantage of it?"

Dana stifled a yawn. "Well, you might not be tired, but I am. Let's wrap it up soon."

Her grandmother carefully studied the large-type guide to the stores, fiddling with her sun visor. It was a nervous habit, reminding Dana of the way her mother was always checking her earrings in the mirror. But she'd never tell her mother that.

Dana's grandmother folded up the map and put it back into her oversized shoulder bag. "I just want to look in Saks at their men's bathrobes. That rag your grandfather shuffles around in is embarrassing. The material has worn so thin at the back I can practically see his ass."

"I would have thought you'd like that," Dana teased.

"I love him, but have you ever seen an old man's ass?"

"No."

"It's not a pretty sight. Trust me on this."

Dana, ever dutiful, spent another half hour traipsing around behind her grandmother before she finally couldn't take it anymore.

"Why don't we make a plan to meet by those benches across the street in half an hour? That way, you can continue robe hunting, and I can just close my eyes for a few minutes."

Her grandmother clucked her tongue. "You're too young to be so tired."

"In case you haven't noticed, I've been working long hours to make sure the launch of the store goes off without a hitch."

Her grandmother smiled proudly. "It will."

"I hope you're right." *Because if it does, I could wind up in Paris.* She couldn't tell her grandmother that, though. She'd freak out. There was no point mentioning it, anyway, since it might not happen at all.

"Half an hour," her grandmother said. "If I'm going to be longer, I'll call you."

Alone and finally able to relax, Dana sat on the bench, content to people-watch.

"Life's rich pageant," as Shakespeare wrote, though in this case, the operative word was definitely *rich*.

Her eyes lit on a tanned, lithe, blond woman who looked like she'd stepped out of a Ralph Lauren ad. She was holding the hand of a little girl who looked to be about three, all blond curls and big, curious brown eyes, wearing an adorable rosebud-patterned sundress and white sandals. Dana's eyes welled up with tears as she struggled with envy, the same forlorn variety she'd struggled with at Lois and Johnny's wedding. *I'll never have that,* was all Dana could think. She knew she was being ridiculous. She was nowhere near the age when her eggs started to shrivel into white raisins and the universe started banging on the door, yelling, "You better have a kid soon." But she couldn't stop fixating on the worst-case scenario.

Was it so much to ask? A partner to spend her life with? Children to love? Self-hatred welled up inside her. If that was what she wanted so badly, then what the hell had she been doing spending time with Josh Green? Worse yet, why the hell was she thinking about him right now? She knew why, and she hated it: because in another time and place . . .

"Oh my God. Honey, what's wrong?"

Dana looked up into her grandmother's fear-stricken face. She had no idea how long she'd been people-watching before the beautiful mother and child had walked by, nor was she aware of how indiscreetly she'd been crying. The only thing she was sure of was that she was glad she had sunglasses on.

"Just my period, Gran," she lied, pulling her glasses off for a moment to swipe at her eyes. "You remember what it's like: I could watch a commercial with adorable kittens tumbling out of a box and I'd burst into tears."

"Except it's not kittens. It's babies." Her grandmother deposited herself beside Dana, offering her a crumpled tissue from her purse.

"Talk to me," her grandmother pressed gently.

Dana stared her grandmother down over the top of her sunglasses. "As long as you don't say a word about Josh Green."

"I can't promise you that."

"Forget it, then."

"All right, all right, all right," her grandmother capitulated resentfully, passing Dana another crumpled tissue that she waved away. "I'll try not to. But remember, I'm old. That makes me very forgetful sometimes."

"That might be the biggest lie I've ever heard come out of your mouth."

"Talk, Dana."

Dana took a deep breath, more to stall than anything else. The last thing she wanted to do was break down in front of her grandmother. She was fairly certain if she confessed just how strong her longings for a family were, her grandmother would be calling every wannabe matchmaker she knew within a fifty-mile radius. Then again, maybe that wasn't such a bad thing, if you ignored the fact she was leaving in two weeks.

"Okay, you asked for it: I'm crying because I'm single with no prospects, and the thing I want more than anything is a family. Don't tell me I haven't tried looking hard enough. I've been set up on blind dates. I've done speed dating. I've done Match Dot Com. I met one guy I really liked on JDate, but there was just one hitch: on our third date, I found out he was married.

"I know that all the traveling for my job hasn't helped. But my job is all I have." Dana squeezed the tension out of the back of her neck. "I'm weepy because I'm tired, and when I'm tired I get depressed, and when I get depressed, I become totally pessimistic. From where I sit right now—alone on a bench in Florida with my grandmother—I can't imagine getting what seems to come so easily to everyone else."

"If it comes so easily to everyone else, then why are there all these dating services out there?"

Dana had no reply to that.

Her grandmother looked pleased with herself as she fiddled with her visor. "Got you there, didn't I?"

Dana smiled faintly.

"Love doesn't come to everyone in the same way," her grandmother continued. Dana was about to protest, and then remembered her grandfather's advice. "Sometimes it sneaks up on you."

"I don't like to be snuck up on. I like to know what's going on."

"Some people have a whirlwind romance. Ever hear of that?"

"Yes, Grandma, I'm familiar with the expression."

"Maybe you and Josh . . ." her grandmother suggested tentatively.

"Done," Dana said tersely.

"Before it even started," her grandmother rejoined. Dana had already told her what had happened at the salsa club. Her grandmother had been uncharacteristically quiet. Perhaps she'd felt guilty because Dana had made her an omelet. But whatever the reason for her silence had been, the moment had obviously passed.

"Let me ask you something."

Dana steeled herself. Those five words meant danger when spoken by Estelle Fine.

"Weren't you the tiniest bit flattered when Josh was upset?"

"No."

Her grandmother lifted her eyebrows. "You know what happens to little girls who lie, don't you, Dana?"

"They get no jelly donuts for dessert," Dana muttered in tandem with her grandmother. It had been a running joke between them since Dana was small.

Her grandmother pulled a Lifesaver out of her purse and popped it in her mouth, looking at Dana expectantly.

"Okay, I was flattered," Dana admitted. "In retrospect. But that's just biology, or pheromones, or whatever."

"Which tells me something."

Dana rolled her eyes, glad her grandmother couldn't see behind the sunglasses. "What does it tell you?"

"It tells me you really like him. Because if you didn't, you wouldn't have felt flattered, even if it was in retrospect. You wouldn't have felt flattered at all. You would have been nothing but disgusted. And quit rolling your eyes."

"Why are we even talking about Josh Green? I was telling you about how I want a family, and somehow you turned it into me and Josh Green."

"Got you again, didn't I?" her grandmother said triumphantly.

"I don't want to talk about Josh Green. I want you to go back to the part where you tell me love comes to people in different ways, and you're not referring to Josh Green."

"He's perfect for you. You're just too damn stubborn to see it."

"I've known him for a week," Dana snapped back, prompting passersby to look at her askance. "How can he be perfect for me? You know, Mom once told me you said Dad was perfect for her. Look how that turned out."

"How was I to know the man liked to wear his pants around his ankles in the office?" her grandmother protested. "Bastard," she added under her breath.

"I'm just saying, your hunches and intuitions aren't always right."

"What if Josh lived in New York?" her grandmother tried. "Would you have been so quick to pull the plug?"

"There's no plug," Dana said wearily.

"But there is fate."

Dana rose. "I'm exhausted. Can we leave now?"

"Sure." Her grandmother grabbed Dana's forearm and hoisted herself up. "Just think about what I said."

"Which part? About old men's asses?"

"No, wiseass," her grandmother said, laughing. "About whirlwind romance and fate."

"I will."

"You won't. But I love you anyway, you brat. Now come back to Saks with me: I want your opinion on a bathrobe."

CHAPTER EIGHTEEN

"I'm sorry."

Dana stood at her grandparents' front door, staring at the handsome man in front of her. His curly hair was damp, his body clean, and his face freshly shaved. He was even wearing cologne.

Dana wasn't sure what to say. Her first reaction to Josh was desire cascading through her body. Perhaps it was the intoxicating brew of masculinity and humility. Or maybe Josh was simply sexy no matter what.

She took a moment to readjust. She'd been on the phone haggling with the trucking company that was delivering the rugs and furniture to the boutique. Dana wanted them there by seven the next morning. They claimed the earliest they could be there was nine, despite her being the first client of the day. She'd been about to "Push the up button" to speak to a manager when the doorbell rang.

"Can I come in?"

Dana ushered Josh in politely. "Sure."

He pulled off his topsiders, carefully lining them up on the inside doormat.

"You can see which toes you mashed if you look close," he joked.

Dana couldn't help cracking a small smile. "How did you know I'd be home?"

"Saw the rental car parked outside." Josh cocked his head,

listening, but there was no sound but the hum of the air conditioner. "Where are your grandparents?"

"It's five o'clock, Josh. They're at the Cheesecake Factory
for the Early Bird Special."

Josh chuckled. "I barely finished lunch a little while ago."

"Me, too." They stood awkwardly in the hallway.

"Water?"

"That would be great."

Dana led him into the pristine kitchen. It was only a few
feet from the front door, but it was far enough for her to feel
his eyes on her back, taking in her hiking shorts and her old,
stretched-out *Phantom of the Opera* T-shirt. She felt self-
conscious, even though she knew that was silly. *The guy has
seen you stark naked.*

"I'm surprised to see you here so early," Dana remarked,
reaching into one of the cabinets for a glass. "Usually you're
whacking at this time." Mortified, Dana closed her eyes.
"Oh, God . . ."

"Don't worry," Josh assured her. "I know what you meant."
He took the glass she offered and started running the tap.
"It's too hot and humid out there right now. We wrapped up
early."

Dana wasn't sure if she was treading on dangerous ground
when she asked, "How is Eduardo? Are you and he okay?"

Josh gave her an odd look as he thrust his glass under the
tap. "He's great. We talked about what happened at the salsa
club, called each other assholes, and tomorrow he's replacing
some sod by Building Eleven." He looked at her with be-
musement as he took a long drink of water. "What? You
thought we'd have a big fistfight?"

"No," Dana replied, mildly insulted. "I just wanted to
make sure everything was okay between the two of you."

"Everything's fine." Josh finished his water and refilled his
glass, quickly finishing that one as well. "Hits the spot."

Dana nervously ran her index finger back and forth across

the kitchen table. The room suddenly felt very small with Josh there. "So—?"

"I'm sorry," he repeated softly. He took a step toward her, his expression so grave Dana was worried. "I've been thinking about what happened a lot. In fact, it's all I've been thinking about.

"What I did was wrong. I think you're gorgeous and really special. That's why I reacted the way I did. Does it excuse my behavior? No. But that's the explanation for it."

Dana's emotions began kicking up. "I appreciate your honesty." *Which is why you should return it.* "I realized, after thinking about it, that I kind of liked your jealousy."

"Yeah?" Josh looked oddly pleased.

"Yeah," Dana mumbled.

"So, I'm not a total jerk," he suggested playfully.

"I'm not so sure about that."

"No? I can prove it to you if you want." He grabbed her into an embrace and kissed her, hard. "How's that?" he asked, playfully nipping the tip of her nose. "Need more?"

Dana felt the world tilt a little. "I think I do."

She led him into her bedroom. They lay down on the bed, wrapping their arms around one another, Dana allowing herself to melt into the hard press of his kiss. When he bit her lower lip, she gasped, surprised by how much pleasure it gave her.

"You like that," Josh murmured sexily.

"I do."

"I can do more, if you want."

"You can do whatever you want with me," Dana murmured, feeling bold as she slid a hand down between them, running her palm up and down against Josh's bulging zipper.

He began to groan.

"How about you, Josh? You like that?" Dana whispered.

"Can't you tell?"

It amazed Dana how quickly the sound of Josh beginning

to breathe hard was making her wet. Her own breath started to catch as she undid his fly, snaking her hand down his briefs to grab his cock, hot in her hand. She began moving it up and down slowly, watching his face. Groan after animal groan rose up in Josh's throat as she squeezed, quickening the pace ever so slightly. He seemed on the verge when he stilled her hand.

"You have to stop or I'm gonna come," he said hoarsely. He removed her hand and, rolling onto his back, pulled off his jeans and briefs.

Dana leaned over, licking the pre-come at the tip of his dick. Josh couldn't take it. "Take your panties off now. Now. If I don't come inside you, I'm gonna lose it."

Aching, Dana hurriedly did as he asked, throwing her panties off the bed as she straddled Josh's hips. Pressing her hands against his shoulders, she rose up slightly, rubbing herself against the tip of his dick. Shock waves went through her body each time the pulsing heat hit her clit. Slowly, so she could savor it, she grabbed him, and began using him to excite herself. Josh was panting, hard.

"That's it, yeah. Use me to come."

Dana let out a tiny cry as heat slammed through her body. "Oh, God. Jesus," she whimpered.

She pushed her hair off her face, looking down at Josh. Smiling seductively, she very slowly, very teasingly, began to lower herself onto his cock.

Josh was panting hard now, his hands burning as he roughly grasped her hips.

"Ride me," he commanded.

The mere words sent her into a state of erotic rapture. She began riding him as commanded, each meeting of their hips sending Josh into a series of animal grunts. He raised his head to look at her riding him, his eyes intense. And then he put his fingers to her heat and began rubbing, his fingers matching her rhythm. Dana's eyes rolled up in her head as the second wave of orgasm smashed her to bits, more intense than

the first. Josh smiled and, taking his soaked fingers from between her legs, sucked them clean. He was still moving inside her, pushing harder until with one final cry, he rammed
deep, coming to a shuddering climax. No man had ever
turned her on the way Josh did. She had a feeling no man
ever would.

CHAPTER NINETEEN

"That was pretty amazing."

Dana lay deep in her lover's arms, both her pulse and breathing taking their time returning to normal. For once, the condo's air felt cool to her as it played over their naked bodies. Dana relished the temperature drop; it was helping calm her down, her excitement lingering far past the point of orgasm.

"I agree," Dana said. She lifted her head and looked at him, his gleaming damp hair pressed on her pillow, that fine body of his now at rest. Having seen him naked twice now, she'd yet to find any physical flaw on his body, save for a scar down his left calf, which he'd said he'd gotten mowing the lawn as a kid. Maybe she was crazy, but the contrast of the thin white stripe against his cinnamon-colored skin was sexy.

"Really amazing," Josh continued.

"Why do you keep saying that?"

"I don't know . . . I guess I'm wondering if you've had a lot of experience."

"What?" Dana spluttered. "Not at all!"

Josh looked at her quizzically. "How many guys have you slept with?"

"Few enough for me to be able to give you the number right off the bat: four." All of their faces materialized for a moment in Dana's memory, then just as quickly faded as she regarded Josh with interest. "What about you? How many women have you slept with?"

Josh groaned.

"C'mon," Dana cajoled, winding a curl of his damp hair around her index finger and tugging it. "What's fair is fair."

Josh closed his eyes, his lips moving as he silently counted . . . and counted . . . and counted.

"You've got to be kidding me."

Josh opened his eyes, flashing that wiseass smile of his that she found both maddening and charming. "Of course I am. Christ, I'm not that much of a dog."

Dana snuggled closer to him. "So, how many?"

"Do you really want to talk about this?"

"You brought it up! Besides, I want to talk about everything in the world right now! That's how good I feel."

Josh looked delighted. "The Goofy Dana has returned." He kissed her shoulder. "I like that Dana."

"Actually, I was fibbing," Dana confessed, changing her mind. "I don't want to talk about how many women you've slept with. It'll just make me jealous of them."

"But they're in the past!"

"I don't care. I don't want to know."

"Then the subject is closed."

"But I still want some info. How old were you when you got your first kiss?" She was clearing a big space in her mind for Josh info.

"Three," Josh said. "Actually, it was more of a bite. My two-year-old cousin set out to kiss me, but somehow her teeth got in the way."

"That doesn't count!"

"Okay, okay, hold on," he said, scrunching up his eyes as he concentrated hard. "Sixth grade. Cheryl Kaiser's Hanukkah party. We were using the dreidel to play spin the bottle. You?"

Dana felt awkward. "I was a really late bloomer. It was in

tenth grade. There was a cast party after the drama club's production of *Guys and Dolls,* and I was invited because one of my friends was in it. The guy who kissed me was named Gerard Beck. He played Sky, and everyone thought he was so talented and gorgeous."

"And he wasn't?"

"Total jerk," Dana supplied without hesitation. "He asked out one of my friends a week later."

"He had to be a jerk to do that to you." Josh stroked her hair. Dana loved it; it was so intimate and tender. She should have been able to predict what would come next, but she was clueless.

"Have you ever been in love?" Josh asked quietly.

Dana was slow in answering; she needed to calm the thrill flying through her body. She wasn't sure how much she should tell. She decided to go the "less is more" route, even though she knew Josh would want more info.

"I was engaged once," she revealed.

"What happened?"

"He cheated on me about six months after we got engaged. When I confronted him, he begged and pleaded for another chance, but there was no way I was going down that road. I'd seen it played out too many times with my own parents." She hesitated, running an index finger along his jawline. "What about you?"

"I'm not sure," Josh answered honestly as he took her finger, sweetly kissing the tip. "I thought I was. But she was always telling me how I needed to improve."

"You don't need to improve on anything! You're fine!" Dana blurted indignantly.

Josh looked at her, making Dana feel at once stupid and exposed. She started to look away, but Josh gently cupped her chin so there was nowhere for her eyes to look but into his.

"You don't need to improve on anything, either."

Dana kissed him softly. "Thank you."

She opened her mouth to speak but Josh shushed her, putting his index finger to her lips. "I can hear the wheels in your head turning. Don't analyze our being together, or pick it apart, or try to decipher subtexts. Words make things more confusing sometimes. Let's just allow ourselves to fully enjoy this."

"I agree."

"One of my clients is having a cocktail party tomorrow night," he went on. "Do you want to come with me? That way I can show you what I do when I'm not maintaining condo communities."

"That would be wonderful."

Josh smiled sadly. "When do you leave Florida?"

Dana felt a crack in her heart. "Nine days or so." She wrapped her body tighter around his. Neither said a word.

CHAPTER TWENTY

Dana's jaw nearly hit the floorboard of Josh's car as they pulled up in front of his client's home for the house-warming party. This wasn't a house. This was a three-winged, four-story mansion. It reminded her of pictures she'd seen of the Palace at Versailles: breathtaking and opulent.

"Wow," was all Dana could manage as Josh eased into a parking space with the other vehicles ringing the circular driveway. She couldn't stop gawking. When Josh came around to open the door for her, all she could do was stare at him with a stunned expression.

"I know," he said. "The first time I came here I thought: *holy shit.*"

"*Holy shit* doesn't cover it, Josh."

"No, it doesn't."

"How many rooms?"

"Sixty-five."

Dana was truly taken aback as he took her hand. "Who needs sixty-five rooms?"

"Rich people who want to make sure you know they're rich?"

"Got it." Dana looked out over the beautiful rolling lawn, so green it almost didn't look real. Walls of well-groomed hedges lined the property's edges, providing complete pri-vacy. Hot pink flowers bloomed in large potted urns, perfectly spaced along the lip of the verandah. She turned to Josh. "You?"

"All me. It took a long time to convince them roses wouldn't do well in the planters. C'mon, let me show you where the really good stuff is."

Dana felt like Cinderella before her transformation as Josh led her along the slate path leading to the back of the house. She'd never been to a place like this in her life, and odds were she never would again.

"There are two courtyards," he said, showing the first one. A gorgeous mix of lush tropical plants and dazzling flowers encircled a five-tier fountain in the center of the courtyard. There were also strategically placed flower beds of both wild and more popularly known flowers along the courtyard's borders. Marble benches provided a place to sit and appreciate the beauty, the only sound being that of the breeze stirring leaves, and the cascading water of the fountain.

"This is really beautiful," Dana marveled. She walked over to the flowers around the fountain and sniffed a small, white bloom with a sweet scent. She looked at Josh questioningly. "Jasmine?"

"Yup."

She pointed to a group of flowers across the way. "And that one with hanging pinking clusters?"

"Orange spike."

Josh walked her around the perimeter of the courtyard, pointing out more flowers. "That's a nerium oleander . . . that blue orchid—well, more purple—is called Blue Vanda. This deep coral-colored one is a passiflora called Coral Glow."

Dana stole several sideway glances at him as he gave her a quick lesson in botany. The pride in his face was moving. What a little snob she'd been to call him a "glorified gardener." The thought embarrassed her now, reminding her how judgmental she could sometimes be, one of the less attractive traits of her personality. Dana got the distinct sense Josh was reading her mind when he joked, "It took a helluva lot more than weed-whacking to pull this together."

"I bet."

Dana closed her eyes and turned her face up to the sun, reveling in the intoxicating scent of the flowers as she inhaled deeply. "Can you imagine having all these scents wafting into your bedroom window at night? It must be amazing."

"Not amazing at all," Josh said casually. "Just Florida."

There was no mistaking the hint. Dana opened her eyes. "I think we should go into the cocktail party," she said.

Josh stood in the marble entrance hall of the Sadlers' home, sipping champagne, feeling trapped as he chatted with an extremely tanned, extremely squat woman named Mrs. Hastings, who'd introduced herself as the head of the Garden Club of Palm Beach. Their talk was less a chat than an inquisition, with the small bronze woman demanding to know his opinion on everything from the hardiest flowering trees to the longevity of orchids during the summer months. Josh was polite and accommodating, but he was growing annoyed as the conversation dragged on. She was eating into valuable mingle time; she was also keeping him from Dana.

Even so, Josh wasn't going to let Mrs. Hastings's endless gum flapping spoil what was turning out to be a great evening. A lot of the guests had asked for his card after Mrs. Sadler gave them a tour of the grounds. *Soon you'll be a weed-whacking mogul,* Josh joked to himself. But deep down, he hoped it turned out to be the truth.

Answering Mrs. Hastings's never-ending questions on automatic pilot, Josh let his eyes sweep the room until they lit on Dana. She was standing at the base of one of the two magnificent staircases, talking with Mrs. Sadler. Dana hadn't been exaggerating when she'd told him he needn't worry about her clinging to him all night. If anything, it was the opposite: she'd been moving easily from group to group, effortlessly charming the guests with her poise and beauty. If she was nervous, she was doing a good job of hiding it.

Feeling his gaze, Dana raised her eyes to his, and they shared a small, secretive smile across the room. *I love you,* Josh thought, immediately tamping the emotion down. He was buzzed on champagne, high on how well the evening was going. No need to get ahead of himself.

He kept his eyes glued to her, his gaze a silent plea for rescue. Dana excused herself and joined him and Mrs. Hastings, who was now interrogating him about bougainvillea.

"Hello, I'm Dana." She extended a friendly hand to the older woman, who smiled cordially.

"You must be Josh's wife."

"Actually—"

"She is," Josh cut in. "In fact, tomorrow is our third anniversary."

Mrs. Hastings's eyes crinkled up with pleasure. "How lovely." She looked at Dana with interest. "Are you a landscape architect as well?"

"No." Dana's voice was polite as she fixed Josh with a glare. "I'm in retail management." She made a point of not looking at him as she explained what she did for a living.

"Well, best of luck to the two of you," Mrs. Hastings said, as her equally bronzed and squat husband made a show of pointing to his wristwatch from across the foyer.

"Josh, you'll definitely be hearing from me about the landscaping needed around our homes," Mrs. Hastings assured him. "And Dana"—she grasped Dana's hand warmly—"I'm looking forward to La Belle Femme's opening."

She released Dana's hand and waddled across the foyer to join her husband. Dana turned to Josh in astonishment.

"What on earth was that? Telling her I'm your wife?"

"I just thought it would save us a lot of inane chat—you know, 'Oh, you're boyfriend and girlfriend! How did you meet?' It was my way of simplifying things."

"Why don't I believe you?"

Josh took up the challenge in her eye. "I don't know. You tell me."

Dana flushed and broke eye contact. "You're unbelievable, you know that? And dumb in that way only men can be."

Josh lifted an eyebrow. "Excuse me?"

"If her husband hadn't given her the high sign to go, she most definitely would have been asking us how we met, and much more! That would have been fun, spinning out the lies."

Josh drained his champagne glass, eager to get off the subject. "Well, she's gone now. I vote we leave and take a walk on the beach."

"Oh, darling, what a wonderful way to begin our anniversary celebrations," Dana said sardonically.

"My thought exactly, Mrs. Green." Her barb had stung, but Josh would be damned if he'd show it.

"You're unbelievable."

"I know. That's why you like me so much."

Dana opened her mouth in protest but quickly clamped it shut. Her mood seemed to shift from annoyed to skittish, her eyes quickly darting away from him. "Let me just use the bathroom and we can go. Okay?"

Josh nodded, smiling. He still intended to proceed with caution; but in his gut, he knew he was almost there.

CHAPTER TWENTY-ONE

Dana was a tangle of emotions as she walked down the beach with Josh. She'd been stunned when Josh told Mrs. Hastings she was his wife, then angered, and finally, unnerved. Now she was juggling all three feelings, along with two or three others that were definitely not welcome.

To be honest, she'd been edgy all day, between the impending boutique opening and her confusion about Josh. She was beginning to feel overwhelmed with doubts about her profession, unable to stop herself from playing the "What If" game.

Dana was proud to have assembled an exceptional sales team at La Belle Femme. She was particularly pleased with the manager, Suki, who had years of experience running small, personalized boutiques. Dana reminded herself that none of La Belle Femme's stores had ever performed less than fabulously. She was silly to worry.

She and Josh strolled silently beneath a radiant moon, white clouds slowly floating past like beautiful, languid ghosts. Josh appeared lost in his thoughts. She let him continue his contemplation for a good while, but eventually, the quiet began to make her uneasy.

"You okay?"

"I'm fine," Josh said distractedly.

"What're you thinking about?"

"Us," he replied bluntly.

Dumb question, followed by an obvious answer. Dana couldn't think why she'd even asked. Josh stopped walking, and taking off his jacket, spread it out on the sand for Dana and sat down.

"You're very good at unexpectedly dropping emotional bombs on me," Dana informed him lightly as she settled down next to him, arms clasped around her knees.

"They're not bombs. They're truths." Josh's expression was so intense, Dana almost couldn't look at him. "I don't want this to end when you leave Florida. I know we've only known each other a short time, but right from the start, I had a feeling about you. I don't know how to explain it without sounding like some mystical asshole, but you opened a door inside me that's been closed for a long time." He paused. "Don't deny you feel the same way."

Dana looked down at the sand, evading his eyes. "I do, but it's not that simple."

"Seems simple to me. We just do the long-distance thing."

Heart beginning to pound, Dana forced herself to look at him. "We'll be too far from each other to do that," she informed him softly. Her throat tightened. "I'm moving to Paris."

Josh just stared at her.

"I got a phone call today," Dana continued, determined to keep her tone neutral. "Originally, the job had been dangled in front of my face as a reward if the Palm Beach launch was successful. But now the company has decided to open a permanent branch, located in Paris. They want me to be director of retail expansion for Europe."

Josh's gaze betrayed nothing. "And this is what you want."

Dana's heart was banging against her ribs. "I do. This kind of opportunity doesn't come along every day. Plus, I've earned it. And I love Paris."

She was going to continue, but Josh held up his hand. "I get it."

Brooding silence returned. Dana was glad she'd been able

to deliver the news without becoming emotional. It had been weighing on her all day.

This time it was Josh who broke the silence. "Distance is distance," he pointed out calmly. "I'm my own boss. I can fly to Paris whenever I want."

Dana felt queasy. "I'm not so sure that's a good idea."

"Why not?"

"Because I'm viewing this as a fresh start for me. It hurts me to say that, but it's true."

"I love you, Dana."

Dana screwed her eyes shut. "Please don't say that."

"Why? Because it complicates your life?"

She forced herself to look at him. "Yes." She locked her arms tighter around her knees. "We're infatuated with one another. It's not love."

Josh looked irritated. "I'm not a kid, Dana. I know the difference between infatuation and love."

Dana rested her forehead on her knees. This was awful, much harder than she'd expected. "Don't."

"You bring out the best in me."

"You have to stop."

"I'll stop when you look at me and tell me you don't feel the same way."

Dana reluctantly lifted her head. What she was about to do wasn't unforgivable, she told herself. It would save a wonderful man a good deal of pain.

"I love you, Josh," she said gently, "but I'm not in love with you. I'm sorry."

Josh was quiet a second, then rose to his feet. "Ah. The old 'I love you but I'm not in love with you' distinction. Classic."

Dana's thoughts raced in circles. *He hates me now. But he has a right to. But I don't want him to. I want him to love me. He does, you little bitch. And you just—*

"I think we should take off," Josh said wearily. "I'm kinda beat, and I'm sure you must have a lot of last-minute stuff to take care of before the opening." He extended a hand to help her up, picking up his jacket and shaking the sand out before wrapping it around her shoulders.

"Friends?" Dana asked tentatively.

Josh nodded curtly. Dana reminded herself that sometimes, doing the right thing hurt. That's what her mother used to tell her, and Dana had scoffed, having no use for platitudes. But once again, it turned out her mother was right. The problem was, doing the right thing gave her no comfort. It just made her feel awful, especially since she was now something she'd never thought she'd be.

A liar.

CHAPTER TWENTY-TWO

"**O**h my God. I am so tired."

Dana flopped down on her grandparents' couch, kicking off her shoes. The La Belle Femme opening had been insane: wall-to-wall well-dressed women of all ages, each in search of something unique, whether it was an article of clothing or a piece of jewelry. Judging by how fast the inventory moved, money was no object, which was what the company had been banking on in choosing this locale. La Belle's first day was a triumph.

Early in the day, Dana had been helping an extremely persnickety woman try on a pair of original Art Deco earrings when Suki, La Belle's manager, tapped her discreetly on the shoulder.

"Some flowers have just been delivered for you. I put them on the sideboard."

"Thanks." Dana redirected her attention to the woman. "How are we doing?" She smiled approvingly. "They're very sexy."

The customer looked pleased by Dana's observation as she tilted her head this way and that, admiring herself in the handheld mirror. "You're right. I'll take them."

Delighted, Dana waded through the thick throng of women, escorting her customer to the antique Victorian desk at the back where the cash register was located. Then, as best she could, she wended her way to the ornately carved sideboard where her flowers sat waiting. The bouquet was beautiful, with tall gorgeous pairings of pink, white, and deep blue flowers. Dana recognized the pink flowers as orchids, but the flowering white blossoms and ocean-blue buds were a mystery to her. She knew before even opening the small white envelope nestled among the flowers that Josh had sent it.

She was right. The card inside read: "Congrats on both the store opening and your impending job in Paris. I know you'll shine wherever you are. Josh."

A lump formed in Dana's throat as she pocketed the card. It was such a lovely thing to do. Pure Josh. Her eyes began filling up, but she blinked the tears back with determination. She knew she had no right to self-pity. She'd made her decision.

"You look tired."

Dana looked up into her grandmother's face. "I know," she replied, stifling a big yawn. "I'll sleep well tonight."

"I'm sorry Molly and I didn't stay long at the store." Her grandmother took off her reading glasses and rubbed her eyes. "It was just too crazy for us. Some Amazon stepped on my foot, and when it got so crowded Molly couldn't see the front door, she started to have a panic attack."

"It's okay," Dana assured her. "You two can go in a few weeks when the hubbub has died down a bit."

"It won't be the same without you there." Her grandmother put her glasses back on, pretending to return to her crossword puzzle. "Did Josh stop by?"

"No. He was working."

Her grandmother's eyes casually slid to hers. "You two up to anything tonight?"

"No."

Her grandmother lowered her gaze. "Did something happen?"

"Not really. I'm going back to New York on Monday."

Her grandmother sucked her cheeks in with displeasure. "That's it, then. Poof. No more Josh."

"That's a pretty flip way of putting it, but yes, that's it."

"No hope of a long-distance relationship?"

"No."

Her grandmother's expression was imperious. "May I ask why not?"

Dana matched it with a steely look of her own. "No."

"I'm your grandmother, Dana. I have wisdom."

The wisdom line again, Dana thought unhappily, until her grandfather's voice came into her head, reminding that her grandmother genuinely wanted to help.

"Okay," said Dana, reversing course. "Hit me with some wisdom."

Her grandmother glared at her. "Don't be facetious, Dana Marie."

"I'm not! I want to hear some of your wisdom."

"All right," her grandmother said, still not entirely convinced. "I think you're being silly not to consider a long-distance relationship with Josh. People do it all the time."

Dana hesitated, then decided it was time to let her grandmother know the full truth. "I'm moving to Paris, Grandma. La Belle Femme is finally opening up headquarters in Europe. I'll be the director of retail expansion there. It's exciting. A new life. I don't want any complications."

"Love isn't a complication."

"I don't love Josh. I mean, I love him, but I'm not in love with him."

Her grandmother frowned. "I don't believe that for a minute."

"You can believe what you want to believe, but it's true." *That's great,* Dana thought, *keep those lies coming.*

Her grandmother was undeterred. "There are things called airplanes, you know."

"I know that, Grandma." Dana's voice sounded sharp in the otherwise silent room. "But I just told you. I'm not in love with Josh, and I want a fresh start."

Her grandmother peered at her over the top of her glasses. "Call me senile, but I could have sworn you were bored with your job."

"I never told you that."

"Josh told Molly."

Dana laughed curtly. "Molly must have tortured the details of our conversations out of him." Dana let down her hair, shaking it out. "Bored is different from tired. I'm tired."

"I thought you wanted to settle down? Get married?"

"I do. But this kind of career opportunity only comes along once in a lifetime."

"A man like Josh Green only comes around once in a lifetime, too. Trust me on this."

"Gran." Dana slid down the couch toward her and took her hand. "Maybe if the circumstances had been different, Josh and I would be together, but obviously, it wasn't meant to be. I know you're sad, and I am, too. But that's just the way it is."

Her grandmother shook her head obstinately. "You're not hearing me."

"No, you're not hearing me," Dana countered, testier than she would have liked, but she couldn't help it. "And the more you pester me, the more it just makes me want to dig my heels in."

"You're worse than your mother. You really are." Dana used to take this as an insult. Now she saw it as a compliment.

Dana could hear the wheels turning in her grandmother's head as she sat there, her eyes staring into the middle distance, concocting God knows what.

"Let it go, Gran."

But her grandmother was unable to help herself. "What if you weren't going to Paris? Would you have a long-distance relationship with him then?"

"Probably not," Dana lied. She'd thought about that herself. And then she'd made herself un-think it.

"What if he moved to New York for you?" her grandmother wheedled.

Dana pressed a thumb against her right eyelid, trying to counter the pressure building behind her eye. "He would never do that. And I would never want him to do that."

Her grandmother shook her head. "You say you want to get married and have a family, but when you find a nice guy, you run away to Paris. Every obstacle you've named can be overcome. Every single one.

"You want to know what I'm afraid of? That if you don't find a husband by the time you're forty, you're going to panic and settle." Her grandmother's eyes welled up. "And I would hate to see that, doll. You deserve the best. Every woman deserves the best."

Dana swallowed, her mouth suddenly dry. The ineffable sadness in her grandmother's eyes was hard to look at. She had a sinking feeling her grandmother was giving up on her in some fundamental way. All the more reason to prove her wrong by being a huge success in Paris. But deep in the part of her brain where she stored the truths she didn't want to deal with, she knew her grandmother was right.

CHAPTER TWENTY-THREE

"We should leave for the airport soon!"
Dana's grandfather's voice was fraught with concern as it rang through the condo. Her flight to New York didn't leave for three hours. But in typical fretful fashion, he wanted to leave now, having convinced himself they were likely to hit afternoon traffic. Rain had also been forecast, upping the ante even more as her grandfather imagined widespread flooding and hurricane-force winds.

Leaving her grandparents was hitting Dana harder than she'd expected, since she didn't know when she'd see them again. Rosh Hashanah was a little less than two months away, but it was unlikely she'd be able to take time off from her new job. Maybe she'd get a few days in December, but her grandparents didn't like to come up to New York in the winter. That left Passover in the spring.

Dana centered herself, determined not to catch her grandfather's restlessness. She'd been in no mood to go running this morning, even though she knew it would clear her head. Instead, she lay in bed when the alarm went off, reviewing all the things her grandmother had said.

Eventually, the buzz of a lawn mower outside had penetrated her thoughts. Josh. As discreetly as she could, she pulled back the curtains to take a peek. It was Eduardo. Dana was just about to give her e-mail a quick check when her grandmother appeared in the doorway, bearing a medium-sized manila envelope. "This just came for you in the mail. Maybe it's La Belle Femme and they've changed their mind about Paris!"

"You'd be happy if I got bad news?"

Her grandmother looked down at the carpet sheepishly. "No, I just meant . . . you wouldn't be so far away."

"Grandma."

Dana tossed the envelope on the bed and put her arms around her grandmother. "It's not like I'm never going to see you again."

"I know. But it was so long between visits this last time . . . ."

Dana felt a spark of guilt. "That won't happen again. I promise."

Her grandmother pulled back to look at her eye-to-eye. "Promise me the next time you see me isn't when I'm being lowered into the ground."

Dana rolled her eyes. "I promise you the next time I see you won't be when you're being lowered into the ground." Dana shook her head in admonishment. "Don't be so morbid, Grandma."

"I just like to keep my bases covered."

Her grandmother broke their embrace, craning her neck past Dana to check out the manila envelope on the bed. "That looks business related."

"I'm sure it is."

"Aren't you going to open it?"

Dana gently turned her grandmother so she faced the bedroom doorway. "In private." She pressed her lips to her grandmother's shoulder, kissing her there gently. "If it's anything earth-shattering, you'll be the first to know, I promise."

Her grandmother harrumphed and left the bedroom, leaving Dana alone with the mystery envelope.

Dana sat down on the edge of the bed, turning it over in her hands, weighing it, trying to guess what it might be. She came up blank, but once again, her intuition told her it was from Josh. Resisting the urge to tear it apart like a child greedy for the money inside a birthday card, she opened the envelope carefully.

She laughed out loud when she saw what the envelope contained: the "Early Bird Special" menu from the Cheesecake Factory. Clipped to it was a note:

> *Remembering our time together will always make me smile. May all your dreams come true. Josh.*

Touched, Dana held on to the menu tightly, her eyes mindlessly skimming the entrées until the words began swimming together, and she realized she was crying.

She tucked the menu at the bottom of her suitcase.

Maybe she should—

Un-think it.

They could—

Un-think it now.

But—

Un-think it now, goddammit!

Head-2, Heart-0. But it was getting harder. Maybe leaving early for the airport wasn't such a bad idea after all.

CHAPTER TWENTY-FOUR

"Are you sure you don't want us to wait with you?" There was an undercurrent of pleading in Dana's grandmother's voice as they stood together inside West Palm Beach's bright, sunny airport. The ride from the condo had proceeded at her grandfather's customary snail's pace. As the car inched along, Dana found herself praying he would speed it up. The sooner she was on her own, the better.

Dana was torn between understanding her grandmother's attempt to draw out their time together, and her own deep need to get the good-byes over with because the parting was going to be painful. Yes, her grandmother could be exasperating. And yes, Dana worried her grandfather was going to drop dead in the driveway one day due to excessive, secret chocolate consumption. But she'd enjoyed staying with them. She wouldn't change who they were for anything.

Dana hated to do it, but for her own sanity, she was going to disappoint her grandmother.

"You don't have to wait with me," Dana assured them with false cheer. "I'll be fine."

"Are you sure?" her grandfather asked.

Dana squeezed his hand. "Yes, Grandpa."

"Okay, hon. You know what's best for you." Her grandfather forced a small smile, but Dana could tell he was disappointed. It was there in the way his shoulders slouched just that tiny bit more, in the way he pressed his lips together and studied the floor, not wanting her to see the sadness in his eyes.

"All right, then." Her grandmother's voice was light, an attempt to mask her misery. "You'll call us as soon as you get in, right?"

"I promise."

Her grandmother squeezed her before holding her face in her chilly hands, gazing at Dana with overwhelming love. "You know you're welcome any time, right?"

"Yes, Grandma."

"Be good. Let us know what's going on with Paris."

Dana swallowed. "I will."

Her grandmother had no sooner released her than her grandfather stepped in, his embrace all-encompassing. "I hate seeing my girl go. But life goes on, eh?" He gave her a big smack on the cheek and whispered, "The chocolate remains our little secret, right?"

Dana grinned. "That goes without saying."

Dana's grandmother gently tugged at her husband's sleeve. "We should go."

Her grandfather released her reluctantly. "We love you."

"Love you, too," said Dana.

She watched them as they walked away, her grandmother reaching for her grandfather's hand. Sam and Adele Fine, who'd once been young like she was, but who now were old. They'd held on in sickness and in health, and had been together so long they could read each other's minds, as well as finish each other's sentences. Their gait was slow, their skin was no longer taut, and their eyesight got a little worse with every passing year. But the only thing that mattered was that Sam loved Adele, and Adele loved Sam, and it was forever. . . .

"WAIT! Grandma! Grandpa! WAIT!"

Dana's grandparents turned slowly, twin expressions of alarm on their lined faces.

"I'm coming with you."

Her grandfather looked perplexed. "Are you all right?"

"Yes, I'm fine. Better than fine. I'm coming back to the condo with you. And then I'm going to find Josh Green and tell him I love him."

Her grandmother threw her hands up in the air, hooting with joy. "Ha! I knew you'd come to your senses."

"It's true," her grandfather confirmed, looking at his wife with admiration. "She said that."

"I know my Dana," her grandmother continued proudly. "Stubborn, yes. Stupid, no."

"Let's get a move on, then," said her grandfather. "Love shouldn't have to wait."

"Grandpa! Slow down!"

Dana had never raised her voice to her grandfather in her life, but right now, it was warranted. Leaving the airport, he'd morphed from the slow driver everyone on the road cursed to the reckless fool behind the wheel who seemed to think rules didn't apply to him because he was old.

"Sam, slow down!"

Dana and her grandmother exchanged glances as he shot through one red light, then two. As they zoomed toward the third, her grandmother lost patience.

"Sam! I know this is your version of not needing Viagra, but slow the goddamn car down!"

The plea fell on deaf ears. To take her mind off the possibility that this ride could end in a visit to the emergency room, Dana focused on one thing: Josh.

Chapter Twenty-Five

Back at Huerto de Naranja, her grandfather threw the car into Park before it had come to a complete stop, jerking them all forward in their seats. Springing out the driver's door with astounding agility, he tossed Dana the keys. "Go find him."

"I hope his crew is still here."

"It's Wednesday. They always stay late on Wednesdays," her grandmother informed her.

"Do you want one of our walkie-talkies so you and I can keep in touch?" she questioned eagerly.

"Gran—"

"I know, I know, I know. Now go."

Dana drove around the complex slowly, which wasn't easy: her entire body was trembling with adrenaline. She understood why her grandfather had just acted like a NASCAR driver: when spurred on by an overwhelming feeling of urgency, sometimes you couldn't fight the need for speed.

But since she was behind the wheel of her grandparents' car, and there was a strictly enforced speed limit of 20 mph in the development, she kept her adrenaline in check. All she needed was to plow into an old couple puttering down the road in a golf cart and it would all be over. She'd be jailed and her grandparents would be exiled, or worse, shunned.

Around and around she drove, but she couldn't find Josh. Close to giving up hope, she finally spotted him mowing the lawn of one of the freestanding houses. Dana's heart surged wildly at the sight of him. There was no time to lose; she'd wasted enough of that precious commodity already.

Dana pulled up to the house, tires screeching as she threw the car into Park and jumped out, running across the lawn toward Josh.

"I LOVE YOU!" she shouted, waving her arms above her head like a maniac. "I love you, Josh!"

Josh looked alarmed as he caught sight of her and killed the mower, whipping off his headphones. "Dana—? Did something happen?"

"Shoot, you had your headphones on. You didn't hear what I said." She threw her arms around his sweaty neck, giddy with emotion. "I love you, Josh! I love you, I love you, I love you!"

"Whoa there, girl." Josh peeled her arms from around his neck and put his hands on her shoulders, gazing at her steadily.

"I love you," Dana repeated, shifting away from his grip. She couldn't hold still. "I love you. I was dumb to fight it. I'm not going to walk away from the love of my life for a job!" She launched herself at him again, twining her arms around his neck and her legs around his hips. Josh laughed, his hands sliding beneath her butt to hold her up.

"You're acting very goofy, Dana. You realize that, right?"

"I don't care!" Dana proclaimed exuberantly. She looked at him for a long second, then kissed him hard on the mouth, surprising him completely. She drew back, breathless.

"Marry me."

Josh's eyes doubled in size. "What?"

"Marry me, Josh. I'm not kidding." She unwound herself from around his body. "I'll go down on one knee if you want." She started to kneel, but Josh gently pulled her up.

"I want you to take a deep breath."

"I'm not crazy," Dana insisted.

"I know that, honey. I just want you to take a nice, deep breath and then we're going to talk about this calmly."

"Okay. Okay." Impatient, Dana took two quick breaths. "So—"

"Deep. I said deep."

Dana scowled at him in frustration, but did as he asked.

Josh remained concerned. "We okay now?"

"I'm fine. Better than ever! Really."

Josh looked around, his eyes lighting on a tree up the street. "Let's go over there and talk about this, okay? Better yet, why don't I pick you up around seven—"

"No." Dana was adamant. She couldn't wait. They had to talk now.

"The tree it is."

Hurry up! Dana silently implored as she practically skipped down the road, Josh's usual pace suddenly seeming maddeningly slow. He looked like he was going to burst out laughing as he sat down, but Dana remained standing, rocking on her feet. "I'm not sure I can sit," she explained.

Josh sighed. "Dana, please don't make me Taser you."

Dana capitulated and sat. Josh looked like he wanted to hold her hand, but he was holding back, so Dana did it for him instead. "I don't care how grubby you are."

Josh smiled slowly as he pulled a handkerchief from the back pocket of his jeans and mopped his forehead. Dana envied his equanimity; she was dying to do cartwheels.

"All right." Josh stuffed the rag back into his pocket. "Tell me what's going on. Slowly."

"I love you and I want to marry you," Dana said simply. "I was being stupid and stubborn and frightened."

"I'd agree with that." His teasing smile turned into one more serious. "You love me."

"Yes."

"And you want to get married."

"Yes."

Josh looked skeptical. "And how's this going to work? Long-distance marriage?"

"No. I'm turning down the job in Paris, and I'm resigning from La Belle Femme. I'm moving down here and we're going to get married and be happy forever!"

Josh blinked at her uncomprehendingly. "What?"

Dana's heart plummeted. "Oh, God. You don't want to."

"Of course I want to, you crazy woman. I just need to process all this."

Dana sighed impatiently.

"You've got to fill in the blanks here, honey. Because they're huge."

He was right. Dana shifted so she was facing him and took both his hands in hers, clasping them tightly.

"It's simple. I told you, I was tired of my job. The only thing keeping me there was the promise of Paris. But that was before we met. I don't want to be apart from you, Josh."

Josh looked mildly perturbed. "You're going to quit your job? For me?"

"For us," Dana corrected. "Look, I've had no life for years. I hate to admit it, but it's true. The only positive thing about that is it's allowed me to save up tons of money. My thinking is that we get married, and then I can use that financial cushion to take time to figure out what I really want to do. From the first time I met you, I envied your freedom to make your own rules. I want to do that, too. And now I'll have a chance to."

"What about starting a family?" His gaze had gone from apprehensive to absolutely sober. Dana wanted to laugh. Mr. Planner, making sure things were mapped out and all the pieces fit together beautifully.

"I want that," Dana murmured, kissing his knuckles. "More than anything."

Josh was still looking at her with uncertainty. "What if you hate it here?"

"I won't. You're here." Dana took one set of their clasped hands and pressed it to her cheek. "Trust me on this, Josh. Please."

Josh took a long look at her, and burst out laughing. "Maybe I'm batshit crazy, but I do."

Dana let out a squeal of delight. "You accept my proposal?"

Josh pulled her onto his lap. "Not only do I accept your proposal, but I also know the perfect time to get married."

Dana was so electrified she could barely catch her breath. "When?"

"Today."

Dana frowned. "This isn't some joke, Josh."

"I know it." His expression was deadly serious. "I think we should get married today."

So, he thought this was all a big joke, huh? Well, two could play at that.

"What time works for you, Josh?" Dana noticed a few of her grandparents' neighbors walking by, and waved feebly. She could just imagine what they were thinking: *There's Adele Fine's granddaughter sitting on the weed-whacker's lap.*

Josh squinted, looking up at the sky. "Five is good."

"Five," Dana played along. "Go on."

"Yeah, five," he repeated, sounding absolutely serious. He pointed to a small row of detached bungalows two streets over.

"You know who lives down there?"

"Who?"

"Rabbi Stern. I'm going to walk over to Rabbi Stern's, and I'm going to ask him to marry us at five."

"Five today."

"Yeah."

"What if he's not home?"

"He's home. He's always home."

Dana began to feel dizzy. "Let me make sure I'm following you here: we're getting married today at five o'clock by Rabbi Stern."

"Yup." Josh rested his forehead against hers. "Five o'clock," he whispered. "Early Bird Special time."

"You're insane. You're being as impulsive as I am. What

happened to Mr. Architect and his need for perfect planning?"

"This is perfectly planned," Josh replied, lying down in the grass and pulling her on top of him. "I'm going to ask the rabbi to marry us. He'll say yes."

"And then?"

"Then I shower at your grandparents' house and change into the spare set of clothes I keep in the truck."

"In case you might get married."

"Exactly."

"Looks like I'm going to need a shower, too," Dana said with a light laugh as she gave Josh's shoulder a short, sweet lick. Salty sweat . . . Josh . . . .

"Dana, I'm not joking. I'm deadly serious."

Dana was dumbstruck.

"I'm not joking," Josh repeated ardently. "I've waited a long time for the right woman, and I'm not going to wait any longer. I love you, and if I could marry you this second, I would. But I can't, so I'm going to have to wait until I'm done with work, and then marry you in the clubhouse as per Huerto de Naranja tradition. We can talk about doing a big wedding and reception at some point in the future. Right now, all I care about is being able to call you my 'wife' as soon as possible. So get back in the car and do whatever you need to do at your grandparents' house. See you at five."

CHAPTER TWENTY-SIX

"I got to hand it to you, Josh. You shocked the shit out of me."

Josh was restless as he milled around Huerto de Naranja's banquet room, waiting for Rabbi Stern to arrive. When the rabbi had first opened his front door to find Josh standing there, dirty, sweaty, and smelling of earth, the poor guy looked afraid. But once Josh explained the situation, the rabbi's face lit up. He would be honored, he said, to preside at the wedding of the granddaughter of Adele and Sam Fine.

Josh wound up showering at Eduardo's since he lived nearby. It made sense, killing two birds with one stone: it saved him the drama of being with Dana's grandmother, and it added an element of tradition to the ceremony, since he wouldn't see Dana until the wedding. That was one of the things he most looked forward to, knowing she'd look more beautiful than ever. All brides looked radiant, right? Which meant that Dana—

"Did you even hear what I said?"

Josh looked at his friend. "Nope."

"I said you shocked the shit out of me," Eduardo repeated. "Mr. Architect, acting on impulse?"

"It felt right."

"I guess I get that," Eduardo allowed. "The feeling that sometimes, you just gotta go for it." He began rocking on his heels, hands stuck in the front pockets of his pants, whistling some tropical-sounding tune Josh didn't know. Josh just watched; he knew what Eduardo was waiting for. Finally, the whistling stopped, replaced by a glare. "Don't you need a best man?"

"Subtle." Josh clapped him on the back. "Goes without saying."

Pleased, Eduardo busied himself with making sure the rows of fold-out chairs were in straight lines. For whatever reason, he was nervous, too, which made Josh even more anxious. He looked at his watch again. The rabbi was late. Josh had a fleeting fear the old man had stroked out, or worse. He dismissed the notion. Nothing was going to get in the way of his marrying his woman today. Nothing.

Watching Eduardo, Josh thought back on all the weddings, baptisms, and communion parties he'd gone to over the years as Eduardo's friend. But this was the very first time Eduardo was attending any kind of ceremony for him.

"Hey, Ed, you ever been to a Jewish wedding before?"

"No." Eduardo looked unfazed. "All I know is I have to wear a beanie."

"A *yarmulke,*" Josh corrected with amusement. "But yeah, you have to wear one. All the men do."

"I don't have one! What am I supposed to do? Throw a napkin over my head?"

"Don't be a douche bag. You think I keep one in the truck? There will be a box of 'em here someplace."

Josh glanced warily at the banquet room doors. No Rabbi Stern.

"Anything else I should know?"

"Yeah. Jews get married beneath a wedding canopy. You're going to hold one of the four poles."

"Who's holding the other three?"

"The rabbi said he'd take care of it." Josh frowned worriedly. The rabbi. He refused to check his watch again. Everything was going to be fine.

CHAPTER TWENTY-SEVEN

"I can't believe this is happening. I keep pinching myself. Look, I'm giving myself bruises."

Dana's grandmother thrust a bony arm under Dana's nose for her to inspect. Returning to the condo after proposing to Josh, Dana wasn't surprised to find both her grandparents waiting for her at the front door. Gleeful, she told them she and Josh were going to be married later today. Her grandmother looked as if Dana had smacked her face. But it took only a few seconds for her to recover and begin the interrogation. Dana told her the details of what had transpired—within reason. No way she was going to tell her grandparents that the minute she'd spotted Josh, she sprinted across a lawn toward him, her arms madly chopping the air like helicopter blades as she screamed her love for him. It made her sound crazy, which, perhaps, she was. She'd heard that love could do that to people. Now she knew it was true.

Dana decided she'd wait until tomorrow to let her parents and friends in New York know about the wedding. She didn't want them to be disappointed, or try to talk her into waiting, since none of them could be there. Dana kept waiting for disappointment to bubble up to the surface over their absence, but so far it hadn't happened, probably because she knew she and Josh would be having another, more traditional wedding in the fall.

Leaving her grandmother in the living room to put makeup

on her burgeoning bruises, Dana went to check on her aunt Molly in the kitchen. Molly was sitting at the table, fiddling with her camera as she drew deeply on a clove cigarette, the last vestige of her younger "bohemian days." Molly was the designated photographer, a smart move since she actually had an eye, unlike Dana's grandmother, who'd only ever taken pictures of the different cats she'd had over the years.

Molly smiled up at her. "Nervous?"

"Not at all."

"Good," Molly said, peering at Dana through the lens of the camera. "There's nothing to be nervous about."

Dana's grandmother appeared in the kitchen doorway, unable to leave her alone for a single minute. A second later, Dana was treated to the crackle of her grandmother's walkie-talkie. "Sam? Adele. How are things going?"

"Fine."

"Good. See you in twenty, ten if you can get them to wrap it up faster."

For the first time all day, Dana's stomach gave a small flip. "What are the two of you up to?"

"You'll like it," her grandmother replied enigmatically. "I promise."

Dana's eyes shot to Molly. Her face was conveniently hidden behind her camera as she fiddled with the lens.

Sighing, Dana headed off to her bedroom. She had only one option of what to wear: her business suit. Would she look silly standing next to Josh in his jeans and tennis shirt? Yes. Did she care? Nope.

"Dana?"

My shadow, Dana thought. Time to do some major cutting of slack.

"What's up?"

Her grandmother perched on the edge of the bed. "I've been thinking: do you remember what you wore to Lois and Johnny's wedding? You know, the first night you and Josh went out?"

Dana nodded with a burgeoning sense of dread.

Her grandmother grew animated. "That outfit was beautiful." Her eyes began to grow misty. "You looked so beautiful in that blouse I bought you."

Dana's smile slowly faded as the walls closed in.

"It would mean a lot to me if you wore it. Plus it would count as something new."

"I . . ."

The epaulet shirt. Josh would probably salute her when he saw her. But her grandmother was holding her breath, looking so hopeful that Dana couldn't turn her down.

"Great idea, Grandma. Thank you."

"You're very welcome." She bounced once on the bed like a little girl. "Now. I've got something old for you." She opened her palm, revealing a tiny velvet drawstring bag that she handed to Dana. Dana carefully opened the bag, pulling out a delicate pair of emerald teardrop earrings.

"Those belonged to my mother," her grandmother managed, choking up. "I wore them on my wedding day."

"Grandma," Dana whispered. "I don't know what to say."

"Your mother didn't like them, so she didn't wear them when she got married. That's why she's not going to get them when I die. You are."

"Grandma!"

Her grandmother quickly swiped both eyes. "You know me: I pull no punches." She put a hand on Dana's forearm to steady herself as she stood up. "Molly's going outside to pick some flowers for your hair."

Dana started with alarm. "She can't do that. Josh planted those."

"Bah. He can plant others later."

Dana backed off, unable to hide her amusement. "Gotcha."

"I'll leave you to it, doll." She gave a small sniffle as she tightly clasped Dana's hand between hers. "I know you and Josh are going to be very happy together. I know it."

Dana felt a wave of untamed joy roll through her. "Me, too."

CHAPTER TWENTY-EIGHT

Dana sat in a small dressing room just off the banquet room with her grandparents, waiting for Rabbi Stern to pop his head in to let them know when the ceremony was about to begin. She still didn't feel nervous. If anything, she felt exultant—goofy even, though that didn't seem a very dignified word to describe a bride.

Her grandfather, looking handsome in a pinstriped suit, had taken to smoothing his hair back every few seconds, a nervous tic Dana had never seen before. Finally, her grandmother grabbed his hands.

"Calm down, old man," she chided affectionately. "Anyone would think it was you getting married."

His eyes filled with adoration as he looked at Dana's grandmother. "You looked so beautiful that day, Adele. You still do."

They exchanged a look of such intense love that Dana felt her heart spark. *That'll be me and Josh in fifty years: our eyesight worse, our hearing fading, the passage of time stealing a few inches from our height and adding them to our waists, but it won't matter. All we'll see when we look at each other is love.*

There was a quick knock on the door that sent Dana's pulse surging as the rabbi poked his head in with a smile. "Ready when you are."

"I'm ready."

"Quite a crowd you've got out there."

Crowd? Dana's pulse shot up higher as she stared hard at her grandparents.

"This is your first surprise!" her grandmother burst out, sounding like a little girl who'd been holding in a secret all day. "We've packed the place! All our friends, Molly's friends—"

"Neighbors—" her grandfather put in.

"All here to see our beautiful granddaughter get married," her grandmother beamed.

"And," her grandfather continued proudly, "we've also taken care of the music."

"When the music starts up, the three of you come on out," the rabbi instructed warmly.

Music? Dana thought.

"Got it," said Dana's grandfather. "Thanks for doing this on such short notice, Gary."

"Please, Sam. It's an honor." He winked at Dana, quietly closing the door behind him.

Dana's grandmother started rubbing her back. "You doing okay?"

"I'm doing great, Grandma. Honestly."

Rather than have just her grandfather walk her down the "aisle," Dana had decided she'd have both grandparents do it. She couldn't imagine her grandmother taking a backseat in this, anyway.

Dana opened the door a sliver, waiting. Finally, it came: the first two notes of the traditional wedding march, followed by the third and fourth, which were jarringly wrong. Confused, Dana opened the door a bit wider. Sitting in a chair directly across the room from them was an old woman in glasses whose lenses were thick as hockey pucks. She was balancing a miniature Casio keyboard on her lap, her wooly eyebrows scrunched together in intense concentration.

Dana waited and winced her way through three false starts before her grandmother thrust her head out the door. "I thought you knew how to play that thing, Phyllis!"

The old woman looked up from the keyboard, her voice quavering. "I do! I'm just rusty. Give me a minute or two."

Dana made sure not to look at Josh, afraid that if their eyes met they'd both burst out laughing.

"Can you believe this?" her grandmother asked, rummaging through her purse.

"Calm down, Adele," said Dana's grandfather. "There's no need for a Valium. This wedding is going to be perfect no matter what happens."

"Grandpa is right," Dana chimed in.

"I hope you're right," her grandmother said.

Finally, feeling like a few years had been clipped off her life, Dana heard Phyllis's reedy voice call out. "Ready, Adele!"

She took each of her grandparents by the hand. "We ready?"

"Ready," they replied in unison.

Dana started up the makeshift aisle toward Josh, accompanied not only by her grandparents and the shaky notes playing on the Casio, but a chorus of approving "Ooh's" and "Ah's." Seeing Josh waiting for her at the front of the room, his handsome face incandescent with happiness, Dana was tempted to ditch her grandparents and break into a run. But for decorum's sake, she stuck to tradition.

Giddy as she was, she managed to calm herself as she took her place beside Josh beneath the *chuppah*. "You look so beautiful," he murmured, taking her hand firmly in his. "Though I do wonder what rank you are."

Dana squeezed his hand hard. "I knew you'd say that."

"I couldn't resist," Josh whispered. "It's really sweet that you're wearing it for your grandmother."

"Very sweet," Dana whispered back.

"Think of it this way: our kids will have a really good laugh at us when they look at the pictures one day."

"God, I love you."

Dana could barely concentrate on the rabbi's words as the

ceremony began, so completely was her attention fixed on Josh. Reciting vows felt almost superfluous; they already belonged to one another. Dana knew that in the future, the memory of Josh's loving, unwavering gaze was something she'd be able to conjure perfectly anytime she needed or wanted to. In sickness and health, to have and to hold. One day her children would ask how they'd met, and she'd tell them, adding that when it's the right time, love will find you.

The proclamation of "You may now kiss the bride!" sent joy rocketing through her as Josh pressed his lips to hers in a passionate kiss. That a gesture so simple could fill her with so much love amazed her. Her love for him was spilling over the brim, its miraculous tide threatening to carry her away.

Kiss completed, the guests broke into applause. Josh put his mouth to Dana's ear and murmured, "If you ask me, this is our best Early Bird Special ever."

Dana laughed. "I couldn't agree more."

Weddings, Ink.

CHRISTIE RIDGWAY

CHAPTER ONE

Mulling over her first appointment of the day, Charlotte Bond considered the wisdom of adding whiskey to her morning latté. The benefit: making the next hour of doing business with her teenage nemesis more bearable. The drawback: liquor invariably unleashed her inhibitions. Who knew what might come out of her mouth?

She was still pondering when she heard the outer door to her workplace open. Her gaze flicked to her desk clock. Nine o'clock on the dot! Since when had Audrey Langford ever been punctual?

Footsteps made it clear her visitor was moving into the small reception area. Charlotte had a part-time assistant—a nineteen-year-old from the community college where she taught writing courses two afternoons a week—but she didn't arrive until ten. So Charlotte immediately rose from her desk and moved toward the half-closed door to her private office, mentally preparing a friendly greeting. Though she'd spent four years waiting for the un-punctual "Princess" Audrey, Charlotte took pride in her professionalism. No way would she make the other woman wait.

When you ran your own company, you had to deal with all kinds of people. Despite their shared past, Audrey was just another client of Charlotte's personalized wedding vows business and she would be serviced just like every other client, too. Meaning Charlotte would do what she must to write vows that would be both personal and elegant. Her company's motto, after all, was "I do-ing it with style," and she guaranteed 100 percent satisfaction.

Nothing would compromise that.

Anyway, a mere sixty minutes from now she'd have Audrey Langford once again gone from her life. Following their meeting, furnishing the words the other woman would speak on her wedding day required only a simple e-mail. And if Charlotte managed to hustle Audrey out in a short forty-five ticks of the minute hand, maybe she'd even give her the friends and family discount.

Her hand on the door, she pushed it open. "Welcome to—" Charlotte swallowed the last words, her professional smile dying.

Luke Harper stood in her reception area, not Audrey Langford. Dark and lean Luke Harper, the most recent man in her life to walk away.

"Y-you." Her fingers clutched the soft folds of her empire-waist dress. She hadn't seen him in more than twelve months. After their big blowup, she'd heard he'd signed on for a year with an engineering firm operating in Qatar. When he'd abandoned her, he'd run to the other side of the earth.

"How are you, Charlotte?" Luke wasn't smiling, either. His hands slipped into the pockets of a pair of dark jeans. He wore a dress shirt with them, crisply ironed and the exact same green as his eyes. The color was perfect for him, the shirt one she didn't recognize.

Her fist went to her chest, pressing against a sudden pang. Stupid, how it hurt that he'd done something as commonplace as shopping without her.

Or perhaps a girlfriend had purchased it for him. The pang stabbed deeper.

"Charlotte?" He frowned.

She realized she'd been staring. Restoring her friendly

smile, she moved forward and held out both her hands. "Luke, how lovely to see you." *Why the hell are you here?*

Before they could make contact, the outer door opened again and a familiar voice sounded. "Yoo-hoo," Audrey Langford said, stepping inside. "Where's my prize? I was almost on time."

Charlotte's hands fell to her sides as she took in the woman who'd been her stepsister during their high school years. Following the divorce of her mother and Audrey's father, she'd heard snippets about her here and there, but she'd never set eyes on the petite blonde since the family breakup.

She'd changed little. Her hair might be a shade more platinum, her makeup more expertly applied, but she appeared not to have gained an ounce since turning eighteen. She wore a size two silk shantung suit the color of lemon sherbet.

Audrey's looks had rocked Charlotte's self-esteem from the beginning. Standing at five feet, eight and one-half inches, she felt like an Amazon in comparison. Her hair, the color of bittersweet chocolate, was nothing special when measured against those sunny angel tresses. Then there was the other uncomfortable contrast, she thought, pulling together the edges of the little black sweater she wore over her knee-length dress.

With her natural air of superiority, Audrey had always claimed she was a " 'D' cup—D as in dainty." Charlotte was nowhere near that delicate. Up-top she was an actual, honest-to-God D—as in double helpings.

Her glance cut to Luke. Not that he'd ever seemed to mind.

That's when her thought processes froze. Luke was here. Audrey was here. Could that possibly mean . . . ?

As her brain tried absorbing the implication, she watched the bride-to-be greet him with an enthusiastic hug and a lingering kiss on the cheek. Luke was smiling now.

Oh, God. Could it be true? Was he Audrey's groom?

Then Charlotte was subjected to her own, much more perfunctory hug from her ex-stepsister. When the other woman moved back, her mouth parted to exhibit a blinding display of white veneers. "What? No congratulations?"

"It's 'best wishes' to the bride," Charlotte said, her lips feeling numb. Her part-timer had taken the booking, so while she'd seen Audrey's name in her appointment book, this was the first opportunity for the two of them to speak. " 'Congratulations' go to the groom."

The wound in her chest spilled acid as she realized what was expected of her now. Steeling herself, she turned toward her former lover and hoped the curve she forced on her mouth looked like a smile. "Congrats, Luke."

A strange expression crossed his face. "Thanks. I'm pretty stoked about the whole thing myself."

"That's fabulous," she said, nodding, though feeling as if she'd just swallowed a cup of the biodegradable confetti that was the latest rage to toss at just-married couples.

Audrey snagged Charlotte at the elbow. "Enough about him," she said briskly. "This appointment is all about *me*."

Of course it was. Charlotte was familiar with that sentiment after four years sharing a bedroom, a car, and a set of mismatched parents. "Let's go into my office and get comfortable."

Luke trailed them inside. He looked around as she settled Audrey onto the black-and-white toile love seat that sat adjacent to a pair of matching upholstered chairs. "You painted," he said.

She blinked. "Yes." He remembered that much about her office? It had been an inoffensive, but not altogether pleasing sage green. Her college student helper had suggested Charlotte color the walls an icy blue.

"It matches your eyes," Luke added. "I like it."

Flustered by the remark, Charlotte dropped into one of the chairs and found herself twirling the ends of her elbow-length hair. Stupid nervous gesture, she admonished herself, and forced that hand to her lap. With the other, she indicated the space on the love seat beside Audrey. "Please sit down."

To her surprise, he took the empty chair.

"Do you want to take notes or something?" Audrey asked. "I don't like repeating myself."

"Right." Embarrassed, because she usually did have her notebook with her during a consultation, she made to rise.

"Let me," Luke put in and he was up and at her desk before she could demur. When he handed over the pages covered in robin's-egg-blue leather—it was her favorite, had he remembered that, too?—their fingers brushed.

Awareness ran like lightning up her arm. Charlotte jumped, then tried to cover the response by crossing one knee over the other. As Luke returned to his seat, she caught him staring at her bare legs. Flushing with heat, she tugged down the hem of her dress and shifted her focus to the bride.

"Your wedding date's June fifteenth?" she asked. "In six weeks, is that right?"

"Yes," Audrey confirmed. "And my wedding planner, AnnaMarie Reed, is the one who recommended your service. Imagine my surprise when I learned that the most sought-after vows consultant in the greater LA area is none other than you!"

What, because Audrey never suspected that Charlotte would get close to a wedding? That she'd never manage to snag a husband? But that wasn't fair. Charlotte had professed her wariness of the matrimonial state even as a teenager. When her mother had announced her impending divorce of Audrey's father—at that time her third attempt at wedded bliss—Charlotte had sworn aloud she'd never be caught dead in bridal white. "We try to keep our services very confidential," she said now. "Not every couple wants the world—or each other—to know they've sought help with this aspect of the ceremony."

"That's exactly what AnnaMarie promised," Audrey said, with a satisfied bob of her head. "It's imperative that my groom not suspect the vows I say aren't completely my own."

Confused, Charlotte's gaze jerked toward Luke then jerked back to the bride-to-be. "But . . . ? Luke?"

A frown dug two lines between her arched golden brows. "But Luke what?" she questioned, and then started tittering. "You mean, you thought Luke? You thought me and Luke?"

Head reeling, Charlotte frowned back. "Well, yes."

"No," Audrey said, still laughing a little. She held out her left hand, displaying a massive diamond on the ring finger. French-manicured nails fluttered. "I'm engaged to Connor, Luke's brother."

"Oh!" Charlotte hoped she didn't sound as—strangely—relieved as she felt. It was almost as if she could breathe again.

"I'm the best man," Luke put in.

"Well." Instead of looking at him, she turned to a fresh page in her notebook and pulled the matching pen free from its little pocket. She would *not* go giddy. "That explains your presence." Sort of.

She returned her attention to Audrey. "I've not met Connor." Luke had wanted her to become acquainted with his family, but she'd always made excuses. Meeting relatives had felt too . . . official for their casual relationship. "What can you tell me about him?"

"I want you to see for yourself," Audrey said. "And see us together, before you get to work writing the vows."

Charlotte barely restrained a bleat of dismay. She'd been hoping the morning's meeting would be the beginning and end of this little reunion of theirs. Forty-five minutes. Sixty, tops. "Oh, that's not necessary—"

"But it's what I want!" Audrey interjected, starting to quiver. "Over the phone, your assistant assured me you'd agree to do this however I said."

Mental note, Charlotte thought, to tell her college student to put some limits on those assurances. When dealing with brides—all of whom were potential bridezillas—it was important to set some boundaries. "Really, Audrey, I can do the job without that."

"No." The other woman slid forward, her expression making clear she was already one toe away from a tantrum. *"You must spend time with us!"*

"Okay, okay," Charlotte said, throwing immediate water on the bridal fire. Experience with Audrey herself, and also with other hyper women on the verge of matrimony, had taught her that at this point appeasement was the only answer. With a little sigh, she mentally paged through her calendar. "Uh . . . coffee on Thursday?"

"Next weekend." Audrey sat back against the cushions, calmer now.

Charlotte considered. "All right, my schedule's pretty open. Which day?"

"Friday, Saturday, and Sunday," Audrey answered. "The entire wedding party is going to a boutique hotel in Palm Springs for bonding time."

Wedding party bonding time? Was this the latest trend? What happened to the guys taking a field trip to a strip club while the girls margarita'd themselves silly during a stay-at-home sing-along of *Mamma Mia*?

"You'll come, too," Audrey added, as if the matter was settled.

Wait. *What?* Charlotte stared at her. "You want me to spend the weekend with you? Uh, I don't think that will work, Audrey."

"Why not? I'll pay you for your time and you just said you were free."

"Yes, I said I was free, except . . ." She turned to Luke in appeal, but he just looked back, offering no help besides the distraction of his gorgeous eyes and handsome face. Her brain stayed on stall for another moment before finally clicking in. "Except won't your fiancé suspect something? A strange woman suddenly shows—"

"I have a plan for that!" Audrey said, triumphant. "It's

why I had Luke meet me here. So you'd know it was okay with him."

Charlotte's gaze slid his way, then slid back to the bride, the one she'd wanted out of her life ASAP. Dread started to rise from the pit of her belly. "What kind of plan?"

"Everybody in the wedding party is bringing a spouse or a significant other. I happen to know that you and the best man have a history. So Connor won't suspect a thing when you spend the weekend as Luke's girl."

Charlotte popped the hood of her trunk and yanked out her small suitcase, all the while trying to shake the notion that this was a very bad idea. For the umpteenth time, she reviewed how she'd ended up agreeing to a long May weekend in Palm Springs—which had the weather forecast of warm temps and sunny skies that signaled high summer anywhere else in the world. She'd been promised three days of lounge chairs by a pool, coconut-scented sunscreen, and fruity umbrella drinks.

Put like that, it didn't sound like torture, of course. But—

"Get that gloomy look off your face," Audrey scolded, coming around the bumper of another of the vehicles in the Park N Ride a short exit off the freeway. The wedding party was going to start their promised bonding by carpooling the ninety minutes it took to travel from LA to the famous resort town known for its golf courses, midcentury modern homes, and frequent celebrity sightings.

The bride-to-be was wearing a cute mint-and-chocolate-striped sundress and Barbie-sized sandals on her impossibly tiny feet. They stopped just shy of Charlotte's size nines. Audrey pushed her sunglasses to the top of her head and peered upward. "Oh. Maybe you just need to do a better job plucking. I can give you the name of my eyebrow artist."

Charlotte stifled the urge to pluck the other woman out of her teensy shoes and wave her around like King Kong did with his little blonde. "Maybe I should just take myself and my brows back home."

Panic widened Audrey's eyes, and she grabbed Charlotte's wrist in a death grip. "No," she whispered in a frantic voice. "The vows have to be perfect. And the vows won't be perfect unless you see Connor. Unless you see me and Connor together!"

Charlotte had witnessed this kind of behavior before. It was well-known in the wedding industry that the bride with the Big Day ahead would find a certain detail to fixate upon. It was always the dress at first, but once the final fitting was scheduled, there had to be a new obsession. The cake was a popular choice. Often there was much hair-tearing (metaphorical, because God forbid the planned half-up, half-down wedding day 'do be endangered) over the seating arrangements.

In Audrey's case, it was clear she'd chosen her marriage vows to go manic about.

Charlotte might have had more sympathy if playing along with her ex-stepsister's paranoia didn't mean *she'd* be playing—

"Good morning," Luke said.

Peeling Audrey's fingers off her forearm, Charlotte glanced at him from beneath her gloomy eyebrows and suppressed a sigh. Yes, she might have had more sympathy for her exstepsister if it didn't also mean she was stuck playing Luke Harper's plus-one.

Hence the very-bad-idea feeling.

His gaze rested on her a moment, then he leaned down to take up her suitcase. "Looking good," he said.

"Oh." Absurdly pleased, Charlotte tried not to squirm inside her little sleeveless A-line dress. It was black, with a geometric pattern of pinks, greens, and yellows cascading down one side. It ended just above the knees in three tiers of ruffles. She'd decided she just had to have the girly thing (as well as several others) on an impromptu shopping expedition the day before. If Luke could have new clothes, why couldn't she?

Yes, he was the reason behind yesterday's assault on her credit card as well as why she'd caved under pressure and agreed on the trip the other morning in her office. Just when she'd been ready to shut down Audrey for good, she'd happened to glance over at Luke and seen something a little . . . smug in his eyes.

In that moment she'd come to the uncomfortable suspicion that he thought she was desperate to escape the weekend because she wasn't over him.

Her pride hadn't let her let him get away with that idea.

And it wouldn't let her act any less than composed and unaffected now. "Are we ready to go?" Charlotte said brightly.

Audrey latched on to her arm again, and started dragging her toward a small knot of people, Luke keeping pace. "You have to meet Connor."

A tall man detached himself from the others and strode toward them. Connor Harper, of course. He was as sexy and handsome as his older brother. He slid an arm around his fiancée and pressed his mouth to the top of her platinum head. "Morning, sweetheart."

Audrey hugged him back and then tugged on his neck to bring him down for a more leisurely, mouth-to-mouth kiss. As it went on and on, Charlotte glanced at Luke and felt the back of her neck go hot. His kisses had been like that, long and all-consuming. Sometimes she'd surface from one and completely forget where she was, what she'd been doing, and why there was anyone else in the world besides herself and the green-eyed guy with the talented lips.

Luke lifted an eyebrow and gave her a look that said he was remembering those kisses, too.

Charlotte abruptly turned away and cleared her throat. Loudly. The bridal pair broke apart and Connor proffered an unapologetic grin. "Hey, bro," he said to Luke, then he held out his hand to Charlotte. "Ah, you must be the elusive lady I never had a chance to become acquainted with before."

His shake was warm and strong. "Connor Harper, I presume," Charlotte said.

"That's right." His gaze shifted to his brother and then back to her. "And I have a small bone to pick with you."

"Con," Luke put in, a warning in his voice.

"What?" Connor sent his brother an innocent look, then redirected his attention to Charlotte and smiled. Oh, he looked so much like Luke then! Both charming rogues. "Okay, okay, since you two are back together, I won't complain about what you put my brother through, though—"

"*Con.*"

Charlotte glanced over her shoulder, noting Luke's tense expression. He'd been "through" something following their breakup? He'd seemed perfectly content to turn his back on her then, going far enough away that any second thoughts she might have had wouldn't do her any good.

Not that she'd had second thoughts. Well, not more than a rare time or two, anyway.

Connor started talking again. "I'm just saying . . ." he began, only to be interrupted by a small guy with a billiard ball head rushing up to them.

"Smile!" he called out, wielding a professional-looking camera. "Show me how thrilled you are about the wedding."

On Audrey, thrilled looked more like irritated. The bride glanced at her watch. "Irv, you were supposed to be here at eight. You're fifteen minutes late."

"Giving you an extra quarter hour to grow in beauty, doll," the photographer said. "I had a dawn shoot at the beach. Ryan Reynolds wanted some photos of himself running with his dog."

The celebrity connection seemed to mollify her. "I see," she said. "Though I'm not sure dog pictures are more important than our wedding album."

Connor pulled his fiancée into his arms. "Nothing is more important than your wedding to *me*, sweetheart."

She leaned back against him and tilted her head to look into his face, the devil-bride replaced by an angel. Irv started madly clicking. "That's it! Show him with your eyes how you feel. How you can't wait to be his wife."

It was all a little too much for Charlotte. Maybe she *was* gloomy. The smooching and the affectionate displays of the future bride and groom were bringing her down. *Think of lounge chairs by the pool*, she told herself. Coconut-scented sunscreen. Fruity drinks with umbrellas.

Luke drew closer, murmuring for her ears only. "Gonna be some good time, huh?"

"I'm surprised they're bringing a professional photographer on a casual weekend."

"I think it's just for the send-off. Though you've known Audrey longer than I have, so you should realize nothing she does is casual. And her daddy only wants her to have the very best."

The mention of Audrey's daddy only dragged Charlotte's mood lower. Peter Langford had been the favorite of her four stepfathers. The one she'd imagined walking her down the aisle some future day. Of course that all changed when her mother divorced him. Then, instead of sticking by Charlotte's side, he'd taken off in the opposite direction—which shouldn't have hurt so much.

It had happened before.

She glanced at Luke.

It had happened again.

"Now for you two," Irv the photographer said, turning to them, camera up and ready. "The best man, right?"

Charlotte shifted to leave Luke free for a solo shot, but he snagged her arm to yank her close. "That's right," he said. "Along with my lovely lady."

"Then show us just how lovely you think she is!" Irv was enthusiasm personified. "Give her a nice big, juicy kiss!"

Before she could bail out of his embrace, Luke's mouth descended. That dread in Charlotte's belly rose again. The very bad idea appeared to be on the verge of getting very worse.

Chapter Two

Luke would have backed off if he hadn't caught that look of anxious alarm on Charlotte's face. She'd been so calm and cool the other day in her office. Like they'd been nothing more to each other than casual acquaintances. It stroked the ego she'd kicked in the knees then to see her uneasiness now.

A kiss would serve his purposes, too. By planting a kiss on Charlotte he could figure out exactly where he was on the continuum of getting over her. He was hoping for Nearly There.

His hand came up to cup her jaw. There was reality surrounding them, a blacktopped parking area busy with cars and people—including the guy hawking rugs out of the bed of his truck in one corner and in another a huckster selling bogus maps to movie stars' homes—but he ignored it for the still waters of Charlotte's clear blue eyes.

She trembled a little. What did she think he was going to do—ravage her? It was Charlotte Bond who had done the ravaging fourteen months ago. Feeling like a fool and frustrated by her hard head and stubborn heart, he'd traveled more than 8,200 miles away to bury himself and his disappointment in hellishly long hours under equally hellish conditions.

Damn it, the *least* she owed him was a welcome-home kiss. She didn't protest as his other hand slid to the small of her back, edging her nearer to him. Her voluptuous breasts brushed the front of his shirt and a bolt of heat shot southward.

God.

Though he'd left Charlotte herself behind, he'd brought with him images of her luscious body to torment him during his tenure in Qatar. There wasn't an inch of it he hadn't recalled time and time again, in agonizingly specific detail. Now he had her in his hands once more and he let himself savor the sensation for a moment, stroking her cheek with the pad of his thumb and breathing deep of her Charlotte-scent.

Then he touched his mouth to hers. Just that. She jerked in his hold, the subtlest of reactions. He murmured a soothing sound, then ran his tongue over the seam of her lips. They softened for him, allowing him to paint the interior of her full bottom one with the wet brush of his tongue. Her body jerked again, then she parted her lips and he followed up on the invitation, thrusting deep.

Charlotte went pliant in his arms, and another bolt of sexual heat arrowed through Luke. He'd forgotten that sweet yielding that was so uniquely Charlotte. She went into his kiss like she'd been waiting for it her whole life.

His ego cheered.

The cavern of her mouth was a wet heat, several thousand times better than any fantasy of her he'd showered with in Qatar. He wrapped his arms around her, drawing her even closer, and then adjusted the angle of his head. "Charlie," he murmured against her mouth.

The word seemed to shatter the spell. The woman he held against him rocked back, then broke his hold, her face blushing pink and her eyes rolling as Luke's bro and the photographer launched into enthusiastic applause. On a deep breath, she ignored the men in favor of the bride. "Audrey, why don't you introduce me to your bridesmaids?"

The women moved off, accompanied by Irv. Connor

watched his blonde walk away, a small smile curving his mouth. Luke shook his head. "You're really gone on her, huh?"

His smile growing, his brother shrugged. "Can't deny it. I know she's a little uptight about the upcoming wedding—so thanks for understanding about that."

Now it was Luke's turn to shrug. Though he rarely spoke of his ill-fated marriage at age nineteen, he remembered the tension the hoopla had placed on his wife-to-be. "A week before the I do's, Jana threw a box of those sugared almonds at my head." Though it had happened twelve years ago, he could still recall their too-sweet candy scent and the brittle crunch of them beneath his feet. "Grooms have it easier than the girls when it comes to wedding prep."

"We deserve it," Connor declared. "The proposal business is burden enough." Then he slid a look at Luke. "Is that where it's going with you and Charlotte? Are you two on the same track, finally?"

Luke didn't know how to respond. If it wasn't for Audrey's use of Charlotte's services and the fact that she wanted to keep her husband-to-be in the dark about it, he would have made no effort to encounter his ex-girlfriend. Yet when his brother's fiancée proposed her plan, he'd gone along with the subterfuge.

It had been a good turn for Audrey—oh, who was he kidding? He'd agreed for purely selfish reasons. Playing Charlotte's romantic interest for a long weekend gave him the perfect excuse to spend time in her company. He stared across the black asphalt, watching the sun spark red highlights in her dark hair.

Yeah, he'd been happy to have the time with her. To prove to himself his sappy feelings for Charlotte were gone—or nearly so.

Connor laughed now. "You might want to roll your tongue back in, bro."

Fine. Yeah, he was staring. That didn't mean anything dire, did it? Any red-blooded male's attention would be snagged by the miles of leg the woman had, light golden now. He wondered if she was still running.

That's how they'd met. Both of them had signed on for a charity 10K. At mile 4, he'd twisted his ankle while avoiding a young mother in front of him who'd abruptly stopped pushing her jogging stroller. After giving his injured joint fifteen minutes of recovery, he'd started limping along the route. Runners passed all around him, but he'd found himself keeping pace with another of the walking wounded.

They'd both stopped at a water station. He'd looked over at the glossy-haired brunette hiding behind a pair of Hollywood-large dark glasses. They didn't camouflage the cute, slightly sunburned nose, the soft mouth, the way her jersey clung to generous breasts. Luke had run his gaze down her long legs and detected her injury.

He'd winced at the bloody heel she'd slipped out of the back of a pair of mint-condition Nikes. "Ouch. Conventional wisdom says you shouldn't wear a new pair of shoes on race day."

She'd turned toward him, and with a pinky, slid the bridge of her glasses down her nose to look at him through amazing, crystal-blue eyes. "I hate when conventional wisdom's right."

Though race volunteers had offered to get them a ride to the finish, they'd both rejected that idea and set off side-by-side. He should have known right then, looking at her bloody foot and determined expression, that she had a mulish streak.

But by the time they'd reached the big time clock at the finish line, he'd been captivated by her good humor and intrigued by the fact she made her living writing. At the city park where the race ended, they'd shared frozen yogurt and exchanged phone numbers. By nightfall, he'd thrown caution to the wind—he had his own reasons to be wary—and invited her out.

Connor nudged him with an elbow now. "From the looks of that kiss, she's just as hot for you as you are for her."

To avoid responding, Luke abandoned his brother, heading toward Charlotte and the knot of bridesmaids. Was it true? Did the blasted woman still lust after him? They'd been compatible in the sack, that was for sure, but he'd wanted her as a partner beyond the sheets.

So sue him, he'd wanted her to meet his family, to share some holiday traditions, to build others that would be unique to the two of them. "I want a relationship," he'd told Charlotte, "that's heading toward a future."

"A future?" Her expression had been horrified.

He'd sighed. "Charlotte, this is like the fifteenth time you've refused to have dinner with my folks. For God's sake, you made an excuse last week to avoid meeting me and my brother for a simple after-work drink. We've been dating for months, but I'm beginning to feel like you're just using me as a bed-buddy."

She'd gone frosty at that . . . but hadn't denied it. Then his hold on his temper had frayed and he'd laid down an ultimatum. Either she'd arrive on his arm as his date to his dad's sixtieth birthday party or they were over. Her face cast in stone, she'd shown him the door.

That same no-expression expression was in place now, just as it had been the morning he'd met with her and Audrey. He strolled closer, just as one of the bridesmaids reached into a huge tote and withdrew gauzy lengths of fabric. With much laughter—and a squeal or two—she passed them out to the other women.

They were—wedding veils? Apparently so, because the women were pinning them into each other's hair with another round of laughter. A small mirror passed from hand to hand.

Charlotte stood outside their circle, the white material in

her grasp floating in the breeze. Her own little island, Luke thought. She didn't need anyone or anything.

Then Audrey turned to her ex-stepsister, cupped palm full of pins. "Your turn."

Charlotte stepped back, her face reflecting her sudden unease. "Oh, no. I'm not the bride-type."

Audrey was having none of that. She might be small, but she had the personality of a bulldozer. Before Charlotte could cut and run, Luke's prospective sister-in-law had hold of her wrist. Going on tiptoe, she attached the froth of fabric on top of the fall of long dark hair.

"Mirror," Audrey ordered, holding out her hand like a surgeon. As it was passed over, she caught Charlotte's own fingers, already reaching to remove the veil. Then Audrey held up the reflective glass so the taller woman could see herself. "Now take a look."

Charlotte rolled her eyes.

Audrey jiggled her hand. "Take a look."

With a sigh, Charlotte obediently directed her gaze. Just then, a strong gust of wind blew the gauzy material over her face. She drew it away, stilled.

Luke did, too. He didn't know what she saw in the mirror. He was only aware of what *he* saw. Charlotte's beautiful face framed by bridal white. It made her mouth more pink, her cheeks more rosy, her eyes more arrestingly blue. As he watched, the expression on her face changed from vexed to . . . vulnerable.

Something turned inside his chest. Vulnerable? It was the one way he'd never seen the obstinate lover who had refused to let him get too close.

As if sensing his regard, Charlotte's gaze lifted. Over the mirror, their eyes met. Beneath his ribs, he felt another painful twist. It was his heart, he realized, in a last-ditch effort to shake off the knowledge that was sinking into his soul.

He wasn't over her. Nowhere near.

Luke Harper was in love with Charlotte Bond. Still in love

with her. It only took another moment for a certainty to surface. This time, by God, he wasn't going to let her shove him away.

Charlotte scrambled into the very back seat of the very first vehicle in the carpool fleet. It was a minivan, and she figured wedging herself into the farthest corner would guarantee she'd share space with one of the other women, leaving the guys the more generous legroom up front. Charlotte was determined to dodge prolonged exposure to Luke.

She'd already risked enough with that kiss!

What had she been thinking? But of course she hadn't been thinking at all. His lips had locked with hers and she'd sunk right back into the familiar sea of lust. She might have drowned in it if he hadn't called her Charlie.

That had saved her. She didn't like to be called Charlie.

Closing her eyes, she leaned against the head rest, then jerked forward as something jabbed her skull. Her hand found an errant bobby pin and she pulled it free, grimacing as it tugged at her long hair. The rest of the women were still wearing those ridiculous wedding veils, but she'd yanked hers off the moment Audrey's back was turned.

Playing bride appealed as little as playing Luke's girl—something she hoped to avoid for the rest of the weekend. The way she figured it, that kiss should have accomplished all the necessary sibling-convincing. Connor now had to believe the old romance was on again and would turn his attention elsewhere. Leaving Charlotte to safely spend the next three days keeping her distance from both Harper brothers.

The minivan rocked as another person stepped inside, quickly followed by another and then another. Before she could let out a peep, she was joined on the bench seat and all the other passenger places were claimed, as well.

It was Luke who settled beside her, damn it.

"Hello there," he said, smiling. "Close quarters, huh?"

Charlotte glared at him as he shifted his legs. There were

seat belts for three back here, but with the length of Luke's limbs and the breadth of his shoulders, there wasn't enough room left over for her to take a deep inhale. She was suddenly breathless, anyway.

"Why don't you find a spot where you'll be more comfortable?" she suggested.

He slid his arm along the back of the seat, his fingertips brushing her hair. "I'm good. You?"

She was not good! With Luke so close she could smell his aftershave and feel his body heat. Without her permission, her nerves reacted to him, the little hairs on her skin rising to the occasion and her memory dredging up all kinds of naughty thoughts. Luke, playing with her hair, drawing the ticklish ends over her breasts as they lay naked together. The morning after the first night they'd made love, she'd left him sleeping while she dashed to the bathroom for a shower and the scent of him on her skin had renewed a need for him so fast and so furious that she'd turned off the spray and run to awaken him, water still coursing down her skin.

"I'm tired," she said, so she'd have an excuse to close her eyes. With his thigh nudging hers, not looking at him was her only defense.

"You can put your head on my shoulder, honey."

The vehicle began to move and she ignored his offer, wiggling farther into the corner. "Ouch!" Something sharp dug at her hip and she reached beneath her to unearth a handful of tiny plastic bricks.

Luke peered at the colored blocks. "You sure have a way of annihilating men, don't you?"

Puzzled, she looked from her palm to Luke's face. Was he implying she'd annihilated *him*? How could that be when it was *he* who'd left the country?

He plucked the objects from her hand. "And here I thought all the girls had crushes on Captain Jack Sparrow. Leave it to you, Charlotte, to be the one woman who crushes a pirate of the Caribbean."

The little speech became clear as Luke deftly handled the pieces, assembling them into a recognizable one-inch plunderer of the seas. Charlotte experienced another of those odd little pains in her chest. Luke would make a good father, she thought. He'd be the kind of dad who joined in his kids' play. She could see him building pretend cities and tree forts and telling ghost stories that weren't too gory, but just scary enough to engender delicious shivers.

Some woman would be the mother to those kids of his. Some other woman.

"Lift up," Luke said to her now.

She stared at him blankly. With a small shrug, he snaked a hand under her bottom. "Hey!" she protested, heat flushing her face.

It was only a quick goose. In a second, his hand was free and he held a tricorn hat-shaped piece of plastic that he popped onto the captain's head. Contemplating the completed Jack, Luke's lips curved in a small smile.

He had great lips. An incredible smile.

"Weddings, Ink. going well?" he asked, his gaze still on the toy.

"What? Huh?" Charlotte started, her brain not on business.

"Your work? It's keeping you busy?"

She cleared her throat and transferred her gaze from the face she'd been ogling. "Sure. Yeah. Turns out the nuptials industry is nearly impervious to economic ups and downs. People want their perfectly romantic I do's."

"Not you, though," Luke said.

"Not me, what?"

"You're not interested in marriage. You made that clear to me."

She shrugged, then looked out the window. She'd wanted to avoid him *and* this kind of conversation. "How about those Dodgers?"

"I wouldn't know," Luke said. "I just got back into the country last week."

"That's right. Qatar." She slid a glance at him.

He raised an eyebrow. "You know about that?"

"Someone mentioned it." She'd dialed his work number when her calls to his cell went unanswered. It had been a . . . relief to know he was out of the country, his absence saving her from herself. Two months after he'd walked out on her she'd had a lonely couple of days, and weak, tried to make contact with him. That he'd been unreachable had been best.

"My year there is how Connor and Audrey met, you know." He tilted his head. "Or maybe the credit all goes to you."

Charlotte blinked. "Why's that?"

"Connor took it into his head that he could patch things up between us. When I wouldn't give him your number, he found his way to your mother."

"My mother!"

"And instead of passing along your contact info, she gave him Audrey's by mistake. The initial confusion quickly gave way to mutual attraction. And lucky for us, that attraction distracted him from his original mission."

"Oh, God." Charlotte rolled her eyes. "Mom will be insufferable if she learns her error ended in a marriage. She'll claim she was the agent of Fate or some similar sentimental drivel."

"Like your clients, she's another believer in romantic I do's?"

"I suppose," Charlotte said, her voice wry. "She's said them herself often enough. She takes credit for my career, you know, because I was pressed into vow-writing service the last three of the five times she married."

"I didn't know," Luke said, his voice quiet. "You never talked about your mom. Or your father. That's the first I've heard of five marriages. I only know that you and Audrey were once connected because *she* told me."

The reproof was clear. Charlotte waved it away. "When you and I were together we had other things to talk about."

Luke caught her hand. "We didn't talk much at all, as I re-member."

There went her naughty thoughts again. Charlotte felt her face heat as she recalled how quickly she'd fallen into bed with him. They'd met at a bar the night after their 10K run. Within moments, Luke had been obliged to buy her a re-placement glass of wine when an obnoxious dude, over-excited about *Monday Night Football,* had bumped their table and knocked over her glass.

When she'd bent to clean up the mess on the floor, Luke had been there first. His simple courtesy had gotten to her. From sodden napkins to a second glass of sauvignon blanc to a scorching night between his sheets. "I never do things like that," she mumbled now. "Never on a first date."

He squeezed her hand. "You mean you haven't made some other man thank the day he was born?"

Charlotte slipped her fingers free and stared out the win-dow. "What about you? Are you seeing someone?" It was merely a polite question.

"Honey, I just spent a year with the same dozen guys who often didn't bother showering, let alone shaving."

"So I suppose any woman looks good to you now." She meant it to sound funny or flip. Casual. But her voice was hoarse and the words were scratchy. Damn air-conditioning.

"I—"

"Who's up for a game of spotting out-of-state license plates?" Charlotte called out to the rest of the passengers. "I'm desperate for something to do to pass the time."

Desperate to stop getting so personal with Luke. She was supposed to be avoiding him, remember?

The other people in the vehicle embraced her suggestion. They played silly road games until they pulled into the courtyard of the boutique hotel. It was a lovely place, the stucco painted a pale pink that was offset by the vibrant green of the ubiquitous palm fronds. Through an ironwork gate, Charlotte could see the sparkling aquamarine pool.

Lounge chairs. Sunscreen. Fruity drinks.

With all that, surely it would be easy to keep her distance from Luke.

They all shuffled up to the front desk, rolling their bags behind them. Audrey took care of the check-in process, then distributed the card keys that were slipped into small envelopes with room numbers written on their fronts. She passed one to Luke. Charlotte held out her hand, received another. Her eyes dropped to the handwritten numerals.

"We're in 12," Luke said, grabbing the handle of her suitcase.

We?

He smiled at her over his shoulder, then glanced at his brother, who was standing nearby. "C'mon, sweetheart. Our room's this way."

Our room?

CHAPTER THREE

Charlotte wasn't feeling very reasonable, even when Luke exhorted her to be so for the fifteenth time. "What's the big deal? The bed's plenty big," he said, indicating the king-sized mattress topped with a white feather duvet and two mountains of pillows.

The Indian Ocean was plenty big, too, but that hadn't stopped Charlotte from yearning for Luke long after he'd strolled out of her life for a stint in the Middle East. "There's got to be a free room," she answered, shifting her gaze from that dangerous place he was suggesting they both sleep for the next two nights.

"It's a boutique hotel," he responded patiently. "The wedding party has filled all the rooms."

"I'll sleep with one of the other women." Her eyebrows slammed together. "Audrey. She owes me."

"Audrey's sharing a room with Connor. And she doesn't want him to suspect your true purpose here, remember?"

Those damn wedding vows. Charlotte crossed her arms over her chest. "I have the words ready right now," she told Luke. " 'I, Audrey Langford, promise to be a self-centered shrew of a wife for the rest of my days.' "

Luke was staring at her.

Embarrassment washed over Charlotte in a flush of heat. "Okay," she muttered, "the self-centered shrew might be me."

He raised a brow. "I just don't get what has you so worked

up. You know me well enough to share a room with me, don't you? I don't have any habits you found disgusting before."

Before was the problem! Before, they were lovers. Before, they'd spent Sunday afternoons playing Scrabble. She knew words like *qintar* (15 points) and *capiz* (18 points). He could take *N, I, V, A, J, L,* find a floating *S* somewhere, and thanks to clever placement turn *JAVELINS* into a triple-letter, triple-word score. Sunday nights, they'd both splurge on ice cream. Luke didn't like her favorite Ben & Jerry flavor; she despised his. Perfect harmony entered a relationship when one's partner could be counted on never to filch the last spoonful of one's preferred dessert.

But "relationship" turned out to be the sticking point. She'd been content with board games and separate bowls of frozen treats. He'd started talking about comingled closet space and shared holiday plans.

Then left the country when she'd shown reluctance.

Okay, she'd told him she was definitely not interested.

But clearly he'd not cared overmuch if he'd been in Qatar less than four weeks later.

Now, Luke threw himself onto the bed, crossing his legs at the ankle and stacking his hands behind his head. He gave her a speculative look. "Charlotte, you're not worrying I'll try to seduce you?"

"Hah." Was that a scoffing sound? She hoped it was a scoffing sound. She didn't dare discern what kind of sound *he* thought it was, because she was keeping her gaze firmly off his long, lean body on that big, comfy bed. Instead, she crossed to the small table in the corner of the room. An agenda of wedding party bonding activities had been left there, little red hearts framing the single sheet of paper.

Charlotte stared at the list, unseeing. With Luke lying like that across the room, seduction *was* on her mind. She was back to that first night, when they'd met at the bar. He'd talked her into coming to his condo—and she *never* went back to a man's place on first acquaintance—by promising he had some special salve and an impossible-to-procure-elsewhere moleskin to protect the heinous blister she'd acquired during the run.

Who could resist a man who wanted to apply TLC to a woman's tender spot?

He'd knelt at her feet to slide off her slip-on sandal. It was as if he'd stripped her of all her clothes. When he held her foot in the palm of his hands, he might as well have been caressing her naked breasts. She'd melted into his couch, melted against him when he'd joined her there, was melted at the core with his very first kiss.

Spending time in this room, spending time in that bed with him, was going to be pure torture. Squeezing shut her eyes, Charlotte pinched the bridge of her nose.

"Sweetheart? Are you okay?"

She wished he wouldn't call her that. The endearment was torture, too. She wasn't his sweetheart any longer. "I'm fine." Opening her eyes, she forced her attention to the heart-embellished piece of paper. Her spirits lifted a little. "Hey. We've got places to be. Things to do."

A room to escape.

"Yeah?"

Turning toward him, she could smile again. "The guys have a golf game scheduled. The girls are going lingerie shopping." Freedom! Maybe in the hours ahead she could figure a way out of this sticky situation.

Luke grinned. "I love lingerie shopping."

She rolled her eyes. "Weren't you listening? The men are golfing. The women are the ones hitting the shops for naughty nightwear."

His expression turned smug. "Heard you the first time. But I have tennis elbow."

Panic fluttered in her belly. "It's a golf game."

"Still."

She stared at the offending joints. With his hands behind

his head, both were perfectly bent—and looked in perfect working order. Suspicion flared. "How often were you on a tennis court during the last year in the Middle East?"

"You'd be surprised."

What could she say to that? Spinning on her shoe, she headed toward the door. "Please yourself, but you'll inhibit our shopping urges if you're hanging around while we look at gossamer teddies and lacy garter belts."

It was his turn to scoff. "I predict there'll be no urge-inhibition. Especially when I'm there to provide opinions and carry the packages."

He was right, of course. The bridesmaids went gaga over having a guy trail them through every boutique in Palm Springs. One in particular, a redheaded giggler who didn't seem to be bothered by the fact that she had her own fiancé in tow for the weekend—"out on the green, out of my mind," she said—was hanging all over Luke.

"He has tennis elbow," Charlotte told the woman, with a pointed look at the possessive hand she'd wrapped around that particular body part.

"I only want to know what he thinks about this," the woman said, lifting a hanger that held scraps of black fabric and a tiny matching robe edged in marabou.

"Why don't you try it on for me?" Luke suggested, as gallant as you please.

Charlotte saw red. As in a red lace teddy and a red satin wrapper. Scooping up the ensemble, she rushed toward a dressing room. She'd burn his retinas with another sight before she let him ogle that shameless hussy. Without giving herself time for second thoughts, she donned the outfit, not daring to check herself out in the mirror until the short kimono-style robe was securely wrapped at her waist.

Oh, she thought, her heart starting to pound as she stared at her reflection. The satin hit her at the top of the thighs, long enough for decency, but short enough to reveal the straps designed to hold up the tops of matching stockings.

The kimono's deep vee revealed her almost X-rated décolletage—her breasts pressed together and propped up by the light boning hidden within the red lace of the teddy's bustier-style.

She would have given up on the whole idea of trotting out in the nearly risqué costume if she hadn't heard the flirty nitwit giggling again. And if Luke hadn't let out a soft, deep laugh in return.

Steeling her spine, she swept the fabric curtain aside and strolled into the boutique. "What do you think?" she said to the room at large.

Several of their party turned toward her. She supposed. But she only had eyes for one. Luke.

He'd gone still. His nostrils flared as his eyes tracked over her body, from her throat to her toes and then back again. She couldn't blame him for getting stalled at the D-cups. The garment did serve them right up, after all.

Then his gaze lifted to her face. She nervously licked her lips as a flush burned over her skin. She could only hope her face wasn't as red as the wicked bed-wear.

Luke's voice whispered in her ear. *Charlotte, you're not worrying I'll try to seduce you?*

No. She was very, very worried it would be the other way around. That she'd be the one trying to seduce Luke. And she didn't know which would be worse—that he'd wouldn't let her . . .

Or that he would.

"Not too fast," Luke's partner cautioned, as they took to the dance floor that had been created by pushing aside the tables in the boutique hotel's small dining room. "You're leading for three."

He glanced down at the matron of honor, Laura, with concern. He had to hold her with his arms fully outstretched to keep from crowding her very pregnant-looking belly. "Are you sure you're all right? Should you be sitting down?"

"I'm perfectly fine, as long as I don't go into labor early. But if the twins arrive before Audrey's wedding date, there'll be hell to pay. My dress is the size of a circus tent, and I don't think we could get it remade in time."

The first bars of Frankie Valli's "Can't Take My Eyes Off You," sounded from the small, iPod-powered stereo system in one corner of the room. "Start dancing," Audrey called over the music. "If anyone's clumsy, I'm bringing in a dance instructor tomorrow night."

Luke grimaced at the threat. As in everything about the weekend, the bride had planned this, too. Wedding dance practice. Audrey had a wooden spoon in hand and was tapping out the beat of the song on a tabletop. As he gently spun Laura in a half-turn, and then whirled her back, his gaze locked with Charlotte's. She was sitting on the sidelines, clearly amused by the command performance expected of the bridal party. Nothing felt funny to Luke. Over the speakers, Frankie was warbling about wanting to hold his pretty baby, and damn, if that wasn't what he wanted, too.

To hold Charlotte. To demand she warm his lonely night.

She was mouthing something to him now, and pointing to her own arm, one eyebrow raised. *Oh*, he thought, *I get it.* Tennis elbow, she was saying, questioning the injury-excuse that had kept him from golf but didn't keep him from twirling his dance partner.

So yeah, he'd lied in order to go shopping with her.

But hadn't he paid for the transgression? He snapped his gaze from hers before she could see what the memory of her in that racy red number did to him. Witch!

It had barely covered her ass, and the top had been designed to display Charlotte's charms in a manner not appropriate for a public venue. No, it should have been modeled in private, with Luke the only audience, and with plenty of time to allow him to remove the wrap of satin and swathe of lace inch-by-inch. Then he'd—

"Switch!" Audrey yelled now.

The command jerked Luke out of his reverie. "What?"

Laura patted him on the shoulder. "It means the fat lady gets to sit down and you have to find yourself another partner. Audrey wants to be sure we can alternate dancers without any awkwardness."

He found himself embracing the redheaded bridesmaid as the music segued into Van Morrison's "Someone Like You." As he'd discovered in the lingerie boutique, she had a tendency to cling like plastic wrap. Though she was thin as a rail, he kept her at pregnant-belly distance as his gaze found Charlotte again. But this time her eyes were closed and she was swaying a little in her seat. Had they ever danced together?

That's what would work, he decided. He'd get her into his arms under the guise of dancing practice. Once he had her that close, she wouldn't be able to deny the attraction was running as hot and hard as always. She wouldn't be able to run from him any longer.

"Switch!"

He dropped the redhead like a hot potato and strode for Charlotte. A hand grabbed his elbow. He winced. Not because it hurt, of course, but because he didn't want to be deterred. But he shifted to meet Audrey's eyes. "My turn," she said. "We'll be expected to partner each other on the wedding day."

Eric Clapton was playing "Wonderful Tonight." Luke couldn't refuse, of course, and so drew Audrey close. She was a little thing and felt as brittle as a peppermint stick. He gave her a tiny shake. "You need to relax."

Her smile was strained as her gaze roamed the dancers around them. "It has to be perfect," she said, clearly distracted. "No cracks in the foundation."

"It doesn't have to be perfect—"

"It does!" Her eyes lasered in on his face. "My marriage is going to last forever," she said, her voice fierce.

"Of course it will," he replied, trying to sound soothing. "But the wedding—"

"When Charlotte's mother married my dad, it was a complete shambles," Audrey said. "It rained, the DJ couldn't find the venue, and my little cousin Dean knocked over the wedding cake. Someone ran out and bought snack cakes to serve the guests. I knew that meant the marriage was destined to be a disaster."

A feather tickled the back of Luke's neck. No, not really a feather, but a sense that some important piece of information had just been laid at his feet. Or perhaps he'd merely discovered the end of a long, tangled thread, one that he needed to follow, to unravel, to find the prize at the center of the maze.

He looked over his shoulder to where he'd last seen Charlotte. Her seat was empty.

His attention returned to Audrey. "Connor won't care how the day goes. He just wants you, like you want him."

"I've wanted other things before."

His neck was itching again. "Yeah?" He was a guy, so he didn't get all the nuance going on here, but he tried stabbing at the dark. "That marriage between your father and Charlotte's mother . . ."

"Put the *Brady Bunch* straight out of your mind," she warned.

"Uh . . ."

"The group did not somehow form a family."

The words made the old TV show's theme song play in his head. Had Audrey expected that? Was a blended family what Charlotte had wished for as well? He couldn't explore the idea any further, because the bride-to-be abruptly swung out of his embrace. "Switch!"

Tim McGraw took over the music-making. "Unbroken" filtered through the speakers. Connor bumped his shoulder and passed his partner. Luke's hands automatically closed over the woman. Charlotte.

His fingers tightened on her shoulders. *Finally.*

"I'm rescuing my girl," Connor said, striding off. A few yards away, a tight-faced Audrey was adjusting the position of a groomsman's hand on the waist of a bridesmaid. A single inch higher, thumb rotated one click to the right.

"He's rescuing that poor couple," Charlotte muttered. "Audrey's officially hit ten on the bridal mania meter."

He looked back at her, using her distraction to draw her closer. With his mouth against her hair, he took her in a dance hold and started the quick-quick-slow-slow of a country two-step.

She fluttered a little in his hands, but he just tightened his grip on her fingers and made his arms more rigid, all the better to continue leading. He knew right where he wanted to take her.

A little sound come out of her mouth, but he continued shuffling his feet, moving her along with him. "You dance?" she finally said, her voice faint.

"Mmmm." His cheek nuzzled the soft warmth of her hair. He curled their joined hands tight to his chest, her knuckles pressed against his beating heart.

They passed his brother and Audrey. Connor had his wife-to-be wrapped in his arms, barely swaying. His mouth was close to her ear and whatever he was whispering eased the tension on her face.

Charlotte's gaze took in the other couple, then she drew back a little to glance up at Luke. "Do you really think their wedding's a good idea? Maybe you should be rescuing Connor."

"I happen to like marriage." He wasn't against the institution, even though his first had ended in a fiery crash. But he'd never expected he'd find a woman he wanted to be that close to again. Then Charlotte had limped into his life, wearing her independence like a crown, yet still unable to completely disguise that vulnerable Achilles' heel of hers.

Charlotte . . . sweet Charlotte, with her sharp thorns and soft petals, had been impossible to ignore.

Impossible to forget.

"I tried to, you know," he said, meeting her eyes.

Prickly woman was instantly wary. Amazing how those pale blue eyes could turn dark with suspicion. "What are you talking about?"

He drew her closer so he could nuzzle the top of her head again. "I didn't want to remember how sweet you taste. Your mouth, your skin, that hot place between your legs."

She jerked in his arms. He didn't loosen his hold. His mouth found her ear. "Haven't you thought of me?" he asked. "Missed our mutual showers?"

"Luke . . ."

"Shh, shh. It's okay. No one can hear."

"*I* can hear!"

He smiled, knowing he was getting to her. "Are you saying I'm tempting you, baby? Because I find that's fair payback for the little fashion show this afternoon."

"That wasn't . . . intentional."

"Oh, lie to yourself, but don't lie to me, honey. You wanted me to see all that I'd lost. Your long legs. Your—well, let's just say stupendous—breasts. No woman owns a sin-red outfit like that unless she wants a man to see her in it."

"I don't own it," Charlotte said quickly. "I put it back on the hanger and left it at the boutique."

"Where I returned this afternoon while you were stretched out by the pool. It's in our room now. Folded and waiting under your pillow."

He didn't think she was breathing. He ensured it by letting his mouth trail down from her ear, pushing aside her dark fall of hair to find the smooth skin at the back of her neck. His lips lingered there.

She trembled and the little noise that escaped her throat sounded like a half-swallowed moan.

"Remember how you liked it when I marked you here?" he murmured. "Leaving just the smallest bruise caused by just the tiniest sting of a kiss?"

"I didn't like it!"

"No lies, remember? But if you agree to come back to our room right now, I won't mark you again."

Another shiver racked her body.

He pushed her away to look into her face. Her cheeks and lips were flushed, her blue eyes wide. "Oh, baby. Am I making the wrong bargain? Come back to our room right now and I *will* mark you again."

"*Luke . . .*"

His forefinger brushed aside her hair to touch that place on her neck, and her skin burned like a fever. "Right here."

Chapter Four

L uke saw that his words were working on her. Whether it was because she was a writer or the other men in her life had been the inarticulate type, he'd learned before that sexy talk mesmerized Charlotte. And he so wanted her as his captive.

Their gazes still locked, he danced her toward the exit. She was breathing fast, hot little exhalations that blew across his chin. "I want you," he said. "Fourteen months is a long time without a woman in my bed."

"You didn't . . . ?" Her front teeth closed over her bottom lip.

"Only when I was all alone. And only when I was thinking of you," he admitted.

The flush on her neck rushed to her face. The pink was such a pretty contrast with the icy blue surprise of her eyes. "You shouldn't say things like that to me, Luke."

He kept moving in the direction of the exit. "I've never been less than straightforward with you, Charlotte. I'm not starting now."

Her mouth opened, then snapped shut. Oh, Charlotte. She wanted to ask what he was up to . . . what he was after.

But that stubborn heart of hers didn't want to know the answer. She wasn't ready for him to declare all the ways he wanted to take her into his life.

Taking her to bed would have to do for now, he decided.

Once they were joined there, she'd be unable to deny they should join all the other parts of their lives.

They'd reached the double doors. He quick-quick-slow-slowed her over the threshold, and then pushed her against the nearest wall. Leaning his weight into her body, he took both her hands in his and bent his head.

Kissed her.

Like earlier, like before he'd left the country, like always, the struggle went straight out of her. It was the most seductive damn thing. Charlotte was all thinking, planning, worrying, until he got his mouth on her. Then she yielded, her taste sugar and fire.

He lifted his head to take a breath and saw that she was gasping, too, her eyes tightly shut, her head resting against the wall. "It's been a long fourteen months for you, too, hasn't it honey?"

Her thick lashes lifted. "Maybe I've had a different lover every night."

"I'll make you forget every single one of them."

She smiled a little. "Silly man. You know how cautious I am."

"But you don't have to be that way with me, do you, Charlotte? You can break your celibacy with me. I'm safe to go wild with, baby."

She laughed. " 'Safe to go wild with'?"

"Isn't that what you need?" He had her hands and walked backward, taking a path toward their room. "There's a lot of energy stored up in this beautiful body. You can release it with me and I'll make sure it's the best night of your life."

She frowned at him, though he noticed she was allowing herself to be pulled in the right direction. "You're sure of yourself."

"I'm sure I know what to do with you. I know how you like your breasts to be teased, how you like my fingers inside you when I suck your nipples, how when you're on top I can touch you in that one special place and you'll—"

"Luke!" Red-faced, her gaze jumped behind him.

Grinning, he glanced over his shoulder to see a uniformed waiter outside their room, holding a tray with a bucket of ice, a bottle of wine, and two gleaming glasses.

"—scream just like that."

She whacked him on the shoulder as he turned to deal with the room service order. In moments they were behind the locked door, with chilling chardonnay beside the bed and thrumming sexual tension filling the bedroom.

Charlotte stood on one side of the mattress, her gaze down, her fingers fiddling with the lace edge of the sheet. Luke leaned over to flip the pillow on its end, revealing the scarlet temptations of lace and satin. "They're for you," he said.

She glanced at him, glanced back at the lingerie. "I should put them on just to torment you."

"I'll enjoy suffering for you." He'd seen her face at the boutique. Donning the garments would be a seduction of their own. He poured her a glass of wine, then came around the end of the bed to place the stem in her hand. She took it, as well as the soft kiss he placed on her mouth. "You're worrying too much," he said.

A moment passed. He could see her brain working, calculating the pros and cons. Desperation made his heartbeat kick up and it prompted him to utter the first lie he'd ever told her. "It's just sex, Charlotte."

The words made her eyes brighten. He saw her spine straighten. Another moment passed. "You're right," she finally said, handing over the glass and swooping up the lingerie in one move. Before his head had stopped spinning, she was behind the bathroom door.

In what seemed like a second, she was out again. He choked on the swallow of wine that was in his mouth. *Jesus.* "You're killing me."

The robe wasn't tight around her waist this time. It flowed open, another frame for her bountiful breasts and creamy skin. The teddy was poured over every curve of her body, displaying the flare of her hips as well as showcasing her magnificent chest. He felt stupid, staring at her. He had a master's degree in math. Professional credentials in engineering and physics.

He had no idea how to traverse the feet between them. How he would manage to hold on to the flaming temptation that was Charlotte's body in that fantasy-wear.

Perhaps she sensed his paralysis, because she strolled toward him. His gaze was drawn downward to her long legs, the tops of her thighs bare, the rest of them covered with sheer stockings held up by garters attached to the lacy hem of the teddy.

"Take off your clothes, Luke," she said.

Were there any more beautiful words in the English language? But he was still floored by the sexiest sight of his life. She frowned. "Do I need to help you?"

He cleared his throat, and was able to move just enough to set his wineglass aside. "Please do," he said.

Her smile caused a tiny dimple to crease her right cheek. She was feeling good, he decided, decisive and confident now, and he grinned in return. He wanted her all-in here.

His all the way.

She drew his sport coat off first. "So handsome," she murmured. "Have I ever seen you this dressed up?" Her hands ran over the navy blue wool as she draped it over a chair. Then she was back, loosening his tie.

His heart pounded in his chest as her fingers worked slowly to unknot the fabric. He wanted to grab the thing and yank it over his head, but Charlotte was so pretty with her tongue caught between her teeth, her focus so absolute on her task. She peeped up at him, a laugh in her eyes.

"Witch," he murmured. "You know you're making me crazy."

She let the strip of silk drop to the ground. "Fourteen months is a long, long time, Luke. We don't want to rush things."

His chest expanded as she attacked the buttons of his shirt.

"We could rush the first time and go slow the second. And the third . . ." The tails of his shirt pulled free and then it, too, dropped to the ground. "I'll take it really slow, then. Lick you all over. Lick you on that very special place you like, lick you until you come on my tongue."

She swayed. He caught her hips, yanked her close.

The kiss was sex in itself. He thrust deep into the hot cavern of her mouth. She rubbed against his chest, and he felt her hard nipples scrape against his undershirt. Still holding her close, he lifted one hand to grasp the soft cotton between his shoulder blades. He yanked it upward and over his head, separating their lips for just the second it took to toss the fabric aside.

Then it was his naked chest to her lace-covered breasts. With a quick swipe, he slid the robe from her shoulders. Then he peeled the cups of the teddy away from her, tucking the stretchy lace beneath her breasts. Desperate for more, he jerked her forward again, groaning as the stiff beads of her nipples met his hot skin.

He was going to go off just with this.

Charlotte twined a leg around his, opening her hip so that her pelvis was flush with his. He rubbed his shaft against her soft mound, watching her eyes close as she moaned and pushed back. His hand pressed the small of her back, anchoring her so that the movement was his alone.

Her frustrated sound was music to his ears. She made another as he lifted his mouth and ran his lips across her jaw and down her neck. As she went on tiptoe, the curve of her ass found the palm of his hand and his mouth met the top swell of her luscious breasts.

He breathed in, taking Charlotte-scent into his lungs. His free hand moved to cup the heavy weight of her as his mouth shifted to hover over her nipple. His tongue reached out to lick the very tip.

Charlotte jerked in his hold. A tremor worked down her spine. "Luke. Luke, please."

He flicked her nipple, a harder touch this time and another shudder racked her frame. Teasing her like this wasn't easy on him, either. There were dozens of things he adored when it came to Charlotte's body, from her elegant limbs to her silky hair, but she liked the attention he paid to her breasts as much as he liked paying the attention.

He curled his tongue around the jutting stiffness and this time she broke, both her hands sliding to his head and holding him right where she wanted him. Her fingernails scratched his scalp, insisting he provide a firmer touch.

So he sucked.

Her moan went straight to his cock. Blood surged there, making it go even harder as his body processed the absolute sexual thrill of his mouth filled with her warm, soft flesh. He pressed her nipple against the roof of his mouth, and then drew on it in a rhythm that he matched with the hand kneading her ass.

She was climbing his body like ivy. He flashed hot, thinking about just freeing his shaft and pushing aside that scrap of red to shove himself inside her body. But it would be over too soon. It wouldn't provide enough Luke-to-Charlotte contact.

He released her breast with a carnal pop and she didn't hesitate to put her mouth on him, her greedy tongue licking across his chest wall until she found his own nipple. She paid him back with delicate licks there and he groaned, his hand sliding down to the fastening of his slacks.

His cock needed out.

Her fingers replaced his. "Let me," she whispered, and it was his turn to shudder as her knuckles brushed him while she worked at the zipper. Then she shoved the fabric away. The pants and boxers fell to his ankles and he tripped trying to step out of them, landing on the bed.

She laughed.

He snagged her wrist and drew her down beside him even as he kicked out of the last of his clothes. She twined her

arms around his neck and they were nose-to-nose. Smile-to-
smile.

He caressed her bottom. "You have the most delectable
soft curves."

"I missed all your hard parts."

"Yeah?" He twined his legs with hers but while the stockings were hot, they weren't the same as Charlotte's own sleek
skin. "My hard parts want you completely naked."

She rolled to her back and let her arms and legs go lax.
"You bought the goods, you get to take them off."

He ignored his trembling hands to do just that. But he
couldn't ignore the miles of flesh he revealed. As he unrolled
each stocking he trailed his tongue down the taut muscles of
her thigh, over her knee, along her shin. A line of fasteners
marched down the middle of the naughty scrap of red and he
kissed her belly as each was undone.

He drew the lingerie away from Charlotte's body and
dropped it over the side of the mattress. The only thing now
decorating the white sheets was the erotic display of her
long-limbed nakedness. His heart walloped against his ribs.
Staring down at her, he rubbed at the spot with his palm.

Then Charlotte, her gaze never leaving his, took his other
hand. She placed it palm-down on the wet, pulsing heat of
her pussy.

If she was trying to send him a message, he wasn't in the
mood to listen. Instead, he curled his fingers and tenderly slid
two into the sleek, giving center of her.

She gasped, and just the glimpse of the pink wetness inside
her mouth made him go harder. Without moving his hand,
he stretched beside her body. Her head turned to his and
their lips met, the kiss going wild as she pushed her tongue
into his mouth. God!

He sucked on it, and then started moving inside her body,
filling her with his fingers as she filled him with her hot, teasing tongue. His hips moved against her, his cock stroking her
pretty flank.

She twisted closer and her breast brushed his chest, distracting him. Demanding attention.

Still thrusting with his fingers, he slid lower, listening to her gasp as he found her nipple and sucked it inside. Her hips pumped into his penetrating touch, her whole body undulating as he dallied at each breast, switching from nipple to nipple.

He was careful to be gentle with them. So gentle.

"Luke. Luke, Luke, *Luke*."

Careful to make her eager for more. Fourteen months had passed, but everything that he'd learned of her body was still fresh in his mind. Gentle, to make her crazy.

He eased up the pressure on the nipple in his mouth. His tongue made soft, lazy lashes against the jutting bud.

His hand moved slower into the soft drenched tissues where his cock was clamoring to take over.

When he moved his head to press a closed-lips kiss on her midriff, she broke. One moment they were both on their sides. In the next, his shoulder blades were flat to the mattress and she had a hand on his belly. "Condom?" she asked, her voice fierce.

His favorite side of Charlotte. The wild side.

"I bought a package when I went out for the lingerie," he said. "Check the bedside table drawer."

She tilted her head. "You didn't come with condoms?"

"Where you're involved, I don't take anything for granted." Back to honesty.

She seemed to appreciate it. Once a foil packet had been located, the action speeded up. Or maybe it was just that his brain could no longer keep hold of all the details. There was . . .

Charlotte.

Her smooth skin.

Her mouth latching onto his.

The teasing roll of latex down his shaft.

Her gaze caught his, a question in them, and he recalled his own promise. "This way," he said, pulling her astride his hips.

They both groaned as he worked his way inside her.

She rode him then, leaving his hands free to play with her magnificent breasts. Allowing him to toy with that bundle of nerves that he'd promised to please.

He was pleasing her. God, what a high.

Her hair swung around her shoulders as she moved on him, counterpoint to the lift of his hips. Her mouth was half-opened, her blue gaze half-shuttered.

Fourteen months' worth of fantasies had never been this good.

And then the crisis was upon him. The burn was shooting up the back of his legs. His balls were tightening. His movements went jerky. Urgent.

And he saw she was urgent, too. He took his fingers from her clit. Her gaze was focused on them. She saw him lift them to his mouth, wet them with his tongue. Her eyes dropped as he brought two fingertips back to that throbbing nub of flesh.

He rubbed her there, firm and sure, and he saw the moment when climax struck. She stilled, then jerked, smacking against his upstroke. As a flush broke across her skin, he reached for one nipple and pinched her there, watching as her head dropped back. Feeling as her internal muscles milked his body.

They both went wilder.

Calm took awhile to achieve.

"I told you," he said finally, not trying to camouflage the satisfaction he felt. She was beside him now, as she always should be. "This was a very good idea."

"You're right," she agreed, nestling her cheek against the hollow of his shoulder. "There's nothing wrong with sex for the sake of sex."

He stilled. *Shit.* Fourteen months had passed, yet nothing had changed. He'd said they should have "just sex" to get her in his bed. But now that he had her there, he'd gotten "just" what he said he'd wanted.

Which wasn't enough at all.

CHAPTER FIVE

Charlotte woke, confused for a moment by the beat beneath her cheek and the hair-roughened legs twined with hers. Then she recognized Luke's scent, his wide palm cupping her shoulder, the sound of his heart.

Heat flashed over her, part-panic, part-passion. She'd had sex with Luke last night. And it had been as intimate and erotic as every other time before. On the tender skin at the nape of her neck—that she prayed her long hair would conceal—she felt a lick of heat that told her he'd left her with a reminder of his favorite kiss in her favorite place.

Fourteen months had passed—but what had happened between the sheets in the preceding hours proved that while a year had gone by, they'd lost nothing of their sexual connection. And she couldn't afford to be connected with any man.

Agitated at the thought, she started to wrench from Luke's hold, stirring him from sleep. Charlotte froze as his fingers twitched and his legs shifted. He settled again and she breathed out a quiet sigh, holding still to give her pulse another minute to quiet. She needed to keep her cool. And she needed to disentangle herself from him.

For now.

Forever.

Moving glacier-slow, Charlotte slipped from his lax hold and slid off the mattress. Her heart jerked as he muttered something then rolled to his stomach, gathering the pillow close. She watched him another long moment, appreciating again his wide shoulders, lean hips, and the deep valley of his spine revealed by the sheet that was pooled across the top of his muscled ass.

Who could blame her for succumbing to temptation? She'd put up a good fight, hadn't she? But he knew all the ways to melt her resistance, and God knows he was a beautiful man.

Still, she could keep passion and emotion separate, she could. A few minutes alone, a cup or two of coffee, and she'd be back to her composed, calm self. Their night together didn't mean that *they* were together.

He was deep enough in sleep that she risked a quick shower. Then she pulled on her swimsuit and cover-up, a floppy hat, and big sunglasses, and departed the room in search of caffeine and a secluded corner beside the pool.

In the open-air lobby, silver carafes and paper cups were provided for early rising guests. Charlotte breathed in the steam of her dose of strong coffee and her spirits lifted. Clearly she was the first to venture from her room, and with a little luck she'd have enough time for the tranquility to settle into her soul.

Leaning against the nearby wall, she closed her eyes as the coffee slid down her throat.

"Charlotte," a man's voice said. "As I live and breathe, Charlotte Bond."

She startled, causing hot liquid to burp from the opening in the coffee's lid. A yelp escaped her and she whirled, seeking a napkin to mop up the burn.

The man hurried close to press a handkerchief into her free hand. "I'm sorry," he said, his voice concerned. "Are you all right?"

She kept her attention on the cooling drips. "I'm fine. It was nothing." *You didn't break my heart.* "How are you, Peter?"

Peter Langford, Audrey's dad and Charlotte's former step-father, ran a hand over his expertly cut steel-gray hair. "This father-of-the-bride stuff isn't for the faint of heart," he said, with an awkward laugh.

"Audrey didn't say you'd be here this weekend," Charlotte said. She handed him back the square of cotton. Though she hadn't seen him in nine years, he'd changed as little as his daughter.

"I have a place nearby that I use on weekends." Tall and spare, with a golfer's tan and a wealthy man's aura, Peter appeared in good health—though he was gazing on her with something that felt uncomfortably close to regret.

Or maybe that was projecting, she thought, embarrassed. It was likely an old echo of her devastated teenage self. Charlotte cleared her throat and gave him her best professional smile, donning her composure like armor. *Treat him like a client.* "Well, it's a pleasure to see you again."

"Is it, Charlotte?" he asked, his voice quiet. Then he cleared his throat. "I've thought of you so many times."

Then why didn't you ever try to see me? Contact me? "How kind of you to say so."

A pained expression crossed his face. "I'm serious, Charlotte. Maybe today we could—"

"There you are!" Another man's voice boomed through the lobby.

Charlotte's stomach clenched, but she spun, pasting on a welcoming smile. At this moment she was glad for an interruption, even if it meant facing Luke before she was quite ready. "I was on a coffee safari." She held out her hand to him. "Have you met Audrey's father?"

His fingers twined with hers. She flashed back to the first moments of wakefulness, when they'd been wrapped around each other. Her common sense told her to pull back, pull away, but Luke tightened his hold and leaned down to kiss her cheek. Then he swept her hair off her shoulder, his mouth finding that little hickey he'd left behind on her neck. He dropped a second, gentle kiss there.

She shot him a look. He reciprocated with a shameless

grin. "Morning, angel," he said, his voice soft. Then he turned to Peter, extending his free hand to shake the other man's. "I haven't had the opportunity as yet. I'm Luke Harper, Connor's older brother."

"You've been overseas," Peter said, with a smile. "You were doing engineering work?"

"When he wasn't playing tennis," Charlotte said dryly.

Luke slid his arm around her waist. "And pining after this girl. We were separated for much, much too long."

Peter glanced at Charlotte. "I could say the same. I haven't seen her since she was a coltish eighteen. She's grown into an extraordinarily beautiful young woman."

"That's right," Luke said. "You were married to her mother for a time."

"When Audrey and Charlotte were high schoolers." Peter looked away. "Charlotte's mother is another extraordinary beauty."

"I wouldn't know," Luke said. "Charlotte is very stingy with her family." Then he snuggled her closer to his hip. "But that's going to change, right, honey?"

She was going to have to change to survive this. With Luke so near, she could feel her nerve endings lighting up like sparklers. Last night was supposed to be scratching an itch or maybe putting a period on an old romance. Instead, she wanted to lean into him, imprinting herself on his skin.

But the possibility of starting up with Luke again was such a bad idea that it made her head ache. On the pretext of re-filling her coffee cup, she moved toward the carafes and out of Luke's reach. "Would either of you like a cup?" she asked.

The man with whom she'd spent the night was giving her a look that said he'd noticed her retreat. "Black, please," he answered, then shifted his gaze to the other man. "So, tell me, Peter, what was our Charlotte like as a teenager?"

"He couldn't possibly remember," she protested. Rehashing any moment of those four years when she'd thought she finally had both a mother *and* a father wasn't the path to calm. The tension churning in her belly was testament to that.

She handed Luke his coffee. " 'Our' Charlotte doesn't quite describe the relationship. Peter never considered me his."

The older man winced, and she regretted the remark instantly. It had been her intention to clarify, not cut. She inspected the lid of her cup. "However, he went to every one of my basketball games."

"I still have all the *Beacon* issues from your senior year, too," he said.

Astonished, her head came up. "The high school literary magazine?"

Peter nodded, then looked at Luke. "She was the editor. It won two national awards."

Charlotte felt her face go hot. She wouldn't have bet Peter would remember that—let alone have saved the magazines! "I . . ." Maybe for the first time in her life, words failed her. Helpless, she found herself glancing around at Luke, a sudden sting of tears in her eyes.

He brushed a palm down the back of her hair, then kept his fingers tangled in the ends. "Yeah, but could she hit a three-pointer?"

It was the exact right thing to say. Peter laughed, and launched into the retelling of a league championship game. That he'd remember a sporting event didn't seem so earth-shaking to Charlotte. In her experience, men had memories for random athletic moments. She'd dated a guy who could describe the 2007 Stanley Cup championship game blow-by-blow, despite the fact that he'd never played hockey, let alone worn a pair of ice skates.

Charlotte's tension eased a little more. Though Luke's warmth was at her back and his fingers were still twined in her hair, she found both more comforting than frightening. And maybe it should scare her, but his touch was centering her, steadying her after the rocking and rolling brought on by this unexpected meeting with Peter.

She was even managing to hold on to her cool.

"You want to see pictures?" Peter asked.

Pictures?

"Sure." Luke grinned. "Is she in braces and zit cream?"

Charlotte could only stare as Peter, the man she'd once called "Dad," reached for his wallet. Inside, he flipped past a couple of shots of Audrey to display face-to-face images of herself, circa ages seventeen and eighteen. In the first, she wore her basketball uniform. She had her hair in a high ponytail tied up with a blue-and-white ribbon—the school colors. In the other, she was holding up one of the magazine awards. Beside her stood an obviously proud Peter.

The men's voices receded as she gazed on the images of her younger, less cynical self. Audrey had been a pain in the ass in the way a same-age, different-interests sibling could be. But Charlotte had suffered her gladly for the paradise of two parents. Of having a father figure in her life whom she thought really cared about her.

Poor kid, with those big smiles on the verge of shattering. Just a short few months away from finally learning the hard lesson that men wouldn't stay. That she couldn't count on love, only herself.

"Honey? Sweetheart?" Luke tugged on her hair.

She started. "What?"

"Peter asked you a question."

The man who'd once been married to her mother gave her a little smile. "I was hoping you'd let me take you to lunch today. Just the two of us."

Charlotte blinked. "I . . . I don't think so." She didn't want any further reminders of her hopeful adolescent years.

"Sweetheart—" Luke started.

She clutched the side of his shirt, panicking again. "We— Luke and I—have plans. All-day plans. We've been apart for a long time, you see, and want to . . . to spend every moment together." Entangled. Inside her head, she groaned, but the words were already out there.

Okay, but at least she'd hung on to her cool, right? She sent Peter another of her businessperson-to-client smiles. "You understand?"

"I suppose I do." Peter folded his wallet, but stared down at it instead of putting it away. "But, Charlie—"

"Don't call me that!" Charlotte's voice was harsh, her feet already in retreat. "Don't ever use that name." It was a knee-jerk reaction she was helpless to prevent. But she didn't care that her cool had evaporated. She only cared about getting far, far away.

"I feel ridiculous and I'm not the one draped in toilet paper," Luke said to the unlucky groomsman who had drawn the short straw. He attached strips of the paper squares to the tiara another of the guys had fashioned from twists of yet more TP. He stood back, eyeing the effect. "What do you think, Con? Does that look like a wedding veil?"

His brother grinned. "It looks like I owe Derrik a keg of beer."

"Yeah," the faux-bride grumbled, batting at the paper the breeze blew into his eyes. "Because when I good-naturedly said I'd participate in some games, I thought we were talking about pool volleyball."

"I had something like that in mind myself," Luke said, glancing across the deck where the women were similarly dressing up one of the bridesmaids. Whatever they played, he'd planned on being teamed with Charlotte. It was imperative he stick close enough to find out what was going on inside her head. The sex had been spectacular the night before, and he'd have liked nothing more than waking up to more of it, but she'd run off while he was still sleeping.

Then he'd tracked her down and she'd looked uncomfortable and embarrassed—even before she'd caught sight of him. Peter Langford seemed like a nice enough guy, but he'd put Charlotte on edge.

Luke glanced at her again, noting she had retreated to a lounge chair and was hiding behind her sunglasses and wide-brimmed hat. He drew his brother away from the other men and lowered his voice. "What do you know about your future father-in-law's marriage to Charlotte's mom?"

"I think its failure was a big disappointment to him. Audrey is pretty close mouthed about it, but I get the feeling that she wanted it to work, as well. Her mother died when she was very small and she doesn't remember her—I think she was hoping she'd finally have one again."

"Is that what happened to Charlotte's dad? Did he die?"

Con shrugged. "You're asking me? You're the one in love with the woman. Why don't you know?"

Luke opened his mouth, then shut it. Why didn't he know? He'd said that Charlotte had been stingy about her family, but he'd never pressed her, had he? That distance he'd allowed had kept *her* distant.

It was time to remedy that, he decided. He was going to make her talk. It was the only way, he figured, to bridge the gap that she kept putting between them.

It looked good for him in the next few minutes. Voting took place on which bride was more beautiful, Derrik with his goatee and elbow-length "veil," or his opponent, who actually knew how to walk in a dress. When they proceeded down the "aisle"—a path around the pool—amid some snickers and several guffaws, at the halfway point Derrik was left in only his tiara and his tattered shorts.

Connie, the bridesmaid, won the prize—tickets to an upcoming Dodgers baseball match-up—which only made Derrik a sorer loser. Over his grousing, Audrey also announced that the other woman would choose the next game, and it would be one that pitted couple against couple.

With Charlotte his designated partner in the upcoming

event, Luke approached her, a mimosa in each hand. He passed over a glass, then wedged his hips onto the cushion of her lounge chair. She hesitated a moment, then shifted her long golden legs a little to the side.

He trailed his cold fingers down her shin, smiling as she twitched. "Ticklish?"

"Mmm."

He couldn't read her expression behind her dark glasses. "I enjoyed last night," he said, his voice quiet. "You're amazing, especially when you—"

"Do we have to discuss it?" she asked in a rushed whisper.

He grinned at her obvious fluster. "I guess not."

"Good." She set her big hat and her champagne and orange juice on the square table to her right and leaned her head against the cushion, a woman on the verge of napping.

He clasped her thigh, right above her knee. "We could talk about the more distant past instead."

The muscle in her leg tightened in his hand. "Why?"

"I'm just curious. Before . . . I didn't press you to tell me things."

"One of your stellar qualities."

Stubborn woman! "Is it so intrusive of me to want to know some basics?"

She resorted to the one-word response again. "Why?"

He might have wrung her neck if the start of the next game wasn't announced at that moment. They were forced to gather poolside with the other couples. The rules were simple and the reaction a mix of groans and ribald comments. The competition would occur simultaneously. Each partner would hold their hands behind their backs. The male half would have a cellophane-covered package of mini powdered donuts in his mouth. It was up to the female half to unwrap the treat and down each little circle without dropping one and without the aid of any fingers. The winners were whoever finished first.

They'd recruited the woman who worked the front desk

to call "Time!" and then the game was on. It was clear right off the bat that Charlotte's height put them at an advantage. Once she lifted on tiptoe, she was at a level to attack the cellophane with her teeth. She started to make headway, but then broke away, laughing.

"I'm sorry," she wheezed out. "But you're looking at me cross-eyed!"

With his mouth full of mini-donuts, he couldn't do more than grunt. So he tried getting his message across by stepping up to her. *Let's win this.*

Hey, he was a big baseball fan and there might be more Dodgers tickets at stake.

She dutifully attacked the cellophane again, then had to take another break for laughter. He uncrossed and then rolled his eyes, stepping close to her again.

"Okay, okay," she said, and went after the plastic with gusto. Around them, several other players had already left the competition, disqualified for dropping donuts or forgetting and reaching with a hand.

Audrey and Con were still in, though, and despite their size difference making headway. The bride-to-be was already swallowing one treat, but then hesitated before taking another as she worried about putting on weight. "In six weeks I have to squeeze into a size zero wedding dress!"

Charlotte sent the other woman a scathing sidelong look, then redoubled her efforts. Clearly she wanted to best her ex-stepsister. In seconds she was chewing, powdered sugar all over her lips.

Luke considered spitting out the rest of the package, just so he could lick the sweetness off her luscious mouth. But she gestured to him with a hand, then placed it once again behind her back. Dutifully crowding her, he presented the open packet.

He realized the game was downright evil when she attempted to suck the next treat out of the plastic. It set Charlotte off again and she had to break away to recover from her giggles. "You should see your face," she said, holding one hand over her belly.

He took a deep breath through his nose. Hopefully she wouldn't look below his waist. Eyeing the competition, Luke knew they had to get a move on or give up on seeing the Dodgers kill the San Diego Padres. Stepping close, he shoved the packet toward her mouth, nudging her lips.

It set her laughing again. She swayed back, losing her balance. Her foot moved to stabilize herself, but it only found air. They'd moved too close to the edge of the pool! Luke reached to save her, his fingers closing around her wrist. But the die was already cast. She was going over and if he didn't let her, he'd be in, too. He loosened his grip and she completed her backward tip into the water.

She came up, sputtering, as applause broke out. Another couple had won the game. Sure enough, baseball tickets.

Luke grumbled about it as he helped Charlotte up the pool steps. She appeared very wet and only somewhat contrite. "Okay, okay, I owe you one," she said, as she twisted her hair to wring the water out of it.

He dropped a beach towel over her head and drew her down to share one of the chaises with him. "Then tell me something about your family situation," he said. "You know mine. Mother, father, Con."

"You grew up with two dogs and a cat. Summer vacations at national parks."

It did sound idyllic, put like that. And her tone was a great big hint that her childhood was not so picture-postcard. "You have any pets as a kid?" he asked.

"My mother collects husbands, not animals."

Luke tilted his head, waited for more. Charlotte let out a sigh. "Fine. My mom and dad divorced when I was two. Then there was Mark. He was around until I was eight. You've met Peter. After that it was Gus. Now she has Vincent. They live in Florida near his kids."

"Ah." So Charlotte was left on this side of the country all by herself. Or was she? "You see your father very often?"

Her gaze cut from his. She busied herself by drying off her sunglasses, which had gone in the pool with her. "Nope. Haven't a clue where he is. He was the first to leave—and the first never to return."

She said it matter-of-factly, but the implication made Luke ache for her. Her dad had walked out of her life, followed by man after man after man . . . including him. Yeah, she'd pushed him away, but he understood why, now, he thought. She donned her prickliness for protection.

He cupped her cheek in his palm. "Sweetheart," he murmured, wanting her to look at him. "Charlie . . ."

Her chin jerked away from his touch. "Don't call me that!" She jumped from the lounge and seemed poised to stride away.

Luke caught her hand, remembering that same reaction when Peter Langford had used the nickname. "What's the matter? Why does 'Charlie' set you off?"

"I was called that as a kid, okay?" She snatched her fingers from his. "I'm not a kid anymore."

Oh, that feather was teasing the back of his neck again. When he saw the tense set of her shoulders, all his alarms started ringing. *Here we go*, he thought. *Tread carefully*. If he could get her to talk about this, he'd get her close enough to keep forever.

His hand founds hers again. "I kinda like Charlie," he said gently. "Why is it so bad?"

She donned the sunglasses she held in her free hand, the overlarge lenses obscuring the expression on her face. "Because . . ." she hesitated, then yanked her fingers from his once again. "Because Charlie gets left, okay? But Charlotte . . . Charlotte is the one who does the leaving."

And then, she—Charlotte—walked away from Luke, taking any hope that he'd been close to winning her back with her.

Chapter Six

Getting away from Luke appeared an impossibility, Charlotte discovered. They shared a room, and even if he wasn't in it with her, the bed was there, a big white reminder of how hot the sex had been between them the night before. Poolside wasn't any better. Though they'd stopped with the stupid games, the banter between the couples only made her remember fourteen months before when she'd had him to play Scrabble with, to go for a run with, to share a meal with at the end of a long day.

It scared her how much she found herself longing to do that again.

So in the late afternoon, when Audrey clapped her hands and said it was time for the next activity—a surprise that was not on the agenda—Charlotte didn't hesitate to be herded toward the parking lot. Anything to get her mind off of him. Anything to get away from her body's demands to cozy up to his lean strength.

This time she ended up beside her ex-stepsister in the backseat of the minivan. She breathed a sigh of relief until Audrey poked her in the ribs with a sharp elbow. "Do you see how it is with us?" she whispered. "Do you understand how things are between me and Connor?"

Diplomacy, Charlotte reminded herself. *She's a client, and a bride, and not the teenage brat who used to steal the last of your clean sweatsocks.* "I can tell he loves you very much." Poor guy.

Audrey let out a little sigh. "I think so, too," she said. "I want us to be happy. I want our marriage to be a strong one more than anything. Do you think I'll be a good wife? That's what Connor deserves. That's what I want to be for him."

Charlotte stared at her. The Audrey she knew had never let a chink in her confidence show. Where Charlotte had attempted covering up her insecurities with a mantle of detachment edged with sarcasm, Audrey's beauty and assurance had always seemed polished and solid. All the way to the core.

Frankly, until now, Charlotte hadn't suspected the other woman had a heart beneath that perfect polish. But . . . wow. Audrey acting like a human being with worries and vulnerabilities was, God, it was kind of touching. "If you put your mind to it, Audrey, I'm sure you can accomplish anything." She surprised herself by believing every word.

Her ex-stepsister sent her a skeptical look. "If I had that kind of power, our parents would still be together."

Shock felt like a slap to the face. Charlotte drew back as far as she could, her mind working over and over that last sentence. "You . . . you wanted that? You hoped their marriage would last?"

"Of course." Audrey looked down, spinning the diamond that she wore on her dainty finger. "I wanted a mother. I wanted my father to be happy. A sister wasn't so bad."

"You hated me."

"I didn't hate you. We didn't like the same things . . . but that didn't matter."

"You took my clothes!"

A small smile turned up the corners of Audrey's mouth. "Only the ones I liked and that fit me . . . which weren't many."

"The sweatsocks," Charlotte grumbled. "Yours were never clean."

"I paid you back in fashion advice." Audrey's gaze flicked

over Charlotte's outfit—a bright racer-backed tank paired with a flounced full skirt that skimmed her knees. "And it looks like you took it. Very cute clothes you've been wearing."

"Gee, thanks." Charlotte felt a little more comfortable with this Audrey, who handed out backhanded compliments. "Without you I might still be in flannel shirts and overalls," she said dryly.

"It wasn't that," Audrey said. "Your mother was always encouraging you to buy things that were more suited to a petite blonde, that's all."

"A petite blonde like you."

"Like me," Audrey admitted. "It's why I always thought she might take to me."

There was an echo of hurt that Charlotte found familiar in the other woman's voice. "She cared for you," she said. "It wasn't because of us that they divorced."

"I never heard from your mother again, though I sent her a Christmas card with my contact info every year."

"Peter didn't call me once either," Charlotte replied.

They both were silent for a moment. Then Audrey clutched Charlotte's arm and started whispering to her in a fierce voice. "What am I doing? Why would I think any marriage could last?"

Charlotte swallowed, trying to think of what to say. She could see that they were turning into a parking lot and if freedom wasn't that close, she might have bailed out the window. "Audrey . . ."

"I'm not kidding. Am I making a huge mistake?"

Their car stopped behind another, already parked. Both Luke and Connor were climbing out of that one. "Look at your groom," Charlotte said, pointing through the glass. "Does he look like a mistake?"

Audrey's expression softened. A glow came into her eyes. It freaked Charlotte a little, to see how she was transformed, just by gazing on the man she was engaged to marry.

Her ex-stepsister's gaze darted back to Charlotte. "But—"
"Who has the gloomy eyebrows now?"

It made Audrey laugh. She glanced at Connor again and
all the tension went out of her. "Thanks," she said. "I think
you're the only person here who could have talked me out
of that little panic attack."

Which freaked Charlotte just a little bit more. She had become the defender of marital possibility? That wasn't who
she was!

But her fears only grew as she comprehended the next
item on the wedding party bonding agenda. They were
parked beside a field. And in that field were large baskets and
long lines attached to slowly filling orbs of parachute-like
material. Audrey announced they were about to embark on
a hot-air ballooning adventure.

Charlotte's heart rose to clog her throat. Suddenly Luke
was beside her, his hand at the small of her back. "Are you
going to be okay with this? I remember you're afraid of
heights."

She glanced at him. "How do you know that?"

"It's one of the few secrets you ever divulged."

Maybe it was stupid to feel more vulnerable that he knew
about her weakness. But she couldn't deny the sentiment, so
she decided to disavow her fear. "I don't know what you're
talking about. I'll be fine. Just fine."

He released a sigh that sounded suspiciously frustrating,
but she had enough emotion roiling around in her belly and
brain and so she declined to think more about it. Quicker
than she liked, they were divided into groups and helped
into the baskets. Her nerves jittering, she waited for them to
leave the ground, unaware of who shared the space around
her.

Then the body behind hers shifted and she knew the identity of at least one of her companions. She shouldn't be relieved to have Luke at her back, but she figured if she threw
up on him, he'd take it better than most.

As the basket lifted in the air, she thought getting sick was a very real possibility. She crossed her arms over her chest, surreptitiously hugging herself. Instinct had her closing her eyes, but that made her stomach's pitching even worse, so she opened them and focused on her size 9 sandals. They were a toasty brown, with a myriad of straps and a wedge heel. She tried thinking back to where exactly she'd bought them . . .

The air seemed to bump them from below, and she gasped, jolted out of her reverie. Her gaze jumped from her toes to the scenery surrounding them. They were really moving now, the ground receding and their cars turning to children's toys. She felt her face go green.

"Honey." Luke drew her back against his chest. "Are you all right?"

The air moving past the basket dried the cold sweat on her face. "With any luck I'll die before I die."

Luke's hands tightened on her upper arms. "Don't talk like that."

His harsh tone had her turning around, for a moment sidetracked from her shakiness. "What?" The bones of his face suddenly seemed to push against his skin. His eyes glittered. "Are *you* all right?"

"Sure." He blew out a breath. "I just . . . Let's talk about something else."

She kept her gaze trained on his face. "Preferably not the great amount of space between my feet and the ground."

"Hah. So you *are* afraid of heights." He seemed completely relaxed now.

"And spiders."

"All girls are afraid of spiders," he scoffed.

She bristled, unwilling to be one of a common horde. "Maybe, but not just anyone is terrified of tripe."

"No one really likes to eat tripe."

"I'm afraid of *looking* at it," she said, clarifying. "Those creepy little chambers. Sometimes sponges can gross me out, too."

He was staring at her.

"Too much information?"

"I'm just pondering how we could have dated for so long without me guessing your fear of a common cleaning implement."

"I keep things to myself."

"I'll say." His voice was dry.

"Well, I'm sharing now." Ironically, it seemed to keep the scariness at bay. "I bet you didn't know it's possible that I was a tin can in a previous life. I'm also afraid of goats."

"That's where you're wrong." He turned her to face him. She didn't notice the earth slipping below them as she looked into green eyes that held a spark of contagious humor. "Don't you remember our visit to the zoo?"

Oh, she had forgotten. They'd gone to the world-famous one in San Diego, just a couple of hours away. Every exhibit had been so interesting, from the meerkats to the hippos, that she'd been lulled into a sense of security. The fact was, Luke had that kind of effect on her. So one minute they'd been gazing on the Galapagos tortoises, the next he'd led her into another enclosure without her actually taking in which it was. Then she'd instantly frozen up, easy prey to the four-legged, forelocked creatures who came nibbling at her clothes.

"They would have eaten me alive!" The memory made her clutch at his shirt. "But you saved me by immediately carting me out of there."

"Glad you remember it that way, sweetheart," he said with an unabashed grin. "I did get you out of there, but not before I took a minute to snap this." His hand reached for his wallet.

When he opened it, they might as well have tipped upside down in the gondola. Her stomach took an elevator fall and that cold sweat broke out all over her skin again.

Luke had photos of her in his wallet. Like Peter, two, face-to-face. In one, she was at the petting zoo, standing statue-still, her eyes screwed tight and her body rigid as a creature of the damned nipped at the hem of her tee. She looked silly and childish and she couldn't imagine why he carried it with him unless it was to remind himself of the mistake he'd almost made by wanting more from her.

"Every time I look at it I think of how you clung to me when I took you from the petting corral," Luke said quietly. "It was probably the tightest you ever let me hold you."

Charlotte's heart was pounding so hard she could feel her blood knocking against the pulse points at her wrists and her temples. Fear tasted metallic on her tongue.

The other picture made her even more alarmed. In it, they were seated at an outdoor table at a pier-side restaurant. Luke had handed his cell phone to their waiter and asked him to press the camera icon. She'd been reading the menu, not paying attention to the request, and only looked up—looked at Luke—when he called her name. The server had caught that moment. Charlotte, her feelings for Luke written all over her face.

She'd been in love with him then.

A buzzing sounded in her ears. He'd kept photos of her just like Peter Langford. All this time, these two men had been carrying something of her around with them.

And she'd never forgotten them, either.

She'd never stopped loving Luke.

Oh, God. *I've never stopped loving Luke.*

He was saying something to her as he returned his wallet to his pocket. "What?" she asked, not wanting him to sense her secret. She had to keep her cover. She had to stay strong. "What did you say?"

"I'm asking if that's all your fears then." He ticked them off with his fingers. "Heights, spiders, tripe, and goats."

"Don't forget sponges."

"I won't forget sponges." He leaned down to kiss her cheek and whispered in her ear. "Nor your terror of commitment."

"Nor my terror of commitment," she murmured in agreement. Because no matter what she felt for Luke, forgetting that would be the scariest thing of all.

When they touched down, the balloon people served champagne and a light dinner on picnic tables set up under canopies in the launching field. Relieved to be back on solid earth and compelled to drown the disturbing self-revelation about her feelings for Luke, Charlotte had her share of the bubbly and then some. Once they were back at the hotel, she stumbled over her own tipsy feet on the way across the parking lot. Straightening, she started forward again, only to be nearly run over by a taxi speeding toward the porte-cochère.

Its brakes squealed, she lurched back, then stumbled again, falling to her knees just inches from the vehicle's yellow bumper. A hand yanked her to her feet—Luke's, she supposed—because it was his voice that yelled at that taxi driver. The cabbie yelled back that it was the woman who wasn't watching where she was going.

Her head was still reeling and her knees still smarting when Connor interrupted and calmed the situation. Whatever he murmured to his brother had Luke going quiet, but even in her slightly inebriated state she felt the menace bubbling in him. With deliberate movements, she extracted her arm from his hold and made her way poolside again, following the rest of the wedding party. Luke stalked behind her.

She glanced over her shoulder at him. His face was set in furious lines. "Geez," she complained. "What's the big deal?"

"You were almost killed," he muttered.

Not even close, she thought, rolling her eyes. "It's just a life," she said lightly. "Just my little ol' life."

She thought she heard his back teeth grind, but ignored it to throw herself onto one of the cushioned lounge chairs by the pool. Luke came to a halt beside her, and hovered. "You're bleeding," he said, his voice sounding strangled.

The fall onto rough asphalt had scraped both knees. Now that she looked at the nasty scrapes, they started to hurt. One had caused enough blood to flow that a trail of it dripped halfway down her shin. Charlotte made a face and stood. "I'll go clean them up. I brought some plastic bandages with me."

Luke was stalking her again. She felt his moody presence like a black cloud following her toward their room. She didn't bother trying to lock him out. Instead she left the door open and moved into the bathroom, where she rummaged for the first aid supplies in her toiletries bag.

Once they were on the counter, he joined her in the small room. Without saying a word, he pushed her onto the closed lid of the toilet seat and went about cleaning and bandaging the wounds. She held back her winces when she saw he still wore that fierce expression.

Déjà vu, she thought, as he tended her. It was just like that night he'd taken her home to look after her blisters. Letting him care for her then had led to all this trouble. "Listen, Luke, I'm sorry you feel this need to patch me up, but I'm actually—"

"Excuse me for caring about your 'little ol' life.' " He tossed the washcloth into the sink and then stomped out of the bathroom.

Charlotte washed her face and hands with cool water and then took another moment to run a brush through her hair. The last of the champagne bubbles had dissipated from her system in her close call and its aftermath. Luke was still nearby, his uncharacteristic anger tainting the air like black smoke. She found him standing by the sliding glass door that led to a small patio, looking out at the greenery surrounding a small glass-topped table and chairs.

She didn't think he saw them. She didn't think he was seeing anything.

When he didn't turn around, she crossed over to him and placed a hesitant hand on his back. His muscles felt like steel. "I'm fine," she said, giving him a tentative pat. "You've made me well."

"Yeah?" His voice sounded like he'd swallowed grated

glass. "Maybe now there's someone else in the room who needs tending. Maybe it's me who needs a distraction from my fears this time."

Puzzled, Charlotte flattened her hand on his spine. "Luke?"

In one quick move he spun and crushed her against him, burying his face in her hair.

"Luke?"

He only answered by yanking back her head and latching his mouth onto hers. His tongue sought immediate entry. She gave it to him, opening her mouth for what felt like a dire, emergency-level kiss.

Her moan only seemed to drive his frenzy higher. He clutched at her as he kissed her, his hands gripping her shoulders, her hips, and then her ass, tilting her pelvis to grind against his.

He was heavy, fully aroused, and his skin was so hot that she thought the smoke she'd sensed earlier was really in the room now, the result of the fire of his passion. He lifted his head to let her get a breath, but she didn't think he needed oxygen, because his mouth didn't leave her skin. It bit at her jaw and sucked on her neck and ran along her collarbone.

He was ripping at his clothes as he kissed her. His shirt was undone and his jeans unfastened when he pushed her down to the mattress. She landed with an "oomph" and then another was expelled from her lungs when he dropped onto her body, pinning her to the bed even as he was pushing up the hem of her skirt.

His hands were hot and hard on her thighs and she felt his fingers curl around the edges of her panties. They ripped and he tore them away.

He was panting; she was panting. The rigid column of his penis was naked against the crease between her thigh and hip, its presence burning like a brand, the tip of him already wet. His mouth was on hers again, his tongue thrusting and dominant, rubbing against hers with carnal, ferocious intent.

Her pulse was throbbing and her clitoris was, too, and she

tried shifting, tried moving so that she could get him to touch her there, where her craving for him was centered. But he resisted, holding her down with his weight as if he thought she meant to run away from him.

But she'd never done that! She'd been the one left behind. For fourteen months, she'd been in her same place, living with the image of Luke turning his back and leaving her.

The memory made a sob crawl up her throat. When he turned his head to string kisses across her cheek, it came out, a little jerk of sound. Luke froze.

"I'm hurting you?"

He'd hurt her. Fourteen months ago when he'd allowed her reluctance to drive him away. But *this* didn't hurt, so she shook her head and took his beautiful face between her two hands and lifted toward him to initiate her own kiss. She could show him carnal. Needy. It had always been safe to be wild in Luke's embrace.

She shoved his shirt off his shoulders and then ended their mouth-to-mouth kiss to begin other ones—her mouth running along the strong column of his throat and across the tanned skin of his chest to find a nipple. It beaded against her tongue and he groaned. Under her palms, she felt the goose bumps rising over his back.

He was hers now. For now. She showed him that by shoving at his shoulders again, so that he was flat against the mattress. She made to turn onto her knees, but he stayed her with a hand. "Your scrapes, baby," he reminded her. "You let me do the work. What are you after?"

Her face burned but she was determined. "I want you in my mouth, Luke," she said, twisting to her side and scooting down the mattress. "Put it in my mouth."

He groaned in answer and kicked off his jeans and boxers. Then she had him in her hands, at her mercy. She cupped him from below and used her other hand to curl around his shaft. Her tongue circled the head, flicked the small slit. Then she took him into the heat of her mouth, her cheek pressed to his belly, her body curled so that she could take him deep.

Luke groaned, one hand delving into her hair, twisting the strands around his fingers. She loved the desperation in his voice, in the flexing power of his grip, in the rising tension she could feel in his body.

If he found comfort in this, good for him. But for her it was pleasure, bliss, ratcheting arousal. Her legs shifted and she squeezed her thighs together to ease some of the ache between them.

Opening her mouth wider, she slid her tongue down his shaft and—

—and then she was dizzy, disoriented as he moved again, until she found her own shoulders flat on the mattress and Luke between her splayed thighs. Another instant and he was holding her open to lick the drenched folds. She twitched, the rough touch of his tongue already almost too much.

"No, Luke," she said, her head thrashing against the pillows.

He looked up at her, his mouth wet, his green eyes glittering. "Yes, Charlotte," he said. "This time, just say, 'Yes, Luke.'"

And he looked so beautiful and so desperate that she said it, over and over, a chant, a song, a sort of healing balm—for him? for her?—as his mouth took her over the edge.

He was there when she landed, his body already inside of hers, his condom-covered shaft spearing through her as if seeking a path to the heart that she'd been protecting for so, so long.

"Yes, Luke," she said again, just as he reached the point of no return, and she figured he was blind and deaf to all but his completion.

And when it was over and his head came to rest on her breast, surely filling his ears with the thudding beat of her heart, she said it one last time, quiet enough so that only she could hear. "Yes, Luke."

CHAPTER SEVEN

The next morning, Charlotte was again awake before Luke. Was he still unaccustomed to this time zone after his months in Qatar? Or had she worn him out with spectacular sex? She smiled a little at that, gazing at his sleeping face from the opposite pillow. His expression was relaxed, the intensity of the night before gone now.

She brushed his hair off his forehead and when he didn't stir, she smiled again. Yep, the spectacular sex had done him in. The idea that she'd bested him with her body had her scrambling out of bed, ready for coffee and a new day.

Showered, she left the room, almost bouncing in eagerness. That made her pause. She couldn't remember the last time she'd felt such sweet expectation.

She'd been a cynic for so damn long. Too damn long.

Once she made it to the lobby, she realized she wasn't the only one who had awoken with a smile. The other guests were gathered poolside, cups of coffee in hand. The only item on the day's agenda was brunch, followed by their return to LA. But instead of chattering as a group, they were arranged in pairs, some sitting beside each other in chairs, other couples stretched out on a single lounge together. Their lazy companionship reminded her of Sunday mornings when she'd been together with Luke.

Together with Luke.

Why, exactly, had she been so afraid of that?

Crossing to the silver carafes in the lobby, she filled two paper cups with coffee. He liked his black, but she took a moment to doctor hers with half-and-half and a dash of sugar. A giggle from behind her made her glance over her shoulder. Connor and Audrey were walking toward her, arms entwined, attention on each other.

The sight of her ex-stepsister didn't grate on her nerves as it had in the past days. As a matter of fact, she enjoyed watching Audrey's interplay with her husband-to-be. Maybe they could make it, Charlotte thought. She hoped they would make it.

It was yet another thought that gave her pause. For so long, for forever, she'd been without expectation for the wedding couples who crossed the threshold of her office. They wanted vows, she'd write them, but the promises had held no meaning for her. She hadn't put faith in the words she'd written.

But now she wanted to believe in them. She wanted Connor and Audrey to find happiness as a couple. Her gaze drifted back to the pool again and the other pairs relaxing there. Optimism made her heart float free in her chest as she took in their cozy poses, their entwined hands, their whispered conversations. More intimacy. More happiness in the making.

She looked down at the duo of coffee cups she'd prepared. Another pair. One for her, and one for Luke.

A couple.

"Good morning."

She turned to smile at Connor, then Audrey. "Good morning." So good. "It's a glorious day."

Audrey leaned her head against her fiancé's arm. "So you're glad you came?"

Aware she was acting completely out of character, Charlotte didn't even stop to assess and analyze. "I'm very glad I came," she said. The time in Palm Springs, the time with Luke, had opened her heart to possibilities she'd run from before. He'd been right to want more from her fourteen months ago. Closing herself off from him hadn't made her safe, only unhappy.

The only safety she'd found was in his arms.

His voice whispered in her mind. *Honey. Sweetheart. Baby.* Casual endearments that were emblems of the affection she craved. He knew her so well. He knew her so well and he'd always been so open with her. If she wanted a future with him, she'd have to be the same.

As Connor reached for the top cup in the stack, he sent her a quizzical look. "You're very chipper today."

"Mmm." If by chipper he meant a weird and wild exuberance blended with sexual satiety.

"Where's my brother?"

"Down for the count." She still felt a bit smug about that. "I'm bringing him back a cup of coffee." Maybe she'd attack him once he got a little caffeine in his system.

Connor breathed out a small sigh. "He got some sleep last night then?"

Odd question. "Uh . . ." She didn't think he was prying into their sexual escapades. "Why wouldn't he?"

He shrugged. "You saw how he was after your near-miss with the taxi. I thought his mood . . . when it gets dark like that, well, you know."

Charlotte stared at him. Yeah, Luke had been in a mood, and she'd not really gotten to the bottom of it, but Connor seemed to see some secret meaning that she didn't fathom. "What?"

Both Connor and Audrey were staring at her now. Luke's brother opened his mouth, but Audrey put her hand on his arm. "She doesn't know," she said quietly. "Con, Luke's kept it from her."

Charlotte shuffled back, her shoulder blades hitting the plaster wall. "What are you talking about?"

The couple exchanged glances.

A shiver ran down Charlotte's spine as the air turned suddenly chilly. It was as if a dark cloud had crossed over that glorious sun. *"What are you talking about?"*

Connor cursed under his breath. "You'd better ask Luke."

Her head whipped toward her ex-stepsister. "Audrey?"

With a glance at her husband-to-be, she stepped closer to Charlotte. "He didn't tell you he'd been married before?"

Married before? *I happen to like marriage.* He'd said that, she remembered. "He has a wife?"

Audrey shook her head.

Relief made her giddy. For a stupid moment she'd thought she'd been contemplating couplehood with a married man. "He's divorced."

Audrey shook her head again.

The giddiness evaporated. Her heartbeat slowed to a dull *thud thud thud.* "I don't understand."

"Sweetheart," Connor said to Audrey, "maybe we should let Luke—"

"Continue to keep my sister in the dark?" Audrey said, shooting him a look.

Charlotte's heart wasn't moving at all. Somewhere in her past she'd given up trusting men, and it looked like she'd been right about that. "Continue to keep your sister in the dark about what, exactly?"

Audrey reached out, her soft hand on Charlotte's forearm. "Luke had a wife. She died ten years ago."

He'd been married. He'd lost a wife. She shivered again as another blast of cold blew across her skin. Her optimism leached from her and she felt herself tumbling, as if she'd been tossed from that balloon's gondola after all.

She'd kept her heart from Luke . . . and then given it, never suspecting he'd kept anything from her.

Luke squinted as he entered the open-air lobby, the midmorning light bright after the darkened room and hall. He put up a hand to shade his eyes, impatient to find Charlotte.

Last night, that bridge he'd wanted to build, those walls he'd wanted to breach . . . well, he thought he'd done it.

He heard voices and followed the sound to the dining room. The wedding party was feasting on buffet goods, and his gaze skipped from table to table, looking for the woman who'd slayed him with sex the night before. They'd slept tangled together—God, how he'd loved that—but sometime in his dreams she'd left him. He needed her close again.

He needed her close forever.

At a table in the corner he spied Connor and Audrey. They were talking with the bride's father, Peter Langford. Ah. No wonder his girl was missing. She avoided like the devil things that had hurt her.

So he wasn't surprised to discover her at a small table by the pool, the newspaper folded in front of her, a pencil in hand. Her dark hair swirled around her shoulders. She wore a pale blue halter dress that exposed the golden slopes of her shoulders. Charlotte had beautiful skin and his palms itched to caress it again. Remembering he owed some attention to her bountiful breasts, he started forward.

As if sensing his presence, she glanced up, then she ducked her head once again, clearly planning to ignore the man who'd slept beside her all night long, face-to-face, heart-to-heart.

Wary now, he approached her slowly. She was working the crossword puzzle, he noted. Her gaze didn't move from the page even as he pulled out an adjoining chair, its legs grating against the concrete.

She avoided like the devil things that had hurt her.

But *he* faced them. So he took a deep breath and stared her down. "What's going on, Charlotte?"

Her knuckles whitened as her fingers tightened on the pencil. "Just trying to . . . solve this."

"Yeah?" Maybe he was wrong. Maybe sometimes a crossword puzzle was just a crossword puzzle.

"Here are the clues. Hypocrite. Dishonest. Heart as cold as a fish."

The crossword puzzle wasn't just a crossword puzzle. Hell. He didn't know how it had come to this. "That's not me."

Her head came up, her blue eyes icy-hot. "What was her name?"

"Who?" Though of course he knew whom she meant. Someone had told her about his marriage. About the woman he'd married. The ache of that loss filled his chest like black ink.

"What was the name of your wife?"

Did he have to say it aloud? She was his private pain. The dream and the disaster of a very young man, a young man that wasn't who Luke was anymore, but he was loathe to share it still. It had hurt so bad.

Charlotte made a disgusted sound. "Fraud. Snake. Cheater."

He jumped to his feet. "I never cheated on her in my life!"

"You cheated on *me*, Luke." She rose, too, stepping toward him until they were toe-to-toe. "If you can't even speak her name, then she's the one cemented in your heart. You tricked me into . . . into caring about you when you're as unavailable as every other man who has played games with my affections."

Instinct had him moving back again, away from her temper, even as he was trying to take in her words. "You care about me?"

"I cared about the man who was so damn determined to heal my wounds. But that's not really you, is it, Luke? Because you're so closed off you didn't want me to know who you really were. You didn't want me to know your hurts. You are so hung up on your wife—"

"Jana. Her name was Jana." Saying it aloud made her image blossom in his brain. She'd been curly-haired and freckle-faced and so damn young. What had their parents been thinking? "We were a couple of teenagers who thought we had the world by the tail. Nothing could get in our way if we *got* our way."

"So you wanted to get married . . ."

Shrugging, he gazed off into the distance, seeing that summer wedding so many years before. "And so we got married. In August, right before her first semester of college. I was a sophomore." Then he could smell September, the scent of dried grass and parched dirt. The sun was hot on his hair and the straps of his textbook-laden backpack dug into his shoulders. The leather bottom had slammed against the small of his back as he'd run from second year Chemistry to the bus stop at the center of campus.

"She had her earbuds in and she liked her music loud. When she crossed the street, she didn't see the bus." He was speaking beside the pool in Palm Springs, but his head was at the campus where they'd both attended college and he was racing toward emergency vehicles and strobe lights. *Red red red.* Then so much blood. "I was too late. Too late to even say good-bye."

"Luke . . ."

He blinked, pulling himself back to the present. "We were married three weeks and two days."

Charlotte stared at him a moment. Her magnificent blue eyes were glittering—tears? He didn't want her sympathy, but he could sense her mood changing. Then she snatched up the pencil she'd been writing with and threw it at his head.

He ducked, feeling it whip past his ear. "Wha—"

"Damn you!" she yelled. There were plastic salt-and-pepper shakers on the table and she scooped them up in her hands.

Startled, Luke leaped back, even as she sent one and then the other in his direction. "What did I do now?"

Her chest was heaving. "*Now?* You did it months ago, ages ago, maybe that day when you limped beside me to the finish line. Damn you, Luke Harper. You and your green eyes crawled inside my heart even when yours has been locked up tight."

Luke retreated again, teetering on the coping of the pool. "What does that mean?"

Her fingers closed over the chair he'd been sitting in, and he eyed it with alarm, aware he had no way to escape. "Don't, Charlotte."

She ignored him, lifting the curved metal legs off the concrete. "It means I love you and you're not capable of loving me back. It means you'll never have me." Then she heaved the chair at him.

There was nothing else that he could do. The day before, he'd saved himself from going in with Charlotte, but he had to take the leap now. Her words replayed as the water closed over his head. *It means I love you and you're not capable of loving me back.*

It means you'll never have me.

CHAPTER EIGHT

To cap off a truly craptastic morning, it was Peter Langford who found Charlotte following her flare-out with Luke. She was loitering in a side garden that she'd discovered when trying to avoid the wedding party. Temper tantrum over, she felt empty. Figured. She couldn't deny now that she'd given Luke her heart.

At least her emptiness made it easier to look Peter in the eye. "Can I help you?" she asked.

He rubbed his jaw. "I guess I thought that should be my line."

"Oh, I'm good." Blatant lie, but Peter was no more to her than a business client—and she supposed he was, since surely he was paying all the wedding expenses—so this conversation didn't require any real depth.

His expression turned apologetic. "I was out on the pool deck about fifteen minutes ago."

"Oh. Well." Meaning he'd overheard her . . . discussion with Luke.

"You remember I lost my first wife."

Audrey's mother. Charlotte looked away. "Yes."

"It's not easy to open yourself up again after something unexpected like that."

She jerked her chin toward him. "That's not my fault! *He* pursued *me*. He shouldn't have done that, and he shouldn't have come back after fourteen months away if he was all locked up tight."

"Fourteen months away?"

Her hand lashed out. "We were dating. He wanted more, I said no. He went away, and then he came back."

"Oh, Charlie," he said.

Tears stung her eyes. "Why did he come back?" Embarrassed by the plaintiveness of her tone, she whirled to run.

Peter caught her arm.

Charlotte found herself huddled against his chest, the heels of her hands pressed to her eyes. *Point guards don't cry,* she told herself. Yet the tears still fell.

Her ex-stepfather patted her back. "Seems like you both tried staying apart but it didn't do much good. You're still in love with him and he's—"

"Stuck on his dead wife!"

"Charlie . . ."

"Why else wouldn't he tell me about her? There were a dozen opportunities, a hundred, a thousand! Damn it, he should have told me about it the very first night when he took care of my wounded foot." She jerked out of his embrace and started for the door leading into the hotel. "He healed my heart only to break it all over again."

"Charlie."

She glanced over her shoulder, but kept moving. "What?"

"A little advice, okay? From the man who enjoyed being your father?"

The regret in his voice made her pause. *From the man who enjoyed being your father.* She swallowed, then asked the question that had plagued her for years. "About that, why . . . why didn't you ever contact me after the divorce?"

Grimacing, he rubbed a hand over his hair, then sighed. "Oh, Charlie. Emotions were running so high and the lawyers said—" He broke off and shook his head. "Your mother and I thought a clean break would be simplest. We didn't want you girls dragged into the marital acrimony where you'd be forced to take sides. Looking back . . . it was the wrong decision. I'm so sorry."

Charlotte took a minute to absorb that, seeing the situation from an adult's perspective. "All right," she said finally. Then she lifted her brows. "And the advice?"

Peter's gaze softened. "Don't expect Luke to be perfect, honey. You know better than anyone that no man is."

She hurried away from Peter and his last words and headed for the lobby. While she wished she could have hailed a taxi or rented a car to head back to LA immediately, she'd made a promise to Audrey and she would see this through. They'd been sisters, once, after all. And Audrey wasn't so bad, "fashion advice" aside.

The bridezilla was starting to grow on her.

As she reached the lobby, her feet stuttered to a stop. Luke was there, leaning against the counter. In dry clothes now, though his hair was still damp, he was focused on his right palm. She took a hasty step forward as she saw the elastic bandage in his other hand.

He was injured!

But he glanced at the clerk, reassuring the young man with a brief smile. "It's nothing. Thought I had something to staunch the bleeding in my room, but we're all out."

They'd used up the supply on her. And for once it was Luke who was bleeding. She found herself staring at him as he deftly tended his wound. Had he been hurt while dodging her temper?

But of course he'd been injured years ago. A teenager, losing his love. A man, losing his wife. He'd kept that from her, but that only went to show how deep the damage went.

Damn it, she didn't want a damaged man!

She didn't want someone who put up walls, because hers were high and thick enough as it was. If she had to love Luke, then he should be . . . should be . . .

Don't expect him to be perfect. You know better than anyone that no man is.

Luke wasn't perfect. Instead he was a man who needed someone to pierce his shell. To heal his wound.

Just like her, he was imperfect. Just like her, he needed to love and be loved.

Meaning, she thought, going cold then hot, that she had to do her part in the relationship. Be a partner and not a parasite.

At the thought, a whole orchestra broke out in her head. A crescendo of sound that made clear it was a momentous idea. One she needed to act upon. But how?

"There you are!" Audrey slipped her arm through Charlotte's. "It's time for brunch and one last wedding party practice session," she said, dragging her toward the dining room.

Leave it to Audrey to want to practice the spontaneous toasting of the bridal couple. Connor hooted with laughter at the announcement and dragged her to him for a big squeeze. "My lovely fiancée, you know that spontaneous means impromptu, right?"

She sniffed, even as she brushed back a lock of his hair. "Of course. I'm very good with words, as you'll see when I speak my personal wedding vows to you." The woman was so good, she didn't even drop a hint by glancing at Charlotte.

For her part, Charlotte's expression didn't waver. She could feel it was set on nervous and with the way her heart was pounding, it was probably trending toward panic. Though she had a plan, her mind was racing at the same fast rate as her heart and she wasn't feeling all that optimistic. The fact that the dining room was small and Luke had taken a table in the farthest corner of the room from her didn't ease her mind.

She might have lost him forever.

She wasn't going to lose him forever!

Audrey, being Audrey, had arranged for a cordless mic and amp to be available so they could get a preview of their tones of voice. "And listen, everybody," she said. "To avoid that popping sound when saying words containing *B, P,* or *S,* make sure you have the microphone a little to the side instead of in front of your mouth." The whole room groaned, but the matron-of-honor gamely volunteered to go first.

"Doesn't the best man usually start these things off?" one of the groomsmen asked, but Luke declared himself unready to speak. "I'm mum, people, until the wedding reception."

The mic traveled the room while the weekend revelers shared ribald or sentimental reminiscences of either Audrey, Connor, or the two of them together. Charlotte didn't absorb any of it really, her attention focused on Luke, who was tipped back in his chair, his eyes half-closed.

She wondered if he'd even be awake when she took her turn.

Everyone in the room had spoken but the best man and Charlotte when she grabbed the mic as it passed by. Audrey half-rose from her chair. "You don't have to talk, Charlie," she said. "We haven't seen each other in years."

Charlie. Peter had called her that earlier. She'd forgotten that Audrey had used it, too, as they lay in their beds in that room they'd shared.

Charlie, do you think I'm the most beautiful girl in the junior class?

Charlie, I think you would look prettier with bangs. I'll cut them for you tomorrow.

Charlie, do you realize we'll be the aunts to each other's children?

"I have some things I want to share," Charlotte said into the mic. Her tongue was clicking against the dry roof of her mouth, so she paused to gulp from her water glass.

"First, I want to thank Audrey and Connor for including me in this fun weekend. I'll never look at mini-donuts in quite the same way again." The crowd clapped in appreciation. "I've enjoyed meeting all of you, and particularly getting to watch Audrey and Connor interact."

She turned to them. "I admire how committed you are to each other. Connor smiles through Audrey's bridal mania, while she is working so hard to make the day the most perfect—no, let's not expect perfection—to make the day the very best for them both."

The room exploded in more applause. Audrey, as relaxed as Charlotte had ever seen her, stood up to curtsy. Then she dropped into her groom's lap, who acted as if a whale had landed on him instead of a smiling piece of dandelion fluff.

Charlotte couldn't help grinning at them herself. They were going to make it. If there was anybody who could, it would be them.

The clapping died down. "And if I could add just one last thing." She turned to face the dark-haired man across the room. "Luke, I've been inspired by the partnership of your brother and Audrey. They don't expect the relationship to rest on just one person's shoulders. They each do their part—sometimes being the healer and sometimes doing the healing."

He'd sat up, his eyes fully open now, his pose alert. "Charlotte . . ." she heard him murmur.

"Let me into your heart, Luke," she said, "as you've found a way into mine. I promise to be careful with it." Tears stung but she didn't care when they overflowed. She wasn't trying to pretend any longer with him. "Let me . . . let me love you."

Her vision was blurry so she didn't see that he'd left his place in the room until he swiped the mic from her hand and swept her into his arms. Her size nines dangled in the air as he brought her close enough to kiss. But first he brought the mic to his mouth—sideways, of course.

"I have something to say after all." He paused, then smiled down at Charlotte, the deep green of life ahead in his eyes. "Yes."

Epilogue

The wedding was traditional in many ways. There were adorable flower girls and one small ring bearer in knee pants. The bridesmaids' dresses were not designed to be ever worn again, though one young woman claimed she might don the lightly beaded, sweeping mermaid-style when it was her turn to be married.

Peter Langford walked the white-gowned bride down the aisle. When they reached the groom, he put her hand in the younger man's, then lifted the elbow-length veil. Peter pressed a kiss to her cheek. "Be happy," he murmured.

She smiled back. "I am."

The ceremony had all the usual elements. And, as was the custom, the groom spoke his vow first.

He grinned at his bride. "I wrote this myself."

Her dimple showed as she whispered up to him. "Stick with math. One plus one equals two will work."

Shaking his head, Luke took another step closer and the humor fled from his face. His hand tightened on hers. "Charlotte, you are my prize, my partner, my passion. You are my spirit, my soul, and the source of all good things to come in my life. I promise to walk with you on the road ahead, sometimes leading, sometimes following, sometimes side-by-side, yet always hand-in-hand." He took a big breath. "I love you. I love you so much. Please, be mine."

Overcome by emotion, Charlotte, the professional in the

vows business, completely forgot the words she'd practiced to say in return. She searched her memory, then scoured it again, but still came up blank. Holding up one gloved hand, she gave the man she trusted enough to marry a rueful yet loving look. "I will."

It turned out to be the exact right thing to say.

All's Fair in
Love and Chocolate

LAURA FLORAND

*Infinite thanks to Jacques Genin and Michel Chaudun,
two master chocolatiers in Paris who allowed me inside their
laboratoires, and answered all my questions.
Thank you also to Sophie Vidal, chef chocolatier for
Jacques Genin, for all her patience.*

CHAPTER ONE

The problem with summer in Paris was the lack of coats, Ellie decided. She hadn't really thought the timing through, when she decided to take her blogging artist career to a whole new level by moving here, but sundresses made it hard to hide a camera. Also, no one else on the streets seemed to be wearing a sundress, which was a little disconcerting; hers, in its white on sunny green flower pattern, had made *her* think of summer in Paris. Exciting new ventures. Seizing life with both hands.

She angled her phone as best she could, trying to look like a farsighted person reading a text message, and took a shot of the luscious display of chocolate in the window.

She loved this man. More than Sylvain Marquis, even, more than Philippe Lyonnais, more than Dominique Richard, she loved *this* one, the severely private Simon Casset. She loved what he did with his chocolate and sugar, the fantastical structures of it, the way they rose and rose in whirls and swirls of colors and whimsy, as if gravity had no meaning, as if the only thing that would ever stop him was lack of oxygen up there in the stratosphere.

She had gone to his exhibit at the Salon du Chocolat in New York last year, but hadn't seen him. She had circled around his sculptures taking picture after picture, just longing for him, for his world, to know how he worked, to see the man who made this. Later, from her photos, she had painted some of her best-selling works. Her readers had snatched them off her blog faster than you could click Pay-Pal.

But now . . . she had done it. Left the safety of New York, made the leap to Paris. Now she didn't have to long from a distance. Now she, Eloise Layne, food blogger extraordinaire, artist, and newly minted *Parisienne*-in-training, was going to awe her readers worldwide by finding out his secrets. First Simon Casset's and then, one after the other, those of every top chocolatier and pâtissier in Paris. She could be exploring the magic of food for years here.

She didn't *have* to long from a distance, but . . . she hadn't quite anticipated how much these superheroes of the Parisian gourmet scene would intimidate her, how embarrassed she would feel to go up and introduce herself, to ask for interviews and photographs. What were her credentials? A blogger. Nobody took that seriously.

And—moving to Paris was all very exciting, but God, did she feel vulnerable, out there floating in midair with nothing to count on. It was hard to get up still *more* gumption.

Maybe a particularly spectacular post would generate enough clicks that she could buy one of those spy cameras with the advertising money and— She took a step back, worried about the light reflecting off the display window, and ran right into something hard.

The hardness closed around her, fingers curling into her bare upper arms. "May I help you?" a voice of steel asked.

She jumped, or would have, except the grasp held her so strongly she couldn't get any upward momentum. Fleetingly, irrationally, something strange took hold of her: a sense of purchase, as if she had just been given something to count on in her gravity-defying leaps. "I"—she fumbled with her phone, trying to switch it from camera to text. The phone went flying from her nervous fingers, hit the flagstones hard, and slid.

"Oh crap," she said in English and looked down—right

into a storm grate. "Crap." Had her last link with stability just slid down the drain? Alone in Paris, no real job, no friends, whole life uprooted, following a dream, unable to sleep from the constant sense of eager panic at what she was doing . . . and now no phone. There was only so much exhilarated terror a body could take before she had to sit down and put her head between her knees.

The firm fingers released her, which felt like the final betrayal. She had *just* started relying on their strong grip. She floundered, twisting to face their owner.

She looked up past a fitted gray T-shirt over hard shoulders to—oh God, that was Simon Casset himself. She recognized him from the rare photos she had managed to track down, usually poorly shot ones at reward ceremonies. Unlike media darlings Sylvain Marquis and Philippe Lyonnais, or the infamous troublemaker Dominique Richard, Simon Casset let his work speak for him and kept the person who made it—him—out of the spotlight.

He could have been a media darling, though, she thought, with a sudden wave of yearning that caught her by surprise, as if she had been playing with her back to the ocean. *This* man made those beautiful, swooping dreams? With his long, lean body, angular, ascetic face, cool, proud cheekbones, steel-blue-gray eyes, and tousled black hair that fell in one lock over his forehead like a cute nerd dragged out of a bout of computer programming? A few choice photo shoots, and he could be plastered up on bedroom walls where women could swoon over him in hopeless longing.

That bare wall at the foot of her bed, for example . . .

She tried to get a grip, wishing she hadn't lost his more effective one, still marking her like a slow stamp of heat. She glanced at her arms, half-expecting to see gold fingerprints against her skin. How did he do that? Grip her so firmly that she couldn't even *jump* a half inch, but with such control that it hadn't hurt?

She looked back up at him, and attraction swept through

her in a high cresting wave again. A man with that lean strength of his should be required to wear baggy clothes like they did in America. To protect hopeless cases like her.

So why didn't he play to the media? Too impatient, too private, too modest? Maybe *she* could be the person who revealed him to the world, the investigative blogger who showed the man behind the creations, the—

"Who sent you?" he asked, with a cool lift of one eyebrow. He stood so close, she felt invaded. Loomed over. *French,* she reminded herself. *Smaller sense of personal space.* Still—*that* small? "Marquis? Lyonnais? Richard? Who wants to spy on my work this week?"

The top chocolatiers-pâtissiers in Paris *spied* on each other? Delighted excitement surged. See, now, this was good stuff. She had been right to move here. She could get all kinds of dirt. Cover story. She needed a darn cover story. If he was a private person, he might not warm up right away to the idea of her plastering him all over the web.

"I'm getting married," she said off the top of her head.

A little, thin, clear sheet of plastic slipped between her and the chocolatier. Barely detectable to the naked eye. But there just the same. Somehow her personal space grew, and she never even saw him shift.

Wait. Oh damn. Had he been *noticing* her? Like in a thinking-she-looked-cute-in-her-sundress way? Stupid cover story.

But that penetrating gaze of his made it absolutely impossible for her to back down from it. She had to be ready for this tough Parisian chocolate scene. Ready to report on the best of the best of the best . . . and *not* get caught skulking on the street because their coolly lofty cashiers intimidated her. And definitely not pour out her soul at Simon Casset's feet because he raised his eyebrows. "And I'm comparing the different chocolatiers in the city so we can decide who we want to do the *pièces* for the reception," she said brightly, putting a little bit of snooty into it, like someone who could afford to have him do her wedding.

Instead of someone who had just installed herself in an apartment the size of a walk-in closet and was praying this would all work out like she had planned and she would be able to make the rent.

He studied her for one moment as if he could see right through to her underwear and maybe the soul underneath. Her soul was not sexy—she couldn't do anything about that—but she sure wished she had worn something better than a white cotton bra and panties.

She forced down that urge to confess all and throw herself on his mercy—*I just threw my whole life over to live this dream, can I come take pictures of everything you do and show the whole world, please, pretty please?* Firmly, she brightened her smile a couple of notches.

His eyes flicked over her, down and up, just once in an infinitesimal shift. She might as well be walking around naked, that one flick made her feel so exposed. "I suppose that means you would like to visit my *laboratoire* and look at some of the previous work I've done." He sounded resigned.

Her breath came in on a rush. "*Reall*—I mean, yes, that would be"—Wait, she had to get a spy camera first. She swallowed and firmed her tone. "I should narrow down my top choices before I"—

His eyes narrowed fractionally. Oh, he didn't like that, to not automatically be her top choice, did he?

"—And—and talk to my fiancé about it. But perhaps we could set up an appointment to discuss it? Tomorrow?" If she could sit on her excitement that long. *Spy camera,* she reminded herself. *Don't waste this opportunity.*

"*Bien sûr,*" he said evenly. He scrutinized her a second more, and she tried gamely to look credible. "Will your fiancé be joining us?"

Zut, alors. Now where could she stash a nonexistent fiancé so she could go invade a superstar chocolatier's privacy? She gave him a smile so bright it nearly bounced off the steel in those eyes of his and blinded *her.* "Of course!"

Simon watched the lithe figure disappear down the sidewalk, a spring in her step, bouncing from exuberance. Her ponytail bobbed against the nape of her neck, all that mass of deep russet brown waves contained at one point by an elastic they clearly resisted. A man could slip his thumbs into that elastic and snap it in two. He would feel like the world's greatest liberator, freeing the rebellious waves so that they spilled out all over his hands in giddy delight.

And her eyes would widen in a kind of thrilled alarm as his hands cradled her skull and dealt so ruthlessly with her bonds, and her lips would part as he bent his head and kissed her until she would tell him the truth just to get more kisses . . .

The vision was so powerful his thumbs tingled from the texture of her hair, from an elastic snapping. His mouth felt softer, almost bruised.

Last year, on an endurance race, just when the going was at its grimmest, he had spotted the palm trees of an oasis in the distance. Oddly, the exact same feeling had shot through him when he took in that excited, bright face, that slightly rounded, not-particularly-muscled body.

A first thrill of exquisite relief and then: determined, focused, and very, very thirsty.

The warm green of her sundress stood out among the cool, clean lines of the Parisians brushing past her on the sidewalk. One of his hands curled into a fist when those more subdued colors finally blocked her from view. One last little glimpse of green and she disappeared around the corner.

Don't be a mirage, he thought.

Or already taken. Although—there must be any number of ways to dispose of an inconvenient fiancé.

A fiancé who had been oh-so-conveniently produced. If

she hadn't been spying on him for one of his rivals, why not pull out a regular camera, introduce herself, and take photos openly?

He crouched, stretched an arm under the nearest parked car, and pulled out her phone. No code protected it. He flipped back through her photos, finding several of his display windows, none inside the shop. His eyebrows flicked together at the next photos, familiar chocolate work, not his own. Had she been visiting Sylvain Marquis, too? *Before* him? Annoyance hummed at her priorities.

Those photos, too, were taken at awkward angles, light often reflecting off glass, like someone who hadn't dared ask to be allowed behind the display cases. That was one shy bride.

He switched to her address book, but she didn't have any of his rivals entered in it. Maybe she was spying for herself? Looking to start her own chocolate shop in the United States?

He flipped to her Recent Calls and found a male name as number one. *Merde, alors.* David Layne. Well, he hadn't been forced through years of English classes in school for nothing. He hit the call button.

"Ellie?" The voice on the other end sounded startled and wary.

"No, I'm sorry. I found this phone on the street, and I am trying to get it back to its owner. Are you a friend?"

"No, her brother."

Simon grinned and turned to look in the direction of the vanished green sundress. A woman could have a brother *and* a fiancé. But the next three most recent calls made on her phone had been to "Mom," another woman, and a company, and that over several days. "If you can tell me how to find her, I can give it back to her."

Unfortunately, her brother wasn't an idiot. "It's probably better if I get your information and have her contact you."

Well, it had been worth a shot. He gave the brother his name and shop address and double-checked her incoming calls for an obsessed fiancé calling her so often she never got a chance to be the one to call him. No, the past four calls, in a twenty-four hour period, had come from "Mom."

In his office, he tried Googling "Ellie Layne," "Ellen Layne," "Eleanor Layne," and every spelling of Elizabeth he could think of. Unfortunately, all variants called up plenty of search results, and after he had checked the photos of one Vegas call girl and multiple Facebook sites, he finally gave up.

No photos gazed back at him with happy green eyes that widened when he looked at her too steadily, or brown hair that practically wiggled with energy, or a bowed lip that curved into an impudently bright grin when she was lying, or skin so transparent that he could see exactly how nervous he made her. He gave up looking, his mind wandering . . . over cheekbones with a suggestion of freckles so faint it was like the gold specks on a ripe pear . . . tracing the delicate white strap that peeked out under her sundress, following it down to the soft, generous breasts it supported. He would bet anything her bra and panties matched: dainty, white, innocent cotton. Arousal closed one lazy, hard hand around his body and wouldn't let him go, as he thought about that white cotton.

He studied her phone, with its screen photo of the Eiffel Tower. Not, for example, of her cheek pressed against some man's while he stretched the camera out and took a picture of them standing in front of it.

He smiled a little. Then that smile broke into a narrow grin, restrained, controlled, and infinitely more dangerous for that restraint. He didn't have a one-track mind for nothing. Control and focus would get you what you wanted every time.

If her fiancé existed, he was a very lucky man.

And his luck was about to change.

CHAPTER TWO

Ellie was so relieved when she got her brother's e-mail about her phone that she had to sit on herself to keep from running out into the night to a closed shop to find it. Yay! Not only did her phone exist, but the hottest chocolatier in Paris was holding it hostage. If only she could bribe him with sex to get it back, all would be perfect.

Alas, he would probably just hand it to her politely and hope she would get out of his way as quickly as possible. He was a nice man, to have tracked her down, though, which was a little bit of a surprise. He had looked at her so penetratingly and suspiciously, she hadn't been sure he liked her very much.

Speaking of suspicions, she needed to bolster her cover story before she waved it in front of that X-ray vision again. So she spent some time scouring baby name sites until she came up with Cal Kenton for her fiancé's name. "High Drama!" she posted on Twitter. "More on my secret investigations later! I TELL ALL about Simon Casset!"

There, that should whet their interest until she got photos and maybe it would draw some extra clicks to her blog. Meanwhile, on that blog, she posted some great shots—taken openly with her real camera—of her apartment view and her adventures finding her feet the first three days in Paris. Bright, fun, full of hope and fear, welcoming her readers into her adventure, letting them live it vicariously. The encouraging comments started coming within minutes after the post. Wishing her all the best, and begging for more of Simon Casset.

Yeah, them and her both.

Buoyed, she headed out first thing the next morning for an engagement ring.

Ouch, did she have sympathy with men after *that* excursion. Who spent *a month's salary* on something so silly? But at the same time, she didn't want to come across as cheap, or unvalued, when she was waving her hands around talking to Simon Casset about his *gâteaux*.

In other words, cubic zirconium was where it was *at*. It felt exciting and romantic, in a weird lonely way, to be shopping for her engagement ring in Paris. She finally came up with an elegant, scrolled, antique-looking silver setting and a large but not too large, beveled-set fake diamond for under fifty dollars. It suited her just perfectly, to think that a man had spotted something so old-fashioned and delicate and pretty and thought of her. Guys usually thought she was very strong, which she was, resilient as a damn superball, but it wasn't as much fun bouncing back from their carelessness as they thought. Ellie never threw superballs across a room. She flinched for them, every single bounce.

Cal Kenton would treat her as something precious. And if he didn't waste a couple of months' Paris rent while he was at it, so much the better. He was a smart guy and knew where her priorities lay, that Cal Kenton. Perfect for her.

Spy cameras, unfortunately, turned out to be a little bit beyond her budget, and not nearly as stylish as what she had expected from James Bond movies. She tried to imagine fumbling with one of those things while Simon Casset's blue-gray eyes rested on her, blushed crimson, and hurriedly handed the "button camera" back to the clerk. She might just have to evoke client privilege and get permission to take her photos.

Leaving the spy equipment shop in Les Halles, she spotted

a little boutique selling pay-as-you-go phones and had a sudden inspiration. Buying one for twenty euros, she sent her own phone a text.

Simon's marketing firm forwarded him the tweet and the link to the blog first thing in the morning, with an acerbic little comment, since Simon was constantly provoking them by refusing to do photo shoots and otherwise display his private life. Simon raised his eyebrows over the title. *TELL ALL about Simon Casset?* Like, what, how he worked his butt off and was such an obsessed geek that he thought a millimeter difference in a line of icing on a *réligieuse* was important? And how he was so completely unable to relax from his perfectionism and have fun that in his leisure time he trained for triathlons? That should keep them on the edge of their seats, all right.

But seeing himself all sparkly with exclamation points made him smile. He liked seeing himself through her eyes. It took no great leap of intuition to figure out who had stamped exclamation points all around his name. Someone who was petrified with nervousness at being caught sneaking photos of his shop and who was capable of wearing a flower-printed summer green dress through the streets of Paris and making everyone else look *coincé* and boring.

A Taste of Elle, she had called her blog. And the taste it offered of her was—sweet and spicy all at once. Not spicy like hot peppers, which, like any palate-respecting French chef, he loathed, but like that little bit of brightness that made the mouth wake up and take notice. She was having *fun* with her life. Every hyper-controlled muscle in his body relaxed as he read her effervescent account of her move to Paris and looked at the pictures of everything she was excited about: a green door; a very ordinary balcony; someone carrying a baguette; the rooftops she could see from her tiny, still-bare apartment; the arrangement of her croissants and coffee on a tray in a bistro.

Laughter, self-mockery, trepidation, delight—her stories about her adventures were full of all of it, spread out before the world with generous good humor, pulling her readers in. And were they pulled in. The comments were full of "Good luck!" "We love you! We can't wait to hear about Paris!" "Who are you going to go see first, Simon Casset or Sylvain Marquis?"

His eyes narrowed a little over there being a choice, and he clicked back further, to a post in the last days leading up to her move, in which she was ecstatic about all the different chocolatiers-pâtissiers she would be able to visit and taste, and promised to tell her readers all about it. Well, *merde,* he was only one of a list. But he got three exclamation points, and Sylvain Marquis only got two.

Ha, take that, Sylvain. Someone can appreciate discipline, focused risk, and quality over a poetic lady's man who likes to smolder for the camera.

Further back in her posts, her subjects were mostly New York chocolatiers, pâtissiers, special little cafés and places, but anyone could spot a growing desire to move to Paris, mentioned more and more often to her readers, with little photos of what tempted her or links to posts by bloggers living in Paris.

What he didn't see, notably, was any mention of a fiancé. Of course, she didn't mention her brother or mother either, so it was possible she was maintaining some privacy. Along the side of her blog page was a list of products and books to click on, presumably a source of income, and discreetly along the bottom, some other ads. Occasional references revealed that she also did art for an ad agency. Regularly inserted into posts were photos of her own watercolors, mostly of delicious tartes and cakes and chocolates. When he clicked on a watercolor of one of his own works from last year's Salon du Chocolat in New York, it had already been sold.

"Chef?" Nathalie, one of his sous-chefs, said from the door of his office, and he looked up lazily, feeling warm and relaxed and golden, as if he had been called back to the world from a hammock in which he had been lounging in the summer sun. Lean and intense and crisp and cool, like him, Nathalie raised her eyebrows. *"Tout va bien?"*

"Hmm?" He blinked and gave himself a shake. He didn't feel crisp and cool at all. He felt drugged by sunlight, as if he *couldn't* make his muscles return to their normal tension.

"Il est dix heures. Are you—do you have anything in particular you want us to work on today?"

Ten o'clock? He had been lost in her blog all morning. Not working. He didn't know he knew *how* to not work. He leapt up, his muscles tensing, oddly invigorated, as if he was jumping from a sauna into the snow. "Of course. Let me show you."

When Ellie Layne's phone made the burping noise of a text received a half hour later, Simon wiped chocolate off one hand, fished it out of his pocket under his pastry jacket, and checked it with no compunction whatsoever. She was planning to TELL ALL about him, so . . . *en amour comme à la guerre, petite.* All was fair . . . "Missed U last night. Why didn't U call?"

He grinned. Apparently she thought all was fair, too. Her phone didn't have any name associated with the number of the person saying he missed her so much.

Half an hour later it burped again. The same unnamed number. "XOXO. Love U!"

Maybe she was trying to convince him that her mother was texting her. Or maybe no one had ever sent her romantic texts, not at least since she was a teenager, and she didn't know what an adult man might actually write? He smiled a little and entered her number into his own phone.

Just in case he had an opportunity to fix that problem for her.

Ellie's heart stopped when she walked into Simon Casset's *laboratoire.* The scent of chocolate flooded her, laced playfully with hints of caramelized sugar and butter and almonds, filling her lungs, until she couldn't think or be anything else but longing for a taste. It rested on her tongue, sank into her hair, settled into her clothes, so that she would have to strip naked to start to free herself of it. So that she would have to stand a long, long time under the shower. If there was a test for chocolate content in the blood, she would lose her license from just one breath of that laboratoire.

Extending around her with its marble counters and stainless steel and white-coated chefs, that laboratoire might as well have been a Versailles Court backdrop for the center of attraction, the Sun-King there. Not that either his kitchens or he himself were opulent, both all long spare lines with no ounce of extra fat. But the piece he was working on . . . his face stern, fine lines from weather and concentration crinkling at the corners of his eyes . . . oh, that was enough opulence for anyone.

It rose and rose, from a tiny chocolate base the shape of a great splitting seed, sweeping out like great swirls of daydreaming, dark chocolate rising higher and higher, twining with white, and then with little spears of colors in spun sugar that must be incredibly delicate. How could he even touch them without shattering them, let alone place them so beautifully in this sculpture? He had paused and was studying it, little figures lined up on parchment paper on the counter before him, ready, presumably, to grace the unbelievably high and slender structure. Dragonflies? Pixies? Their bodies alternately of white or dark chocolate, their spring-green wings of gossamer spun sugar.

She got lost in the structure, trying to make out the pixie-dragonflies from the doorway, and when she looked up, he was gazing at her. With those same crinkle lines of concentration. As if he had been studying her underwear for some time.

She flushed. How did he *do* that, with just a look? And if

he was really seeing her underwear, could he look more lustful about it, and less like a professional radiologist?

"*Bonjour, Mademoiselle Layne,*" he said politely. Today he wore a white chef's jacket over jeans, a blue, white, and red marking on its collar. *Un MOF,* she thought, with a thrill. She knew what that *bleu, blanc, rouge* at his collar meant. He was a *Meilleur Ouvrier de France,* elite among chocolatiers, chosen by his peers in the grueling quadrennial M.O.F. trials, the Olympics of his field. Maybe she should genuflect.

His eyes flicked behind her. That firm mouth curved just a little. "Your fiancé couldn't make it?"

"He broke his leg," Ellie said promptly. "On the way over here. A moped accident. Poor Cal." She adopted the most mournful expression she could.

He gave her an utterly charmed look. "Your fiancé drives a moped?"

Could people who drove mopeds typically afford him for their weddings? "He was crossing the street. An old lady was driving the moped."

"She was probably so busy juggling her baguette," Simon sympathized solemnly, as if he had seen this kind of tragic accident many times before.

"Yes!" Ellie had a brief, beautiful vision. Oh lord, she was going to draw a caricature of that for her blog, she had to. "And her beret slipped over her eyes at just the wrong moment."

Simon had to turn away and cough, which he did with a great deal of respect for the rules of hygiene in food industries, covering his face completely with his elbow for a long moment. When he turned back, his expression was quite compassionate. "And yet you continued on here while he was carried off to the hospital. What a difficult choice that must have been for you."

"Well, um"—Hmm. "I think he was glad to get out of it, to be honest. He hates all this wedding stuff."

His eyebrows rose a little. "To the extent that he prefers a broken leg?"

Well, that . . . that did sound a little odd, didn't it? "He's very stoic. Endurance athlete, you know."

His eyebrows went very high up indeed. He grinned suddenly, a white flash, and then caught his mouth back to its usual firm line. "Is he? How . . . interesting. Being laid up for at least six weeks will be hard on him, then. It's lucky he has such a . . . sympathetic fiancée."

Darn it, she really needed to start thinking her cover stories through. Still, a tough-as-nails reporter *would* leave her fiancé at the hospital for a story, wouldn't she? No need for guilt.

"But it was thoughtful of you to put me first," Simon said blandly.

"Well, of course," Ellie said blankly. Fake fiancés only cost about $35 so far, cubic zirconium being so cheap. A chance to find out Simon Casset's secrets—that was priceless.

Simon Casset's white grin started to flash again and was bitten severely into line. "But I'm so sorry to have forced you to choose between me and him. If only I had imagined something like this could come up, I would have given you my number, so you could call and cancel," he said solicitously.

"I thought of that, but you had my phone," Ellie pointed out triumphantly. See, she did have a good reason for her behavior, didn't she?

"*Ah, oui,* how could I have forgotten?" He slipped a hand under his chef's jacket into the back pocket of his jeans, offering it to her so that she had to walk up to him and that magical dreaming sculpture of his to get it.

The phone felt warm in her hands. Ellie stared at it as if it had been transformed into an alien object by its ride on one of those firm butt cheeks. A flush mounted inexorably, and she had no excuse to offer for it and no way to hide it.

She had kind of thought he would leave her phone lying

on the desk in his office. She was never going to be able to use this phone to call her mother again.

She slipped it into the back pocket of her little white capri pants, where it seemed to burn against her butt, and looked down at the pixie-dragonflies with their filigree wings. The fineness of the work was incredible, as if their wings were made out of bright glowing spiderwebs. The stylized little bodies made it hard to be sure, but, "Are they *fées*? Or humanized dragonflies?"

"Is there a difference?" he asked, amused. She glanced up to find an unexpected gentleness in the blue eyes that had heretofore speared her like a laser, as he watched her study his work. Maybe her interest was just so naked to him, he didn't have to x-ray her anymore. "Which do you think?"

"Something magic," she said definitely. Which could include dragonflies over summer water, certainly. "Is this for a wedding?"

His eyes flickered. "*Une excellente question. I*"—a very long pause—"can't say. No one has ordered it, no, but I felt inspired this morning. I'll probably put it in the displays."

"Could you do something like that for *my* wedding?" Ellie asked longingly, before she remembered that if she tried to go through with this wedding, Cal Kenton would leave her standing at the altar. Bastard. And she had had such hopes for him when he picked out such a nice ring, too.

An odd little smile played around Simon Casset's mouth. "*Évidemment.*"

This was what she needed to write about for her readers, these fantasy wedding pieces. She slipped out her little digital camera, with which she could capture some truly beautiful shots. Nobody might ever hang her in museums, but she had lost track of how many weddings she had been asked to photograph for free. "Do you mind?" she dared to ask this time, from her power position of potential client.

Lying potential client who couldn't actually afford to pay him for anything he might design for her. Oh dear. *Why* had she thought this was a better idea than introducing herself and confessing to being a food blogger and passionate fan?

He looked at the camera for an odd, restrained moment. "For your fiancé?" he asked meditatively.

She nodded enthusiastically. "It will cheer him up while his broken leg is mending!"

"Even though he hates dealing with wedding stuff?"

Why was it that he could keep her story straighter than she could? "If he hates this, I would have to dump him," she said firmly. "This is extraordinary."

He shifted in pleased discomfort at such open praise. She gave him her biggest-eyed, most enthusiastic look, her hands clasping the camera in front of her hopefully.

"By all means," he said, in a resigned tone, and stepped back well out of range. Now why couldn't she be brazen enough to just start wandering around taking more pictures, of every single thing? What if he looked at her with merciless coolness and kicked her out, though?

She would do better at hard-nosed journalism when she did her pieces on Sylvain Marquis, she promised herself. Someone who didn't make her feel so, so . . .

So.

She finished her shots and slipped her camera back in her purse with her iPad.

A lean hand caught hers. Just like that, as if it had the right to.

She stared down at her small hand lying across his palm while pleasure rushed through her. *Oh. Okay, you can have the right.* And a beat later: *Did he want it?*

His thumb touched her engagement ring, wiggling it fractionally on her finger. "So your fiancé finally got you a ring?"

Just how observant was he, exactly? "No, he gave it to me when he proposed."

His eyes lifted suddenly from her finger to hold hers, with that look as if he could see right through to her bones. Note to self: find some silkier, lacier underwear. "Which was?"

She blanked. Which was, which was . . . when *would* it have been logical for her fiancé to have proposed to her, if she was now looking at food for the reception? "Three months ago?"

His eyebrows lifted faintly. "You don't remember?"

"April first," she said firmly. "How long ago is that now? Three and a half months?"

His eyebrows went up a little higher. "He proposed to you as a *poisson d'Avril*?"

A *fish*? What—oh, damn it, had she just said her fiancé proposed to her on April Fool's Day? "That's when we met," she said even more firmly. "It was a romantic reference. The proposal was a very elaborate April Fool's joke, in fact." *Elaborate a joke, fast.* "He managed to hide the ring in an eggshell, so that when I cracked it open that morning, or thought I was cracking a raw egg open, out fell the ring."

"With the raw egg?"

"*No.* He got the raw egg out and—" How the heck would a man manage to hide a ring in an intact eggshell? There had to be a way, right? If there wasn't, one of the top chocolatiers-pâtissiers in Paris would probably know it. "I'm not sure exactly how he managed it."

Simon Casset's lower lip looked just a little odd, as if he might be biting into it. Otherwise his expression was quite serious, as befitted someone seeing through to her bones. "You weren't wearing it yesterday."

Okay, see, *how could he know that?* He had been so busy gazing at her face as if he saw every thought in her head, and then that one glance up and down her body that made her feel she was posing naked for him. How could he possibly have spotted her ring finger? "I forgot to put it on."

"You take it off regularly?"

Why did that make her feel so naughty? "It pokes my eye if I sleep with it."

This time, the corners of his lips definitely twitched. "An inconvenient accessory?"

Well, it was. It felt so odd on her hand and very confining. "If you were married, you would take your ring off every day for work!"

If? Something cold congealed in her. He could very well be taking off a wedding ring every morning. Her phone could have been snuggling up to one in his back pocket the whole time.

He gazed at her a moment, still holding her hand, still playing with her ring, as if debating several paths. "I'm not," he said finally.

She couldn't help her face perking up in hopeful inquiry.

"Married. Or engaged." He released her hand.

Really! Excitement sparked through her in multiple exclamation points. Single hot man who worked well with chocolate plus—oh wait. *She* was engaged.

She cleared her throat and tucked her hand firmly down by her thigh, feeling sulky about it.

He studied her a moment, amused and intent all at once. "Mademoiselle Layne, were you thinking of just a centerpiece or perhaps favors as well? Perhaps we should talk about whether you want a special form for the favors or just a little box of two or four chocolates, and if so, which flavors. Which of mine do you like best?"

She could barely avoid shuffling her feet. "I've—I've never tasted any of them."

He checked. In the first instant, he looked taken aback, offended. Then an odd expression crossed his face, much more mixed. "Might I ask what made me one of your top choices then? Reputation?"

In part. A longing to taste what she had heard so much about, and what was physically so beautiful. She gestured helplessly toward the half-finished structure, so magical, as if something as earthbound as food could be transmorphed into an airy grace that touched the sky. He made her feel like *she* could fly. Like it was all worth it. Eating. Life. This was the kind of thing you lived for. Right? "I'm an artist. Your art is extraordinary."

He smiled involuntarily, that unexpectedly awkward pleasure at her praise. "But you've never tasted anything of mine?"

She would have bought something yesterday, a small something that her budget allowed, except he had flustered her so easily into flight. She shook her head, trying not to show how much she was starving for him.

"Ah." Something happened to his face, something honed, intense, like a hawk that had seen a helpless mouse. In the steel-blue eyes, the pupils dilated visibly. "This is going to be fun."

The oasis was real, Simon decided. Not a mirage. Something he could plunge in and drink from. And he was damn well going to reach it.

It was real, but its nearness was illusory. Because it felt as if he could reach out and take her right there, just sink his fingers into that soft flesh of her hips and butt and pull her against him. She was wearing snug white capri pants through which he could make out the even, no-lace edge of her bikini panties when the light angled against her butt. And over that, a top with tiny straps and a gathered ruffle across her chest and again at her hips, in a soft blue printed with tiny darker blue flowers. Her shoulders looked so soft and smooth and naked, as if she needed his whole body over her to clothe her. How was she surviving, walking around Paris all perky and happy and delectable like that? The *dragueurs* must be nipping at her bare heels in their little white sandals everywhere she went. *Mademoiselle, vous êtes charmante . . .* The bastards.

She was, though. *Charmante.* With her life and color and eagerness and her fiancé run over by a moped and abandoned by her in the street.

It would help if his countrymen weren't such flirts, he decided severely. Now he was going to have to figure out some other way to communicate how charming he found her, one that didn't get him immediately categorized with all the aggressive strangers harassing her on the street.

Reaching out, sinking his fingers into her, and dragging her against him, as much as it felt as if he should be able to— *she's right there,* his atavistic urges cried, *and we want her*—that probably wasn't the way to do it.

And obviously, he couldn't ask her out. She would be honor bound to say no, thanks to that bedridden fiancé of hers. There was only one way to reach a woman who had declared herself out of bounds, committed to someone else.

He grinned a slow wickedness as he turned away from her to pull trays of his chocolates from the racks in the cooling room, feeling more pleasure than with any of the ambitious goals he had set for himself in a long time.

Seduction.

CHAPTER THREE

It was the moment that proved the whole decision to throw her life over a windmill and come to Paris had been worth it. That moment when those long, lean, tan fingers held out a small triangular shape of chocolate, the surface so glossy and gleaming she could almost catch a reflection of her fingers as she took it from him.

She was about to eat one of Simon Casset's chocolates, at last. From his own hand!

The brush of her fingers against his traveled the entire length of her body, in little shivers she couldn't shake off her skin. Even when she broke the contact. Even when she held the chocolate just an inch from her lips, teasing herself with that last anticipation of its taste. She took a breath, letting the chocolate scent caress down the nape of her neck and sink into her body.

Simon Casset watched her. He always looked intense, alert, and as if he could see her underwear, so it was hard to say what this moment meant to him. Probably nothing, why should it? He had seen any number of people eat his chocolates for the first time.

But she—she wanted to hand him her camera and ask him to take a commemorative photo as she bit into it. Except even she wouldn't share erotic photos of herself with her readers, and the moment felt like that. Erotic. Naked. Exotically happy.

"Did you know, they say that eighty percent of the plea-sure in most food we eat is through the scent?" the choco-latier asked, all lean quiet. His focused expression revealed nothing particularly dangerous. But an image ghosted through her of a colorful bird in a yard and a cat coming out from be-hind a bush. "You can save that extra twenty percent, the ac-tual taste, for the things that are really . . . special."

The glossy finish of the triangular chocolate, starting to warm to her hand, blurred in her head with the thought of soft lamplight shining off a broad, bare shoulder. She looked from his chocolate to him. Had he grown closer? The steel-blue was softer somehow, as if rather than seeing through her with a laser pinpoint, his focus had widened and he was holding all of her in his gaze.

"That you really, really want to taste." His voice brushed over her skin.

She looked up at him helplessly, wishing she tasted good.

He shifted an infinitesimal bit closer. "But what those sci-entists don't know how to take into account is that with chocolate, there's a tactile pleasure, too." His thumb traced over the marble counter as he gazed at her, the way she sometimes "drew" people as she was talking to them, on the nearest surface. What contours was he drawing while he looked at her that way? "The way it melts in your mouth, just at the temperature of your body, as if it was made for you and for nothing else. You can bite it, you can feel it yield to your teeth before it starts to soften. Or you can lay it on your tongue and let it slowly melt there. It won't take—" he grew closer still—"long at all. For it to melt."

No. Not long. She was melted already. Just at the thought of his bite, his tongue. She looked at the chocolate and caught sight of the engagement ring and couldn't remember why it was there. A promise. Some kind of promise of for-ever, something to do with this chocolate . . .

She brought the chocolate to her mouth, almost afraid to eat something that beautiful. Somehow biting into it felt like stepping out of a plane without checking her parachute. Her stomach rushing into her mouth, her whole world changing, and maybe, maybe she might be in trouble.

That was ridiculous. It was one of the finest chocolates in the world, not a mile drop.

Carefully, she closed her teeth over it. Felt the cool gloss of the surface on her tongue, warming so quickly, the most delicate resistance, the rushing pleasure of the insides, a ganache so soft and unctuous it felt almost molten, with some golden flavor to the chocolate she couldn't identify.

"*Oh,*" she whispered very softly. A tremble ran all through her. Oh, she really should have checked her parachute.

He took a step forward. He was now completely in her personal space, but that seemed right, since he was in her body. Melting in it.

"You're *beautiful,*" she said on a note of wonder. "Inside, too."

The muscles in his body flicked, one long little whiplash of shock all through him. It seemed to shift him closer, angle his body, so that now her back was to the marble counter and he half-trapped her there. Around them, not near, but it seemed harshly invasive, far too close, people moved, working. Enrobing chocolate at a little machine that carried small squares of ganache through a chocolate-fall, carrying a bowl to weigh while adding something ground fine that smelled of almonds, spreading a fresh ganache between metal frames.

"The—the chocolate," she whispered. "The chocolate's beautiful."

He blinked. "Of course," he said blankly.

That startled her. He truly didn't realize she could mean him, too? That she *did* mean him, too?

He held her eyes, as if he could parse every thought that passed through her mind and it was fascinating reading. His mouth softened, and he ducked his head to her. "You don't know what I'm like inside yet," he whispered.

A haze of heat shut off her vision, so that she could only

see his face bent over hers. Vaguely, in the distance, pots echoed on marble. "I think you're like this," she whispered, holding up the other half of the golden-flavored chocolate.

His eyes widened. She wanted desperately to feel the feathered silk of his short hair, push back that black lock that kept falling over his forehead.

"And like that." She nodded to the sculpture with its pixies.

He looked at it and then back at her. He shook his head definitely. "No. No, I'm not like that."

She frowned, wanting to argue. But he closed his hand around her wrist and used it to bring the second half of the chocolate to her lips. "That sculpture isn't of me."

The rich deep chocolate with its golden undertones melted all over her tongue again and melted every erogenous zone of her body while it was at it: heat spreading out from the nape of her neck, from the insides of her elbows—since when had that become an erogenous zone?—down the delicate insides of her wrists, in her breasts, and of course, of course blooming between her thighs.

She could barely stop herself from grabbing on to him. He seemed such an intense, still center in that melting world.

"I'm not, you know," he whispered. "Like that. I'm all tension. All steel. All the time. I don't have any softness but what I make." He was closing her in entirely now, a hand on either side of her on the counter. He had long arms, a tall lean body, and still the space she had left to maneuver was exquisitely small. His gaze ran over her hair, her eyebrows, her cheeks, down to the curve of her breasts under her little blue top. "Not yet," he breathed.

She took a hard, involuntary breath, and brought her thumb up only half-consciously to suck the melted chocolate off its pad.

Tension grew all around her, in the long arms under his jacket, the shoulders angled over her, the flat stomach, the strong thighs. If she reached out and touched him, would those muscles be as taut as the air between them? Her fingers itched. As an investigative journalist, maybe she should just *check* . . .

He pushed himself suddenly away from her with a little huff of breath and turned toward the racks of chocolates. One hand curled into the wire shelving, and he stood for a moment with his back to her. A white-coated assistant came up to him. It took him a second before he turned his head and looked at the woman, nodding, responding something. His face slowly regained that severe, disciplined look.

He pulled out his phone and walked away, talking into it for a few minutes. At the end of the conversation, he shook his head and rolled his shoulders, rubbed the nape of his neck, then turned and came back to her. His face was all ascetic, but his eyes watched her. "I'm sorry, that was the wife of one of the *pâtissiers* I trained under, asking if I can help out. He was supposed to give a workshop this afternoon at LeNôtre, but apparently had an allergic reaction to raw red tuna at breakfast this morning—please don't ask why anyone would eat sushi for breakfast. He's the one who invented a chocolate filled with foie gras. Anyway, his wife asked if I could go fill in." He stood still a moment looking down at her. Was he too controlled to show frustration or just not frustrated?

He might flirt with engaged women all the time. Every time one came in to talk to him about her wedding, in fact.

Good lord, he might not even have been flirting. He was French, right? Didn't they breathe sex appeal without even thinking about it?

Great. Living in Paris was going to kill her, then. Nobody in bars or at frat parties or even in her old ad agency in New York, where there had been some serious self-marketers, knew how to get to a woman that unconsciously.

"I could show you my sketches," Ellie heard herself say.

Simon's face broke into a smile. His head tilted. She felt so special when he looked at her with such focus. Alas, she was pretty sure that was just his normal look. "What an excellent idea. *Demain?* Do you want to come back tomorrow and show me your thoughts about what you're looking for?"

She nodded emphatically. One lock of her hair escaped from her ponytail and bobbed into her eyes.

His gaze honed in on that, then tracked over her hair like a heavy, petting hand. "And you can try more chocolates."

"Really?" she said hungrily, wonderingly. "Would you let me?" Living in Paris might kill her, but it was a good way to die. This master chocolatier feeding her chocolates from his own hand as she slowly lost her mind to heartbroken desire. It seemed suitably French. Didn't all their films end that way?

Oh crap, he was only offering her chocolates from his hand because she was a potential valuable client. Was she *stealing* from him?

Instead of all those art courses in college, she probably should have taken one on journalistic ethics.

CHAPTER FOUR

CAUGHT in the act. Simon Casset is HOT! read the next morning's blog post.

Simon's hand jerked on his mouse as if it were an electric socket. A geyser of hot, liquid sugar surged through his body. He had to grip the edge of his desk, which was a lousy substitute for soft curves through a thin flower print. Desire hit him in great waves, like being caught wrong as he made it out through the breakers for an ocean swim, and he had to ride it out, let them batter him until he could come up for air.

She thought he was hot? She thought he was HOT!

Help! she told her readers. *What's a girl to do?*

She seemed to have no conception of the fact that she left herself *naked*. That he might read this. Did she think, when she wrote, that she was confessing things to an audience of personal friends? Was that her performance mind-set, the thing that let her blog when otherwise she might retreat into some semblance of privacy? Or did she think the fact that it was in English would hide it from him, somehow? Surely not. She had plenty of comments in French below her posts, proving she knew French audiences read her. She was just all out there, wasn't she? Oblivious to the obvious, that if she blogged about him, with his full name to pop up on Google Alerts, he would find out about it. And realize who had written it.

Did she think he wouldn't *care?* That it wouldn't turn him into a hungry, prowling wolf?

Even if she assumed he would never see it . . . how could she blithely tell her readers she thought he was HOT!

He could only imagine telling one person how hot he found her, and even then only at some very intimate, exposed moments, like . . .

He had to swallow on another wave of desire, as he imagined some possible moments. He could imagine . . . quite a bit.

How had she even gotten that picture of him? He was bent over a marble counter, picking up a chocolate-sugar pixie, and looking up just at the right moment, with a little crinkle around his eyes, warm, a slight smile that now looked as if it had been for the world *entier,* but which in reality must have been just for her.

He didn't know how they did it in America, but here in France it was illegal to publish someone's photo on the web without permission, and he didn't give a damn. *Il s'en foutait royalement, en fait.*

I want her, his whole being said like a small child clamoring for a toy. *I want her.* All the curves and flowers and life of her.

And I'm going to have her. Today.

While she still thinks I'm hot.

"*Monsieur?*" asked Lucie. He peered at his front manager from very far away, trying to make her out through that blinding desire-storm. "The *mademoiselle* is here to see you with her sketches for the wedding."

Oh yes, I'm going to have her. He fisted a hand, making his personal contract, the one he had made before the M.O.F. *concours* and his first iron distance triathlon. *I promise myself I am.*

"Bring her back, Lucie, *merci.* And could you close the door behind us when you leave?"

He turned the lock, so that when Lucie pulled the door

closed, no one else could get to them unless they battered it down.

Ellie's skin was charged before she even reached his shop, as if he was pulling all her positive electric particles to him and she needed desperately to touch him, to rebalance herself with that first huge ZAP!

The outside of the shop was a brown so dark and assertive it was almost black, like old iron, the name *SIMON CAS-SET* stamped above it as if by a merciless press. Inside, the style was so purist, so streamlined, that the contents hit like a miracle. The counters reminded her of his eyes, gray-blue, but such a pale, pale shade of it, that it became the foil for the dark, dark chocolate that contrasted with it, and for the bright, rich fruit colors that lit the dark chocolate as if a Fairy King had passed through the Black Forest, bringing life and whimsy racing out of the darkness in his wake, surging into the sky. Sculptures that were impossible fancies claimed the eye, then let it relax to the carpet of small perfect chocolates, to the flowering bed of pastries, that stretched in the display cases at those sculptures' feet.

She felt—giddy, moving through that shop. Too bright, too beautiful, too hungry. As if it made her into something richer and tried to snare her all at once.

Her heart seized oddly, and she felt sparkly and strange, to see the pixie-dragonfly sculpture. The pixies laughed and played so merrily, she could swear their eyes caught hers in a moment of joyous complicity.

She was so hungry by the time she made it through that shop to the *laboratoire* beyond it, she might eat the first thing that moved. Her skin prickled all over, the hairs stirring on her body. She would have bought a box of chocolates right then, except . . . her tongue curled with longing to be fed them again from his own hand.

Come away, O human child . . .

When the girl who walked her back shut the door behind

her, closing Ellie and Simon into the office, Ellie couldn't breathe. *Just being French,* she reminded herself. Her French teachers in college had told her about this: the French liked to shut doors, it didn't seem intimate to them; leaving doors open seemed overexposed.

That was . . . that was . . . all—

Simon Casset smiled at her. Just a tiny smile. An—intimate smile. Energy crackled off him as if he had just come out of a lightning storm. That self-contained control of his must be all that prevented him from releasing thunderbolts with a sudden movement.

The energy in this small office felt . . . too much. Seriously, if she couldn't touch him soon to release that static buildup, her whole body might crackle apart from the force of it.

"Bonjour." His gaze tracked over her once, a subtle flicker up and down, and again she might have been posing naked. Those blue-gray eyes of his looked a lot darker than usual, some heat blackening the steel. "Your fiancé still couldn't make it?" he asked gently.

He sure showed a lot of solicitude for her fiancé. What, did it seem *that* bad to be engaged to her? That he had to take care of the other man? "Hospital. Remember?"

"Still? For a broken leg?"

Damn, it would have helped if she had ever known personally someone with a broken leg. She tried to call up television shows. "Traction. The old lady was heavy. There were multiple fractures."

"Poor you." His voice might as well have been a flow of chocolate, caressing her all over.

Why? *She* wasn't in traction. "It's all right. I'm happy to see you without him."

A flicker of a grin, oddly carnivorous. "An endurance athlete with his leg in traction is going to be impossible to live with. All that energy he can't expend. You might want to avoid him completely for a couple of months so you won't end up dumping him for someone more . . . self-controlled."

The most self-controlled person she knew was standing right in front of her. In her mind, he lost all that control and his clothes with it.

She looked down at her sketchbook, that penetrating gaze of his making her feel caught *en flagrant délit*. Cheater.

Abruptly, she remembered whom she was cheating. Not Cal Kenton but Simon Casset.

She was going to have to pay him for all this, wasn't she? Take out extravagant credit card debt and somehow manage to pay him for the favors and sculptures for her invented wedding. He was so sincerely offering her his precious time, and she was behaving *execrably*. She hadn't realized that about hard-nosed journalism: the price getting what she wanted might cost other people.

God, he must be hideously expensive.

"Your sketches?" he asked, moving around the desk and in quite close behind her to reach for the book.

She swallowed as every hair on her body strained toward him, guilt or no. Her hold loosened involuntarily on the sketchbook, because she had no more muscles. He had all the muscles in the room.

But instead of taking it from her, he reached past her body and opened it, standing looking over her shoulder.

That exhilirated giddy about-to-jump-off-the-edge-of-the-world fear pressed outward from her middle, swelling like a balloon, until there was no more space for her lungs. He looked at the first page. It was of the Statue of Liberty and part of the New York skyline, and under it she had drawn a bright, sad, excited *BYE!*, decorated with a bow and a tear.

She couldn't see his face or judge his reaction, just feel the stretch of time as he looked at it, the heat of him not touching her but closing all around her just shy of her skin.

He turned the page. The Eiffel Tower, dazzling with sparkles. She had made the sparkles shoot out lines all over the page, like fireworks.

"It's . . . they're at the back," she mumbled, embarrassed. Having him so perfect and controlled so close behind her was leaving her completely vulnerable. It was all she could do not to bend her head, offer the long stretch of her nape, and submit to him.

Well, and she *would* do that, if she thought he would take the invitation.

And not look at her with appalled embarrassment or cynical amusement and leave her to extricate herself from the humiliating moment. She just so didn't seem like his type, with all that controlled perfectionism of his. Life was too much fun for her to slow down and be perfect at any part of it. Even her watercolors were charming and quixotic and would never hang in any museum.

"Mmm." His voice burred softly so close behind her, her skin shivered from it. He turned the next page, taking his time.

He looked through all of them, her sketches of gargoyles, and the doors on all the seventeenth-century buildings, and the displays in bakeries. She stopped protesting as he studied her delighted discovery of his city, because she lost her capacity to protest. Having him so close behind her had slowly stolen so many muscles that she couldn't even control her mind and tongue to speak.

"Is your fiancé Parisian?" he asked suddenly, in that low voice that rubbed all over her.

He had an awfully funny name for a Frenchman, but— "*Oui!*" she realized suddenly. That would be *perfect*. A Parisian who would love her for what she was and sweep her into the heart of his city, but who—might not be *quite* as lighthearted and fun-focused as she was. She had tried relationships with fun-loving men before, and it had been disastrous. "That's why I moved here." He must have gotten the Cal Kenton from a paternal British grandfather.

Simon Casset didn't say anything, but she felt suddenly, oddly, completely wrapped up in someone else's happiness. Like a smile was twining all around her. "A Parisian endurance athlete. How perfect. Does he have any other sterling qualities?"

She racked her brain for what she would look for in a man. "He loves to give me really good chocolate."

"Mmm." His murmur rumbled deliciously against her.

"And he thinks I'm special."

"Of course. How not?" The faint note of surprise in his voice rippled through her whole body. That was—a very nice thing to say. These French were such good flirts. He turned another page.

"The pixies." His voice brushed her with warmth. He had come to the page where she had sketched out his sculpture-in-progress before she painted a watercolor of it for her blog. "It's done now. Did you see?"

She had. In pride of place in his window display, the pixies with their green wings delicately edged with blue, playing in their world of swirling chocolate. Held up high by it and flying. It had filled her with an inexplicable longing and rightness all at once, as if she had glimpsed, through a telescope, a place where *all was right with the world*.

His whole body grazed hers. By accident, surely, as he turned the page, for he eased back again immediately. But her mouth went still dryer. She tried to swallow, to find a place for air in her lungs, but she couldn't.

"That's beautiful." It was her first wedding-sculpture sketch. She didn't really know anything about what chocolate and sugar could or couldn't do, but she had thought—summery. Happy. She had closed her eyes and thought of Simon Casset's styles, all the photos of his works she had seen, and she had drawn swirls and whirls and put in cascades of flowers he could surely make from sugar. "It needs a pixie." He put one lean finger on a spot just above the flowers. "Or a dragonfly. Being lured in for a taste."

His voice curled around the nape of her neck and stroked her there. She had it so bad. "Could you—could you do it?" she asked, for something to say, instead of just melting into him.

"Do you want to watch me? See how it's done?"

She jumped in pure delight, bumping into his body, arched over hers. *See how Simon Casset worked?* "And—and take pictures and everything? Oh, that would be so *perfect.*" She turned around in her enthusiasm, feeling an urge to do something physical with it, grab him and kiss him in excitement maybe.

She froze. The effect of her turn, the rubbing of their bodies with her movement, kept washing in waves all through her, like liquid in a glass too quickly spun. She had just almost kissed him.

He didn't move back. There could be no mistaking the intent in how close he kept himself, his body enclosing hers. He didn't catch her to steady her when she wobbled back against his desk in thrilled terror.

He closed both hands around the desk on either side of her and locked her in.

The sketchbook provided a tantalizingly flimsy shield between their chests.

Was he hitting on someone else's fiancée while she was discussing her wedding plans with him? That was just . . .

That was *so bad.*

These Frenchmen. It was true, then, they had *no* morals and—

And he could look after his own conscience.

She dropped the sketchbook, which got caught between their bodies, a frustrating barrier between breasts and chest. But her hands were already climbing to his shoulders, too impatient to move the sketchbook out of the way. Her fingers flexed into muscle, pulling her body up on tiptoe.

His mouth met hers before she could even reach the balls of her feet. One hand ran hard up her back and pulled her into him. He dove into her like he had been waiting to strike for hours, just still and poised on his branch until the mouse finally exposed itself.

No, the hawk metaphor broke down, those weren't talons gripping her, but warm, hard hands, setting her on the desk, sliding over her, as his mouth rubbed and opened hers, wedded them together. She twisted and arched, the sketchbook barricade driving her crazy. She wanted it gone, but she couldn't stand to let him go.

He reached suddenly between them and jerked it away. Her breasts sprang to fill the space it had left, and his hand pressed up her back, crushing her harder to him.

He didn't seduce. He didn't wait for her to melt. He didn't show one iota of that precise control that let him create impossible sculptures out of fragility. He kissed her all out and open, like he was starving. His hands ran up and down her ribs, her hips and bottom and the sides of her breasts, kneading into softness. She wiggled into his hardness, loving the way she crushed against it. He smelled irresistible, like chocolate and sugar. Pressing herself to him seemed to release the scents all around her, hiding her in their perfume.

She petted the back of his head, the silk of it, down over the whisper-faint scrape of his jaw, over and over, not able to get enough of his texture. She gave herself completely to his mouth, tangling with his tongue, getting lost in the kiss like something she could never find her way out of.

He was the one who eased back, not breaking the kiss, but giving himself enough room that he could run his hands more fully up and down her body, find space to caress over her breasts. Slip his fingers under the straps of her top, cup her shoulders.

She shivered at the slide of his palms over bare skin, caught between two forces, wanting simultaneously to press herself back against him and to lie back, give him all the access he wanted. She tightened her hands around his neck, and her engagement ring bit into her fingers.

Her enga—oh . . . *merde.* This couldn't be good. He must think—he must just want—well, so did she, but—damn it, this was why she had had to stop going to bars and frat parties after the first couple of times in college. She was all-out, delighted enthusiasm, like a stupid, bubbling stream, and the guy would just cup that in his hands for the hell of it, splash his face with it, and drop the leftovers back into the river.

She pushed away. Then pushed again when the first time failed to penetrate. He lifted his head, a deep flush mantling his cheekbones, his pupils dilated so much his eyes were more black than blue, his firm ascetic's mouth all softened, crushed, open.

It took him a long moment to come up. He blinked several times, shaking himself as if emerging from deep water. "*Pardon.* That—may have been a little fast."

Her eyes stung suddenly. Completely unexpectedly, as if he had opened up a wound she didn't know she had. Just once she would like to have a man fall for her like she fell for him. Just—openhearted. She twisted more adamantly, forcing him to either hold her against her will or let her go.

He let her go, moving back. But he set his back against the door, so she couldn't just rush away. Was that on purpose? "I'm sorry," he said again. He was breathing very hard and seemed still a little dazed. His gaze went down and up her body. He swallowed and shut his eyes, fisting his hands against the door and taking a long, deep breath that came out in a rush.

That pissed her off, that he should be sorry. It made her want to stamp her foot in rage. Which was idiotic and juvenile, so instead she made sure her sandals hit really hard on the floor as she walked up to him and grabbed the doorknob, despite his weight against the door. Despite the fact that it made her arm brush his body and brought her right in close to him, nearly touching again.

That bastard moved his weight *off* it. Leaving her free to escape. He had been trapping her by *accident*? Oh, the . . . the *salaud*. He moved a little to the side, not exactly out of her personal space, but allowing more of it than she herself had. "You should be sorry," she hissed at him, infuriated. "I'm *engaged*. But of course, *you* don't care. You and your French morals."

His eyes sparked with surprise and then glittered crystalline suddenly with outrage. He pressed one hand against the frame of the door. Not against the door itself to lock her in, oh no, not him, he had to leave her just enough space to open it and get out. "I think my morals are better than yours," he said icily.

Which, of course, he would, since *she* was the one behaving so illicitly and finding that pseudo-infidelity . . . just a little bit delicious.

He bent his head as she yanked the door open, so that his breath curled warm over her ear, in direct counterpoint to the ice. "A lot better," he breathed like a compliment.

She managed to stalk out, but her ear kept trickling that whisper down through her body in little breaths of arousal for the entire rest of the day. How could an ear do that?

CHAPTER FIVE

M*erde.* It took Simon a good five minutes after she had left to pull his hand off the door frame, palm deeply printed with the wood mark. He had pushed way, way too fast there. Just—the feel of her through her fine white peasant's top, all soft and supple, and the scent of her and that wild happy hair he wanted to free, and—it had flooded him. He had forgotten all about control.

She had, too, he reminded himself. She had, too. But he was pretty sure she had never known much about it in the first place.

She threw herself into things. He wanted her to throw herself into him.

He had to remind himself that she planned, too. Her blog had shown a desire to go to Paris for well over a year before she had prepared the way for her dream enough to actually come here. She hadn't just gotten a whim and jumped out of her old life immediately, with no thought for how she would land. She had been in love with the idea of Paris, with the idea of tasting *him,* and, all right, tasting all its chocolatiers and pâtissiers, for years before she came. She could tell the whole world that he was HOT! and still need time to adjust to the fact that he wasn't some safe, distant fantasy.

If she thought he was HOT!, she could have him, good God.

He sure as hell hoped that she really did want him, that this wasn't just playful dramatics for her readers.

No, she had kissed him. She had definitely kissed him as if she wanted him.

But maybe deciding he was going to have her *today* had been a little ambitious, even for him. If it had taken her over a year to actually pack up her old life and move to Paris . . . .

Paris hadn't really actively pursued her, though, he reminded himself. Just sat there existing. Maybe, with some concentrated effort on his part, it wouldn't take her a year to move from dream to action where he was concerned.

Putain, he hoped not.

He went back to his desk and her sketchbook, full of all its delight in Paris. She just squeezed life to her in one big hug, didn't she? Every part of it she could find.

There was an address on the inside of the cover, an "If you find this please return it, reward," an apartment in the Ninth. She had writing like a smile, rounded in all the right places, but with a little bit of angular, swooping drama, too.

Showing up at her apartment with the sketchbook might push him over the line into creepy stalker. He suspected he wouldn't really know if he was over the line. He tended to focus on so few things so completely and utterly, to the exclusion of all else. It worked fine with triathlon times and chocolate championships, but if a woman didn't want that focus on her, she might find it unsettling.

So he looked through the sketchbook one more time, smiling, because every drawing made him want to pick her up and kiss her again, sink into that eager happiness.

Engaged. The nerve of her to pull that on him. In retrospect, why he had been so insulted at the aspersion on his morals, he didn't know. The accusation was so extremely opposite to his one-track mind—if she let him keep her, he probably wouldn't ever again even *see* any women existed— that it should have been hilarious.

He closed the sketchbook and pulled out his phone.

* * *

I have your sketchbook, the first text said.

Ellie jumped, and desire flushed through her body. It sounded so—menacing. Like *I have your teddy-bear,* from the neighbor boy when she was little, or *I have the secret tapes* from a blackmailer.

She smiled vaguely at the parents and children with their little sailboats whom she was trying to sketch—in her newly purchased sketchbook—if only men would quit hitting on her. One of them had nearly sat on her lap. If this kept up, she was going to switch from pencils and watercolors to oils, so that she could squirt red paint all over the worst offenders.

The phone burped again twenty minutes later. She turned crimson before she even pulled it out of her pocket. *If you want it back, you know what to do.*

That made her body go insane with tension and arousal. *What* did she know to do? He probably wasn't after a million euros in unmarked bills. Which left—whoa. She hadn't realized her mind could come up with that many sexual possibilities in one swooping thought. Like, he could want—or he could want—or then again he could want—

Oh boy. She brought her new sketchbook to her face, trying to get its paper scent to work like a paper bag.

Because she was hyperventilating.

An hour later, she had just finished eating pastries for lunch at Philippe Lyonnais's, with its opulent nineteenth-century salon of which she had snapped exactly three photos before the waiter had started frowning at her, and was composing a tweet to entice her fans to her blog about it later, when there was another text. *The offer still stands.*

What offer? The offer made on his office desk with his body pressed hard against hers? The offer to let her buy back her sketchbook with hundreds of indecent services? Oh wait, he hadn't actually made that offer. He was—maybe her fiancé could just *die* of his wounds in the hospital and leave her a free woman. Hadn't she read hospital infections were a major problem?

She definitely couldn't imagine herself looking Simon Casset straight in those penetrating eyes of his and confessing she had made the whole thing up as a way to infiltrate his *laboratoire* and tell the whole world about it.

And then there was this other worry: Simon Casset might not want her to be a free woman. He was French, after all. She had heard about that whole French extramarital affairs thing. Maybe she was just supposed to be—spice.

How bad was she, that part of her liked feeling—just spicy.

To watch me work, said the next text.

Oh. A few hours ago she had been ecstatic at the offer to watch him work, and now she felt as if he had just stuck a pin in her balloon. *That* offer. That would be—well, it would still be wonderful, but—

I promise not to touch anything but chocolate, read the last text.

Well, damn him. Who asked him to promise something like that? And why did she immediately imagine him marking her body with generous paths of chocolate?

He had better go for a run, Simon thought, when the whole afternoon passed with no response to his texts and no russet-brown head appeared in his *laboratoire,* with her flirty blue skirt and little white peasant top. It was his day for a long run anyway, so he normally wouldn't have even thought about skipping, but today he nevertheless had to force himself. Because her address seemed to stand out in neon Pigalle SEX SHOP letters in his brain, and . . . he had better go for a run.

Ellie grabbed a free Vélib bike for a sunset ride along the quays. Evenings were her most homesick time, when she noticed how very isolated she was in this city. But the plan to ride Vélib bikes through Paris with the wind in her hair had been one of her top one hundred reasons for moving here. After the patisseries and chocolate, of course.

The hem of her skirt danced around her knees as she biked, as if she had slipped back into the 1950s. The road along the lower quay was closed to motor vehicles, leaving bikers and skaters and pedestrians free passage by the great stretches of sand and blue umbrellas that were Paris-Plage, the city's summer transformation of itself into a would-be-Nice.

Ellie grinned in delight. Biking between the Seine and sand, as the sun set beyond the Eiffel Tower in the distance, bathing the horizon in a soft pink light, the wind stirring softly in her hair and making the hem of her skirt stream poetically around her . . . she was *happy,* and tomorrow she *was* going to take Simon Casset up on that offer of his—*both* of those offers of his, maybe.

She would just—she frowned in concentration at the Eiffel Tower as its copper glow grew more pronounced in the dusk—just have to figure out a way to do away with her fiancé.

If he died, though, wouldn't she be grief-stricken? She didn't know if she could do grief-stricken.

She straightened on her bike, brightening enough to rival the Eiffel Tower. That was *it.* He could fall in love with a French nurse. Who wouldn't? Perfect, perfect, perfect—

She swerved just before she ran over Simon Casset.

He dodged and grabbed her handlebars before she could fall over. "*Pardon.* I thought you saw me. I take it you weren't smiling at me?"

She stared at him. His black hair clung to his forehead, damp with sweat, and he was breathing with the deep, efficient, easy pants of a dedicated athlete out for a ten-mile jog. Under her gaze, he ducked his head toward his shoulder suddenly, dragging the sleeve across his face.

"I think my fiancé's been flirting with his nurse," she

blurted, and his head whipped up from his sleeve with a fierce, white grin.

"*Has* he now? *Quel salaud.*"

She toyed with the idea of throwing her ring in the Seine right then and there in some great dramatic gesture. But . . . it was pretty. It had cost thirty-five euros, which was, like, a whole tiny box of Simon Casset chocolates. No small change, given the current unpredictable state of her income. And Simon might feel a lot safer if she was engaged.

Although, come to think of it, why she should be interested in making him feel *safe*, she didn't know.

"Do you, uh, usually run on the quays?" She might need to start taking a sunset Vélib trip *every day*. "In the evening?"

"I usually do a couple of rounds of them twice a week."

A couple of—her jaw dropped. As in fifteen miles or so? She had only gone a few miles on a *bike*, and she was already feeling it in her muscles.

"And . . . and this would be your usual day to run?" As in . . . when could she catch her next sighting of the superhero?

His smile faded, his eyes growing very intent. Although he had stopped running, his breathing seemed to be picking up. "Yes. I like the Seine in the evening. It's beautiful, with all the lights on the bridges and the Louvre, the Musée d'Orsay, the Hôtel de Ville, the Conciergerie, shining off the water. Sometimes, just when you're wondering why the hell you're such a glutton for punishment, the Eiffel Tower will start sparkling in the distance. Just at the right moment. I love it."

She smiled, feeling happy to have that exact kind of evening stretch out before her, minus the glutton for punishment bit. Of course, maybe if she had ever been a glutton for punishment, she could be running along beside him right now, she thought wistfully. Physical misery versus emotional bliss. What an unfair trade-off.

When all her marathon-crazy friends in New York had been trying to convince her that training with them would be good for her *heart,* they could have been a little more specific.

"But you . . ." he said slowly. "I don't know if it's a good idea for you to be biking alone at night, dressed like that."

She gave a blank look down at her clothes. "What's wrong with the way I'm dressed?" A skirt that came to just below her knees and a loose top in the middle of July? It was hardly overly revealing.

"You look edible," one of the most selective palates in Paris said matter-of-factly.

Arousal jolted through every erogenous zone in her body.

That arousal seemed to balance perfectly with the balmy, soft summer night.

His head tilted. His voice softened, to match the night. "You look as if you go around distilling everything that is best in life, and all a man would have to do is grab you to have all that best for himself."

Her lips parted. She sat staring at him. The summer night seemed to rush into her, rush all through her, like some magic breeze.

He looked away a moment, at the darkening water as a barge slowly passed, looked back at her. His hand caressed the handlebars. "Why don't you bike beside me?"

Oh. That would be *wonderful.* But— "You're going to run while I bike?"

He coughed and maintained an oddly neutral expression. "It's a heavy bike. I mean—you aren't a competitive cyclist or anything, are you?"

She looked at him blankly. That was hilarious. She danced for exercise, or another time she had tried rock-climbing, and she had even signed up for that pole-dancing craze but had felt ridiculous. Also, she was signed up to start trapeze lessons at L'École du Cirque in Paris next month. It seemed appropriate, that moving to Paris she would learn to fly. "Do I *look* like a competitive cyclist?"

His mouth curved as he took the invitation to examine her body, from the set of her shoulders, all the way down her thigh muscles, to her toes. "You look delicious. And I think we'll manage."

Not only did they manage, her coasting along dreamily as night fell over Paris and darkened the water beside them, but he barely seemed to exert himself. She had the occasional suspicion that he was actually slowing himself to her pace. He was coasting, too, only on foot at the same speed she could coast on the bike, relaxed, perhaps even as dreamy as she was.

They spoke very little. Occasionally, he would point something out to her or she would ask about something. Mostly they floated, in silence, at peace, absorbing the night falling over the city and the company they kept as it fell.

Oh boy, had she ever made a mistake in moving to a city where a man could tell a woman *tu as l'air délicieux* like that, as if it was a normal part of human conversation. But she would have to worry about keeping her heart safe later. A lot later.

Night fell very late in July in Paris, almost ten before it was dark enough to qualify, and yet it being a warm Friday evening, many people were still out, strolling or skating or biking or sitting on benches or in the sand, conversations floating frequently across each other, in and out, as groups continued their separate ways. The lights illuminating all the great monuments, the Louvre, the Musée d'Orsay, the bridges, felt warm and almost affectionate, as if the city were telling a magic bedtime story to tired children.

Ellie was so happy she had followed her dream to this moment that it squeezed her panic at that dream-following almost out of existence. She might have left friends, family, cultural comfort, and job security, but still . . . you could not get very much better than this.

They rode/ran all the way to the Eiffel Tower and back. Whenever she asked whether Simon was tired, he looked surprised and shook his head. Slightly embarrassing, because Ellie was getting quite tired by the end of the trip, in a happy way.

"I'll see you back to your apartment," Simon said, when they reached the Pont Neuf again. The bridge's grotesque faces grimaced down at her, and she wanted to thumb her nose back at them, because she was happy, and they were just pale silly stone.

She started to fish for her smartphone. "I'm not sure I remember how——"

"It's this way." He headed north through the more crowded streets, full of lit bars and bistros and shop windows, finally slipping into the street she had chosen in part because of its name, Rue de la Lune, past the little church and the tiny children's park to her green building door. He helped her find a Vélib station to return her bike, and she watched it go in its slot with a forlorn little squeeze of her heart. That was it. The evening was over. "Have you eaten?"

She brightened, excited and alarmed all at once. If the evening *wasn't* over, then . . . this was getting seriouser and seriouser.

"I'll be starving in about fifteen minutes. Most places will have stopped serving, but we could find *un Grec.*"

Her stomach was too full of butterflies for hunger, but she nodded happily.

He looked down at her from the other side of the bike in its station. He wasn't invading her personal space right now. He was keeping several discreet feet away. "Do you mind if I use your shower first?"

And, given that he had just said he was starving, it never once occurred to her that he didn't have a clean thing to wear when he got out of the shower.

CHAPTER SIX

It didn't occur to her until she was lying on her little white bed—it was either that or the little straightback chair in front of her easel—listening to him shower. The window was open, for there was no air conditioner and the tiny space would have been stifling without it. The street was rather quiet, with occasional sounds of cars, motorcycles, footsteps. All that lit the room now were the lights from the street, not too many here, and the soft glow of the one lamp she had bought since she'd moved in.

He didn't have a thing to wear, she told the ceiling, which she was thinking of painting with a moon. Not a thing. Surely he wouldn't put those sweaty running clothes back on.

Surely he had only invited himself up to her apartment for one reason.

And the reason ran through her, silky and warm and stealing her breath, while the water ran over him.

He took the shortest shower on record. And when he came out of it, she couldn't breathe. Carelessly dried, beads of water curled lovingly down a hard lean chest with no ounce of softness on it. His shoulders looked like a swimmer's, broad, muscled, his torso tightening to narrow hips. Curls of dark hair narrowed to a fine, discreet arrow disappearing under the blue towel at his waist.

She tried to swallow, but her mouth was so dry. She

dragged her gaze back up from that towel, up his taut belly, the powerful shoulders, to . . . his eyes.

They caught her. She couldn't look away.

Dimly, she realized she was just lying on the bed in blatant invitation, and she forced herself to sit up. "I don't—I don't have any food." Her voice rang dimly in her ears, some idiot talking about nothing.

"I know." He came toward her. There was almost no distance to cross in the tiny space. "I'll just have to starve."

He leaned over her, and the first touch of his warm hands stole her mind. Focused all her being on sensation. He closed his hands over her shoulders and rubbed them in one long stroke down her arms. His stroke ended at her fingers, his own curling into hers, holding on as he kissed her. He kissed her until she was shivering and clinging to his damp skin, and he was making little hungry sounds, his hands petting her everywhere as if that was her reward for her yielding.

He lifted her left hand and kissed up the inside of her forearm, sending frissons of pleasure and naked vulnerability all through her. She curled her other arm around him, holding him as hard as she could to her. Like her safe harbor in a storm, so very ironic, since he was the storm.

He pressed his mouth into her open palm, holding it there, and with his other hand stroked her ring finger out straight. "Let's just take this off, shall we?" he murmured, pulling on her ring.

It tugged against her skin. She stared at it as he put it in the trough of her easel, as if she was watching him tuck a life preserver out of reach. Just before the iceberg collision. She had just moved here. How hard was she going to fall for someone, how fast? How much more overturned could her life be?

He kissed the spot the ring left bare, watching her over the edge of her palm. "Don't think of him," he said roughly, sinking his hands into her thighs and using them to pull her lower on the bed so that only her stack of pillows angled her up. "Think of me." His hands sank into her hair, wisped by the ride. His thumbs slid over the wiggly confined waves until they slipped under the elastic. His eyes glittering fiercely, he jerked his thumbs apart, still keeping his palms curved over her head.

The elastic snapped. Her hair spilled free over his hands with a little ache in the repositioning roots. His fingers sank into it, spasmodic fists. "Mine," he said, and held her with his fists under her skull, caught in her hair, for his kiss. It was very deep, a transference of starving. "You're mine. I want you."

He didn't say it like a declaration of sexual desire, although desire was in every line of his body. He said it like someone staking a claim on what he knew was the flimsiest of bases. Only in a spoiled childhood did wanting something ever give you right to possession.

But he was all adult. All hungry male. He pressed her back into the pillows, kissing her as if he could not sink far enough into her. His body rubbed back and forth over hers as he kissed her, rocked minutely on his elbows, maximizing the feel of their bodies against each other.

She wrapped her arms around him, up over his back to grip his shoulders, pulling herself up into him, writhing her own body in response. The feel of him was so gloriously hard, so immutable. He lifted his head for air, and she pressed kisses over his shoulder, over his collarbone, over the curve and tightness of muscle.

He pulled back enough to stare at her. "You do think I'm hot," he whispered wonderingly.

She laughed involuntarily as she rubbed her face into the join of his shoulder. Such a strong shoulder. Where was his softness? Didn't he have any *anywhere?* "Now what gave that away?"

"You." He slid his hands under her top. Both her muscles and his flicked at the first contact of his palms against her bare ribs. They stared at each other, caught by that second, that promise that she would soon be naked. "You don't hide any-thing."

Her tummy flinched with guilt, muscles tightening under his hand. Her cover story was hiding everything about her-self.

Except how hot and weak and hungry she felt.

She had given up falling for men. It was so bad for her. But he certainly *felt* like a man who could catch her no mat-ter what height she fell from. Maybe even let her down gently, back to the ground.

Maybe—maybe?—never set her down at all. She flinched her face into the nearest place to hide it—his biceps—at the thought. *Please don't get your hopes up. Ellie, remember what we said, that you could dream big about Paris, but no more dreams built on men.*

He rubbed the knit waist of her skirt down, traced his thumb over the edge of her little white panties. She had known she would regret not making the purchase of sexy underwear a top priority. "You're so beautiful," he said. "Are you sure you want to let *me* be the one who gets to eat you up?"

Her lips parted. He brought up a hand fast to cover them. "Forget I said that." He pushed her back into the pillows with his hand firm on her mouth while he bent his head to her breast. *"Sois sûre. Tu es sûre."*

Be sure. You're sure.

She nipped at the inside of his palm to free herself. He slid it slowly off her mouth without lifting his head from her breast, the palm drifting caressingly, until only his thumb kept tracing over her parted lips. Drifting inside them. Invit-ingly. He wanted her to take it into her mouth and suck it.

So she did, and he made a little hard sound, his body tight-ening everywhere against her. *"You're* the one who tastes so good. All chocolate and sugar."

The smile against the curve of her breast was wry. "But in

real life I'm all stringy muscle. No flavor." His hand ran possessively over the curve of her hip.

She laughed out loud, her hands stroking over all that lean delineated muscle. "You're *kidding*."

A fractional pause of his face rubbing between her breasts. As if he wasn't kidding and was thrown for a loop by the fact she could think so.

"You're *perfect*."

His head lifted, his eyebrows quirked. "I don't think so." But there was a hunger in his eyes, as if he wanted to know why she did.

"*Look* at you." She stroked her hands over the swimmer's shoulders and back, over the tight, lean muscles at his waist, slowing at the loosened towel and growing shy, although at a guess from all that running, the muscles of his butt and thighs must be even more defined. Even more tempting . . .

A little shiver ran through him and all those muscles stretched into her touch. He blushed. "You mean— physically perfect." His blush deepened as he forced himself to say it out loud.

"I thought you were perfect before I even saw you," she confessed, her fingers flexing into his waist right there at the edge of the terry cloth. Sneaking it down with just a little nudge of her fingertips. Loosening it just a little further.

He shook his head bemusedly. But waited eagerly for the reason.

"Your art. The patience, the discipline, the time you're willing to spend to make something that's always only temporary, always to be eaten, always to delight everyone who sees it in almost every sense they have. And it's so *beautiful*. Your sculptures—it's like you have this magic imagination inside you. Each one is this exultant, triumphant *dream*."

His blush was adorable. Who had ever seen a dark-haired tan man blush so deeply. Just because he had a half-naked worshipper trapped beneath him. He shifted uneasily, and the

movement rubbed his towel farther apart and his skin against
hers. "I'm really just—technical. Like an engineer. And anal
enough to make sure that everything I work with is exactly,
to the last millimeter, perfect."

She began to laugh, as visions of those sculptures and
chocolates and pastries danced through her mind. The
colors, the perfection, the dazzling flights of gravity-defying
whimsy. "A technician. An engineer. You really think that?
Oh God, you're so *cute.*" She wrapped her arms around those
shoulders to lift herself up and kiss him.

The feel of her arms flexing, pulling her weight up off the
mattress to be closer to him, as his own strength braced to
carry it, that undid him. He held himself off the bed a moment longer just to savor the strength with which she held
herself to him, her mouth seeking his, open, like an offer. He
could take it and drink his fill.

He closed his arms under her back and lett her sink slowly
into them, feeling him holding her, as he took the offer, took
her tongue, her lips, in a twining battle he couldn't get
enough of.

I'm not cute, he wanted to tell her. *I'm not. It's you.* But his
mouth was too busy, suckling and being suckled, as if they
were battling to see who could take the most of the other.

Her body felt so soft under his weight, which was gently
crushing her, as if her curves gave all his unpadded muscles a
resting place. He loved that softness. She wasn't fat, but she
wasn't skinny either, as if she didn't spend one damned second of her life obsessing over anything. Her body was—
happy. She was happy in it, like it could be just whatever way
it happened to become while she was busy having fun.

His hands kneaded over her like a great cat finding and
testing that perfect spot where it would curl up forever.
When her hands ran over his head, found the faint dusting of
fine hairs down the nape of his neck, he shivered, arched,
and his hands dug into her too hard, until he thought she

would pull them off her, cast the cat with its unsheathed claws from her lap.

She didn't, though. She shivered, too, and arched into him, and dragged her hands over his ribs and back, letting her nails flex in just a little. Little bitten-to-the-quick nails.

He sank too hard into her mouth at that, seizing it as if it was his last hope, and then had to drag himself away, twist his head to bury it in her shoulder where he couldn't steal all her breath.

"Wow," she whispered. Her hands were tracing over his shoulders, the muscles of his back, down to his waist, as if she couldn't get enough of his contours. Her fingers grew greedy, pushed past the towel to curve over his butt, and his hips jerked involuntarily into hers. Her fingers caressed him all over and then sank as deep as they could. There wasn't much yield to him, and even less than usual at that moment. "Oh, wow."

"I love it," he whispered to her breasts, hiding his face in her. "I love the feel of your fingers trying to make me yield. Dig as hard as you can."

But her hands were running down over his buttocks to his thighs, gentle now, hopelessly small against him. *"J'adore ça aussi,"* he groaned against her breast, licking at the edge of her bra in frantic little laps, teasing his tongue under it. He found the clasp at her back and opened it easily. Control of his fingers was never really an issue.

Not even now. His fingers teased back around her chest, following the line that the bra had printed on her flesh, loosening it, easing that confined skin. She made a little moaning sound, as if his touch felt just right. He slid his hands up under the loosened cups, cotton grazing against his knuckles as he caressed that full softness. Made it peak to him. Made it beg.

He pushed her bra straps down her arms, tossed it somewhere, brought his tongue to those tight nipples. *You don't have to beg* me. *But I like it. I like it.*

He suckled her in lavishly, almost an apology for how very much he liked it. She was turning him into gold at her touch. He had exclamation points raining down all over him, a storm of them, bright, shining, pelting him like a pulsing shower, just right, just right, it was better than a massage.

Worlds better. He pressed one hard thigh between her legs, drew the other up so that he could feel her hip twisting against it. She *was* his massage. God, but she rubbed him just right.

"You and your *putain de fiancé,*" he muttered, dragging his face down over her belly, which enchanted him utterly by having some flesh on it, not being some concave stretch of skin over bones and muscles like his was. He drove his thumbs under the band of her panties, stretching the elastic away from her skin as he rubbed his hands over her hips, her bottom. "You couldn't let me have *five seconds* to think of a way to start hitting on you before you threw that one out."

She was tracing all the contours of his body, hands sliding and gripping, following the lines and indentations of muscle with utter absorption. "I didn't know," she whispered, probably with no thought at all to what she was revealing. She couldn't even keep in character when she was fully focused on her fiancée role. "I didn't know you would let me in just for me."

"Who would want to keep you *out?*"

She shook her head hopelessly, but with a kind of pleasurable hopelessness as her hands ran all over him, as if she abandoned herself to her fate. "You're so cute."

Those little palms sliding everywhere over his skin—they might be remaking him into golden silk, but under that veil, he was becoming all steel. He tensed with delight everywhere, wanting to just close his eyes and concentrate on the feel of it—except then he wouldn't be able to see her.

Cute. There was that word again. He lifted his head to study her. Maybe it was the language barrier. French wasn't her first language, as her delectable little drawl showed. Did he sound like that when he spoke to her in English, all exotic and adorable? He was never speaking in English again. "I'm not even remotely cute," he said incredulously.

She smiled in a mysterious, cat-licking-her-chops way, as if she knew far more about it than he did. "And you're *Simon Casset*."

Why did she say his name as if he was God? Awkward, reticent pleasure uncurled in a cramped space inside him. He didn't believe in flattery. Growing up, the best comment he received on anything he did was what he could do better, and it was only as an adult that praise had started being heaped on his head. And even now, his peers and critics were quick to point out what could be improved by a millimeter of difference in the fold of a ribbon of cream, the faintest degree more or less of shine in a *glaçage*.

But if it made her happy, he would make an effort to get used to it. *Merde,* who was he kidding, he could definitely get used to it. "And you're beautiful," he said because it wasn't flattery at all. He brushed his lips over those faint, faint pear-speckles on her cheekbones.

She shook her head, but she was glowing with happiness. "Do *you* really think so?"

"Minou." He sank into her. "Yes, I really think so."

She kissed him back eagerly, while his hand explored further under the elastic of her panties, stroked over soft hair there, slid until he gently cupped her. His hand found soft, damp openness. She shivered for him, already blooming. "Wh-what's that?" she asked breathlessly. In the low glow of the lamp, her pupils had narrowed the green of her eyes to a thin rim.

He gave a little low laugh. "My hand." He bent his head close to her ear, brushing his face into her hair. *"Ta chopinette."*

She twisted her head to look at him, confused, and his hand made an explicit movement, illustrating the word for her.

She gasped, her body tightening around him, curling into

him before it relaxed, all her muscles losing their power. Oh yes, his control of his hands was absolute.

"I meant—" she clutched into him again, pressing scattered, lost, hungry kisses on his chest, no control in her at all. But he loved it. He loved that she had no control. "*Minou.* What does that—mean?"

"*Minou?*" He let his fingers slide up and down her, parting her, every helpless clutch and slackening of her body a sweet victory. "It's just"—He tested the precision of his fingers in a tiny, grazing circle.

Her fingernails sank into his arm.

"—a word for someone special." When he was working on an *oeuvre d'art,* a sculpture, a new chocolate, a new pastry, he made sure he got things exactly to the millimeter right. He tested his tiny, grazing circle—to make sure he was to the millimeter perfect.

She made a strangled sound into his chest. Her pants hit his pectorals, warming him, dampening him.

"*Minou.*" Or maybe this way, the circle?

She scrubbed her head against him frantically, her face tucked down so she could watch what he was doing.

"*Chouchou.*" Sometimes, a circle might not be the right shape. Maybe a little brushing back and forth . . .

She made a little sobbing sound.

"*Coeur,*" he whispered, and slid one finger deep inside her as his thumb pressed down. "*Mon coeur.*"

She convulsed around him, dragging at him with a sudden wild burst of strength, as she came to his hand.

So sweet, to feel her body clutching on him so desperately, to let his palm ride her gently down, to catch her as she fell. He kissed her slowly, deeply, her mouth, over her throat, her shoulders, as all her muscles came undone, leaving her body at last limp and quiet in his hold, her hands stroking vaguely over him. He stripped off her panties, shaking now himself. He always had control. He always did. But just in a minute now, he would—he would—

The towel, half-lost long ago, tangled around his thighs. He wrenched it free and threw it across the room.

She drew one thigh dreamily up his, satiated but seeming to enjoy the stroking motion, the softness of her inner thigh running along the gilded hardness of his. Her head had fallen back on the pillows. She gazed up at him langorously, her skin all pink everywhere from his touch, her lips flush and open like her sex was flush and open as he settled his against it. *Putain,* that look of hers, dreamy and happy, blushing and open, sated and yet offering herself to him, one thigh rubbing up and down his, opening herself further.

He drove into her harder than he meant to, a sudden violent surge. Her eyes flared wide, and she gasped, both legs coming up and tightening hard around him.

"*Pardon.* I didn't mean"—

She put her hand over his mouth, and he shut it instantly. Entirely at her command. She shook her head slowly, in that tangle of hair, her eyes smoked emeralds. "Do it again."

Braced on his elbows, he took a deep breath, staring down at her. He didn't mean to, but he did—do it again. Even harder.

She made a little moaning sound and her hips arched up into his.

"*Coeur,*" he whispered again. "*Mon coeur.*"

"Simon," she said, one almost strengthless hand coming up to his shoulder, drifting slowly over it and down his arm, as if she lacked the muscles to keep it up.

He always . . .

He always had . . .

He lost control.

CHAPTER SEVEN

Later, Simon tucked her under him, slipping his weight to the side so the bed took most of it, instead of her soft body. But he kept his hardness curved over her, one arm under her weight on the bed, wrapping her to him. Exclamation points seemed to snow softly down on him, a subsiding storm, golden flakes that fell gently against his skin and caressed it as they melted into him.

He felt exhausted, but in the best way possible, as if endorphins were releasing into his system after some merciless effort. Or as if muscles that had been working far longer than he realized had suddenly relaxed, abandoning him completely as they wallowed in the rest. Even with the open window, her small cube of an apartment was too hot on this July night, and, now that more important hungers were no longer overwhelming him, he was starving for actual food. But he curled over her just a little bit longer, because he liked it here.

He liked being snowed on by exclamation points.

He liked being part of her dream.

Ellie fell asleep, but Simon's movements woke her again. He had pulled the towel back around himself and was sitting in her little chair in front of her easel with his elbows on his knees and his hands clasped, gazing at the easel as if he might eat it. He looked over at her when she rolled to her side.

"I'm absolutely starving," he confessed, shame-faced. "The running. I think I'll try to catch that *épicerie* at the corner before it closes." He glanced at the heart-rate monitor on his wrist for the time, which must be close to midnight. "Otherwise I might gnaw off a leg. Literally, in a way. My body's breaking down muscles right now. Is there anything you would particularly like?"

For just one heart-wounding second, she had thought he was looking for an excuse to escape. But the last question meant he was coming back. She relaxed happily. "I can make some pasta. I've got some gruyère and petits lardons." She had been so delighted with the presence of those last two items in grocery stores as basic staples, not as costly luxuries. "And some yogurt."

He smiled at her, and her heart flipped over. It was such an open, relaxed smile, so different from his usual controlled tension. He was naked but for a towel, showing all that spare long body, the narrow waist and strong shoulders and not an ounce of fat on him anywhere, it made her want to hide her curves under a sheet how little fat he had. His hair was flopped over his forehead every which way, and . . . he was smiling at her. As if he liked every curve about her. "That would be perfect. I'll just go get something to supplement it."

"Perfect" seemed a little generous from one of the world's top chefs toward boxed pasta with gruyère grated over it. And yogurt for dessert. She wrapped her arms around her knees, hugging that generosity to her. It seemed to indicate he was willing to put up with a lot to spend more time with her.

He went into the bathroom and came out pulling on his running clothes, grimacing as their old-sweat dampness hit his skin. She started to push out of bed, feeling around for her shoes.

"No, I'll go." He smiled at her again. The tenderness in it seemed to just wrap her up and tuck her back into the bed. "Don't get dressed."

Oh. She subsided, clutching the sheet to her chest, her heart thudding against the heel of her palm. That made him smile again. She hadn't even known he had it in him to look so relaxed and so very, very happy. "I'm sorry I don't have more food in the place," she offered as he pulled on his running shoes. "I just moved here last week, and it's so small, there's not much storage." She had mostly been eating pastries since she got here, to tell the truth.

"I like it." He paused with his hand on the doorknob, his gaze drifting to the corners of the small space and back to her, as if he was following light back to its source. "It's full of a dream."

They ate the midnight supper on her bed, for lack of a proper table. Simon came back with two full bags, cherries and peaches, packages of ham and the kind of *charcuterie* you couldn't find in the States, some more cheese, and a baguette for which he was very apologetic. Something about its crust being *mou*. "I'll feed you better than this next time. I promise."

Next time? Maybe her fiancé had just ceased to exist, like the figment of her imagination he was. She blinked as Simon pulled his shirt back over his head, stripping immediately naked again, in front of her, as if there was nothing to that at all, while her mouth dropped open, not even remotely accustomed to the impact of that body being unveiled. He didn't even notice. He laid his clothes over her windowsill to dry and wrapped a towel around his waist again. Then started preparing sandwiches to accompany her pasta, with the efficiency of a man who could not wait anymore. She marveled a little at his discipline in not biting into one of the peaches while he worked, given how starving he clearly was. He might be starving, but he ate when the meal was ready, and *with* her, not while she was still draining the pasta.

Simon acted embarrassed from time to time—at the fact that he was feeding her packaged ham and a stale baguette on her bed rather than taking her to a nice restaurant, at how much he ate—nearly the whole pound of pasta, to start. But he seemed to have fun, too, grinning sometimes like a boy camping out.

She had fun. The night lights and soft noises of Paris coming through her open window. Someone to share it with. Him. He seemed to center himself in the middle of her dream and make it true. Like its lodestone.

When they finished, he gathered the sheet up carefully from each corner so nothing spilled out, took it to the window, and shook out all the crumbs. Turning back, the sheet floated open between them, a fine white separation.

That suddenly enveloped her completely, as if she had been kidnapped by a ghost. Only this ghost was warm and hard, all real through the sheet. He toppled her back onto the bed, laughing, and let her pull the sheet off her face, as he held her tight, his face just above hers, his body pressing her into the bed.

He was laughing, but his focus grew slowly more intent, as his eyes traced over her hair, her face. He pulled one arm out from under her and slid the other one up so that her head was cradled on it. His breaths grew deep.

He drew one finger very carefully down her arm, the whole length of it, over her shoulder, down past her elbow, down the side of her forearm to her wrist, watching the path of it with absorption. "You know, I'm such a geek, that I really might touch every millimeter of your skin," he said ruefully.

Her breath came in on a little rush. His eyes lifted to hers, focused on what he saw there. The ruefulness faded away before a fascinated wonder. "To see if you react differently to this—" he drew his thumbnail faintly down the inside of her wrist, making her shiver and stretch. "And this—" he repeated the gesture . . . a millimeter to the left. "Or this." He used his whole thumb, a broad stroke of the slightly callused pad.

She made a little shivering sound of pleasure, her eyes

closing, her face turning into the arm that curled under her head. When she opened them again, he was watching her. That intent look of his, but something so much softer in it.

"Just to give you fair warning." He lowered his head.

From her open window the next morning, he could see rooftops and a narrow glimpse of street below, and lines of casement windows with iron balcony railings. It seemed a very ordinary view to him. He remembered her ecstasies about it on her blog. "Are you going to tell him?" he asked without looking around, his voice absurdly grim.

Absurd because there was no *him* to tell, but her willingness to admit that right now would mean—whether she was playing or not. Whether she was even thinking about letting him keep her vivid happiness in his life. Or whether he was the French chocolatier who completed a food blogger's perfect Paris postcard. He liked being part of her dream, but not if he didn't have any dimensions in it beyond "French lover."

How the hell Frenchmen had gotten the reputation for being so good at casual affairs, he did not know. He, personally, was *merde* at them, and he felt an icy dread that he was about to find himself forced into the role.

She sat up slowly in the bed, drawing up her knees and pulling the sheet around her. Now he did turn his head enough to see her face. She looked at a loss. Her hair spilled around her shoulders in exuberant waves that had been tangled into a mess by his hands, and her face was flushed from—him.

I'm not going into that pigeonhole, Ellie. And if you don't like it, you should have looked before you leapt, because I do long-term impossible goals pretty damn well.

"I . . ." she said slowly, and his hands clenched over her balcony railing.

She climbed out of bed, taking the sheet with her, clutched to her chest, and he followed that movement involuntarily. Wistfully. The sheet draped softly, precariously between her body and his, and left her entire backside naked. Within grabbing distance. Why the hell had he started this conversation? *Ah, oui*—he had thought she would confess all.

Where had the humor in that farcical fiancé gone?

"I—I don't know if we need to bring my fiancé into this at *all*, really," she said.

His hands tightened on the railing. He drew in a breath, pulling the blow inside him, deep, keeping his outside still, controlled. "Ah. I beg your pardon. So it was that kind of evening."

Her eyes flickered. "No, I didn't mean—" She floundered to a stop. Gave her head a shake and gathered herself. "I mean, what kind of evening was it for *you*? Are we . . . are we dating?" Her voice dropped to a shy, scared whisper.

What the hell? Why scared? Was she afraid she had just attracted the attention of an insane stalker? The only difference between the way he felt right now—ready to pursue carefully and relentlessly a woman who barely knew him—and the way a stalker felt was the degree to which *she* wanted or resisted the attention.

Probably a pretend fiancé counted as resisting.

"We're not dating," he said flatly.

She reached out and closed her hand around the easel. "Oh." She looked as if he had just struck her.

"You're cheating on your fiancé. I believe it's a time-honored tradition: the affair in Paris."

She blinked. Her eyes sparkled suddenly. "Like a story!"

A hard spear of rage drove through him. This was *fun* to her, wasn't it? And it was completely outrageous for him to have played on that sense of fun starting out and now be furiously wounded by the same thing.

"Not like a story."

She pulled her lip in under her teeth nervously. "No?"

"Here's an idea: think about it a little bit and tell me if you figure out any differences between our situation and a story."

She mulled that over so long, he went to the door and put

his hand on the knob, which, being hard metal, was safer to strangle.

"I'm real?" she offered tentatively.

He stared at her grimly. And waited.

She shook her head definitely. "You are not real. There's no way you can be. You're too perfect."

He gaped at her, dumbfounded, fury growing so powerfully even he had a hard time controlling it. *He* wasn't real? What the hell? How much more real could he be? His muscles ached everywhere from having added thirteen kilometers extra onto his twenty-kilometer run the night before, a radical violation of his training schedule that was probably going to ruin his chances at the Vichy triathlon next month. He sure as hell felt real to *him.* "As opposed to your fiancé?"

She nibbled more on her lip. "Cal's not *perfect.* I mean— there's that French nurse."

He was going to kill her. His teeth bared. "You're well-suited, then."

She startled, clearly having forgotten somehow, even in the midst of this discussion, that she should perhaps not throw stones at cheating fiancés.

At least he could have beaten out a real fiancé. Especially one who flirted with his nurse. Instead of which, he was boxing with someone else's daydream. He scrubbed his hand over his face, feeling drained, as probably befitted a man who had run thirty-three kilometers, stayed up all night making love, and then discovered he was second best to a *fictitious fiancé who had been run over by a damn moped.* "So where does that leave us?"

She nibbled on her lip some more. She was going to drive him crazy, nibbling on her lip like that, with only that barely clutched sheet between him, and her entire back and *fesses* exposed to the air just where he couldn't see. "Where exactly do you want it to leave us?"

He began to dress quickly. Someone preferred to work with a safety net while she left her partner venturing out over some drastic drops, didn't she? On the other hand, he could see why she had a right to not want to let that sweet, soft vibrancy of hers hit any brutal rocks below. He looked at her a long moment. "I'll tell you what. You let go of that fiancé of yours, and throw yourself at me, and I promise I'll catch you."

He jerked the door open and headed downstairs.

Chapter Eight

Why hadn't she just told him? What was wrong with her? She could have enough courage to uproot her life and move to Paris, but a gorgeous man showed some interest in joining her in that dream, and she hid behind a fiancé who couldn't even dodge an old lady with a baguette?

The odd thing was that fiancé over there in—she needed to look up some Paris hospital names—flirting with nurses, was starting to feel very reassuring. Like the teddy bear she had hidden between the bed and the wall last night, but which was now safely back on her pillow, something she could hold on to, that kept her world from becoming entirely topsy-turvy.

If she just returned to single and available status all of a sudden . . . she would be working without a chute. And if she hit the ground in broken bits this time, there would be no friends or family to bake her cakes, to take her out clubbing, to help her bounce back.

It was all very well of him to say he would catch her. But—if he *didn't*—he would be just fine.

The person who strolled out of the way of someone falling off a building so he didn't get crushed under the body always came out of things just fine.

That fiancé of hers could just keep flirting with that nurse a little while longer.

★ ★ ★

The wait for her blog post was excruciating. Simon kept checking his phone the whole trip back to his place, after he showered and changed into something that didn't stink of day-old sweat, and all the way to his shop. By the time he got there, something finally showed up: *La vie est belle.*

His heart seized with the sweetness of that. For her, too, then? *Life is beautiful.*

Beyond the title, the post had no words. She had posted the sketch he had gazed at on her easel that morning, as he lay with her curled against him in a bed far too narrow for two, her sketch slowly becoming clearer with the dawn. It was fanciful and full of Paris, half-caricature, half-exuberant joy, with mopeds and baguettes and poodles and the Eiffel Tower dancing everywhere. There was an old lady in a beret with a baguette on a moped in one corner of it, running over a lanky guy with glasses. And in the middle, now, she had added a little caricature figure with brown hair in a ponytail and a green dress on, jumping high with arms and legs spread wide, a big grin on her face.

Her dream of Paris. An alarm bell sounded somewhere deep within him, not the first time, but maybe the other times it had been muffled by desire, easy to ignore. *Was* he just her French lover? He was making love to her, and he was French, but . . . why did it sound so different if he put the terms together, made them an identity?

Putain. He didn't want to be a French lover.

But that joy in her, in that little caricature flinging her arms out wide . . . he did want to be the cause of that.

He found his thumb running against the side of his index finger, as if seeking out a texture that was not there. The paper of the sketch. Her skin. Her hair.

He moved, before he could start clicking *refresh* over and over to see if she added anything else, before he could send her a text, or call her, or act obsessive. *She's a person. Not an award. A person wielding a fake fiancé like some kind of shield. Pursuit is okay, but not* relentless *pursuit.*

He went back into the heart of his *laboratoire* and began to create an impossibly delicate chocolate, which he would produce by hand in the hundreds to keep his more obsessive tendencies occupied.

Round. A hazel-green outer shell, blurring golden-brown and green, and so glossy it reflected light. Inside, a rich, warm chocolate ganache, something cozy you couldn't stand not to linger with. A bottom shell of dark chocolate. And precisely, just off center of the top of the gold-green, pear-speckled dome of it, a tiny off-white flower, with six minute, perfect petals, formed from sugar, and placed by hand, one after the other.

"You know how Dominique Richard likes the simple square ganache, just a print on top?" Nathalie said. "That are so much simpler to produce?"

Simon gave her a cool look, his eyebrows raised.

Nathalie cleared her throat. "I'm glad you're not him. Of course. Who wants an easy job? Show me again how you managed to get the speckles that faint."

Half an hour later, Simon was showing his team how to get the effect he wanted. "Just the faintest misting, pass the mold through quickly—no. Start over. It has to be just a hint of an idea of fre—of speckles."

"*Oh,*" Ellie said behind him, and every nerve along his spine flashed. He held himself still.

"That's so *beautiful,*" she said incredulously, coming up so her arm brushed his. She bent to the marble, trying to see the underside of the tiny flower posed on the small domed chocolate.

Without presuming she had the right to pick it up to get a better look.

He scattered his white-jacketed staff to other posts with a gesture of one hand. "You touched me," he said dryly, pitching his voice to keep them out of earshot. "I'll let you touch it. Taste it, too."

She blushed, her cheek still pressed against the marble counter. "You're both works of art, true."

And *he* blushed. *Sérieusement?* Well, he supposed he did treat himself like a work of—well, *some* kind of merciless perfectionism. He hadn't thought of it as art, not often, only maybe during those euphoric highs you could hit sometimes on the long runs.

She straightened. "What did you mean by 'catch' exactly?"

His hand shot out and locked around her wrist. "There. You're caught."

She started and stared from him to his hand on her arm. After a second, she tried to twist her wrist and couldn't budge it a millimeter.

"Don't bruise yourself. Let me know when you want me to let go."

She kept looking at his hand and didn't say anything.

"You're not wearing your ring," he mentioned. "I like that in a cheating fiancée."

Her jaw went out rather sulkily. "I couldn't find it. We must have knocked it out of the easel in the night somehow." She sent him a shy, fugitive glance.

"How Freudian. And in that tiny apartment, you can't find it anywhere?"

She narrowed her eyes at him. It made him want to kiss her. Or strangle her. Or both at once.

"Vas-y, goûte." He nodded to the green-gold flower chocolates, sublimating.

She was so careful as she closed her hand around one, as if she touched some rare, priceless artifact. He stared at her little fingers, nails bitten to the quick, against that glossy chocolate, and everything in his world suddenly settled into its purpose, its right place.

He waited until her teeth had sunk into it. "I'm calling it 'Elle.' "

And while its chocolate-warm insides melted in her

mouth, she stared up at him. Her eyes grew wider and wider until a man could drown in them. Even a man who didn't drown very easily at all.

Suddenly and unexpectedly, her eyes filled with tears.

Putain. He dropped her wrist and grabbed her shoulders instead. "Ellie. Are you—I'm sorry—did I—" *Merde,* maybe she had a boyfriend in New York. A recent breakup. Maybe this whole fiancé story was a cover for more fragile emotions than he had first realized. How could he? His imagination didn't work well enough to think up someone who would not take good care of her if he had the chance.

"Here, come here." He cast a glance at his *laboratoire,* his sense of privacy deeply violated to be the subject of his team's discreet glances—and they all knew it, too, hiding the glances as fast as they could—and drew her into his office.

She dashed a hand across her eyes. "No, I'm sorry. It's just—I've never—it's like *magic.* To move to Paris and have you"—she faltered—"and have you. And then to have *you* make a chocolate named after *me.* I can't believe you want me to believe this is real."

He dropped her shoulders in incredulous exasperation. "Look, Ellie, it's not a fairy tale to *me.*"

That sulky set came back to her jaw, and she looked a little wounded.

"The chocolate! Paris! Those are just my daily life. *You,* now. You popping into this achromatic world, that's a miracle, yes."

She frowned suspiciously, so suspicious that she completely failed to appreciate he had just called her a miracle. "*What* achromatic world?"

His mouth twisted wryly. "I don't think you can see it. The black and gray and tension, the obsession with perfection. You just filter it out to the rest of the world full of color and joy. That clear glass of water that turns light into a rainbow."

That made her happy. He could tell. She curled her arms

around herself as if hugging the words to her, but smiled at him indulgently. "That's what *you* do. Take cool, intense perfectionism and produce something so beautiful it's like—I don't know—I want to be in the heart of you where you come up with these things."

The truth of it hit him so hard he couldn't get his breath back. He stared at her wordlessly. *You are.*

He turned away before he could say that out loud, his insides trembling under the outside he kept so cool. "*Viens.* I told you you could watch me work."

CHAPTER NINE

It would have helped if he wasn't quite so incredible at his work. If you were trying to get your insides to calm down from all the whooshing, it probably wasn't a good idea to hang around honed perfection, blurring sexual desire and memories of touch with the scents and sights of chocolate melting and being re-formed into something ethereal, of sugar stretching and arching between two competent hands like some Fairy King making a world.

And tossing it over to his Titania with a little smile just for her.

Ellie curled her fingers delicately around the crystalline rose he had just made from a ribbon of sugar for her, whimsically, in the middle of his more complex work. Her breath came in and out. Oh yes, the world was whooshing.

She curled the thumb of her other hand around the base of her ring finger, missing the fake ring like she might miss a worry stone. Something to calm that crazy world.

The rose shattered in her right hand.

Simon looked up from what seemed to be a surreal fairy-tale treehouse he was making out of chocolate and caught her hand. She stared at the red shards clinging to her palm, feeling horrible.

He laughed, leaned across the counter, and kissed her quickly, regardless of the gazes of his team. Picking the shards off as carefully as if they had been actual glass, he gave her a caressing smile. "It's very fragile. Didn't you know?"

"I barely even touched it!" He was deftly manipulating these bits of blown and pulled and spun sugar into gravity-defying art, and she couldn't even let one rest on her palm? Good God, how controlled *was* his touch?

Heat suffused her body as she thought of the answer to that question. He lifted her palm to his mouth, cradled it there, and—flicked his tongue out and teased the last bit of red sugar dust off her palm. Over the edge of that palm, he raised one eyebrow at her. "Did you notice that what I hold never gets broken?"

Yes, she had noticed that. In his hands, things just soared.

"How's that French nurse working out?" Simon asked the next night, after having thoroughly adulterized her in the big bed in his apartment.

Ellie frowned at him. He sure did harp on her fiancé a lot. Was it her, or was he starting to sound quite fond of the man?

If he decided *he* liked hiding behind a fiancé, too, she didn't know what she was going to do. Would it be at all plausible if, just when Cal finally healed enough to walk out of the hospital, he tripped trying to get down the stairs into the Métro and had to go right back in?

"Are you sure she's really French? I would have thought she could move faster than this."

"Yes, well—he's in traction." She defended his country's honor.

"Exactly. If you can't seduce a bored man with no chance to get away . . ."

A vision flashed through her mind of Simon bored and bound and completely vulnerable to seduction. She only realized she had dimpled when Simon's thumb gently caressed over the little hollow. He bent and kissed her, long and deeply, as if to reward her for what he could read straight out of her mind.

Her laughter faded before arousal. She lost all focus, except her attention to his mouth, taking hers.

He lifted his head. "Of course, maybe she has," he said thoughtfully. "He might not be admitting any more to you than you are to him."

She blinked a moment to try to remember what they were talking about. Oh. She shifted uneasily, her hair stinging her scalp. He eased his forearm up enough to let the captured strands slide free.

She tried to hold his eyes sincerely. Anyone would think that once a man had you naked a few times, all while assuming you were a complete tramp, it would be much easier to face an X-ray gaze.

Instead of which, it was getting *harder.*

"I'm not usually like this," she promised him.

He raised his eyebrows in polite query. How *did* he manage to look still so polite and controlled when their bodies were naked against each other from a recent bout of intense lovemaking, and his mouth still soft and damp from that kiss?

She cleared her throat. "I wouldn't, you know, umm—" She frowned very severely toward the night outside the window. He began stretching her hair over her naked shoulders strand by strand. "I don't believe in cheating."

"That's all right, we all know about American morals," he said kindly.

She blinked and then gaped at him indignantly. *"American—"*

"I saw *French Kiss.* She didn't even wait until she was off the *plane* before she was picking up a French lover." The longest strands of her hair reached just to the swell of her breasts. He put some effort into his stroking, trying to coax one to unwind enough to reach her nipple, but the hair resisted. He finished the rest of the route without it, curving his hand around her.

Ellie opened her mouth and closed it several times, cycling through multiple unsatisfactory retorts.

"At least you waited a few days," Simon said approvingly. "You're not as bad as *some.*"

As bad as—okay, that—he teased his tongue around her nipple and she lost the protest.

He lifted his head to regard the results of his work with satisfaction. "I mean, it's not as if you were just going after any Frenchman that moved. You already *have* one, and he just sounds so perfect for you—a Parisian endurance athlete who gives you great chocolate—so you must see something else in me."

He leaned over her, his eyes soulful and sincere, his hand stroking the length of her, breast, belly, thigh. "After all, surely," he breathed, "you're not sacrificing all sense of shame just for sex."

CHAPTER TEN

Simon focused on the creamy white chocolate petals he was peeling off paper and curving with the help of the mini-torch he held in one hand, offering tiny bursts of just the right amount of warmth. He was building an impossibly high twining garden of great wildflowers, like some mythical swamp, each blossom to hold a miniature cake at its center.

He remembered, vaguely, the days when working chocolate provoked tension in him. These days, he had won his laurels—Meilleur Ouvrier de France, Champion du Monde, all of that—and he was so used to chocolate doing exactly what he wanted, that he found it an intense, demanding challenge, exactly the way he liked things, but not stressful, not the same way.

In fact, right this second, the fun challenge wasn't keeping his focus at all.

Ellie was watching him. He never found it hard to keep his focus, no matter the bustle of activity his team made around him as they carried out their own tasks, but the way Ellie watched him . . .

Made him feel hot.

Made him hot, also.

So hot that every time that damn camera of hers flashed, he felt vaguely as if he had been posing for porn shots, despite the chef's jacket.

He glanced at her, losing his focus again. She gazed at him—as if he was posing for a porn shot.

Putain. How the hell could she look at him that way, so that his whole body melted faster than chocolate and then hardened worse than tempered steel, and still pretend she had that *putain de fiancé?*

The made-up one whose every element corresponded exactly with him.

"He's not exactly perfect," she said suddenly, startling him considerably. She had mentioned the day before—after the assignation he had set up with her via erotic text messaging, as if her fiancé might catch her at it if he didn't—that he looked at her as if he could read her mind. She underestimated how convoluted her mind was, but in any case, he had never once had the impression that she could read *his.*

"The *perfect* boyfr—fiancé wouldn't flirt with anyone else. I wouldn't have to worry about him cheating."

Someone certainly liked to pad the ground before she leapt, didn't she? Some bad falls in her past? "I worry about that, too," he said, thoughtfully, and ever so casually slipped his arm between her hips and the counter, sliding down to open a stainless steel cabinet and pull a completely unrequired utensil out, just so the whole length of his arm would rub directly over her sex. There was no sense tormenting someone on only one level. "A lot these days, *en fait.* That I might end up with someone who would cheat on me."

Her face was a picture of guilty consternation. That would teach her to crouch on the edge of that emotional cliff, looking down at him as if she was afraid she would land in something icky.

"When I'm at my most vulnerable," he added for good measure.

She opened her mouth and almost started to say something, to *tell him,* he hoped. But then her eyes widened with fear again, and she caught her lip under her teeth.

Merde.

"Maybe I should stop dating Americans. You're all just after one thing." He tried to look virtuous and innocent and a little embittered, which wasn't that hard. If she thought he was good material for a sexual fling, then he *did* feel violated.

Worse material for a sexual fling just didn't exist. Once his mind settled on a track, it could not be derailed.

"What do you mean, stop? Have you ever dated an American before?" she asked jealously.

He hid the grin inside him, a hot little lancing victory at that jealousy. "No, but it's proving a corrupting influence. American, engaged . . . the next thing you know I'll be sleeping with someone who's married."

She frowned instantly. "Who?"

He gave her an astounded look. "You, of course. You weren't planning on dumping me after the wedding, were you? Ellie."

She floundered visibly, flabbergasted, and he looked wounded and sorrowful. She closed her hands in fistfuls of her hair and yanked. He placed the wide swooping petals on their tall stem, with perfect controlled grace, hoping that yank had stung.

"There's probably even a way we could sneak in something on the wedding day itself, since I'll be bringing the centerpieces. Would you like that?" He put a little evil kinkiness into his tone. "Maybe while you're wearing your wedding dress, even."

She made a little choking sound. See? There was more than one way to strangle an infuriating woman.

"Just before you say your vows or right after? Which do you think? Or maybe both?"

She flushed crimson. "That's *awful.*"

He placed a tiny chocolate mound in the center of the flower petals, its heart. "But admit it turns you on."

"I will *not.* I wouldn't cheat on my—I wouldn't—" She broke off, clearly stymied by the fact that she *was* cheating on her "fiancé."

He gave her a malevolent smile. "When you think about it, if it's just before your vows, morally it really isn't that different from what we're already doing. Can I help you pick out your wedding dress? Because I'm getting a vision . . ."

"I've already picked it," she said quickly, repressively.

It always pissed him off when she added another layer to her lie. Was she just going to keep digging that hole forever, or would she someday tell him the truth? "*Ah, oui?* What does it look like?"

She got the blank look she always had when pulling details out of thin air.

"What color is it?" he asked helpfully.

"White," she said instantly and with a complete lack of creativity.

"Ooh. Perfect."

She gave him a fulminating look that faded, as she looked away, to something very troubled.

"Do you think you should invite his nurse so she can keep him distracted?"

"Simon."

He smiled involuntarily at his name in her voice, the trouble she had with the *N*. He liked the anxious frustration in her tone. *Figure it out, Ellie. Come out from behind the fiancé. We're not playing hide and seek.*

"*En fait,* if this were a movie, there could be a happy ending to this story."

She peeked at him through her lashes, a shy, hopeful curiosity.

"The French nurse and I could fall for each other when we meet, and you and your fiancé could realize how much you really love each other and how close you came to losing something perfect, and everyone could live happily ever after."

Her face fell dramatically. She looked as if she was about to cry.

Making him immediately feel like a bastard. "Or, you know, the offer still stands."

"Which offer?" she asked warily, blinking hard and crinkling her nose as if it stung.

He closed his hand around her wrist. "This offer, Ellie. To catch you."

But she had to have enough trust to throw herself off the cliff.

Chapter Eleven

Ellie was dancing with temptation. Her fingers itched to fly over her keyboard. She couldn't believe she was keeping this from her readers: the whole story, spying on him, getting caught, the fiancé—oh God, her readers would have a field day with that one!—her being crazy in love, and all those lovely, luscious shots of him working chocolate, of his creations, the inside scoop on a top Parisian *chocolaterie.*

Her readers were beginning to wonder what the heck she was up to, too. She could have claimed Internet problems if Paris had been a little more backward, but since the city insisted on having the greatest wifi access in the world, she was mostly reduced to filler: a few stolen shots of Philippe Lyonnais, all kinds of shop windows, and meanwhile, all those posts she had written about Simon Casset just sat there on her computer, clamoring to be published.

Sometimes she had to bite her own hands to keep from hitting the button.

She couldn't just publish him to the world while tricking him, though. She couldn't. She had to tell him the truth.

And risk—how chilly could those eyes get, if he learned she had lied to him to get under his skin? Would he freeze her where she stood and drop her?

Did superballs still bounce if they were frozen when they fell?

* * *

"So what would you have to worry about?" Simon asked. They were sitting in the Luxembourg Gardens, in the shade of plane trees down one of the gravel paths, tucked out of the main pedestrian traffic. Simon's *chocolaterie* was closed on Mondays, but this summer Monday was so beautiful, the gardens were drawing crowds despite the workday, both tourists and native Parisians, lots of mothers with their children. Simon was lounging, half-prone, his legs propped up on another green chair, his knees lifted to form an easel for his own "sketchbook," a small leather journal he had pulled out once or twice already that day, to sketch something he had seen in a shop window. "Ideas," he had told her briefly.

Ellie also had her sketchbook out, happily dabbling with different ways to express the pure joy of having sunlight dappled over her in this elegant, peaceful heart of Paris, while Simon Casset sat angled toward her with a little smile on his face. She tried to catch the play of light and shadow, doodled caricatures of herself jumping for joy in the margins, and didn't even try to draw Simon because, as much as she would love to be able to capture his sculpted body on her pages, she knew he was well beyond her skill. Simon, on the other hand, kept glancing at her as he drew.

"Me?" she said, startled. "Worry?" Right *now*? Who could worry at a moment like this? The air was just perfect, its heat cooled slightly by the shade, the sound of children laughing reaching them from the play area, a group of men sitting at chess tables just faintly glimpsed through several ranges of trees.

"From your ideal fiancé. You said you wouldn't have to worry about him cheating. What would you have to worry about?"

She frowned severely. What *was* the matter with him? Could he not just enjoy a beautiful day when he had it? "If he's perfect, I shouldn't have to worry about anything."

"There obviously must be something you worry about more than being cheated on, though. Since you're willing to stay with someone who might cheat on you, rather than face that worry."

Ellie contemplated hitting Simon over the head with her sketchbook. She didn't even have an engagement ring anymore. What part of *let the fiancé wink out of existence when the moment felt right* did Simon not understand?

"What are you drawing?" She redirected the subject firmly, getting up to see.

He closed the journal and slipped it into his pocket before she could get close. But he tilted his head back against the green metal of the chair and smiled up at her lazily, as she stood over him. Ellie's own mouth softened helplessly at that smile. She didn't know—but she almost thought—that Simon hadn't smiled like that before he met her: as if life was very good and he could take a long, long time lingering in it. "You did promise to dump your fiancé if he didn't like my sculptures, didn't you?"

"He wouldn't be that stupid," Ellie said decisively.

Simon snagged her wrist with a hand she didn't even see move, all without losing his lazy ease, and pulled her onto his lap. "Cheating on you with a French nurse is pretty damned stupid, Ellie." He settled her body effortlessly, finding just the right spot so that her weight snuggled against his chest. It moved under her in a long, deep breath as he rubbed his nose into her hair. "There. Now this day is just about perfect."

"Just about?" she checked uneasily. See, that was one of the things that worried her. His standards must be incredibly high. "What else do you need?"

His hand stroked her back as if he was reassuring a small child. "A clean conscience," he said promptly, in direct prickly opposition to that stroking hand.

If she could find enough loose skin on those ripped ribs of his, she would *pinch* him.

His face tucked into her hair, his arm cradling her to him. "All right, I lied," he murmured. "There's more than one kind of perfect. This is one."

She relaxed her head against him, smiling. He smelled so good: clean, golden warm, and a hint, as if it had been showered off but just kept breathing through his pores, of chocolate.

He went back to stroking her. "So what worries you, Ellie?"

Not much, just then. She took a deep breath of him and nuzzled her face more deeply into him.

"Because . . . I might know of a—Parisian—endurance athlete—who gives you the *best chocolate* in the world—who wouldn't cheat on you with anyone. Actually, might have far too exclusive a focus on you for your own sense of freedom. If, you know, you're still in an—exploring your freedom stage."

Suddenly and to her complete chagrin, her eyes filled with tears. She fought it back, steadied her voice: "Bouncing."

Oh crap, that made it worse. Two tears actually welled up and managed to spill out onto her cheeks. Her face was against his chest, he wouldn't notice—but then her nose stung so much that she had to sniffle.

His arms tightened. "Bouncing?"

She nodded, pinching herself hard to give herself something else to think about and quit being such a public baby. It didn't work. She had to sniffle again, and two more tears spilled out.

"Minou." One hand stroked firm and gentle all the way up her back, and he cradled her neck, pulling her back to see her face. "What's this?"

Her lip trembled. The eyes that had been so cool and penetrating on their first meeting were so tender. "I don't want to do it anymore. Bounce back. I'm here, in Paris, and *this time* I'm going to *fly.*"

He pulled her ponytail out gently, letting her hair spill, so that it slid between his skin and hers when he kneaded his hand against the nape of her neck. "Of course you are. You have pixie dust." A thumb skated, barely touching, over her cheekbones. How had he even noticed she *had* freckles? They were so faint. "*Minou.* There's nothing I handle that's resilient. *You* might be, yes, I can believe that you can handle absolutely anything and come out more beautiful for it, but this"—his hands flexed into her waist and pulled her closer against him—"*you with me*—trust me, I'm not going to drop it and hope it bounces."

She kneaded her hands into his chest, insofar as the hardness under his silk-soft T-shirt allowed for kneading. His words made her so blissful, like a cat finally settling down into the perfect lap, that it was a belated second before it occurred to her: she was still playing him, in an elaborate lie that got more extended every day. Oh *crap.* "What if you got mad?"

He gave a crack of laughter. "Let me think. Mad like during the Championnat du Monde, when I discovered that the premade pieces we were allowed to bring had been lost by the airline? Watch the old videos of the competition. See if I dropped anything. Mad like when I finally, finally qualified for Hawaii, and my wetsuit ripped, and my bike tire blew, and I banged the shit out of my knee just before the run? My time was lousy, but I didn't quit."

She knit her brows, against his shirt. "Have I mentioned that I think a long walk is plenty of exercise?"

His hands flexed into her. "One where you gaze around with your eyes all bright and stop and take pictures of everything? I think I figured it out. I don't know if you can put up with the way I am, but Ellie—*j'adore comment tu es.*"

I love how you are . . . It wasn't the first time a man had told her that he loved her the way she was, or even that he loved her. But maybe it was something about her position— cradled safely in iron hardness, being handled with such delicate care—but this time, she actually felt as if he might mean something more than the enthusiasm of the moment.

"Put up with the way *you* are? You're perfect."

He wound his hand in her hair and pulled her head back

enough to look her in the face again. "Yeah, but I'm a pure bastard about the cap on the toothpaste. We can have separate bathrooms, if you want."

The leaves dappled shadow and sunlight over her as the implications of that slowly sank in, her eyes growing wider and wider. She had just settled into her own apartment in Paris, of which she was ecstatically proud, and she didn't entirely know if she *wanted* to give up the independence of her adventure yet, and—

"Oh, I beg your pardon." Simon kissed her, a warm stamp of possession. "I forgot you were marrying someone else."

CHAPTER TWELVE

If she couldn't talk to her readers soon and get a little feed-
back about all this, she was going to go completely nuts.
Maybe she could beat around the bush: "I think I'm in
love!" she caroled on her blog, showing photos of chocolate
sculptures, pastries, little chocolates named *Elle*. Everyone
who knew her knew she could be in love with a chocolate.
"More later!" she said at the end. "Maybe. Wish me luck!"

And felt a flood of relief when the comments started coming in, teasing, curious, complaining *she* was being a tease, or
just thanking her for the pictures to brighten their day. It
helped her, the blog, made her feel that when she flung herself out there to the world, well—the world liked her.

Oh, really? Simon rubbed one hand over the back of his
neck, and a slow, slow smile grew, deeper and deeper, until
it was lodged in him somewhere from which it could never
be knocked out. She thought that, did she? He had hoped,
but—*putain,* but she made it hard to be sure.

Every damn one of those chocolate works under that "I
think I'm in love!" was his.

It looked as if he was just going to have to go head-to-
head with that fiancé of hers.

Fighting an imagined man for a woman's heart. He
knuckled his crazy head but then had to grin. Just when he

had been thinking he had mastered most of the challenges in his life . . .

Come kiss me, the text said.

Ellie, who had been trying to sneak a picture of chocolatier Sylvain Marquis's display when her phone burped, gave the woman behind the counter a guilty look. The woman raised her eyebrows disdainfully.

Ellie frowned at her, lifted the phone and snapped a picture openly, and turned to stroll out of the shop.

She nearly ran into an absolutely gorgeous poet as he stepped inside, black hair tucked behind one ear, chocolate eyes laughing down at her with vibrant curiosity. "May I help you?" he asked. He bent and picked up her dropped phone, taking in the text as he did so. His eyebrows lifted, and he grinned a little.

Sylvain Marquis, she thought with startled pleasure. It was amazing how she kept running into these famous chocolatiers around their shops. It was almost like they were real humans or something. Somehow, when she went into Notre-Dame, she didn't expect to have a physical collision with God.

She really should seize this opportunity to introduce herself, like the dedicated journalist she was, but—she glanced toward the text.

Her phone burped again as Sylvain handed it back to her: *I think I have the perfect* pièce *for your wedding.*

Would he *drop the subject of her damn wedding*? "Do you know Simon Casset?" she asked the top chocolatier smiling down at her.

Sylvain looked a little disappointed. "Sure. We were on the same team for the Championnat du Monde. Why? Are you his?"

Ellie frowned at him.

"Apprentice," Sylvain clarified, with the lift of one supple eyebrow, his eyes dancing. "Spying on me." His lips twitched. "Being paid with kisses."

Really, she had to get more details on this practice of chocolatier espionnage. Maybe after she had beaten Simon over
the head with something. And why didn't anybody in America ever pay people with kisses? The greenback looked so
sordid in comparison. "Did you often want to strangle him?"

"Simon?" Sylvain looked startled. "No. Too much of a
professional. Dominique Richard, now, if I ever have to
work on a team with him again, I'll kill somebody."

"Dominique Richard?" Ellie fished, briefly diverted. She
hadn't had a chance to go see the wild chocolate rebel's *chocolaterie* yet, but she could tell good gossip when she got a whiff
of it.

"No, not him," Sylvain said regretfully, misunderstanding.
"You can't go killing good chocolatiers. We might be able to
transfer him to a remote location far from human habitation,
though. No, I'll kill the next committee that thinks we should
work together. Poisoned chocolate." He paused a moment to
contemplate the vision. "Not mean enough, is it? They would
probably die happy."

O-kay. No false modesty here. "And when you worked
with Simon, he didn't have a perverse and sadistic sense of
humor?"

"Simon?"

"Obsess on ideas he should just let drop?"

"Oh, that, *oui, bien sûr. L'idée fixe, c'est Simon.*"

"Hmm." Ellie gave that some thought and then abruptly
thrust out her hand. "Eloise Layne, blogger. It's nice to meet
you, Monsieur Marquis. I would love to do a story on you
soon, if you have the time."

"Of course," said the media's darling. "I always have time
for beautiful journalists. Just give me a call to set it up."

Belles journalistes. There really was something to be said for
France.

"Passez Simon le bonjour de ma part," Sylvain called after her
as she headed for the door. *Tell him hello from me.* He smirked.
"It will drive him absolutely crazy."

CHAPTER THIRTEEN

"Your fiancé and I might not see eye to eye on this one,"
Simon told her.

Ellie studied the cloth-covered sculpture on his desk and
wondered why they were in his office for this unveiling.
Simon never had any concern about showing his *work* in
public.

"You'll have to give me his honest reaction. Remember,
if he doesn't like it, you did promise to dump him."

"Well, that was really just rhetoric—" Why did she keep
defending her relationship to a fictitious man she was cheating on? "Sylvain Marquis sends his love."

"Not to me, he doesn't," Simon said dryly. "Was that *salaud*
flirting with you?"

Ellie considered. Maybe a little.

"What the hell am I saying? Of course, he was. Were you
flirting back?"

"You kept sending me texts about kisses! Who can flirt in
that context?"

"I'll keep the technique in mind. This sculpture might
be good timing." Simon reached for the fine cloth that covered it.

"Is it normal to actually *make* the different centerpieces
you are proposing for a wedding reception?" Ellie asked uneasily. "Instead of sketches?" How much exactly was she go-

ing to owe Simon for his work when her fiancé ran off with the nurse?

"No, but I was inspired. I sketched it yesterday in the gardens." He held her eyes, so much strength in that steel-blue that she could cling to it, vastly reassured. "Don't worry, Ellie, no matter what you think, you really can afford it."

He pulled the cloth off.

The woman sat in the shelter of a great chocolate tree. Violets and ferns of translucent sugar grew around her. She was completely naked, her knees drawn up and her arms around them, so that the most private parts of her body were concealed, her toes pointed as if she was dipping them into something delightful: a stream, or life. She was made of pure white chocolate, no color to her, like a marble sculpture, but the incredible detail of the hair spilling wildly around her face, the bright smile as she looked upward, the curves of her body, made it clear who she was. Made it clear that the sculptor knew her intimately. The quality of the art was incredible, as if Michelangelo were working in a new medium. And—she looked so beautiful. So happy.

A dark chocolate ribbon had been curled once around the body, a spiral, the end of it fluttering past her shoulder as if it had been caught in a breeze. That end was inscribed in gold lettering: *Mine. S.C.*

Ellie's mouth dropped open. She stared at the claimed naked body, while her heart thudded until she couldn't think through its rhythm. That was—so arousing.

Outrageous, she reminded herself as sternly as she could. Completely and utterly outrageous, could not be stood for a minute, and—she glanced at the lock on the door, contemplating attacking him.

Look, was it her fault her outrage seemed to want to express itself sexually?

Simon gave a very mean, self-satisfied smile. "Think he'll like it?"

She tried to force herself to breathe. To not sexually assault Simon in his own office as an expression of her outrage at being stamped *Mine*. First of all, he would be horrified—later—at his staff knowing he was having sex in his office. And second of all, she suspected her feminist message might not come across.

"Can I take a picture?" she asked instead, jerking the provocation out in some last-ditch random grab for what had once been her world.

It wiped the smug smile off his face. "Don't tell me you're going to—" He broke off.

"To show him. I can't possibly take this on the Métro to the hospital."

"Oh, come *on*." Simon threw the cloth hard against the wall. "Are you *still*—" He pressed his lips together. Hard. They straightened out like some steel blade, and she could feel anger mounting in him, an anger that was pressing against all his control, like steam against a lid that had no outlet to siphon it off. Anger like the pressure against a mountain face just before a volcano blew; it had been building a long time, but only now did you suddenly realize the danger.

"If he doesn't like it, I'll dump him, as promised." She could probably keep up the fiction of Cal Kenton's brief presence in her life indefinitely, right? And never have to tell Simon the truth, that she had actually dumped someone who hadn't existed?

A vein throbbed in Simon's temple. He looked—scarily grim.

Ellie felt her insides knot in anguish. She hadn't realized he was that near the brink, over sharing her. That he might get fed up and break it off, as—as would be his right, really. Cal Kenton was such a ridiculous farce on her end, that maybe she had never quite realized what it would feel like to Simon, believing he was real. "I promise!"

"Ellie." Simon gripped the edge of his desk, in pure rage and . . . despair? "What am I going to do with you? I'm the first to understand why you want to protect—all this." He made a little gesture that meant . . . her. "After all, *you* must know you're precious. But, Ellie—I think you're precious, too. Can't you trust me a little bit?"

Trust him. Not to drop her. She huddled her arms around herself, kneading. "I think you'll be really mad." More mad. Good lord. The room already felt as if steel was trying way too hard to hold in an explosion, disaster imminent for everyone in that steel's vicinity when it blew.

He leaned forward, poised, tense. "Try me."

She took a hard breath and closed her eyes tight. She held that breath inside her so long that she had to let it out to get more oxygen, and into its violent expulsion she packed all the words: "I-don't-have-a-fiancé-never-did-I-was-just-trying-to-find-a-way-in." There. She had to breathe in again. She peeked at him.

All the tension was collapsing out of his body. He looked almost exhausted from its departure, as if it had been carrying him for a long time.

"I write a food blog," she said low, hanging her head. "When I came to Paris, I was just so excited, and embarrassed, and then I just . . . it felt a lot safer to have the perfect fiancé."

Her eyes pricked. That was pathetic. She forced her chin up, so she wouldn't play the pathos card to someone she had been tricking all this time, and met his eyes.

He was smiling at her. He had sunk onto the edge of the desk as if he had no muscles left, and he looked . . . utterly relieved.

She frowned a little uncertainly. "Are you—I mean—" She cleared her throat. "You might be a little too self-controlled sometimes. Why don't you go ahead and yell at me, and then we can talk, and *then* you can realize I'm really not so bad and get over it?"

His smile grew blinding. He reached for her, and Ellie was so surprised, her hands got stuck under her elbows, and she couldn't get them untucked fast enough. He caught her by the upper arms and pulled her against him. "*Minou,* I love you. I especially love the part of you that doesn't give me the option of *not* getting over it."

"Well." She set her jaw mulishly. He *had* said he would catch her, no matter what. Sometimes a woman had to hold a man to a promise like that.

He kissed her until her mouth lost its stubborn set, and then he kissed her for a lot longer still, as if he needed to. When he at last lifted his head, he had snapped yet another of her hairbands, and her hair was spilling all over her shoulders. The man had some kind of personal crusade against ponytail holders.

"I want to tell the whole world about you," she whispered into his mouth, losing her last bit of sense. Idiot, she didn't have to confess *all* her flaws, all at once.

"I know," he breathed. His kisses were growing wilder, like a person who had thought he might starve suddenly given free run at a feast. "I know you do."

"You don't—you don't mind?" He couldn't realize how many hits she got a day. "When I said the whole world—I wasn't exaggerating by that much."

He dragged his hands through her hair, clutching fistfuls of it. "I'm resigned to it. I'll stand it. Don't tell them about our sex life, all right? And no naked photos."

"Of *course* not!" she said indignantly. Show him naked to all those hungry females? Did he think she was an imbecile? Actually, now that she thought about it, maybe *any* pictures of him might be . . . maybe she should just concentrate on his chocolate. And stress how ugly he was.

He teased her mouth apart with his thumbs at the corners, kissed her some more. "If I get over this, can you get over something on my part?"

Ellie's mind scrambled wildly for possible crimes. Cheating on her with a French nurse? No, wait, that was his alter ego. Or was Cal Kenton more like his evil nemesis? "Y-es," she said hesitantly.

"Now, please try to take this as well as I'm taking your news." He stroked her back, pre-emptive soothing. Started to speak, then paused, reached into a box stamped with his name, silver on black, on his desk, and slipped something into her mouth. The flavor of one of his chocolates burst on her tongue, just where his own tongue had been a second before. "I knew you were lying. From the first. You're not very good at it."

She stared at him for a long moment, forced to absorb that news with the most luscious chocolate melting in her mouth, claiming her body. She finally swallowed, and just before she could speak, Simon rubbed his thumb across her upper lip, smiled at the chocolate on its tip, and sucked it off. That— she had to learn how to manipulate *him* that well. "God damn it. You really could see through to my underwear, couldn't you?"

"White cotton, no lace, sexy as hell," he said promptly. "You really shouldn't wear that kind of thing in public. Makes a man think all kinds of things. You might try—" He paused and considered. And considered. Against her body, she could feel his arousal growing ever more pronounced. "I'm not sure what you could try, *en fait*. So far, it's all looking good."

"And I am, too, a good liar. It's just *you*. No one can lie to you."

"Well. You can't, *c'est sûr*."

She frowned at him. "I think I'll be madder about this after it's had time to sink in." All the times he had tormented her with mentions of her fiancé . . .

"While it's sinking . . ." He brought a little box out of his back pocket. "Before it has time to settle . . ."

It was her engagement ring. The one with the antique scrolled setting and the beveled-set diamond, that she had found for $35 in a shop full of fake jewelry in Les Halles, that slightly sordid center of Paris.

"I stole the other one," he said, falsely apologetic. "You don't mind if I keep it, do you? This is a copy I had made." His lips compressed a little, his eyes alive with laughter. "It's a real diamond now. And I believe the silver won't turn your finger green anymore. *Merde,* Ellie, don't *cry.*"

He pulled her into his arms again.

But she cried anyway.

He patted her rather helplessly on the back and talked her through it. "We can have a long engagement, so you can come to terms with the toothpaste thing. I even thought— we could maybe have two apartments side by side, with a connecting door like a suite, I'm just throwing this out there, it's an option if I drive you too crazy to live with me. I'm going to take the crying as a yes, all right?"

He took her hand and slid the ring very, very carefully onto her finger. Ellie, who had almost gotten herself under control, opened her eyes to see his expression as he looked at her hand and started crying again.

"*Allez, minou, arrête.*" He stroked her hair. "All right, don't stop, if it makes you—is this happy?"

She nodded, her face sliding in her hair against his chest.

"The ring is all right? I thought . . . since it was the ring the perfect man for you had picked." She snuck a peek at him suspiciously and caught the bitten-down grin. "Endurance athlete and all that . . ."

"I just made that endurance athlete thing up off the top of my head!" She began to pull herself together, mopping her eyes and pulling back a little from his chest.

"So it must be true." He lifted her left hand to his mouth and pressed a kiss into the center of her palm, holding it there against his mouth a moment, his eyes closing. "I might cut back on that, though. Do only half distances, maybe."

She scrubbed her eyes some more, trying to focus. "Why? Uh—did I hurt you the other night? You know, I did ask if that position wasn't hard on your thighs, but you wouldn't *listen . . ."*

He grinned into her hand, then opened his eyes and gazed at her, still holding her hand to his face, so that his voice buzzed against her palm. "I work ten or twelve hours a day, and training for four more doesn't leave much time to be with you."

She opened her free hand and closed it uncomfortably on emptiness. She never wanted anyone to give up any dream or ambition for her. Not a *dream*. But the thought of evening after evening with him out running or swimming or biking or otherwise occupied felt . . . scarily bare. "You don't have to change for me."

He shook his head, his jaw scraping faintly against her palm. "I'm very self-centered. That might develop into a problem over time. This is for me." A breath against her palm, a flush. "I can't get enough of you."

Now she was the one who blushed. "I'm sure that will calm down eventually—"

He smiled and finally lowered her hand so that he was no longer hiding behind it. "I didn't mean just sex. Although that's a very enjoyable facet of it. You light up my life," he said simply.

Her mouth softened open. Her eyes widened and stung again.

His flush deepened. This man clearly found it easier to express himself in chocolate. But he kept on. "All those sculptures." He nodded to the photos of award-winning swoops and swirls and color and deliciousness on the wall, made a sweep of his hand that seemed to indicate his whole *chocolaterie,* or perhaps his whole life. "All that time." He pulled her tightly against him again. "I was just trying to make you."

If you enjoyed Laura Florand's "All's Fair in Love and Chocolate," take a taste of *The Chocolate Thief,* coming this August.

Sylvain Marquis knew what women desired—chocolate. And so he had learned as he grew into adulthood how to master a woman's desire.

Outside, November had turned the Paris streets cold and gray. But in his *laboratoire,* he brought his chocolate to the temperature he wanted it, smooth and luxurious. He spread it out across his marble counter. With a deft flick of his hand, he stroked it up and spread it out again, glowing and dark.

In the shop, an elegant blonde whose every movement spoke of wealth and privilege was buying a box of his chocolates, unable to resist biting into one before she left the shop. He could see her through the glass window that allowed visitors a glimpse of the way artisan chocolate was made. He saw her perfect teeth sink into the thumbnail-size chocolate and knew exactly the way the shell yielded with a delicate resistance, the way the ganache inside melted on her tongue, the pleasure that ran through her body.

He smiled a little, bending his head to focus on his chocolate again. He did not see the next woman as she entered his shop.

But as it turned out, she wasn't about to let him miss her.

The scent of chocolate snuck out onto the rainy street. Boot heels broke their rapid rhythm as passersby, bundled in long black coats, glanced toward the source and hesitated.

Some stopped. Some went on. Cade's momentum carried her inside.

Theobromine wrapped around her like a warm blanket against the chill. Cacao flooded her senses.

She hugged herself. The odor brought her home, belying her own eyes, which told her she couldn't be farther from the steel vats of the factory, the streams of chocolate ejecting without break in tempo from spouts into molds, and the billions of perfectly identical bars and bold-printed wrappings that had formed her life.

Something, some tension she carried with her, unknit in her shoulder muscles, and the shiver from its release rippled all the way through her body.

Someone had molded chocolate into giant cacao bean halves that graced the display windows and added drama to the corners of the shop. She could imagine the hand that had shaped it—a man's hand, strong, square, long-fingered, capable of the most delicate precision. She had a photo of that hand as her laptop wallpaper.

On the surface of each bean, he had painted a scene from a different country that produced cacao. And on the surface of the horizontal "beans," he had placed thumbnail-size chocolates, exactly where he wanted them.

She looked around. Tucked in corners here and there, black brands on shipping crates spoke of distant lands. Real cacao beans spilled from the crates, reminding customers that chocolate was an exotic thing, brought from another world. Cade had seen those lands. The black brands brought their scents and sights back to her mind, the people she had met there, the sounds of machetes on cacao trees, the scent of fermenting cacao husks.

He had scattered cocoa nibs here and there, as a master chef might decorate a plate with a few drops of sauce. He had spilled vanilla beans and cinnamon bark on multiple surfaces, wantonly, a débauche of raw luxury.

Every single element of this décor emphasized the raw,

beautiful nature of chocolate and thus the triumph of its ultimate refinement: the minuscule squares, the *chocolats* worth one hundred fifty dollars a pound, from the hand of Sylvain Marquis.

Sylvain Marquis. Some said he was the top chocolatier in Paris. *He did, too,* she thought. She knew he had that confidence. She knew it from that picture of his hand she carried on her laptop.

His boxes were the color of raw wood and tied with shipping string. The name stamped on them—SYLVAIN MARQUIS—dominated them, the color of dark chocolate, the font a bare, bold statement.

Cade breathed in, seeking courage from the scents and sights. Heady excitement gripped her, but also, in strange counterpoint, fear, as if she was about to walk naked onto a stage in front of a hundred people. She shouldn't feel this way. Chocolate was her business, her heritage. Her dad often joked her veins ran with the stuff. A significant portion of the global economy actually did run off the chocolate her family produced. She could offer Sylvain Marquis incredible opportunity.

And yet she felt so scared to try she could barely swallow.

She kept seeing her family's most famous bar, milk chocolate wrapped in foil and paper and stamped with her name— 33 cents on sale at Walmart. Those 33-cent bars had put more money in her family's bank accounts than most people could imagine. Certainly more than *he* could imagine. And yet her soul shriveled at the thought of taking the one in her purse out and displaying it in these surroundings.

"Bonjour," she said to the nearest clerk, and excitement rushed to her head again, driving out everything else it contained. She'd done it. She'd spoken her first word of French to an actual Parisian, in pursuit of her goal. She had studied Spanish and French off and on for most of her life, so that she could easily communicate when she visited their cacao plantations. For the past year, she had also paid native French

speakers to tutor her toward her purpose, an hour a day and homework every night, focusing on the words she had come here today to use—samples, marketing, product lines. And *chocolat*.

And now, finally, here she was. Speaking. About to put *la cerise sur le gâteau* of the whole new line she was planning for the company. The cherry on the cake . . . maybe they could do something with *La Cerise* as one of the new line's products . . .

"*Je m'appelle Cade Corey*. I'll take five samples of everything here, one of each kind per box, please." Only one of those boxes was for her. The others were to send back to Corey Chocolate headquarters in Corey, Maryland. "And while you are boxing that up, I have a meeting with Sylvain Marquis."

Her French sounded so beautiful, she couldn't restrain a tiny smile of pride. It just came *tripping* off her tongue, with only the merest stutter getting started. All that work had paid off.

"Yes, madame," the crisply attired young man answered in English, as coolly and precisely as a pin.

She blinked, her balloon of happiness shriveling, humiliated by one word in her own language.

"M. Marquis is with the chocolates, madame," he said, still in English, setting her back teeth. Her French was *much better* than his English, thank you. Or *merci*.

A young woman began to fill boxes with Cade's chocolates while the snobbish young man guided her through a door in the back of the shop.

She stepped into a magical world and almost managed to forget that slap of English in her face as her happiness balloon swelled right up again. In one corner, a lean man in glasses with the fine face of a poet or a nerd, poured generous ladles of white chocolate over molds. In another, a woman with her hair covered by a transparent plastic-brimmed cap, used a paintbrush to touch up chocolate owls. Two more women were filling boxes with small chocolates. More women still were laying finely decorated sheets of plastic over chocolates grouped by the dozen and tamping down on each chocolate gently, transferring the decoration.

At the central table of rose-colored marble, a man took a large whisk to something in a bain-marie that looked as if it must by itself weigh forty pounds, a faint white powder rising in the air around him. Across from him, another lean man, this one with a tiny dark beard on his chin, squeezed chocolate from a pastry bag into a mold from which lollipop handles protruded. His wedding ring glinted in a ray of light from the windows.

They were all lean, in fact. Surprisingly so, for people who worked all day with chocolate only a bite away. Only one man, tall and burly, stood out for his paunch, and he seemed entirely cheerful with his weight. Everyone wore white, and everyone had a paper cap, styles differing according to role. It was a world with a hierarchy, clearly defined for all to see.

Over the sinks hung brushes, spatulas, whisks. On the marble counter stood a large electric scale and an enormous mixer. On a counter to one side were all sizes of containers and bowls. Filled with raisins, candied oranges, sugar, they surrounded those working at the great marble island.

Everyone glanced up at her entry, but most focused on their work again. Only one man, expertly stroking chocolate over marble, spared her a lingering gaze that held greater authority and perhaps more dismissal.

Tall and lean, he had black hair that fell in slightly wavy locks to his chin. He had tucked it carelessly behind his ear on one side, clearly exposing his strong, even features. A white paper toque minimized the risk of any of the rest of it falling into some client's chocolate. Chocolate smeared the front of the white chef's jacket he wore.

He was beautiful.

She swallowed, her mouth feeling dry. All the scents, the activity, the realization that the best chocolatier in Paris was, in person, even more attractive than in his photos, it all swirled around in her, surging up in ever-heightened excitement. She was here. In her dream. *This was going to be so much fun.*

And Sylvain Marquis was hot.

Maybe she was overexcited. He wasn't that great, was he? Okay, he had looked sexy in his photos, and that shot of his hand had filled her dreams for nights on end, but she had tried to take all that with a grain of salt.

But here, in person, she had a sense from him of energy and control, passion and discipline. It fed into her excitement, provoking an exaggerated sensitivity on her part. She felt like a can of Coke being jostled, building up a fizz that was pressing against its limits.

"*Bonjour, monsieur,*" she said, as her French tutors had taught her to do, and confidently walked forward to thrust out her hand.

He proffered an elbow in return, which threw her off. She stared at it, then stared up at him.

He raised his eyebrows just enough that she felt abruptly slow on the uptake. "*Hygiène,*" he said. "*Je travaille le chocolat. Comment puis-je vous aider, Mademoiselle Co-ree?*"

She translated all that in her head, growing more and more excited as she realized that she *could,* that this language thing was working. Hygiene. I am working the chocolate. How can I you help, Mademoiselle Corey? He sounded so elegant she wanted to hug his voice up to her in delight. Instead, she found herself awkwardly brushing his elbow, flushing despite herself. How the heck did you shake an elbow?

It dropped away from her. He touched the back of his pinky finger to the chocolate he was tempering on the marble, concentrated. And none of his focus was on her.

That didn't make sense. He knew who she was. This wasn't a surprise visit. He had to realize she could up his income by millions. How could he not concentrate on her?

Yet he seemed to consider her less important than a batch of chocolate. She braced against the presentiment that someone might try to put her fizzed-up Coke self in the freezer.

"Do you have somewhere we could talk in private?" she asked him.

He twitched his eyebrows. "This is important," he told her. Meaning the chocolate and not her.

Did he think she was just here as a professional tourist? "I'm interested in finding someone to design a new line of chocolate products for us," she said calmly. *Now who's important, Sylvain Marquis?* She had practiced that line at least fifty times with her French tutor, and actually saying it out loud in this place and for the reason she had practiced it made her feel giddy with success. "We're interested in going into premium chocolates and are thinking of something very elegant, very Parisian, maybe with your name on it."

There, *that* had got his attention, she thought smugly, as he stared at her, long, thin spatula freezing on the chocolate. She could almost see the euro signs flashing in his head. Had he just added a few zeros onto the end of his account balance?

"Pardon," he said very slowly and carefully. "You want to put *my* name on one of *your* products?"

She nodded, pleased at finally making an impact. Excitement resurged like Old Faithful inside her. This would be her gift to her family, this gourmet line. She would be in charge of it, and it would involve all the luxuriating in high-end chocolate making and Paris she could possibly want. "Maybe. That's what I want to discuss with you."

His mouth opened and closed. She grinned at him triumphantly. What would his hand feel like when they shook on the deal?

Warm maybe. Strong. Sure. Full of the energy and power to turn something raw into something sensual and extraordinary.

There she went with the fizzing again. She glanced around

at the small *laboratoire,* a miracle of intimacy and creation, so different from the chocolate factories in which she had grown up.

"Vous"—Sylvain Marquis broke off, shutting his mouth firmly again. Something was percolating up into his eyes, breaking through that cool control.

Rage.

"You want to put my name on your products?" he repeated, trying hard to keep control of his voice, his expression, but his eyes were practically incandescent. *"My* name?" He flung out a hand to where box after enticing box stamped with that name was being filled, closed, and tied a couple of counters away. "Sylvain Marquis?"

"I—"

"On *Corey Bars?"*

Thirty-three cents at Walmart. She flushed down to her toes and thrust her hand into her purse to close it around a rectangle in gaudy gold and brown wrapping, using it as her talisman-strength and hiding its shame all at the same time. "It would be a different line. A gourmet line—"

"Mademoiselle—" His mouth hardened, freezing her fizzing Coke bottle so fast she could feel an explosion building up. "You are wasting my time. And I am wasting yours. I will never agree to work with *Corey Bars."*

"But just list—"

"Au revoir." He didn't move. He didn't stalk off. He stood over his half-tempered chocolate and pinned her with eyes the color of cocoa nibs and *made her,* just by the look, the words, his mastery of his own domain, made her turn around and walk out.

She was trembling with embarrassment and rage by the time she got five steps back toward the door into the shop and realized she had *let him.* She had let him keep control of his world and drive her out of it. She wasn't the kind of person who got dominated. She should have stood there and stood up for what she wanted.

She tried to get herself to turn around and brave that humiliation again, but the door was only three steps away. She closed her hand hard around the Corey Bar in her purse and tried to make those three steps scornful. But you couldn't be scornful in retreat. Nobody was fooled by a scornful back.

To hell with you, Sylvain Marquis. There are other chocolatiers in Paris and probably better than you. You're just the fad of the moment. You'll regret it.

She let the door between the *laboratoire* and the shop slam behind her, garnering multiple disapproving looks from clients and employees alike, all of whom expressed their opinion of barbaric Americans by a subtle downturn of their lips.

America could buy and sell them any day of the week.

Damn it. If only they would put a price sticker on themselves and take the money.

She strode toward the glass door onto the street.

"Madame," said a young woman near it, a large sack the color of raw wood sitting beside her cash register, stamped with SYLVAIN MARQUIS. Her expression—neutrality buoyed up by an underlying conviction of superiority—made Cade want to smack her. "Your chocolates."

Cade hesitated. Her credit card might as well have been barbed wire, it galled her so much to pull it out and hand it to the clerk.

Glancing back, she saw Sylvain Marquis watching her through the glass window, one corner of those supple, thin lips of his twisting in amusement, annoyance, dismissal.

She pressed her teeth together so hard she was surprised they didn't break. He returned to his work, forgetting her.

Her rage went to incandescent.

She signed off on a credit card payment into his bank account of nearly a thousand dollars for five measly boxes of chocolate and strode out into the street.

She desperately wished to sweep dramatically into a limousine or at least stride off into a Parisian sunset. Instead she walked ten paces across the street, through a dark green door, and into an elevator so tiny she finally understood the *real* reason French women didn't get fat. Claustrophobia.

Her bag of chocolate squashed against her legs. The elevator creaked to a halt six floors up. She let herself into an apartment less than half the size of her bedroom back home, threw her bag of chocolate on the bed, and glared down at Sylvain Marquis's shop below. She had been so excited to find this little apartment for rent right above his *chocolaterie*. It had seemed so much more real, so much more what she wanted to do, than a luxury hotel off the Champs-Elysées. It might come with some sacrifices, like the fact that she was going to have to figure out how to use a Laundromat, but that had seemed a reasonable price to pay.

Until now. Now here she was, stuck just above the *chocolaterie* of a real jerk.

She could still go to a hotel, she supposed. But then, what was the point of her being here, if she just went to a hotel like she did on all her business trips?

She snuck a glance at the bag of chocolate on the bed. *No,* she told herself firmly.

She went back to scowling down at the Sylvain Marquis sign below.

The scent of chocolate reached her from the boxes. Her home town smelled of chocolate all the time. Not this kind of chocolate, though. Not this exquisite quality, the work of one person's imagination and hands.

Maybe she would try just one. To prove how overrated he was.

As flavor pure as sin burst on her mouth, and her whole body melted in response, she pressed her forehead helplessly against her window, trying to keep her mouth in a scowl. Which was hard to do around melting chocolate.

He was so delicious.

How unfortunate that he was such a jerk.

GREAT BOOKS, GREAT SAVINGS!

When You Visit Our Website:
www.kensingtonbooks.com
You Can Save Money Off The Retail Price Of Any Book You Purchase!

- **All Your Favorite Kensington Authors**
- **New Releases & Timeless Classics**
- **Overnight Shipping Available**
- **eBooks Available For Many Titles**
- **All Major Credit Cards Accepted**

Visit Us Today To Start Saving!
www.kensingtonbooks.com